HER UNDYING THIRST

Inspired by J. Sheridan Le Fanu's "Carmilla"

Reina Callier

ARTES REGINAE PRESS

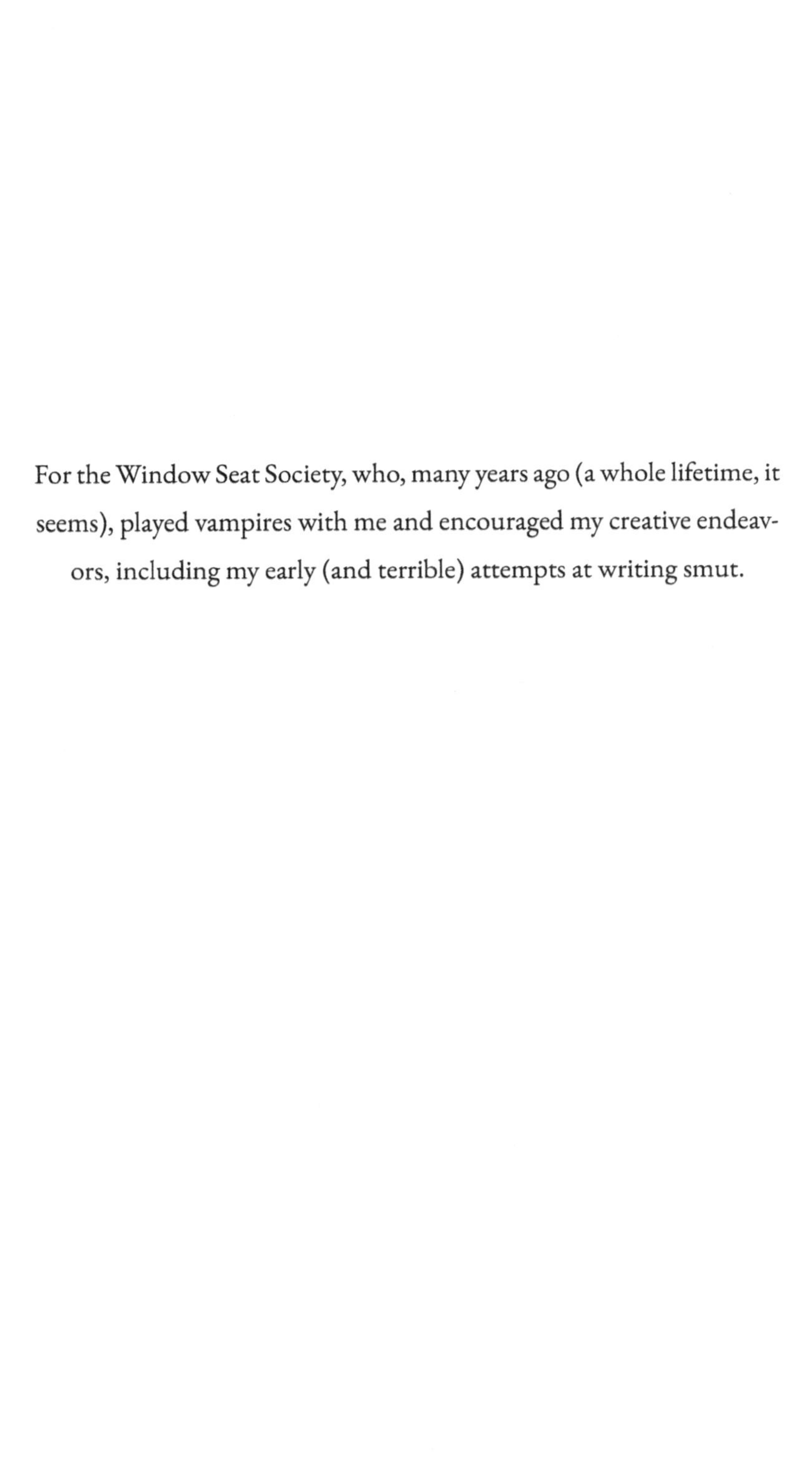

For the Window Seat Society, who, many years ago (a whole lifetime, it seems), played vampires with me and encouraged my creative endeavors, including my early (and terrible) attempts at writing smut.

Content Warnings

In addition to open-door sex scenes and typical horror-genre fare (e.g. strong language, violence, blood/gore, supernatural terror, and lots of death), this novel includes instances of sexual assault, unwanted pregnancy, and death in childbirth.

PROLOGUE

8th September, 1886

Dear William,

You are certainly not the first person to wonder how I dream up such ghastly stories. Indeed, I couldn't help but laugh after reading your last letter, for I have heard that same question countless times over the course of my career, including from your own father, when he first began to publish my work.

You may not be the first, but you *shall* be the last.

Somehow – very much against my will, I might add – I seem to have grown old, and I long to see more of the world while I still can. Unfortunately, this means that I must put aside this writing business. Yet I do not wish to withdraw from the limelight without telling the truth about myself. Perhaps it's because I want my fame, the only chance I have at outliving my mortal body, to be rooted in my true identity. Or perhaps I wish my story to serve as a warning to others. You see, the monsters that spring forth from my pages are far less dangerous than the *real* monster I encountered in my youth, and every morbid fantasy I have concocted since then has been inspired by that terrifying encounter.

And so, my friend, please find enclosed the answer to your query: my memoir. Do with it what you will; I understand, however, if you deem it unsuitable for publication. The first thing I must tell you is this: I am not Johnathan Karnstein, though this *nom de plume* has served me well these past decades. My real name is Laura Bancroft, and fifty years ago, I loved – and killed – a vampire.

CHAPTER ONE
INTO THE WOODS

The story begins with my mother's death.

Believe me, I wish it didn't. Indeed, I'm tempted to apologize for making such a sad and horrifying start. But the story really *does* begin there, for it was my mother's death that occasioned our relocation to Austria and brought us within the vampire's reach. Furthermore, among those who study the craft of writing, one truth is (to draw an apt phrase from one of my *own* favorite authors) "universally acknowledged": it's best to let your readers know right away what kind of story they're committing themselves to. By beginning with grief and terror, then, I'm warning you of what's to come. Thankfully, I do not think this will be a deterrent to *everyone* (in fact, my success in writing stories of the gruesome and macabre suggests that some people will be *drawn* to it).

So, the death of my mother.

I was five years old. Outside our London home, the sun was shining, and the crowds were going about their daily business. I had been awake for two days and nights, trembling on a chair in the hallway while my mother screamed at regular intervals from her bedroom. When I looked out the window, the sheer disregard of the outside world for our predicament seemed ludicrous, like a cruel joke God was playing to deepen our misfortune. I was curled up with my arms around my shins, the fabric of my dress warm and wet from the hot tears falling onto my kneecaps. I thought that eventually I would run out of tears, that eventually my mother would run out of screams, but both kept coming.

I knew the situation was dire because, despite the constant movement of people in and out of my mother's bedroom – my father, my nursemaid, a priest, several of our servants, the midwife, and, finally, the doctor – no one seemed to notice that I was there. Finally, as the bright noon sun streamed through the window, my mother's screams became weaker. The thought that this might signify the situation's improvement was dashed from my mind before it was able to take root, for my nursemaid Hannah came running from the bedroom, her sobs echoing down the hallway as she headed for her own quarters. My father and the doctor emerged from the bedroom then, talking in hushed tones. I could not understand what the doctor was saying, but my father's face – his red-eyed, stubbled face, pale beneath unkempt blonde hair – fell from exhaustion into abject grief, and he cried out "No! No!" as the doctor grabbed his arms to try to keep him from collapsing.

The doctor whispered, "There is nothing we can do to save her, Edward. God is calling her home. But if we do this, we might be able to save the child. We must act quickly."

Hunched over, clinging to the doctor's arms, my father sobbed with anguish and disbelief. For a moment, he turned his eyes up to the heavens in accusation, as though he had been betrayed by a dear friend. Then he looked at the doctor and nodded. One of our servants, tear-stained and sniffling, came out of the bedroom carrying a silver basin, over which a towel splattered with dark blood had been draped. "Bring that basin back quickly with clean water, as hot as you can get it," the doctor said to her, "and some clean towels and sheets, if there are any left. And fetch the priest."

There was a flurry of activity then, during which my father and the doctor disappeared into the bedroom, followed by the midwife and servants bringing supplies. I could still hear my mother, though she was moaning hoarsely now rather than screaming. Then the priest slipped into the bedroom, and, for a few minutes, everything was silent. I unfolded myself and moved to the door. Pressing my ear to the wood, I could hear the priest's murmured intonations and my father's low sobs. My mother was saying something too, in short, rasping outbursts, but I couldn't make out her words.

Then the doctor's voice: "Hold her down." A piercing shriek ripped through the house. I staggered back from the doorway and covered my ears with my hands as though I could shut out that unrelenting, fatal noise. I couldn't.

It stopped. The house seemed to be holding its breath, waiting for something. Now that I have more experience in the world, I know what it was waiting for: the cry of a baby, the proof of a life miraculously produced from pain and peril. But that sound didn't come.

Instead, there was only a male voice weeping. Softly at first, then with a harsh desperation.

After a few minutes, my father stumbled from the room and hurtled down the hallway to his study. The servants began to move to and fro, removing blood-stained fabrics and bringing in more basins of water for cleaning. The priest murmured to a servant as they went back out into that bright, shining world outside; I heard something about "making arrangements for the body." The midwife, delicately holding a bloody, baby-shaped bundle of rags, made her way down the hallway and out of sight.

I was alone, and I wanted to see my mother.

The heavy door creaked as I pushed it open. An acrid smell washed over me, and I paused for a moment, fear dripping down my spine like icy water. The room was dark; they had drawn the curtains closed, no doubt to prevent the outside world from witnessing her pain. The dying fire provided a meager light by which I could survey the scene. The doctor was hunched before the fireplace, cleaning his instruments in a basin of water. *Drip...drip...drip.* Something wet was hitting the stone floor.

I tore my eyes away from the fire and looked at the bed, where a blood-stained sheet covered a motionless form. My feet moved me stiffly toward the form. As I grasped the edge of the sheet, my fingers brushed against damp tendrils of hair. I pulled the cloth down, exposing what lay underneath. The husk of my mother was splayed in a dark puddle of blood. Her glassy eyes were fixed on the ceiling, her mouth open, its cracked, gray lips twisted in a silent scream. Her near-black hair clung to the cooled sweat on her pallid skin. Her fingers and toes were bent like claws, as though she had been fighting not to be ripped from this realm. Her abdomen gaped wetly where the doctor had cut into her, and blood seeped from it still, soaking the bed and dripping from the corner of the sheet onto the floor below.

I screamed and staggered out of the room into the hallway, where Hannah found me and carried me to my nursery as I sobbed, "She didn't want to go! She didn't want to go!"

My father was never the same. For one thing, once we had made the journey to Styria to lay my mother to rest in her birthplace, my father found he did not have the heart to return to the noise and industry of London. Thus, he moved us to a derelict schloss thirty miles from my mother's grave in Gratz (which had not yet lost the "t" in its name and become Graz, as it is now). He was a loving father, to be sure, and he provided me with nearly everything I could have desired, but the moments in which he found joy were fleeting. He often wandered the halls like a ghost himself. At other times, he sat in his office for hours, staring out the window into the woods, as if waiting for her to emerge from the shadows.

I, too, was deeply affected by my mother's death. How could I not be? For one thing, I decided shortly after the funeral that I would never marry, not wishing to subject myself to the risks of childbirth. In this decision I never wavered, and my father was more than willing to indulge me. But also, after the trauma of my mother's death, night terrors and horrific flights of fancy plagued me throughout my life.

Our schloss was enormous. Between his patrimony and the pension he received from his military service, my father was considered fairly wealthy by London standards. In Styria, however, his money went much further, especially in the remote region in which we settled. Situated in a thick, mountainous forest that stretched for miles in every direction, the property had been empty for years, and much effort was expended in preparing it for our tenancy. Even the paintings on the walls, obscured by dust and smoke for decades, were sent (at no small cost!) to a refurbisher in Gratz. The nearest settlement, three miles north of us, had once been a bustling village under the aegis of the Karnstein family. Now, it was nearly a ghost town. A few families had managed to maintain a small community there that thrived upon bartering, but the immense home of the Karnstein family had long been abandoned, standing hollowly across from a blackened church whose rafters teemed with bats.

Twenty miles to the southeast of us (two-thirds of the way to Gratz) lay the palatial estate of General Josef Spielsdorf, an old friend of my father's. Twenty miles was no mean distance, especially given the poor condition of the roads, which made journeying by carriage quite unpleasant. Thus, though the General was our closest friend, we saw him only rarely in the beginning.

While our household was much smaller than General Spielsdorf's, our large property still required the employment of several servants. The main house had two stories. On the top floor were several bedrooms, including mine and my father's. A third bedroom was occupied by Sophie De Lafontaine, a formidable and unusual young woman – half German, half Haitian, and more educated than most men – whom my father had taken on as my governess. The other upstairs rooms remained empty and cold, their furniture covered with cloth to ward off the dust. Downstairs were the entrance hall, the dining room, the kitchen and its pantries, a parlor (complete with a dusty, long-unused piano), a library-cum-office which my father claimed as his own, and the servants' quarters. Our cook, Maria, stayed in these quarters with Bettina, her ward and assistant. Bettina was only a few years older than me. Maria had found her, orphaned and starving, at the market in Gratz shortly after our own arrival at the schloss.

Our property was closely surrounded on three sides by the dense woods, but the grounds stretched somewhat farther to the south, encompassing gardens, a stable, a barn, a small chapel, and a caretaker's cottage. The caretaker, Martin Fischer, was married to Adeline Perrodon, a French woman. Their son Elias, a jovial and energetic boy five years my elder, served as Martin's assistant. Adeline had traveled to Styria with her family as a young woman and, after meeting Martin, had decided not to return to France. As one might expect of a woman with such a story, Adeline was a romantic at heart, and I remember her warm smile, round face, and soft embraces with extraordinary fondness, for she was not only the housekeeper but also my new nurse. My former nursemaid, Hannah, could not bring herself to make the journey to our new home; she told my father that seeing me every day would only deepen her grief for my mother. I often wondered if my father felt the same way, although he never would have admitted it. It was true that my physical resemblance to my mother – in every aspect except my hair, which was blonde like my father's – was uncanny. Of course, I only knew this from comparing my reflection to the painting of my mother in the parlor. There was no one else who might remark upon this resemblance besides my father, who avoided the topic entirely.

Our household was unusual in many ways, not least because of the mixture of languages spoken within its walls. My father and I preferred English, but French and German were more common among the others. Since the isolated nature of our existence made traditional social distinctions feel unnecessary, our servants ate meals with my father and me, and they spoke to us as equals. We also did not observe religion the way other households did. When we first arrived, a priest named Father Schmidt made the journey to our small chapel every weekend to lead us in prayer. But grief is a funny thing. Sometimes it turns people *toward* God; other times it turns them away. One day I heard my father speaking with Father Schmidt, explaining that he could no longer bring himself to worship God, as prayers had done nothing to help my mother. When Father Schmidt suggested that continuing to pray would help him avoid eternal punishment, my father shrugged, remarking that he could not imagine any punishment worse than what he had already suffered. Father Schmidt was a compassionate man, with eyes that crinkled when he smiled, but he understood that his efforts would be better appreciated elsewhere. After that, he stopped coming to our property, though Martin, Adeline, Elias, Maria, and Bettina – devout Christians all – continued to venture to the small chapel to pray every Sunday.

The effects of my father's agnosticism were compounded by the things I learned from Sophie, who had acquired a love of all things metaphysical from her father, an infamous Haitian mystic. This was an odd quality, perhaps, in a woman who was also acutely analytical, and under whose tutelage I received an education that rivaled what I might have gotten at the best schools in England. But her obsession with the spirit world accorded well with my own, and after the day's schoolwork was done, she would indulge my requests for tales of the supernatural and unexplained, relating to me everything she had heard about spirits, werewolves, fairies, and the like. One day, as rain darkened the sky and thunder shook the eaves of our house, she told me of her father's seances. Her eyes flashed as she described the shaking table, the sputtering flames of the candles, and the eerie voices that had emerged from her father, who was held limp as a rag doll in the arms of the spirits.

My father had interrupted us then, his face a stormcloud of anger as he dismissed Sophie for the day, and later I heard him warning her against such stories in the future. He was right in thinking that Sophie's stories did little to ease the fear that shook me awake, screaming, in the middle of the night. Yet there was something oddly comforting in them, too. Maybe, as a young child who felt the absence of her mother like a wound, I liked the idea that some things exist in the world even though we can't see them. Looking back now, though, I understand my father's aversion. In many such stories, the creatures and spirits of the "other world" are hungry and angry and alone. It must have pained him to think that the realm beyond, the realm to which my mother had been consigned, might be a place of torment rather than peace.

While my father had made an admirable attempt at gathering a loving community for me, our existence was still quite lonely. My mother's family had once lived in the area, not far from General Spielsdorf's estate, but her parents were now dead, and her siblings had long since moved elsewhere. My father seemed unbothered by the solitude, but for me, a girl with an active mind, the emptiness needed to be filled. When I wasn't in lessons with Sophie or playing with Adeline, I would roam the halls, gazing at the family pictures that had been left by the house's previous inhabitants and making up stories in my mind about their subjects. I read extensively, and, once I had learned enough to do so, began to write my own stories. Occasionally I sought companionship by helping Maria and Bettina in the kitchen or tending the gardens with Martin and Elias. But my restless energy still was not appeased.

I started to wander our property alone, despite the protestations of my father and Adeline. At night, when I woke from a nightmare and found myself unable to sleep again due to my pounding pulse and racing mind, I would take to the grounds, making a large circle along the border between the moon-bathed grasses and the shadowy woods. One night, three years after we moved in, I experienced my first taste of the evil that lay beyond our walls.

As the stars above me glittered, clear and cold and so numerous in the yawning sky that they took my breath away, I saw something move in the woods beside me. I stopped for a moment, staring into the shadows, the darkness so profound that it was as though I had gone blind. There was no movement now, but the sensation of someone – or something – staring at me was impossible to shake. I stood motionless and struggled to control my breathing so that I could hear it, whatever it was. After several trembling exhalations, the grip of fear loosened, and the sensation of being watched disappeared. I tried to convince myself that it had been a figment of my overactive imagination, but I walked briskly back toward the house and repeatedly turned my head to glance behind me. Just before I reached the front door, the wind picked up, whistling past my ears and driving me forward. Leaves skittered along the ground like small, clawed feet. I ran the last few steps and tore the door open, then drove it shut against the breath of darkness that seemed to be reaching for me.

Once I was safely ensconced in my room and had slipped beneath the warm blankets, the terror that had seized me slowly ebbed away, and exhaustion pulled me into the realm of dreams.

I dreamed of my mother. I was nestled in her arms, as small and helpless as a baby. She was stroking my hair lovingly. The light around us was golden and warm, and her dark brown hair haloed charmingly around her smiling face. Her voice was soft and sing-songy as she murmured, "My darling...my darling...my Laura...my dear one...my sweet one." Her warm fingers caressed my eyelids, my cheeks, my earlobes, my neck...The utter joy and love I felt in her arms was achingly bittersweet, for even my dream-self understood that it was not real, that it could never be. My mother smiled and kept whispering her endearments as she lowered her face to mine and brushed her lips along the path her fingers had taken...my eyelids, my cheeks, my earlobes, my neck...

A sharp pain stung the base of my throat, and I felt the searing sensation of blood being pulled from my body. I screamed and woke up.

I couldn't sit up. Something was sitting on my chest and pressing my head down into the pillow. I wriggled to free myself, but it pressed me down even harder, until I could not draw a breath. The weight suddenly disappeared, and I looked down and saw (even now, words fail me as I try to describe it) a seething mass of shadows, writhing and spreading itself upon me, with two eyes that shone like the black carapaces of beetles in the scant moonlight. Beneath the eyes, the shifting darkness pulled itself apart into a leering grin with long teeth as sharp as needles and tinged red with my blood.

Footsteps thundered down the hallway, and the dark mass slid to the floor, scuttled to the window, seeped under the sill, and disappeared. I shot up from my bed and ran to the window, pressing my face to the glass. The mass – still as dark and ill-defined as a shadow but now sprouting protrusions that were reminiscent of a head and arms and legs – moved swiftly to the edge of the woods. As my father and Sophie burst through my bedroom door, casting weak light throughout the room with their candles, the shadow creature turned its gleaming black eyes toward me and vanished into the woods.

Father knelt beside me and grasped my arm. "What is it, Laura? Another of your dreams?" He turned me to face him and saw the blood dripping from my throat.

Behind him, Sophie dropped her candle and screamed.

The house was in an uproar. A doctor and Father Schmidt were summoned from Gratz, and they made me repeat what I had felt and seen many times over. Even though the puncture wounds on my throat healed quickly, I was fatigued and listless. They whispered to each other, glancing worriedly at me and my window. Father Schmidt, his gentle face floating like a pale moon over his black cassock, prayed over me with his kind, soothing voice. The doctor, who was pallid and elderly, with a long, slightly-pitted saturnine face and a chestnut wig, brewed smelly herbs into a tea to help restore my blood. At one point, as I was drifting off into sleep again, they said something to my father that made him cross himself.

After the priest and doctor had left, Sophie paced in my room, muttering to herself that she knew exactly what had happened. When I asked her what she meant, she shook her head. "Your father would not want me to say." I was frustrated by her refusal, but she promised that some day, when I was older, she would tell me. Too exhausted to push the matter further, I collapsed back onto the bed and let myself drift away, encircled by Adeline's pillowy arms. When I woke up, I saw that someone had hung a rosary on the window latch.

For the next few weeks, I wasn't allowed to sleep alone. Adeline shared my bed, and each night someone else – Sophie or Bettina or Martin or my father – was posted to keep watch outside my room. Eventually, my youthful energy returned, and everyone was allowed to sleep in their own beds again, though Sophie urged me to leave the rosary hanging on the window. I did not see the creature again for over a decade, and when I did, I did not recognize it until it was too late.

CHAPTER TWO

ELIAS

Being five years older than I was (and a *boy*), Elias, who had been urged by his mother to keep me occupied, was initially a reluctant companion. But he soon found in me an apt fellow-adventurer. I was always so excited to be out of the cold, stagnant rooms of the house that I would follow him anywhere without complaint and help him carry out any mischievous plan he concocted.

His duties as his father's assistant generally kept him busy from dawn to dusk, and I had my schooling to complete, but sometimes, when the weather was warm, he would find me and ask, "Would you like to come on an adventure with me, Laura?" I would get my riding boots and jacket while Adeline prepared a picnic of fruit, cheese, and flatbread, wrapped in cloth and nestled into a basket. This basket would invariably be emptied to make room for berries or interesting sticks or flat rocks for skipping in ponds, the cloth-wrapped food relocated to our pockets. I would scramble to keep up with Elias, whose long-legged strides were unhampered by the fishing pole or bow slung over his shoulder. Once we reached the riverbank, I would entertain myself by climbing trees or drawing pictures in the mud while he cursed at the fish and birds and hares who seemed entirely uninterested in the bits of crumbled cheese he had to offer them. I usually returned home soaked, muddied, and covered in bruises and scratches. Most wealthy households discouraged their young girls from such activity, but Adeline considered the dirt and exercise beneficial.

"Look at her," Adeline said one night, gesturing at my rosy cheeks as I shoveled dinner into my mouth following a day of outdoor exploration. "She's not sickly and weak, like the other noble girls I've seen, closeted away as though they are made of the finest crystal. It's no wonder they break so easily!"

"Some might say it's unseemly," my father muttered in a half-hearted protest as he pushed his food around his plate.

Adeline looked around the room dramatically. "Who?"

I giggled at this, and my father cracked a begrudging smile. After that, no one minded if I came home needing to be scrubbed.

At first, Elias and I barely talked (I was too young to make good conversation, he said). But as the years passed, we found common ground, whether I was dramatically reenacting a book I had read or he was describing in gory detail how he had killed the family of hares laying waste to our vegetable garden. He taught me how to ride the two horses we kept in the stable, though the density of the woods made riding them anywhere but down the path to the main road an arduous task. Soon we had enough shared experiences to provide us with an endless stock of inside jokes. Once, for example, he inadvertently hooked a duck while fishing in the river, and he tasked *me* with holding it while he extricated the hook from its bill. The duck wriggled and kicked and quacked uncooperatively in my hands, and I shrieked as I struggled to keep hold. After that, whenever we saw a duck, he would scream in falsetto to tease me, making me laugh so hard that my stomach cramped.

He grew taller and lankier, and his voice dropped. Our adventuring took us ever farther from the house, until one day we came to the ghostly village north of us.

Coming over the crest of a hill, I gasped at the empty schloss and blackened, dilapidated church below us. "Do you know this place?" I asked.

"I come here sometimes to barter," he said. "We don't need much, but there are skilled woodcutters here, and one family that always has a good supply of pigs."

"Where do these people live?" I asked.

He shrugged. "Here and there. See?" He pointed to a small group walking into the area that had once been the town square. "They live in cottages around the outskirts of town or in the woods. They don't like to sleep near the Karnsteins' old place. I wouldn't either."

I looked at the silent, vine-covered building and shuddered. "What happened to the Karnsteins?"

He gestured that I should follow him as he headed down into the town. I hesitated for a moment before obeying. "They were here for centuries," he said. "According to my Da, there had always been rumors about them, as there were far too many mysterious deaths around their schloss. Then, over a hundred years ago, someone tried to root out the evil."

"Root out the evil?" I asked. "What evil?"

He shrugged again. "I'm not exactly sure." I suspected he knew more than he was letting on; Adeline had probably warned him about my night terrors. "But the townspeople banded together to destroy the family's graves."

"How awful."

"I suppose if they went to the trouble of doing that," Elias said grimly, "the alternative must have been worse."

"What do you mean, the alternative?"

"I mean *not* destroying their graves. There must have been something that made them commit such a sacrilege."

I gulped and stared warily at the huge, abandoned house.

"It's alright now, though," Elias promised. "I've been here loads of times. Come on, I'll take you to Matthias." He folded my small hand in his larger one and pulled me down a road that led to the far edge of the village.

Matthias, a young man near Elias' age, was the son of the woodcutter who sometimes helped Martin clear large trees around our property. Because of this, he and Elias had interacted on several occasions. I couldn't help but feel dismay now as the boys fell into an easy camaraderie that mostly excluded me, though they allowed me to play hide and seek around the village with them for over an hour. "He's the closest thing I have to a friend," Elias said to me as we made our way back home.

It was like a blow to the chest, and my voice quavered. "I'm your friend."

"I mean a friend my own age," he explained. "Besides" – here a broad grin spilled across his face – "you wouldn't want to spend time with me if you had other options!"

At the time, I had no way to refute his claim, there being no other options available. I only knew that we *were* friends, our affection fueled by the laughter we shared. To some, this may seem an inadequate foundation on which to build a lasting friendship. But laughter is a balm that can lighten even the most pain-bound souls, and that is no mean feat.

My father had such a friendship with General Josef Spielsdorf. Though we only saw Josef a few times a year – at least, until Emma arrived, as I will describe two chapters hence – our visits with him were delightful. He was a large, red-faced man with a loud voice and a jovial demeanor, who loved to entertain anyone within earshot with anecdotes from his life that became more fanciful each time he told them. At first, it had surprised me that my father – quiet, grim, and unassuming as he was – cared for the General as much as he did. But their fondness for each other was undeniable. My father became a different person when he was with Josef, a person who drank and chatted and chuckled. I knew, because Sophie had told me, that much of their attachment arose from their shared experiences in the war. My father had served as a medic in the British army when it allied with Austrian forces against Napoleon; Josef had served under the command of Archduke Charles. When Father had been wounded at the devastating Battle of Wagram in 1809, he had retired to Josef's family estate in Styria to recuperate. It was there that he had met my mother.

It was far more common for us to visit Josef at *his* estate, which was larger and better equipped for visitors. But I found the commotion of his house – bustling with his numerous servants and other guests – overwhelming, and so I was especially charmed whenever he came to visit *us*. On one such occasion, we retired to the parlor after a fine dinner. I was curled up in a chair near the door, marveling, as always, at the way Josef had coaxed my father from his shell with brandy and good-natured chatter. I basked in the glimpses of who my father really was, or, at least, who he *had been* before my mother's death. Sophie was playing the piano quietly, her fingers moving over the keys in their usual proficient but unremarkable way. She had dressed up for the occasion, as we all had, for Josef's visits provided a welcome excuse to do so. Her amber dress accentuated her coffee-colored skin. Josef's eyes kept moving in her direction, until finally he stood up and moved toward the piano. Sophie scowled, and Josef, noting the expression, swerved away from her, standing instead before the picture on the wall beside the piano. A portrait of my mother in her wedding dress.

"Dear Emilia," he said somberly. "She was so beautiful, wasn't she?"

"She was," my father replied. The mirth occasioned by Josef's presence vanished from his face, and he became drawn and pale again, his eyes unfocused as he sipped from his glass.

Josef was an observant man, despite his inebriation. He immediately sought to alleviate the gloom. "Laura," he said, turning toward me, "did your father ever tell you how he met your mother?"

"No," I replied. I sat up in my seat eagerly.

"Oho!" he shouted with glee. "Well, allow me to rectify *that* situation."

My father groaned, but he was smiling.

"Emilia and her family lived not far from my family," Josef began. "I knew her from when she was a child. She was a spitfire, wild and adventurous, and she refused to take anyone's nonsense, especially mine."

"Lord knows that's a *lot* of nonsense," my father quipped.

Josef chuckled. "So of course when I met your father, the most serious and withdrawn person I'd ever encountered, I knew they'd be perfect for each other." There was a wry gleam in his eye. "When we were convalescing at my estate after Wagram, I invited Emilia and her family to join us for a visit. She didn't like him at first. Too quiet, she said. But he fell for her hard. And I mean that literally."

My father shook his head, his lips pressed together in a knowing smile.

"Oh?" I asked.

"Emilia had many suitors at the time, you see," Josef continued, "and she wasn't interested in another. But your father tried to impress her anyway, accompanying her around the house and trying to keep up the conversation, though he was no match for her in wit. His leg was still quite painful at the time, and he needed a cane to move around. It caught on a rug in the hallway, and he tumbled down beside her."

"Oh, no!" I cried out.

"Any other man would have been embarrassed," Josef continued, "but your father stood up calmly, reassured her that he was unharmed, and shrugged it off as an unfortunate consequence of his wound. That impressed Emilia, accustomed as she was to young men who were all bluster and misplaced heroism."

"Men like yourself?" my father asked.

Josef guffawed. "Undoubtedly!" Even Sophie couldn't help but grin at this. "At any rate, she started to look at your father differently. And soon, he won her over."

I leaned forward, eager to glimpse more of the hidden world that was my parents' youth. "How?" I asked.

"After several visits, your father asked if he could court her. She rejected him. As I said, she had many other suitors at the time. But his response to her refusal surprised her. Other men would pout, or argue, or continue to press her; your father simply said 'Very well, then,' as though no offense had been laid between them, and continued to be a constant and loyal friend to her. A month later, she realized she was head over heels in love with him."

My father was smiling, bathing in the warmth of his memories. Tears stung my eyes. Josef's words had brought her to life, and now the silence was snatching her away again.

It was late now. Sophie stood, announced that it was past time for me to go to bed, and shooed me out of the parlor. As we left, I heard Josef suggest to my father that he ought to find a woman to warm his bed. I flushed, not quite understanding what he was referring to and yet aware that it was something indecorous. Sophie shooed me faster, but as the parlor door closed behind us, I heard my father's response: "I'm not like you, Josef. Besides, there isn't much choice out here, is there?"

Josef was the only person who could draw my father out from the shadows, who could make him smile and laugh and forget his pain. Elias was the same to me, and he maintained this ability even in the direst of circumstances: puberty.

I was thirteen when the solitude of our life at the schloss began to chafe in earnest. As I read books about the bustling life of city-dwellers and the foibles of ordinary families, I began to resent my father for robbing me of these charms. My father could occasionally be convinced to play chess or wander the grounds with me, but he was still distracted, often staring off into space or cocking his head as though hearing a song in the distance. Perversely, I blamed myself for this, wondering if there was something wrong with *me* that made me unable to capture his undivided attention. Again and again, I revisited the few scraps I had of my mother: the portrait of her on her wedding day, a letter she had written to my father when he had gone to London to arrange their move there, and a blue silk hair ribbon that had once smelled of her perfume. Her voice came to me like a half-remembered dream as I read the words written in her delicate hand. A terrible thought came to me then: if my father were to die and the few relics of her were to be lost or destroyed, would her only foothold on existence be my faint and terrifying memories?

When I dreamed of her, she was always just out of reach. I would catch a glimpse of long, dark hair passing through a doorway ahead of me, and by the time I reached the threshold, the room was empty. I would wake up, the emptiness of the dream spreading from my belly into my throat. When I paced the grounds at night, I sometimes thought I saw her in my periphery, hovering between trees. I learned that I could hold the apparition there by *not* looking directly at it, keeping my gaze fixed firmly upon the ground in front of me while I steadied my breath, the hair on my arms bristling and my legs shaking beneath me. A few times, I even ventured to speak.

"Mama, is that you?" But there was no answer except the sigh of leaves, and, when I finally turned, I could see nothing but shadow. "Where have you gone?" I whispered to the empty air.

These occurrences led me to search my father's library for answers, poring over everything from the Bible to ancient Greek philosophers to modern treatises on metaphysics. I withdrew into myself, as sullen and preoccupied as my father.

Elias, bless him, tried his best to restore me. Encouraged by his parents, who worried about me excessively and decided that cheering me was a more pressing concern than any of the other work their son might do, Elias invited me on more outings.

One day, we hiked to a clearing that had long been one of our favorites. It was surrounded by deep woods on all sides but one, which sloped upward before jutting steeply into a sharp, craggy mountain that Elias and I had named Wolf's Tooth. On the far side of the mountain, a cliff dropped precariously to a small valley below. Nestled in the side of Wolf's Tooth was the entrance to a deep cave, hidden by rock formations. We had only attempted to explore this cave once, giving up quickly when we realized – from the cold and utter darkness that stretched before us and the way our voices echoed endlessly – that it was much larger than we had fathomed. The passage curved down and away from the cliff, into the belly of the earth below the clearing.

Now, as Elias set rabbit traps in the dense undergrowth, I wandered slowly around the base of Wolf's Tooth. I skirted around a rock formation and paused at the mouth of the cave. Cold air swirled from the dark maw and snatched at my skirts, and I shivered and moved away. I stood at the edge of the cliff, peering down at the tops of the trees below. It was not a particularly windy day, but without the shelter of trees to soften it, even the slightest breeze was bracing. One gust caught me off guard, and I stumbled a bit. Small rocks slid out from beneath my feet and disappeared over the edge of the cliff with a clatter.

A harsh laugh escaped my throat. "Is it so easy, then?" I asked the air, and I found myself leaning over the cliff, trying to see where the rocks had landed, though I knew full well they had disappeared into the thick foliage below. A perverse feeling shuddered through me, not a desire to die, exactly, but an impulse to surrender myself to the empty space.

"Laura!" I heard Elias' panicked voice behind me. "What in God's name are you doing?" His hands seized my arms and pulled me away from the edge.

"I'm sorry," I said, another strange laugh bubbling up from within me.

His hands gripped my arms even more tightly, and the genuine concern on his face sobered me. "Why were you standing so close to the edge? You could have died!"

"I'm sorry I worried you." I softened in his arms and pulled him into a hug. His arms relaxed around me. Then I released him and turned to face the cliff again. "It's just...don't you ever wonder what it would be like?"

He took my hand and drew me farther away from the precipice. "I'm fairly certain that falling to my death isn't something I need to experience firsthand."

"Are you scared of death, then?"

He shrugged. "It doesn't matter how scared you are. You have to do it anyway."

The image of my mother's corpse splayed on her bed came to me unbidden, and I shut my eyes as if to banish it. My childlike voice sobbing *She didn't want to go!* rang in my ears.

I shook my head and breathed deeply, calming myself. "Are you scared of what comes after? Don't you ever wonder what it's like? Not to die, I mean, but to be dead."

"Well," Elias said warily, reluctant to engage on the subject but not wishing to dismiss me, "I believe in Heaven and Hell, as the Bible teaches us."

"But once they're there, do you think the dead have any recollection of the living? Can they still see and hear those who love them, do you think? Do they grieve what they've lost?"

Elias didn't say anything for a while, focusing on the path that was taking us back around the mountain. "I don't know," he said finally. "I don't think anyone ever can. The only way to know is to go yourself, and there's no way back."

As we passed the large rocks that shielded the open mouth of the cave, we heard a sound like a groan coming from deep within that cold belly. It must have been the wind playing in the cavernous passages. Still, an eerie chill raised gooseflesh on my arms. Elias' words reminded me of Aeneas' journey to the underworld, a recent topic in my lessons with Sophie. I whispered into the void: "facilis descensus Averno: noctes atque dies patet atri ianua Ditis. Revocare gradum superasque evadere ad auras, hoc opus, hic labor est." *The descent to Avernus is easy: night and day the doorway to black Hades lies open. To recall your step and escape to the upper air, this is the work, this is the toil.* As if in response, the cave emitted a sound that sounded perversely like a laugh.

"What?" Elias snapped. He hated it when I spoke Latin, having no education in the language himself.

I hurried away from the mouth of the cave. "It's no matter. Shall we attend to your snares?"

"Laura," he said, "I don't know why you're so troubled these days, but I'm your friend. I want to help if I can."

"How *could* you know? You have two parents who dote on you. I have a dead mother and nightmares and a father who can't find joy in anything, not even his own daughter."

He turned away, his jaw set in a stiff line as he busied himself with his snares again.

I immediately regretted my harsh tone. "Forgive me," I said, placing my hand on his forearm. "I didn't mean it. I truly appreciate your compassion and friendship. What would I do without you?"

He grinned. "I mean, obviously you'd be *really* sad. There'd be no point in living, would there? Why, you'd probably already be at the bottom of that cliff..." He grunted as I punched him playfully in the ribs.

CHAPTER THREE

THE SEANCE

A few months later, while my father was in Gratz on business, I woke from a dream of my mother writhing and wailing in her bloody sheets to find my own sheets stained with blood. I screamed, tore myself from the bed, and huddled in a corner. Adeline rushed in, took one look at the bed, and came to embrace me. "Hush, girl. 'Tis only natural."

"What do you mean?" I sobbed.

"Oh dear." Adeline patted my hair as my tears fell against her ample bosom. "I suppose you wouldn't know, would you? I'm so sorry; I should have thought to tell you."

She told me everything while Bettina changed my sheets, brought water for washing, and presented me with a pile of rags. I sat in a state of shock, my mind racing with questions that I couldn't bring myself to ask.

When Adeline left me alone, however, my shock became rage. Like a thunderbolt from a stormcloud, I made my way to Sophie's room and rapped on the door.

"Come in." She was sitting at her dresser, checking the mirror as she put the last pin in her tight, dark curls. Her welcoming smile morphed into an expression of concern when she saw my face. "Laura? What on earth?"

"You told me that your father used to hold seances," I said.

"Yes," she said nervously.

"I need you to help me hold one."

She sat in stunned silence for a moment before responding. "That's out of the question. Your father would not approve."

Rage boiled up within me. "I don't care what my father would approve of. I need to speak to my mother."

Adeline, who had heard our words from the hallway, rushed in. "You can't be serious, child. If he finds out, both Sophie and I will be sacked."

"I am entirely serious," I replied, jutting my chin forward in determination. "He's not here. He'll never know."

Adeline threw her hands in the air. "What will we do with you, child?"

"You don't have to help, Adeline," I said. "I'll do it with or without you. Without Sophie, even. I just thought it'd be best to ask someone who has some notion of how to go about it."

Sophie cleared her throat. "Laura, it's very likely that nothing will happen. These things are unpredictable at best."

"And dangerous at worst," Adeline added under her breath.

Hot tears rolled down my cheeks, and my tongue felt thick in my mouth. "I don't care; I have to try. I just need..."—a sob shook me—"I just need to talk to her. Just once."

They looked warily at each other, and some sort of understanding passed between them. "Very well," Sophie said matter-of-factly. "I'll do what I can."

"And I'll help," Adeline added. "Even if it means I'll need to find a priest to absolve me later."

Years later, Sophie told me that she never expected the séance to be successful, given her own lack of experience. Indeed, if she and Adeline *had* expected it to work, they would never have agreed to it. Rather, she had hoped that it might allow me to express some of my fears and anxieties by releasing them into the empty air. And she had expected that, when nothing came of it, the disappointment would deter me from trying such things in the future.

That was not how the situation unfolded.

It took a day for us to get prepared. Sophie consulted some of her father's old books from her personal library and made a list of the materials we would need: candles for light, herbs and dried flowers to create fragrant smoke to attract the spirits, a round table, a mirror, and various charms and crystals to arrange around that mirror.

I was given the task of gathering the herbs and flowers. Some I found in the garden and at the edge of the woods. Others – like myrrh – had to be procured from the kitchen. Maria had gone to Gratz with my father to make purchases for our pantries, and Bettina was occupied with the laundry, so I knew that the kitchen would be empty. There was stew warming in a pot over the coals and some bread loaves wrapped in napkins on the counter. My stomach gurgled, and I tore the end from one of the loaves and ate it while I searched the cabinets.

"Miss Bancroft?" I jumped in surprise to see Bettina coming into the room, her eyes wide. "Can I help you with something?" Her voice was thin and quavering. She had always reminded me of a timid little mouse, or a wren, with her nondescript brown hair, small eyes, and pointed nose. She was shorter than I was, even though I was three years younger, but her sixteen-year-old body was full and voluptuous, her curves swelling beneath the simple dresses she wore. More than once, I had seen Elias eyeing her when she passed him.

I swallowed the bread and cleared my throat. "Oh, I was looking for myrrh. Madame Perrodon and Mademoiselle De Lafontaine are asking for it."

"What do they need it for?" Bettina asked. She opened a drawer and selected a jar from it.

I realized suddenly that, despite Bettina's constant presence in our household, I didn't know her very well. Could I trust her with the truth? Would she help us? Would she even be willing to join us? Or would she be terrified and refuse to help?

"They're airing out the bedrooms," I said, "trying to ameliorate the musty smell. They said myrrh would help."

"Oh?" Bettina frowned. "I hadn't noticed an unpleasant smell." She looked down, embarrassed. I chided myself. It was one of her duties to help Adeline clean the rooms; of *course* she would see it as a failing if she hadn't noticed something amiss.

"It's no matter," I said, holding out my hand for the jar and smiling. "It's not too bad, it's just…well, what else is there to do around here, anyway?"

She smiled nervously and handed me the jar. "Do let me know if there's anything else you need, Miss Bancroft."

"Please, call me Laura."

"I cannot bring myself to, miss," she said, "but I thank you for saying so." Her smile was wider this time.

"Very well." I lifted the jar. "This will do for now."

"Then I must get back to the laundry." She scurried from the kitchen. I headed back upstairs, clutching the jar of myrrh in one hand and the herbs and flowers I had gathered outside in the other.

We began the séance after dinner. We were lucky, Sophie said, that it was a full moon; her father had told her that this was the best time to contact the spirits, who would be naturally drawn to and energized by that light. We closed most of the dark, heavy curtains in my bedroom, leaving only a single opening for the moonlight to spill through and light our work.

Sophie arranged the mirror in the center of the table and put the charms around it; Adeline lit the herbs in the bowl and the candles positioned throughout the room. They kept glancing at each other nervously as they worked. I sat in my chair, gazing into the mirror and *willing* it to reveal my mother. Sophie cleared her throat and opened a musty book on the table before her.

"Come," she said, "we must all hold hands."

She and Adeline took their seats and offered their hands to me. I grasped them. Sophie's hands were ice cold, Adeline's as warm as always. We were silent for a minute while Sophie got her bearings. The thick, sweet-smelling smoke from the bowl and the golden, flickering candlelight enveloped me, and I felt my heart pounding in my throat and hands.

Sophie began to speak, her voice low as she intoned the Latin words from the book. Adeline's brow furrowed for a moment – she, like Elias, did not know Latin – but then she breathed deeply and returned her focus to the mirror. Its surface was glowing with the rays of moonlight streaming in from the window. I was vibrating in my seat and looking wildly around the room and into the mirror, anxious that I would miss the appearance of something in the shadows if I were looking in the wrong place at the wrong time. I caught a few of the Latin words ("threshold...death...spirits...we beseech..."), but my mind was racing too fast to process the rest. Sophie continued chanting for several minutes, the words rising and falling in a hypnotic rhythm that grew more intense as she continued.

Then she stopped, her eyes closed and her head slightly tilted as though she were listening to something. "The gateway to the spirit world is open," she said. "Now, we must be careful to summon the right one."

Adeline shuddered. Too late, I realized how dangerous a séance could be in a house as old as ours.

Sophie's voice was like a bronze bell cutting through the smoke, "I call upon Emilia, wife of Edward and mother of Laura. Emilia, find your way through the veil and show yourself in the mirror. Emilia, come to us. Your daughter calls you, Emilia..."

She kept repeating the name and the exhortations, over and over again. At first, nothing happened. After a minute or two, however, the candlelight suddenly wavered, and I felt a cold prickling at the back of my neck. Adeline gasped, wide-eyed, and when she exhaled her breath was visible in a small cloud of condensation. Sophie's eyes were wide, too. "Laura," she whispered, "look into the mirror."

I looked.

It wasn't my mother. It was a young man, standing behind my shoulder. Adeline and Sophie tightened their hands on mine, and Adeline whispered sharply to Sophie that we should stop. The man's skin was ashen, his eyes black pools. His pupils had stretched out and swallowed the whites. Blood was seeping from a wound in his throat, which he touched tentatively with a finger. He looked at it with dismay in the silvery reflection. Then his eyes locked on mine, and though his lips moved soundlessly, I heard his warning in my head like a scream: *You must go. It is not safe here.* He grew more agitated, clawing at his throat and then at me, though I could not feel his touch. *Go! Go! You must go!*

Behind him, other spirits began to materialize, as soundless as fog creeping over the forest floor, rolling over each other like thunderclouds as they rose up behind the young man, their faces gaunt and stretched in pain and sorrow.

"So many," I breathed. But none of them was my mother.

"We must stop," Sophie said. Her voice was edged with panic. "We must close the gate and break the circle."

"She's not here yet," I protested. My heart pounded with fear as the spirits continued to pour in. They clambered on top of each other, reached toward the moonlight, filled the dark corners of the room with their shadowy, half-corporeal forms. The young man continued to scream in my head *Go! Go! You must leave this place!*

"Laura, we must stop!" Sophie cried. Beside her, Adeline was weeping. Sophie started the closing incantation, bidding the spirits farewell and urging them to find their way back through the threshold.

"No!" I pleaded. I focused my gaze on the young man's face. "Where is Emilia?" I demanded of him. "Where is my mother?"

He did not answer. Behind him, the spirits were beginning to fade, like smoke being sucked into a chimney. He, too, turned away from me and began to dissipate, sinking into the stone floor. I tried to let go of Adeline's and Sophie's hands, to follow him, but they grasped me harder. "Don't break the circle," Sophie warned. "Not yet." She kept chanting the Latin words.

When the spirits were almost gone, a shadow fell onto the mirror. I snapped my head in the direction of the window.

My mother was outside.

Her face was obscured by darkness, but I recognized the waves of dark hair against pale skin. She was hovering outside the second-story window. She put a hand to the glass, her slender fingers outstretched.

Adeline screamed. Sophie cursed.

"Mama!" I shrieked, ripping myself from the circle and hurtling toward the apparition.

"No!" Sophie shouted. The energy that we had summoned into our circle was sucked from the room. The candles flickered and snuffed out from the sudden change in atmosphere.

My mother's ghost sank out of sight below the window. By the time I had pressed my face against the glass, she was gone. A visceral scream ripped from my throat, and before Adeline and Sophie could stop me, I was running out of the room, through the hall, down the stairs, and out into the yard. My bare feet were muddied, rocks and sticks inflicting bruises and cuts on my tender flesh, but I was insensible to all except the disappointment of having lost her again. There was no sign of her. I stopped at the edge of the woods, sobbing and shaking with disappointment.

Then Adeline and Sophie were there. They embraced me and murmured comforting words as we made our way back into the house, but Sophie kept glancing warily behind us until we were safe behind our heavy wooden door.

It is a mark of their integrity that, when my father returned a few days later, Adeline and Sophie immediately told him what had happened. I was still wallowing in my room – I was thirteen, after all – so I didn't see his initial reaction, but at the very least Adeline and Sophie were *not* sacked, and by the time my father had knocked on my door, there was no trace of anger in him.

"Come in," I said sullenly from my armchair. The book I had been trying to read lay neglected on my lap.

I almost couldn't bear the sympathy on his face as he entered and made his way toward me. I didn't stand up, so he had to embrace me awkwardly in the chair. Then he sat on a footstool nearby.

"My dearest," he said.

"They told you?"

He nodded. "I'm afraid so."

I jutted my chin forward. "I'm not sorry we tried it, only that it failed."

He smiled and took one of my hands in his. "You know, sometimes you are very like your mother."

I tried to swallow back the tears that were rushing unbidden to my eyes. "I just wanted to talk to her, Father. I...I can barely remember her."

He considered this. "I sometimes wonder if it is more painful to remember or to forget. If only I could give you some of *my* memories; perhaps then we might judge more fairly."

"You *could* give some to me. Or, at the very least, share them." He was silent. I continued. "Father, I feel like I haven't just lost *her*. I've lost you, as well."

His face crumpled, and his breath caught in his throat. "I'm sorry. I never meant for it to be this way. When she died, I told myself I would have to be strong, that I would have to be there for you." He dashed the tears from his eyes with one hand, his other hand still holding mine. "And I will never forgive myself for how much I have failed in that regard. You see, even when we were in London, even when she was with me, I was prone to feeling helpless and alone. It has been that way since I was a child. I'm not sure how your mother – may she rest in peace – put up with me. She was fierce, and stubborn, and she loved me more than I deserved, and every time I was consumed by sadness, she made it her mission to bring me joy. Most of the time she even succeeded. Without her, though...without her, life became unbearable again. As much as I love you, as much joy as I find in you (and do not doubt for one minute that I *do* love you and you *do* bring me joy) it is in my nature to feel lonely even when I am surrounded by other people. And I *so* wish, for your sake as well as my own, that I could change that, that I could uproot the sadness from my very soul."

"You struggle with feeling lonely, and you moved us...here?" I asked.

He chuckled. "Strangely enough, there is something here that soothes me. In London, I always felt like I had to put on a mask, to hide my true self and converse with people as though I had not a care in the world, and the strain of that exacerbated my sadness. Here, though, the forest and the mountains and these echoing halls do not expect anything of me but what I am." I realized I understood precisely what he meant, and I nodded. Then his brow furrowed in concern. "Are you unhappy here? Say the word, and I will take you wherever you wish to go."

The thought was tempting at first. But then I considered how unhappy he would be in a busy city, how much I would miss Adeline and Elias and the others. And even though I had often wished to experience the bustle and society of city life, I knew I would miss the beauty of the woods and the mountains.

"I do not wish to leave," I assured him. "But I *am* lonely."

He stood and kissed the top of my head. "I will do better. I promise, my dearest one."

He was true to his word. From then on, in the evenings after dinner we sat in the parlor together, playing chess or reading. Often he told me stories of my mother, a practice which benefitted us both, for it allowed me to come to know her while it lightened the burden of his sorrow.

As it turned out, my loneliness was about to find another remedy, as well.

CHAPTER FOUR

EMMA

When I was fifteen, we received a letter from Josef announcing that his fourteen-year-old niece, Emma Rheinfeldt, had come to live with him. She had tragically lost both of her parents to influenza, and she herself was still recovering from her own bout with the illness. But he was sure she would be cheered by some company, and would we like to come and stay with them for a few weeks? He was planning to throw himself a lavish birthday party at the end of the month, too, at which he would appreciate our presence.

I could not contain my excitement, even as I acknowledged how sad the girl's circumstances were. We set an arrival date for the following week. I was an anxious mess in the interim. Knowing that there would be a party at the end of our stay, and that Josef's household was more formal than ours, Adeline and Sophie hurriedly tried to find enough fine clothes for me to wear. I had sprouted in various ways over the past year. I was tall for a woman, and my bosom seemed to be growing larger by the day, and so while Sophie gave me etiquette lessons and taught me how to arrange my hair, Adeline sat in the corner, sewing frantically.

One afternoon, Elias brought a freshly-slaughtered chicken into the house while I was in the hallway trying to walk in heeled shoes and wearing an old dress from Sophie's closet that Adeline had tailored to fit me. When he saw me, his eyes widened. He had had his twentieth birthday recently, and his beard had grown surprisingly thick. It was hard to imagine that this was the same skinny boy who once reluctantly befriended me. The awed look in his eyes suggested he was thinking something similar about me.

He cleared his throat. "I heard you're going to meet the General's ward?"

"Miss Rheinfeldt, yes," I said, smoothing out the front of my dress. "We'll be there for a few weeks."

He nodded, then cast his eyes away from me, suddenly very interested in the pictures on the wall. "You look...different," he said.

I couldn't think of an appropriate response, so I took my leave.

Josef and Miss Rheinfeldt were outside waiting to meet our carriage when we arrived. He was dressed in copper-colored velvet that heightened his ruddy features, and he howled with joy as Martin helped us descend from the cramped compartment. Miss Rheinfeldt – Emma – was like a crescent moon to Josef's sun: small, lithe, and pale. And yet she smiled genuinely at us both.

"Come, come," Josef said, motioning to his servants to get our bags. "Our cook is nearly finished with dinner. Edward, why don't you and I retire to the parlor? I've got a fine brandy that I've been saving for this visit. Dearest Laura, my Emma can show you to your room, if you'd like to freshen up before the meal."

I glanced at my father for approval. He nodded. "That would be lovely," I said.

Despite Sophie's attempts at bolstering my understanding of etiquette, the years of isolation from any peers had put me at a severe disadvantage in comparison to Emma, who had been raised among high society in Vienna. I found myself overwhelmed and unable to respond as Emma chattered away, peppering me with questions. Unbothered by my nervousness, she showed me into the guest room where I would be staying. She gestured for me to sit in one of the lavish chairs; she herself sat – or rather, collapsed – in the other, looking suddenly rather pale.

"Are you alright?" I asked.

"Not really," she sighed. "This recovery seems interminable. I'm fine one minute and exhausted the next."

"I heard you lost your parents," I said softly, hoping it wasn't a mistake to broach the topic. "I'm so sorry."

Her brows drew together in a frown, and I noticed with alarm the shadows beneath her pale blue eyes. Her face was thin, her short nose bedecked with a pleasant constellation of freckles. Her hair and eyebrows were copper-colored and wispy. All in all, with her slight stature and delicate features, she gave the impression of a nymph of the air, about to blow away in the slightest breeze.

She took a deep breath. "I heard about your mother, too." She managed a rueful smile. "It's nice to have someone who understands. True friendships have been built on less, I think."

Her words opened my heart like a ray of sunshine parting the clouds. I swallowed the lump rising in my throat and tried to change the subject. "So, can you tell me all about life in Vienna?"

"I'd be happy to. But I have to ask *you* something first."

"Of course. Anything!"

She raised an eyebrow. "How exactly does one manage to stay sane around here?"

I laughed. "I'm not sure one does!"

We fell into our friendship instantly, as girls often do. It was Emma who introduced me to the glorious world of court gossip, and every time she received a rumor-filled letter from one of her acquaintances in Vienna, she would wait until I was with her so that we could relish its contents together. Emma was particularly fond of romance novels, and her doting uncle spent an ungodly amount of money making sure that the latest publications were sent to their estate. Emma and I read them together in her drawing room, vigorously acting out the part of the dashing young nobleman and the destitute (though secretly noble-born) lady. Being bigger and stronger than she was, I played the part of the nobleman. She swooned in my arms as I carried her across the room, where we collapsed into a warm tangle of limbs, breathless with laughter. Her color was slowly returning, and I found myself gazing at her rosy cheeks and lips, feeling inexplicably as though I wanted to kiss them, until I extricated myself from her embrace and tried to regain my composure. She taught me how to dance several courtly dances, too, though I laughingly complained that I would embarrass myself at a party if I only knew the man's part.

The weeks flew by, and soon it was the day of the General's party. We watched as the servants cleaned and decorated the house in a whirlwind, and Emma trembled with excitement beside me. I was trembling, too, though with anxiety rather than joy. I had never been around so many people. Emma sensed it in me and clasped my hand warmly in her own. "I'll stay with you all day and night," she promised. If I hadn't loved her before, I surely did from that moment.

After my father and I left Josef's house, Emma and I wrote to each other constantly and arranged frequent visits at both their place and ours. Once her health had fully returned, she was amenable to all sorts of activities, from riding horses to painting in the parlor. One day I even convinced Elias to take us on a picnic, though he didn't seem as charmed by the idea as I had hoped.

He took us to the clearing below Wolf's Tooth. Emma and I relaxed on the blankets after enjoying the picnic, our heads beside each other and our feet stretched out in opposite directions. She reached up with one hand and teased the curls on the side of my face. Elias was uncharacteristically glum, not saying a word while Emma and I chattered endlessly about the latest installment of our favorite serial romance in Gratz' premier newspaper.

"What's wrong, Elias?" I asked. "Are you not entertained by the story?"

He shrugged. "I don't understand why you young women are so interested in stories of tragic love and outlandish adventure."

Emma sat up and narrowed her eyes at him. "What is it that *you* read, then?"

Elias flushed, and I bristled at Emma's condescending tone. Elias *could* read, but only well enough to get by, and certainly not well enough to enjoy it. I saw his jaw working with frustration.

"Don't tease him, Emma" I said earnestly. "He's my friend."

"He's a *servant*," Emma protested.

"He's my family, as is everyone who lives under our roof. Please, be as kind to him as you would to me."

Emma sighed and shrugged, giving in. Elias flashed me a look of surprise and gratitude, then addressed Emma once more. "Please forgive me, Miss Rheinfeldt. I did not mean to suggest that there was anything *wrong* with reading romances. It's just that...well, Miss Bancroft used to quote Latin at me, and now she giggles about women tricking their lovers."

Emma feigned shock. "Are you saying I'm a bad influence?"

Both she and I laughed. Elias studied us quietly for a moment before answering, "No. No one in their right mind would ever say such a thing. I've never seen Laura so happy." Emma smiled at this and leaned down to plant a kiss on my cheek, her lips warm on my skin. Elias looked away.

So the years to my adulthood passed.

Elias left for Gratz to apprentice himself at a forge, with a tearful farewell from his mother and father. He hugged me somewhat stiffly before settling into the carriage with all his earthly belongings beside him.

And Emma and I became old enough to attend parties outside of our own homes.

Styria did not have as many opportunities for such events as Vienna or London, but there were several noble families in Gratz. Thus my father and I – or sometimes Sophie and I, since my father was reluctant to attend social events – would arrive at the Spielsdorf abode for a few pleasant days of conversation and preparation, after which we'd all set out together in Josef's finest carriage, making our way to Gratz in comfort and luxury. Once there, we made use of a flat that Josef had retained in the city for precisely this purpose. It was strange and unsettling to be surrounded by the noise of the sleepless city.

Josef and Sophie taught us more dances. Emma and I giggled behind our hands to see the General's enormous frame moving gracefully as he demonstrated the steps.

And Emma, it turned out, was an incorrigible flirt. After a particularly opulent spring celebration at the home of one Sir Waldemar, while Emma and I sat nursing our aching heads at the breakfast table, the General brought in several letters that had arrived with the morning's post.

"No fewer than four of the young gentlemen who attended the party last night have already invited you and Laura for dinner tonight!" he exclaimed. "You splendid creatures, how on earth did you manage it?"

In truth, it was all Emma's doing. At such events, I rarely spoke and never flirted. I merely followed Emma around, marveling at the ease with which she interacted with so many strangers.

"Oh, how can I ask such a question?" Josef continued. He scooped Emma up into his ample embrace. "They would be out of their minds not to want to see you again!"

Soon, one of those four gentlemen, a young man named Franz Kepner, began a serious courtship with Emma. They wrote letters to each other constantly, promising to meet at every party and to dance only with each other. It is a credit to Emma that, unlike the heroines in our romances, she did not allow her dalliance with Franz to consume her entirely. Indeed, she remained an attentive friend to me, showing the same interest in my life as she always had and only speaking of him when I asked her to.

I, meanwhile, found the attentions of the young men who expressed interest in me – of which there was no shortage – to be grating.

"When will we find *you* a beau?" Emma asked one night as she braided my hair in preparation for dinner at her estate. "Both Hans and Paul have been pestering Franz about you."

"They're nice enough," I admitted.

"And handsome enough!"

"Indeed. But, well, I…I don't know. I have no desire for a beau. You know I don't want to be married."

"Yes, but a little flirtation never hurt anyone. It's fun, you know?"

The thought of flirting with Hans or Paul, of kissing them the way Emma kissed Franz, held no interest for me. I frowned, suddenly realizing how unusual this was. At parties, the young women our age giggled giddily, draped themselves on the young men's arms, and rarely spoke of anything but their courtships. Was there something wrong with me? In the mirror, I studied Emma's face as she arranged my hair. My eyes wandered to her small, plump lips, heart-shaped in her pale, freckled face. The pull of her fingers against my scalp sent a pleasant sensation down my spine. Heat suffused my cheeks, and I searched my own reflection for answers. I cleared my throat and added a teasing lilt to my voice. "I'm just not sure it's all worth it. I mean, the amount of time you spend writing to Franz...it's *exhausting*."

Emma tossed back her head and laughed. "It'll all be worth it when he proposes."

"And when precisely do we think that will be?"

She shrugged. "Not soon enough, to my mind. He's quite young to take a wife, and he insists on establishing himself in a legal practice in the city first. He says he wants to be able to support his family properly. Which means it could be years." She sighed melodramatically. "I suppose that's what I get for attaching myself to such an upstanding young gentleman. Why couldn't I find myself a rake?"

"It's not too late," I remarked dryly. "They're not exactly scarce."

She giggled.

When I was nineteen, Emma and I were invited to a gathering at the Kepners' villa in Gratz in honor of Franz's father's birthday. We took Sophie as a chaperone, both the General and my father being otherwise engaged. It was an elegant party, with many of the Kepners' friends and family in attendance. Franz's family were kind and generous people, and it made me smile to see Emma, more beautiful than ever in a pale pink dress, sitting beside Franz and talking to him with an expression that radiated genuine affection. It was clear that he felt the same way about her, though there was a tinge of desperation in his regard. At times his amiable façade faltered, and he looked at her the way a starving man looks at a hot meal, his eyes slipping down to the neckline of her dress, where her small breasts were pressed up into pretty white mounds.

As the night wore on and the effects of the wine began to manifest themselves, some people wandered up to their bedrooms, others to the drawing room for a game of cards, and still others – myself and Sophie included – to the main hall, where a flautist was playing for a small audience that was scattered languidly on various pieces of furniture.

Sophie and I sat on a small couch and listened for a few minutes, watching in amusement as people began to doze off. With a start, I realized that I had lost track of Emma. I nudged Sophie, who was stifling a yawn, and inquired as to my friend's whereabouts.

She glanced around the room, puzzled, then whispered, "She excused herself about a quarter of an hour ago. She said she needed to get something from our room."

"I'll check on her," I said. Sophie stood up as if to join me, but I waved her down. "Please. You've been on your feet all day. If I get lost, I'll get one of the Kepners or their servants to help me."

If she hadn't been drunk and exhausted, she would have insisted on fulfilling her responsibility as chaperone by accompanying me through the hallways of this strange house full of strange men. Instead, she sank back down onto the loveseat in relief.

The Kepners' house was large, but not labyrinthine. The room we were staying in was on the ground floor, tucked behind the kitchen. Rowdy guffaws erupted from the parlor as I passed it; the men didn't seem ready to retire from their card-playing any time soon.

The kitchen was empty (at least the servants had the sense to get a good night's sleep, I thought). Beyond the kitchen was a small hallway that led to two guest rooms, one of which was ours. As I rounded the corner, I heard whispers. I retreated quickly back into the main hallway before peering around a sconce to see what it was I had nearly interrupted.

It was Emma and Franz. Emma was leaning against the doorway to our bedroom, gazing up into Franz's face, her arms thrown around his neck. From the side, I could barely see the dark hunger in his eyes, but the taut energy of his body was clear enough. His arms encircled her back and he pulled her hips against his.

"Please," I heard him say huskily.

"I can't let you in," she said. Her eyes flitted toward the handle of the door. "You know that would be *very wrong.*"

Her voice was playful, teasing. She smiled and drew his head down, opening her mouth beneath his. He groaned and curled his fingers against her back as he pressed her closer. They broke from each other, breathing raggedly.

"It's wrong out here, too," Franz noted.

She didn't answer. While I watched in horror, she unbuttoned his trousers and reached her hand down the front. Franz grunted and put one hand on the door behind her to steady himself, then swayed slightly as she started moving her arm.

"Wait," he said. He extricated himself from her grasp just long enough to crouch down and slip one hand beneath her skirts, then rose and found her mouth with his own again, his arm buried between her legs in the voluminous layers of fabric. She gasped and whimpered softly, then slipped her hand into his trousers again.

My cheeks burned as I watched, and a matching heat began to pulse between my legs. I was painfully aware that my voyeurism was just as inappropriate as the clandestine tryst before me, and I tried – unsuccessfully – to tear my eyes away.

Franz gasped sharply and shuddered, his arm trembling against the door. Emma removed her hand from his trousers, put both arms around his neck, and pulled him down into another kiss.

"Don't you stop now," she said. She rocked her hips against his hand.

"Yes, my love." He began his ministrations anew. She sighed and leaned back against the door as he worked his hand faster, until finally she arched her back, one hand clapped over her mouth to stifle a moan. She pushed him away and collapsed against the door, her body shaking with ragged breaths.

He smiled at her, took her face in his hands, and gave her a lingering kiss. "You're an angel. Goodnight, my darling."

Realizing that he was about to head back toward the main hall, I turned and dashed into the kitchen, hiding myself in shadow as his footsteps approached. I heard him stop in front of the parlor and pull open the door. A wave of raucous voices spilled out into the hallway until he closed it behind him.

Then I stepped out of the kitchen, startling Emma, who was standing at the end of the hallway to watch her lover's departure. The satisfied smile instantly vanished from her face.

"Before you ask," I said, "I saw everything."

She lowered her eyes. "I'm sorry. I didn't mean for you...for anyone...to see. Please, don't—"

"I won't tell anyone," I assured her. "Not that I...not that I really know what I was looking at."

It was true. I knew about the carnal act and pregnancy. But I knew nothing about the myriad ways in which lovers could find pleasure in each other's bodies.

Seeing my confusion, Emma ushered me into our guest room to explain it to me.

A few minutes later, I asked, "So you and Franz don't..."

"Oh, no!" Emma exclaimed. "My uncle would kill me if I became pregnant out of wedlock, and I imagine Franz's parents would be none too pleased, either. But there are ways to get the pleasure of lovemaking without the consequences."

My body prickled with an unfamiliar sensation. Anticipation, perhaps?

"How do you know this?" I asked.

"Helen told me after I caught her doing the same thing with one of the stable boys," Emma giggled. I raised my eyebrows, imagining how Josef would react if he heard that Emma's maid was teaching her such things.

"Aren't you worried about getting caught?"

"Yes," she admitted. Then she grinned. "But the way I see it, life's too short to defer pleasure." She grabbed my hand. "Come on, let's go back to the party, or what's left of it, anyway."

CHAPTER FIVE

FIRST SIGHT

In the autumn after I turned twenty-one, we attended the party that changed my life irrevocably. Six leagues northwest of the old Karnstein village, Count Carlsfeld hosted a fete in honor of Archduke Charles. It was an elaborate and well-attended affair, with nobles from throughout Austria flocking to see the illustrious man.

Josef had convinced my father to join us, given the notable personages who would be in attendance – not the least of which was the Archduke himself, under whom both Josef and my father had served. But once there, my father was discomfited by the sheer scale of the festivities. He stayed close to me and Emma, saying little but smiling occasionally at Emma's chatter.

The opulence of the Count's ballroom was staggering. Hundreds of charming paper lanterns hung like stars above us and illuminated the jewels and silks of the dancers swirling below. A full chamber orchestra played lively waltzes one after another without pause. My father and Josef went to pay their respects to the Archduke, while

Emma and I danced until our feet were sore and we could no longer catch our breath. Then Emma led me and Franz to our assigned table, where my father was already seated. We were on the opposite side of the room from the Archduke and the Carlsfelds, which meant that we could gossip without repercussion, though my father frowned more than once at the tone of Franz's and Emma's banter. Josef was nowhere to be found.

A low, thrilling voice suddenly came from behind me. "Excuse me, but would you mind if we sat with you?"

I turned. A pair of night-black eyes, ringed with thick, dark lashes, was fixed on me. They sparkled above a full, wry mouth, in an oval face that was as white and smooth as porcelain. Dark hair – the same color as my mother's, I realized with a start – fell prettily over her smooth shoulders. Her dress of garnet-hued silk dipped dangerously low, revealing the round tops of her breasts. My heart pounded loudly in my ears, and she arched an eyebrow and tilted her head as if she could hear it. "I do apologize, but our RSVP was misplaced, and our poor host and hostess have not assigned us seats."

There was a woman standing beside her, older but no less beautiful. This woman offered her hand to my father and said, "I'm Countess Anna Mueller, and this is my daughter Carmilla. We are most pleased to make your acquaintance."

My father stood awkwardly, took her hand, and bowed over it. "Edward Bancroft," he said. He gestured toward me. "This is my daughter Laura."

The others stood to make their formal introductions just as Josef appeared, both hands occupied with shining crystal goblets full of wine. "Oh, my dear lady!" he said to the Countess, somewhat too loudly (Emma and I exchanged a glance, wondering how much wine he had already consumed). "I am glad you found your way to the table after all! Here," he said, placing one of the wine glasses at an empty place setting. "Edward, you oaf, pull out the lady's chair for her!"

My father hastened to obey; Franz pulled out the remaining chair for Carmilla.

She hadn't taken her eyes off me. They moved brazenly from my eyes to my stiffly-coiffed golden curls, from the earrings glittering in my ears down my neck to the neckline of my emerald-green dress. Then her eyes returned to mine again, and the tip of her pink tongue came forth, moistening her lips before they curved upward into a knowing smile.

I shivered, though heat was flooding my cheeks, and I landed on my chair rather less gracefully than I intended when we all took our seats.

The rest of the night passed in a blur. I watched in amazement as the two ladies Mueller managed to coax my father out of his shell. After a sumptuous appetizer we all danced again, laughing boldly in the candlelight and then running outside to gulp fresh, cold air under the shimmering stars. Carmilla engaged everyone in conversation with a charm that was so easy it was almost languid, and when she threw back her head and sent forth her deep, throaty laugh, it sent a thrill through my body, like lightning striking fire into the very roots of a tree.

When we had settled at the table again to enjoy the main course, Emma aimed her attentions at a young woman across the room. "Do you see that dress?" she asked conspiratorially.

"Which one?" Franz asked.

"*That* one." Emma gestured with her head until we had all taken note of the yellow dress that was somewhat ragged and *very* out of fashion. She giggled. "I wouldn't be caught dead in that thing."

"Emma," I chided. "You shouldn't be so unkind. We don't know the poor girl's situation."

"You're right. I'm sorry." She stuffed a bite of venison in her mouth.

I glanced at Carmilla, who was appraising me with frank admiration at this exchange. My eyes returned hastily to my plate, and I took a bite of roasted vegetables.

Emma was not too drunk to notice my interest. "No one could fault Miss Mueller's fashion, though," she said. "Tell me, Carmilla, where have you been all these years? You seem so comfortable! One would think you had been to thousands of parties, though you cannot be much older than Laura and myself."

Carmilla smiled. "You aren't asking me to confess my age, are you? I might be older than you think."

"With a mother so young and beautiful, it cannot be so!" Josef protested. His leg was pressed against the leg of the aforementioned mother, who bowed her head in acknowledgement at his compliment. "It is strange, though. We have not seen you at other events, and yet everyone here seems to know you."

The Countess laughed. "I cannot say why they find us so familiar. Perhaps we have common faces."

Nothing could be less likely, I thought to myself.

"But I can explain why you have not seen us before," the Countess continued. "My poor child suffers from a terrible illness."

Carmilla's confident smile faltered a little.

"Surely not!" Josef interrupted. "I've never laid eyes on a woman so radiant!"

His brazenness occasioned an embarrassed glance from Emma, but there was no denying that he was right. Carmilla glowed as if lit by an inner fire, her words sparkled with wit, and she moved as gracefully as a trained dancer.

"It comes and goes," Carmilla explained. "When it has me in its clutches, I can barely move for days on end, and I think to myself that death must be preferable. But when I am freed from its grasp, life is all the sweeter."

"Oh, you poor thing!" Emma said. "I know exactly what you mean. I nearly died from influenza a few years ago, and it was so ghastly that I wished for death more than once." She put her arms around my waist and pulled me into an awkward sideways embrace. "If it hadn't been for my dearest Laura, I don't think I would have *ever* recovered." Then she kissed my cheek.

Hot blood suffused my face. If I hadn't been entirely incapable of tearing my gaze away from Carmilla, I wouldn't have seen the slight, momentary narrowing of her eyes.

"Do you two live together?" Carmilla asked.

"Oh, no!" Emma cried. "Although that *would* be lovely indeed, wouldn't it, Laura? Only if we stayed at *my* house, though. The Bancrofts' schloss is so quiet and deserted," she explained. "I don't know how she stands it!"

"It's not so bad," I said softly.

"Oh?" Carmilla asked. "Tell me more." She leaned forward, her eyes bright and warm. The intensity of her gaze made me tremble, and I lowered my eyes before answering.

"Well, there's a sort of wild beauty to it. The solitude, the quiet, the cold. I feel like I can actually *think* there."

"Unlike here!" Emma said. Carmilla glared at her as though she had interrupted me, although in truth I was glad to let someone else carry on the conversation. "But we're not meant to *think* here," Emma continued. She grasped my hand and Franz's and pulled us up from the table. "We're meant to dance! Come on!"

I watched halfheartedly as Emma and Franz whirled around on the dance floor, but I couldn't stop thinking about Carmilla. Again and again my eyes were drawn to her of their own accord. Though she was talking to my father, her eyes kept flickering in my direction, her gaze locking onto mine for a moment before she smiled slyly and returned her attention to their conversation. Her mother, meanwhile, was laughing drunkenly with Josef and sitting so close to him that it bordered on impropriety.

"Your turn, Laura!" Emma said. She left Franz panting beside the dance floor and pulled me forward to join her for the next song. We spun wildly among the couples around us, ignoring their looks of consternation. Emma was drunker than I had realized; she stumbled a few times and laughed when I caught her. As the song came to an end, I guided Emma back toward the edge of the floor and glanced back at our table to see if Carmilla was watching me.

She wasn't there. My heart sank. Then that low voice came from behind me: "May I have the next dance?"

The music started up again, a slower song this time. The dancers clasped each other closely, moving together gracefully rather than in a giddy whirl. My hand burned at the soft touch of Carmilla's fingers as she led me out onto the floor, and I was suddenly self-conscious, convinced that everyone could see the heat in me. When I looked around, however, no one seemed to have noticed us at all. Carmilla faced me and put her left hand on my shoulder, leaning into me and guiding my right arm around her waist. And then we were dancing. The music swelled around us, enclosing us in a world in which only the two of us seemed to exist. We were nearly the same height, and her bosom brushed tantalizingly against my own. She was slender, but I could feel her power and grace as her body moved beneath my hand. A slight smile played upon her lips, and her gaze slipped occasionally down to my mouth before returning to my eyes and locking upon them with an intensity that made me want to look away. But I didn't look away.

All too soon, the song ended, and she leaned forward, her breath warm on my earlobe as she whispered, "You're a wonderful dancer." Then she released me and stepped away. The space between us felt unbearably cold, and I fought the urge to clasp her to me again. "It looks like it's time for dessert," she said. She gestured to the servants who were moving among the tables with platters. "Shall we return to our table?"

The night was over too soon. When the musicians stopped play-ing and our host announced an end to the festivities, Carmilla and her mother excused themselves. My stomach clenched and my breath caught in my throat as I watched her leave, the pain of her absence lodging inside my chest like a sharp needle. As Count Carlsfeld's estate was quite remote, many of the guests were staying the night there, and so everyone who was not planning an overnight carriage ride back to their own homes – ourselves included – headed toward the guest rooms.

The house was spacious, but it had not been built to accom-modate quite so many guests, so Emma and I were forced to share a room with a young noblewoman and her mother, Miss and Madame Schneider. The two of them took the bed, while Emma, who was small enough to do so, slept on a chaise. I was assigned to a makeshift mattress of pillows and blankets that Count Carlsfeld's servants had heaped up appealingly before the small fireplace, which cast a warm and pleasant glow.

But even after my chambermates had begun to snore softly, and despite the glasses of wine I had consumed at dinner, sleep was elusive. I kept thinking of Carmilla. Her long, white neck as she threw back her head and laughed, the dark hair brushing her shoulders tantalizingly, the feeling of her body beneath my hand as we danced... I kicked the blanket away from me, feeling over-warm. I turned onto my side, curled my knees toward my chest, and began breathing deeply, making each breath slower and deeper than the last. It was a technique that Adeline had taught me as a young girl, a trick to keep the terror of the shadowy unknown at bay and to force relaxation into my restless limbs. Now, as always, it worked.

I dreamt that I was visiting my mother's grave in Gratz. It was so dark that I could barely see the path before me, but a small light was drawing me toward the gravesite. As I approached, I saw that it was a lantern, illuminating the lettering on the stones that identified my mother and baby brother. The lantern belonged to a tall, thin man, who was furiously shoveling dirt from the grave and heaving it over his shoulder. His face was contorted with effort, and he was breathing in harsh, shallow gulps.

"What are you doing?" I asked. The man dug himself deeper and deeper, moving implausibly swiftly, as people do in dreams. He did not answer me, but I saw that he was beginning to uncover the coffin itself.

"Stop it," I said. "What are you doing?"

I tried to grab the shovel as he heaved it up behind him, but he paid me no mind, and I spit furiously against the dirt that was filling my mouth.

"Stop!"

I jumped into the grave, throwing myself on him. He shouldered me off and shouted with a hoarse voice, "She is a monster! She must be destroyed!"

"No," I sobbed. "You have the wrong grave!" He had uncovered enough of the coffin to grasp its edge, and he threw the shovel away and heaved on the lid. "Leave her alone!" I continued pleading, "She's been dead for years! She's nothing but dust and bone now!"

But my voice stuck in my throat when the coffin lid creaked open, dirt slid off the wooden surface with a hiss, and I saw my mother lying peacefully on the ivory silks, as whole and beautiful as if she were sleeping.

Fear and joy warred within me. Had we been wrong? Had she secretly been alive all along? Or was the man right? Was she a monster? I reached out my hand to touch her, but before I could, the man reached up and grasped his lantern, and I realized with a shock that it was my father. Then he threw the lantern hard against my mother's body, shattering the glass, spraying oil and flame all over her.

She opened her eyes and sat up, shrieking with an unearthly howl. Her jaw opened wider and wider, her lips stretching and cracking as the gaping black maw expanded slowly, impossibly, down to her belly. Her gaze, glowing red as the flames consumed her, turned suddenly upon me, and she reached for me...

My own scream rang in my ears as I shuddered awake. My breathing was panicked and shallow, and my heart pounded like a drum in my ears. I tried to remember where I was, to bring myself back into the world. Within a few moments, the panic had receded, only to be replaced by overwhelming grief. I sobbed as quietly as I could into my pillow.

Thankfully, it seemed that neither my scream – had I actually screamed? – nor my sobs had awakened my companions. I lifted my head to be sure. Dim moonlight spilled from the window onto the bed, and it bathed the figures of the two Schneider women. Both lay unmoving. The light from the fire flickered on the chaise, and I could see that Emma's face was slack with sleep. I was about to lay my head back down when the thin, silvery light from the window suddenly disappeared, casting the bed and its inhabitants entirely into shadow.

Perhaps a cloud is passing over the moon, I thought to myself, but my nerves prickled with the deep, inexplicable instinct that it was more than that.

Someone was standing outside the window.

Icy terror sank into the pit of my stomach. Something compelled me to get up from my makeshift bed and move toward the window, though every muscle in my body was screaming that I should go – *quickly* – in the other direction.

When I looked outside, it was utterly dark. No gardens, no trees, no moon, no stars. It was as though the window had been shuttered closed entirely. Then the darkness *shifted*, like smoke billowing, and black carapace eyes loomed at me from within the shadows. I staggered backward, hitting one of the bedposts sharply and gasping with pain.

"What was that?" Madame Schneider mumbled, still half-asleep.

The mass of darkness, its eyes still glinting dully from the light of our room, slowly coalesced in the air outside, gathering into itself and allowing the moon and stars to become visible around it. It took a shape that was vaguely human, then darted away from the window. I ran to the glass again and watched the creature slip silently across the garden. It paused by the door to the servants' cabin, loosened its human form, and stretched to funnel itself through the keyhole. Then I saw it no more. I cried out in alarm.

Madame Schneider sat up, bleary-eyed. "My dear," she said hoarsely, "whatever is the matter?"

"There's something out there," I said, my voice edged with panic. "I think the servants are in danger."

She looked warily at the window, then back at me. "You must have had a nightmare, child. Come, go back to sleep. I assure you, Count Carlsfeld would not let harm come to his household. Especially not with the Archduke here!" She lay back against her pillow and turned away from me.

I stood at the window for half an hour, watching and listening for any further indications of peril or disturbance in the household. But all was still and silent, and eventually I convinced myself that it had been a figment of my imagination and allowed myself to return to my makeshift bed.

The next morning, there was no organized gathering for breakfast, only a slow trickle of hungover partygoers taking pastries from the silver trays that were laid out in the great hall, saying their farewells to the Count and the Archduke, and bundling themselves and their belongings into their carriages.

Emma and I piled into the General's carriage and waited, yawning, for my father and her uncle to join us. When they finally did, their countenances were grim, and Josef barked at his driver with uncharacteristic sternness.

"What's wrong, Uncle?" Emma asked.

"It's nothing you need concern yourself with, child," he answered. His large grey eyebrows were knitted with anxiety.

"Father?" I asked.

He sighed. "We might as well tell them, Josef. No doubt they will hear about it at the next event."

The driver clicked his tongue, and the carriage jerked and began rolling forward. Josef nodded at my father in reluctant agreement.

My father cleared his throat, opened his mouth, and then closed it again, as though unsure how to begin. "Two of Count Carlsfeld's servants were found dead in their quarters this morning," he said finally.

"What?" Emma exclaimed.

I said nothing. My skin crawled as I remembered the shadowy creature entering the servants' cabin. How had I convinced myself that it had been a product of my imagination? Why had I listened to Madame Schneider and ignored what I knew to be true? Why hadn't I roused everyone in the house and warned them?

"How did they die?" I asked.

"Why does it matter?" My father said sharply. Then he softened, seeing the anxiety on my face and misconstruing it as fear rather than regret. "Don't worry. It doesn't seem to have been a violent death."

"You saw them?" Emma gasped.

His lips were pressed together in a pale line. "Doctor Schumann called me to consult on the matter first thing this morning. I don't know why; I was only an army medic, and it's been years since then. At any rate, they appear to have died peacefully. It's the strangest thing, though. There was no mark or wound on them, but they were very pale. It was as if they had lost a great deal of blood."

CHAPTER SIX

A PROPOSAL

Two months later, my father left for Gratz to consult with his accountant. In his absence, Adeline, Sophie, and I spent a good portion of each day in the parlor, reading, sewing, and warding off the early-winter chill with a blazing fire.

"This is excellent, Laura," Sophie said, looking up from my latest composition. "Very imaginative, and the imagery is quite chilling."

Adeline was sitting by the fireplace, embroidering a handkerchief for Martin. "It scared *me* out of my wits," she commented. "Werewolves, indeed. Where do you come up with such things?"

"I hardly came up with werewolves," I noted. "But as to the content of the story, well"— I made a broad gesture to indicate my surroundings —"put a girl in a remote location in the wilderness, and I suppose there isn't much she can do to avoid flights of fancy."

Adeline chuckled.

"Have you had any word from Emma?" Sophie asked. She set my story and her reading glasses on the small table beside her.

I shook my head. "None. It's so strange. She's never gone this long without responding to me, and father hasn't heard from the General, either, though he's written to him repeatedly to invite him to Christmas."

"It's very unlike both of them," agreed Adeline. "I do hope you hear from her soon."

"Perhaps father will stop by their estate on the way home." I pitched my voice as though it were a casual suggestion, but in truth I desperately hoped he would. Whenever I thought of my friend, I felt a sinking anxiety that mirrored what I had felt that night at Count Carlsfeld's party, when I had seen the shadowy creature move toward the servants' lodge.

"Perhaps," Adeline agreed. Then she brightened. "Oh, I forgot to tell you: Elias will be here for Christmas!"

Elias. I felt a wave of guilt at how little I had thought of him over the past few years. I realized suddenly that I missed him. I smiled. "It will be good to see him."

Adeline had been looking at me with a strange intensity, as if my response was of the greatest import. Now she grinned, her round, motherly face beaming with joy. "Truer words were never spoken!"

To my surprise, Elias appeared the very next day, having hired a driver to bring him from Gratz. A shock ran through me as he stepped down from the carriage. His body had grown broader, and the spirit of adventure in his eyes had hardened into earnest diligence. I would barely have recognized him were it not for his sandy hair and the way his mother and father had wrapped him in a tight embrace. The wide smile and chuckle of joy he emitted in response briefly brought back the boy I had known, until he looked at me and sobered, inclining his head with unwonted formality. "Hello, Laura."

"Elias," I said warmly, "it's been too long."

"Indeed it has!" Adeline agreed, her face as rosy and full of delight as a child's on Christmas day. "Come, son, let's put your things in the hut, and then we'll join Miss Bancroft and Sophie for dinner, shall we? Maria has made a delightful roast!"

At dinner, Elias regaled us all with tales of his life in Gratz as a blacksmith's apprentice, good-naturedly obliging his parents' overzealous questions. I listened with rapture to his descriptions of city life, my chin propped on both hands on the dining room table, despite Sophie's disapproving glance at my elbows. Maria and Bettina joined us, too, in a departure from their usual practice of eating at their own quiet table in the kitchen. Much to my surprise, Bettina kept glancing at Elias from under her lashes, her cheeks flushed with pink.

"And did you see Mr. Bancroft?" Sophie asked Elias.

"I did not," he replied. "Gratz is a big city, and our forge is not in a part of town that Mr. Bancroft would wish to frequent."

"You knew he'd be there, though. He always is before Christmastime," Adeline chided. "You ought to have sought him out."

"Leave the boy alone," Martin said mildly. "He has his job to think of."

Sophie nodded. "And Mr. Bancroft could just as easily have sought *him* out, too."

"Well, I suppose that's true," Adeline conceded. She took another sip from her wine glass.

There was an uncomfortable silence for a moment, then Elias cleared his throat and directed his gaze toward me. "What about you, Laura? How have you been occupying yourself?"

I raised one eyebrow. "Not so usefully as you have. Though I suppose that's only to be expected, given my sex." It was easy for me to be bold and witty here at home, surrounded by people I knew so well.

"What do you mean?" Adeline protested. "Are you saying women aren't as useful as men?"

I refilled my glass. "You don't suppose *I'd* ever be allowed to apprentice myself at a smithy, do you?"

"No more than my father here would be allowed to be a governess," Elias quipped, gesturing at Martin with his glass.

The table erupted with laughter, and my heart glowed with genuine affection for this family of mine around our modest dinner table, so far removed from the glamorous ballrooms of the grand noble houses with their strangers and elaborate food and round after round of exhausting turns on the dance floor...

I gasped suddenly as the memory of *her* came flooding back. Her slender fingers tracing the rim of her glass, the flashing white teeth, the eyes that smoldered like fire as they met mine, igniting an answering blaze deep within me...

Elias looked at me, puzzled, and I tried to shake the vision from myself, sending what I hoped was a reassuring smile in his direction.

"Oh!" Sophie exclaimed. She rose from her seat, her gaze fixed on the windows that opened out onto the gardens. "I just saw a shooting star!" The sun had just set, and a low swoop of orange light hung over the tops of the trees, gradually fading upwards into an increasingly dark blue. Bright stars were just beginning to peek through the firmament. "Come! Come!" she urged. She pushed her chair back and rushed out into the gardens.

We hastened outside and stood in silence, watching the sky darken and the stars brighten, feeling the cold breath of the night settle upon us.

"Oh, dear," Sophie sighed finally. "I was hoping it might signify a meteor shower, but perhaps it was just an errant, solitary fellow."

I shivered, and Elias put his hands on my arms. "You're cold," he said. "Here." He took off his dinner jacket as though to give it to me, but I protested.

"No," I said. "It seems we won't be out here much longer anyway." Seeing his face fall, I added, "I appreciate your generosity, though."

"Look!" shouted Bettina, pointing southwest. I caught the briefest flash of brightness upon the dark canvas before it disappeared, like a firefly.

We murmured appreciatively and eagerly waited for the next occurrence, turning our gazes here and there lest we miss something by looking in the wrong direction. Elias slipped his jacket onto my shoulders, and his hands lingered for a moment upon my arms.

For the next few days, Elias helped Martin with winter tasks, chopping firewood and reinforcing the barn and the animal pens. Feeling altogether too anxious about Emma's silence and my father's absence to stay inside (where the indolence of my body seemed to encourage my mind's most morbid fancies), I "helped" the men by sitting nearby and engaging them in conversation whenever their exertion allowed. Elias and I soon fell back into our easy camaraderie.

Once we had exhausted the topic of his life in Gratz, his apprenticeship, and the colorful acquaintances he had met through the years, he inquired about my studies. I told him about the stories I had been writing, which both Adeline and Sophie had urged me to send to Gratz or Vienna or even London. They were confident that I would find a paper interested in publishing them, under a male pseudonym, of course. Indeed, now that Sophie and I had reached the limits of what she could teach me, she encouraged me to spend most of our "lesson time" writing on my own; any time that remained was devoted to a more rigorous study of the accomplishments expected of a lady, such as embroidery and music. We had found to our chagrin that my musical abilities were quite limited, no matter how much time I spent practicing.

Stepping back from the fence post he had just straightened and secured, Elias brushed the dirt from his hands and chuckled. "I'd love to listen to you play sometime."

"I promise you wouldn't," I warned.

He shrugged. "Well, not everyone can be perfect like me."

I laughed and pushed him playfully, and he staggered back, clutching his arm as though I had stabbed him, his face an exaggerated imitation of pain. This quickly morphed into real surprise, however, when he tripped over a shovel behind him and went sprawling. We laughed until we couldn't breathe. The pigs on the other side of the fence trotted over and stared at us in silent confusion.

Then Adeline came running out of the house.

"Laura!" she shouted. "Laura! It's a letter from the General's house manager!"

I looked at the envelope lying on the dining room table. The seal had been sloppily applied to the wax, and the lettering on the front was uncharacteristically haphazard. It was addressed only to my father.

"I can't open this," I said.

"You shouldn't," Sophie agreed.

"Was it one of the General's servants who brought it?" I asked.

"I don't think so," said Adeline. "It was the usual weekly messenger."

I ran my finger along the edge of the envelope, as though I could absorb the hidden words through my skin. "I'm worried," I whispered.

"How long until Mr. Bancroft returns?" Elias asked.

"He should arrive tomorrow night at the earliest," I replied. "Perhaps the day after, depending on whether he stops at the General's estate."

My heart was pounding in my chest, and my ears were ringing. I couldn't shake the feeling that something was terribly wrong with our friends. What if I took a carriage there? I cursed under my breath, realizing that this was an impossibility. My father was using our carriage, and Elias' hired carriage had left immediately. It was too late to send a message. Even if I knew where and to whom to send it, the messenger had already left. And even if I should open the letter and find my fears confirmed, there was no recourse for me until my father arrived.

I would have to wait.

One would think that my years of solitude and quiet would have made me into a patient woman. They hadn't. I paced the halls anxiously, chewing on my fingernails and muttering to myself. I pushed the food around my plate at dinner, barely slept the whole night, and the next morning found myself unable to consume anything but tea.

As the clock struck ten, Elias found me sitting in the drawing room, trying to read but passing my eyes uncomprehendingly over the same sentence again and again. He gently moved the book from my lap to the small table beside me, took my hands, and pulled me to my feet.

"Would you like to come on an adventure with me?" he asked. When I hesitated, he added, "At the very least, it will help pass the time until your father's arrival."

I gave in and followed him. Adeline had packed us a basket just as she used to, and Elias held it in one hand as he led the way through the forest. It had been a long time since I'd walked the woods in this way, and I was soon out of breath and flushed. But he had been right to suggest an adventure. The air was cold, and I was glad for the coats and gloves we had donned before leaving the house, but the sunlight peeking through the trees was warm, and the brisk activity warmed the muscles of my legs. And taking in the sights and sounds around me – while keeping a careful watch on the uneven path – proved to be a marvelous distraction from my anxieties.

After nearly an hour of heading due north, we came upon one of our old haunts, a grove high on a hilltop. From here, we had a magnificent view of our schloss and the woods around it, which were sugar-dusted with snow.

"I haven't been here since you left," I said, struggling to catch my breath as he found a flat, grassy spot where he could lay the basket down. "It's more beautiful than I remember."

"The same could be said of many things," he said. He took a small blanket from the basket and spread it on the ground.

"Hmmmm?" I asked. I smoothed my dress before I sat.

"Never mind," he said.

We ate in silence, enjoying the sounds of the winter birds around us. I noticed that he wasn't eating much, and that he kept looking at me with what seemed to be nervousness, though I couldn't fathom why.

I finished the last piece of cheese and sighed with contentment. "Your mother is truly an angel on earth."

He smiled. "She is. I miss her dreadfully. And my father too."

"Are you considering coming back here? Once your apprenticeship is done?"

He frowned. "It wouldn't make much sense to learn a trade I wasn't planning to use."

I nodded. "I suppose not."

"But I do think about asking them to come join *me*, whether I end up in Gratz or somewhere else."

"Oh?" I was stunned. It had never occurred to me that Adeline and Martin could live anywhere else; they had been part of our household for so long that they seemed to have been grown from our very gardens. I swallowed, feeling the hollow ache of what life would be like without them.

"In truth, they're not the only ones I wish would join me," Elias continued tentatively.

"What do you mean?" I asked. When I think back on it now, I am startled (and embarrassed) by my own naivete.

He moved closer, knelt beside me, and took one of my hands in his own. "Laura, I have not stopped thinking about you since I left for Gratz. You're my dearest friend, and I don't want to live a life without you in it."

Now I realized what was happening, and I shrank away from him, though his hand still gripped mine tightly. "Elias," I protested.

He ignored my horror. "Laura, will you be my wife?"

I sat frozen, thunderstruck, wondering if it was a cruel joke he was playing on me. But his eyes were earnest, pleading.

I tried to keep my voice from shaking. "I told you long ago that I don't want to be anyone's wife."

He cast his eyes down. "I know you did. But I was hoping that maybe you'd changed your mind over the years, or that maybe I..." He trailed off, but I knew what he had been about to say, and anger rose in my throat unbidden. I pulled my hand from his.

"You thought that *you* would be different somehow? That *you* could change my mind?" I didn't know why I was getting angry. Could I fault him for asking, for hoping? What was the harm in it? And yet it galled me that he seemed to think that he knew my mind better than I did. Or that I could be easily swayed, like some silly girl. I stood. He followed me up. I took a breath to calm myself. "I have not changed my mind about marriage, Elias."

I should have left it at that. I should have refused him without drawing blood. But I felt betrayed by the burden he had put on me, by the rift he had caused in our relationship by trying to change it, and so I continued: "Besides, even if I had changed my mind about marriage, I would not choose you." He breathed in sharply, as though I had punched him in the stomach. I instantly regretted my words, and I chased them with more, trying to explain, trying to change the pained look in his eyes. "What I mean is, you're my friend. Nothing more."

His face was turned away, looking fixedly at anything but me. If this had been one of Emma's romances, he would have begun shouting about his undying love for me and begging me to reconsider, his eyes wild. Perhaps that would have made it easier.

Instead, he looked at me with eyes full of desolation and disappointment, and his voice trembled when he spoke. "I see. I'm sorry to have misunderstood your feelings." He bent to fold up the blanket and pick up the remains of our picnic, studiously avoiding my gaze.

"Elias," I pleaded. I didn't like seeing him hurt, but I could neither unsay my hurtful words nor say the words he wanted to hear instead.

His voice was cold. "I think it best if we don't spend time together anymore." My heart sank. I wanted to curse at him for destroying our friendship, but I held my tongue, knowing it would only exacerbate the situation. "Please understand," he said, softening a bit. "It's not that I'm angry with you. It's just...I meant what I said. I love you. And knowing that you do not return my affections is...well, seeing you would only reopen the wound. I'll be heading back to Gratz as soon as your father returns with the carriage."

In the span of a few minutes, I had lost one of my only friends in the world. I was about to discover that I had already lost the other, too.

CHAPTER SEVEN

A TRAGEDY

I lay in bed, my heart aching as I revisited what had taken place between Elias and me. I squeezed my eyes shut and wished that I could drift into sleep and awaken in a world where he and I had simply gone out for one of our usual picnics and returned unchanged.

Then I heard hoofbeats coming up the path.

Father, I thought. I rushed to the window to confirm that it was his carriage (it was) before slipping on my shoes, grabbing the letter from the table where I had left it, and running to meet him outside.

His face was a mask of anguish, stark and darkly shadowed. My stomach dropped. He tossed the reins to Martin and climbed down from the driver's seat slowly, as though his joints were aching.

"What is it, Father?" I reached for his hands. They were ice cold.

"Laura, I..." A sob wracked him, and he doubled over, his hands on his knees.

"What is it?" This time, my voice trembled. Anxiety sat like a stone in my belly, and I swallowed down my nausea.

He shook his head. "I don't...I can't..."

"Tell me!" I didn't recognize my own voice. So shrill, so childish.

He took a deep breath and steeled himself. Then he took my hands again, his expression grave. "I stopped at Josef's estate. I knew something was wrong when no one greeted the carriage as I pulled up. When I knocked, Madame Leitner — she's the house manager, do you remember, Laura? — answered. The sound of lamentation hit me as she opened the door. Her eyes were red and swollen from crying. She told me"—his voice caught in his throat—"she told me that Emma was dead."

I staggered backward, shaking my head. "No. It can't be."

My father's face broke, anguished tears streaming down his cheeks. "I wish to God it weren't true, but it is. I...I saw her body myself." He gripped his chest with one hand, as if he could stop the pain there.

The earth tilted beneath me. The sky spun. "No," I said again, in a whisper this time. Someone was grabbing my elbows from behind to keep me from falling. I looked down at the hands holding me. They were big, rough. Elias' hands.

"What happened?" Sophie asked urgently.

"I don't know," my father cried. "They said they can't remember anything from the past several weeks, that it's all blurred and unclear. Like they'd been drugged, or had too much to drink. They only know that Emma is...is dead, and that Josef is nowhere to be found."

"He's gone?" Adeline asked. "With his ward dead?"

"I couldn't believe it either. I looked for him. I thought maybe he had shut himself away, but he wasn't anywhere in the estate. And his favorite carriage was gone. I accosted all the servants, trying to get them to tell me something, *anything*. All they could tell me was that Emma was murdered by someone—"

"Murdered!" Adeline interrupted. Her cry went through me like a knife.

My father squeezed his eyes shut and lowered his head, as though the very words pained him. "Murdered by a guest that they had welcomed into the house. But they couldn't even remember what the guest looked like. It's...I don't know what's going on. I don't know what to do!" His voice was desperate.

"A letter came," I said. A dreadful numbness had crept over me. I felt my hand reach into my pocket, pull out the letter, hand it to him.

He tore it open, read it, and threw it on the ground. "It's from Madame Leitner. It only says what I already knew!"

I picked it up. Though I had been desperate to read its contents just the day before, I had the sudden impulse to turn my eyes away, to tear it to shreds and pretend it had never come.

Dear Mr. Bancroft,

I do not even know how to begin to write these words. Miss Rhein-feldt, the light of our lives, is dead. I cannot imagine a worse blow to our household. We are all inconsolable in our grief. But, even worse, we find ourselves in an untenable situation: the General has left suddenly – where and for what purpose we don't know – and we need to do something to lay Miss Rheinfeldt to rest. None of us can remember what has happened; it is as though the last month has been but a dream that

we have all forgotten upon waking. Please help us. Help us bury our dear
ward, and help us find the General. We do not know where else to turn.

Your Humble Servant,

Bertha Leitner

Until this moment, a part of me had hoped that my father was mistaken, because it just *couldn't* be true. Now, seeing it in Madame Leitner's own hand, a piercing scream ripped forth from my lungs. My knees gave way despite Elias' strong arms behind me. The ground was hard beneath my hands and my face, but I was shaking too hard to push myself up. "No!" I screamed.

The letter had fallen beside me in the dirt. I sobbed as Sophie lifted it and began to read, with Adeline and the others peering over her shoulders to see it too. When they had finished, Adeline crossed herself, while Martin stepped back and looked accusingly at the woods looming around us. Elias stood for a moment in stunned silence, then helped my father lift me from the ground.

"Take her to her room," my father said. "This is unbearable. This cannot be endured!" His voice shattered, and he dissolved into tears.

It was Adeline and Sophie who helped me hobble to my bedroom. Neither of them tried to speak words of comfort. Their tear-streaked faces said enough: this was unbearable. It could not be endured.

I stayed in my bed for days, only moving when Adeline or Sophie came in and urged me to use the chamber pot or take a bit of tea or soup. They were wise enough to leave me alone, though I heard them frequently outside my door, debating whether they should try to persuade me to get up in earnest.

"It won't help none, her lying in bed like this," Adeline chided. "It will do her good to take in some fresh air."

"Give her some more time," Sophie pleaded. "The poor girl has had more than her share of sorrow."

The poor girl. As if any of this were about me. Emma was gone, the shining light of her spirit snuffed out like a candle. The whole world, not just I alone, would suffer from the loss of her. And *Josef.* My heart wrenched painfully in my chest at the thought of his grief. I remembered the way his face had glowed whenever he gazed at her. I was overwhelmed with nausea, and I crawled quickly to the chamber pot to retch into it, though there was nothing in my stomach but bile.

Lying awake did nothing to relieve my feelings of shock and grief, but neither was I able to sleep more than a few minutes at a time. I tossed fitfully on the bed day and night. When I did manage to snatch a few moments of slumber, I dreamed of Emma. She was sitting across from me, just beyond my reach. At first she smiled at me wistfully, but when I tried to speak to her, she turned her face away, standing and walking out of the room while I remained rooted to the bed, unable to follow her.

I woke with a start, the residue of the dream still lying upon me and covering the reality of the world, so that, at first, I wondered if she really *was* standing just outside my door. But before I could gather the strength to call out her name, the truth crashed over me like a wave and knocked the breath from me.

One night, I woke to see that the light from the full moon was streaming into the room and reflecting in my mirror. With a start, I realized that Emma had not been dead long. Her spirit might still be near the threshold, lingering in the land of the living as she waited to take her leave of those who loved her.

I threw off my blankets and rushed over to the mirror, pulling it from its stand and laying it flat on the floor where the moonlight was brightest. I peered into the space behind me in the reflection. "Emma," I said urgently, "Emma, are you there?"

I waited for several minutes, but I saw nothing except my own walls and curtains. I closed my eyes and tried to calm my breath and racing mind. It had been so long ago, I couldn't remember the incantations that Sophie had used exactly, but there was something about opening the doors of death and walking through. I looked frantically around my room for candles. There was only one, but it would have to do. I lit the candle from the embers in my fireplace and set it on the floor beside the mirror. *Charms!* I realized. I went quickly to my jewelry box and took out anything that could serve as a symbol. I arranged the charms around the mirror. Some of the gemstones caught the moonlight and reflected it prettily.

I knelt again, gazed into the mirror, and intoned my best approximation of the Latin Sophie had spoken all those years ago. Nothing happened. I tried again, my voice becoming edged with desperation as I alternated between the words of the chant and repetition of Emma's name, a plea that grew in intensity until I became worried that I would wake everyone in the house. I stopped, peering into the mirror and listening with all my might.

There was nothing but silence and stillness, the latter obscured by the tears that were falling from my eyes onto the smooth glass.

I must not have done it quite right. I sat up abruptly. *The herbs!*

I stood, threw my dressing gown over my shoulders, and padded silently out of my bedroom, down the stairs, and through the front door. The night was cold, but I didn't care. I headed straight for the gardens, trying to remember what I had gathered for the séance years before. The horses in the stable whinnied anxiously while I tore through the gardens. One of the pigs in the sty grunted at the disturbance, then squealed when it saw me. Elias had told me once that pigs were surprisingly intelligent animals; this one seemed to be eyeing me with suspicion.

Elias. I had heard him leave yesterday, three days after we had received the news about Emma. Was he being cruel, leaving me here without a friend in my time of sorrow, or had he simply been unable to stay here any longer without losing his apprenticeship? I was sure it was the latter; I could not think ill of him.

It was not Elias but his father, Martin, who came out of the caretaker's cottage and found me wandering in the garden. His kind eyes wrinkled with sympathy. "Dearest child," he said gently, "whatever are you doing out here?"

"I don't know." I tried – and failed – to stop the tears that were bubbling up from deep within me.

Martin took off his jacket and wrapped it around my shoulders. "Come. Let's get you inside."

I struggled to compose myself. "Yes, I think that would be best."

We walked toward the main house, the gentle grip of his hands, both solace and guidance, never leaving my arms. As we reached the front door, he cleared his throat and spoke. "You know, Miss Bancroft, time does heal all things. It won't be a comfort to you to hear it right now, of course. No, right now you must mourn her as she ought to be mourned, charming young lady that she was, and so kind to you. But someday the pain will be a scar instead of a fresh wound. It will still be there, and plenty noticeable, but you'll be able to run your mind over it without opening up the wound again."

He released my arms and opened the front door for me. I wondered at the truth of his words, given what I had seen of my father's seemingly unending grief for my mother. But the caretaker's face was so earnest, his eyes so compassionate and hopeful, that I wanted to believe that he was right. "You sound like you are acquainted with grief," I said.

"I don't think it's possible to live on this earth and *not* be so," he replied bitterly. Then he sighed. "But to tell you the truth, Adeline and I have experienced what no one ought to suffer. Before Elias was born, we had another child. A daughter. She was so beautiful, so perfect. She was not yet two years old when a cough took hold of her, and she was dead within three days. Adeline and I didn't think we would recover. But God must have seen some purpose in it, else he would not have burdened us so."

I could see the pain still clinging to him in his slumped shoulders, his lowered eyes. "I'm so sorry," I said, my voice breaking.

"At the very least, it has taught us to take nothing for granted," he continued. "We have Elias, and we know we must cherish each moment we have with him. And we have you." He blushed and smiled sheepishly.

His words did not lessen my pain, but I was grateful for them anyway. I threw my arms around him and kissed his cheek. "Oh Martin," I whispered. "Thank you."

When I got back to my room, I put the mirror back on its stand and the jewelry back in its box, blew out the candle, collapsed on the bed, and slept until morning.

Sleeping did me good. When I awakened, I bathed and dressed myself, shocking Adeline and Sophie with my appearance in the dining room for breakfast.

"Are you well?" Sophie asked tentatively as I poured myself some tea.

"No," I replied. "But I am getting better. Where is my father?"

"In his office," Adeline responded. "Would you like me to ask him if he wants to take tea with you?"

"No, thank you. I'll take my tea with *him*." I stood and carried my cup and a biscuit down the hallway to the office. I could feel Adeline's and Sophie's eyes on my back.

To judge by my father's haggard face and deeply shadowed eyes, he'd had as many sleepless nights as I had. He was reading a newspaper, but he stood and moved toward me as soon as I opened the door.

He clasped my face in his hands. "Laura, are you well?"

I sighed and gave him the same answer I'd given to Adeline and Sophie. He nodded, tight-lipped, in response.

There were newspapers strewn all over the floor. We always received several at a time, since the messenger only came to our schloss once a week, and my father appeared to have torn through them all. "What are you doing?" I asked. I put my tea and biscuit on a nearby table and peered down at the papers.

He shook his head and ran his fingers through his hair. "Looking for more information. For anything that might help me understand what happened. There's nothing of her death in the papers, nothing about any sort of disturbance at the Spielsdorf residence. I haven't heard anything from Josef either. I've sent messages to friends in many different cities, asking them if they've seen him and, if not, to keep an eye out for him. I just feel so helpless."

"Father, how...how did she die?"

He shook his head. "I don't know. She was very pale, and she had small puncture wounds at her throat. But I couldn't see any wounds that would have caused death."

"I want to see her."

He scoffed, his eyes steely. "What good do you think *that* will do, exactly?"

"I..." I bit my lip. "I just..." I couldn't put it into words.

His voice was low. "Laura, do you really want your last memory of your friend to be her corpse?"

The image of my mother's body splayed in those bloody sheets flashed through my mind. I shuddered. "Do we know anything about...funeral arrangements?"

My father sighed. "I need to go back to the Spielsdorf estate. With the General gone, they need me to make some decisions." He glanced at the newspapers again and chewed his bottom lip. "Where *is* he?" he asked the empty air.

We were silent as our eyes roamed uncomprehendingly over the tiny print.

A realization hit me. "Oh, God," I said, sitting down hard in the nearest chair, "we have to tell Franz." Father nodded and lowered himself into his own chair, overwhelmed with the burden of it all. "I will write to Franz," I offered. "It's the least I can do. Though I'm not...I don't..."— I swallowed down the tears threatening to choke me —"I don't really know what to say. She told me he was getting ready to propose. He thought she didn't know."

My father didn't respond. After a few minutes, he cleared his throat: "Adeline told me about what happened with Elias."

I sighed, rested my head on the back of the chair, and looked fixedly at the ceiling.

"I'm not surprised at your answer to him," he continued. "You've always told me that you do not wish to marry, and I understand why."

"No one should ever have to feel the pain we felt when we lost my mother." I left my fear of death in childbirth unvoiced.

My father nodded, considering my words. Then, hesitantly: "You know, I've had many years to think about this. And in that time, my opinion has changed. If you had asked me fifteen years ago if loving her was worth the pain, I would have said no. Back then, I thought that if God could somehow give me another chance at my youth, I would choose never to meet your mother at all, never to love her, never to marry her, never to lose her. But now...now I believe that pain as deep as mine cannot exist without an even deeper joy, and that the joy was worth it all. And you! You are evidence of that joy. I don't want to imagine a world where I never met her and we never created *you*. To live a life without such joy...well, it is no life at all."

He meant well. I knew he did. But it sounded like he was suggesting that my refusal of Elias had been a mistake. And I did *not* want to talk about this when my best friend still needed to be buried. Anger flared in my chest. "No life at all, you say?" I spat. "Isn't that what my mother is consigned to? If only we could ask her whether *she* thinks it's better to be alive and unmarried or dead in childbirth. You say I bring you joy, and I am glad to hear it. But I cannot bring *her* joy, nor can my brother, whose conception came to naught after all. Do you think, if she had had a choice in the matter, she would have chosen to die?"

I rushed from the room, ignoring my father's pained protestations.

CHAPTER EIGHT

AN ARRIVAL

For the next two weeks, the schloss continued to be funereal. My father briefly returned to the Spielsdorf estate to help the servants bury Emma, promising them – and me – that there would be a real funeral once the General could attend. Christmas and the New Year came and went without fanfare. Restless and still mired in grief, I wandered aimlessly outside, my boots crunching in the cold grass.

One day, I was pacing the grounds and thinking – again – of my conversation with my father, specifically the things I had said about my mother. *She didn't want to go,* I remembered, my mind conjuring up that terrible scene that had plagued me for sixteen years. I would have screamed the same thing beside Emma's corpse, too, if I had been given a chance. *She didn't want to go.* Suddenly I couldn't breathe, and my heart was pounding in my chest. The fear of death that had long informed my nightly anxieties came roaring back into my mind, into my very limbs, and I trembled until my teeth chattered.

But now thundering hoofbeats came echoing up the path. I took a deep breath to steady myself before I ran toward the house. As I approached, Bettina, Maria, and Adeline came outside, and then Sophie and my father, who had not even bothered to put on a jacket. I sidled up beside him, panting from the exertion.

It was not the General's carriage, we could see plainly enough. It was smaller and less ornate, of a much older style, though it seemed to have been impeccably cared for. It was drawn by two large black horses with shaggy forelocks and fetlocks. A young man sat stiffly in the driver's seat, neither speaking to nor guiding the horses, who seemed to be heading toward us of their own accord. The carriage stopped just in front of the house, and the driver hopped down and opened the door of the box.

Out stepped Countess Anna Mueller, dressed in plain, dark clothes and looking utterly distraught.

"Oh, my dears," she said. She extended her hands so that my father and I could take them. "I'm *so* glad you're here! We went to General Spielsdorf's house first, you see, but he was not there, and his house was in such disarray!" I craned my neck to try to see who else might be in the carriage. A little jolt of warmth tingled in my belly at the realization that it was very likely Carmilla.

"Yes, I'm afraid a terrible tragedy has befallen him," my father said stiffly. "I cannot tell you more about it, as I know nearly nothing myself, except that his young ward Emma has suffered an untimely death."

The Countess gasped and drew backward, her hand covering her mouth. "Oh, Mr. Bancroft! I cannot believe it! She was so young!" She dashed a tear from her eye. "But you see, it is for a similar reason that I was seeking the General's help, and now I am seeking yours."

"Please," my father said, his melancholy warming a bit in response to her vulnerability, "tell me how we can help you."

"Do you remember that night at the Count's schloss, when I mentioned that my dear daughter Carmilla" – here she gestured at the carriage, and a thrill went through me to have my suspicions verified – "has a terrible illness?"

"Of course," my father replied.

"Well," continued the Countess, "I'm afraid that she is in the throes of it now, and it is worse than it has ever been. She can barely stand, the poor thing, and she sleeps all day. I cannot abide it any longer. I cannot watch my daughter waste away thus. We have sought the advice of every doctor in Austria, but none has been able to give us any answers. And so I have finally decided to leave the country, to seek help in Paris or – if I must – to cross the waters and go to London. I hear there are very fine doctors there." She paused, waiting for confirmation from my father, but he said nothing. When she realized a response was not forthcoming, she continued. "But my poor girl cannot travel in this state. I fear it will do her in entirely. I thought, if only I could find a place where she could rest in the company of friends, I could try to find a doctor and bring him back to her."

My heart was leaping in my chest. To have her *here*, in my home? I kept looking at the carriage, hoping she would emerge.

My father cleared his throat. "For...for how long?"

"I'm not sure, but it won't be for more than a few months. If I haven't found a solution by then, I will return. I do not wish to leave this matter in God's hands – He does not often take the feelings of mothers into consideration, it seems to me – but, if I cannot find a doctor, I will take it as an indication that that is exactly what I must do." My father and I, accustomed as we were to our own blasphemous thoughts, were unbothered by the Countess's irreverence, but Adeline crossed her arms sternly.

My father addressed me in English. "Laura, I imagine this decision will affect you more than anyone else; as you are Carmilla's age-mate and mistress of the household, it is *you* who must entertain her and direct her care. What do you think of the Countess's proposal?"

I tried to calm the excited quaver in my voice before answering in German. "I think we must help the Countess and her daughter. It would be heartless of us to refuse!"

My father nodded, then looked slowly around at the rest of our household, as if waiting for objection. Finding none, he turned to Madame Mueller. "Countess, we are pleased to oblige you; your daughter will be cared for assiduously until you return."

"I knew I could rely on you!" she exclaimed. Then she grew serious. "Oh, but I must ask for your help in retrieving my daughter and her luggage. I must depart immediately; there is no time to lose!"

The driver untied a heavy chest from the back of the carriage and handed it to Bettina and Adeline, who struggled under its weight as they took it into the house. The Countess gestured for my father and Martin to follow her to the carriage where Carmilla lay. My legs seemed to move of their own accord, bringing me closer to *her*.

I gasped when I saw her lying on the cushions in the carriage. Her skin was pale by nature, but now it had taken on an almost grayish tinge, and the rosy redness of her lips and cheeks was gone entirely. She was sprawled as if dead across some cushions on the carriage seat, her chest rising and falling in small, shallow spurts. Her simple linen dress clung to her clammy skin, and her dark hair was wet with perspiration.

"Mama," she said, as the Countess lifted her head from the pillow and guided her into the waiting arms of Martin and my father. "Where are we?"

"We are at the Bancrofts' schloss, my dear," the Countess replied. "Mr. Bancroft – and Miss Bancroft, naturally – have been kind enough to agree to take care of you while I am away."

"Oh?" Carmilla asked, energy suddenly suffusing her limbs. She lifted her head up as my father and Martin eased her out of the carriage, and her eyes found and fixed upon mine. Her pallid features livened. She lifted an eyebrow and flashed me that wry smile. "How utterly marvelous."

Sophie was standing just outside the front door. To my surprise, she narrowed her eyes at Carmilla as my father and Martin brought her inside. Behind us, the Countess's horses had already begun to trot away.

After Carmilla collapsed in exhaustion in one of our guest bedrooms, my father instructed Bettina to check on her frequently. She didn't stir all that day or even into the next morning, at which point we wondered if it would be prudent to send for a doctor. And yet she looked peaceful and untroubled in her sleep, her limbs relaxed on the bed and a hint of a smile on her face, her breathing slow and steady.

When she finally awoke near tea-time of the second day and ventured into the parlor with Bettina's help, Father broached the subject.

"Oh, no," she said. "I have had doctors all my life. None of them can help me, and so there is no use in troubling yourself. I merely require rest; this episode will pass, as the others do. I *do* appreciate your concern, though." She took a few sips of tea and a tiny nibble of a biscuit, and then, as if even such a meager conversation had exhausted her, she retired back to the bedroom.

There were several more days like this, and eventually our anxiety about her strange schedule abated. Nevertheless, I wandered the hallways with a knot of complicated emotions tightening my innards and making it difficult for me to eat. On the one hand, I longed to see our guest. On the other, I was still reeling from Emma's death. The pain of losing my friend was magnified exponentially by the inexplicability of that loss, and often a wave would hit me as I completed the most mundane tasks, sending me, sobbing, to my bedroom.

After five days of brief and unsatisfying interactions, however, there was a change in Carmilla. She was no longer as pale as the moon when she awoke, and she took the trouble to dress herself fully and arrange her hair. Unaccompanied by Bettina, she came to find my father and me in the parlor, where we were playing chess. My father had been unusually active since Carmilla arrived; it seemed that having a guest to care for had given him a sense of purpose. Though his face was still tight with worry and grief from Josef's news, he did not simply wander the halls aimlessly, but took a keen interest in the conditions of both Miss Mueller and the household. Just this morning he had heard Martin and Adeline whispering in an agitated manner, and when they explained that a pig had been found dead in the sty with no obvious cause, he promised to send for another immediately, and to summon the nearest veterinarian as soon as he had the chance.

Sophie and Adeline were in the parlor, as well, the former watching the chess game while she embroidered, the latter dusting above the fireplace, which was roaring with warmth against the icy chill of winter that threatened to settle deep in our bones.

Carmilla entered, wearing a gown of deep sapphire that was too fine for our simple surroundings, her dark hair arranged elegantly atop her head. Her eyes were bright and her step lively as she approached us, clapping her hands with excitement.

"A game of chess!" she said. "How wonderful!"

My father stood awkwardly, struggling in vain to mask his shock. "Miss Mueller, you look much improved!"

She waved her hand as if shooing away a fly. "My illness is like this. It goes as quickly as it arrives. And do please call me Carmilla."

I stood, too, and gestured to the board. "Would you like to play? My father and I have nearly finished our game."

"Have we?" My father glanced at the board. "Good lord, I suppose we have! My daughter has me in check, it seems!" He chuckled.

"Oh no," she said. "I was hoping to enjoy tea with you, if you would be so kind to indulge me."

"Tea sounds lovely," my father said. "Adeline, would you ask Bettina to bring the tea service?"

"I'll bring it myself, sir," Adeline replied. "Bettina is unwell today."

Everyone in the room turned to her in surprise, except Carmilla.

"Don't know what's wrong with her," Adeline shrugged. "It doesn't seem to be anything of real concern, but she's pale and exhausted. She couldn't get herself out of bed this morning!"

"That's unlike her," my father said.

"It is," Adeline agreed.

"Shall I send for the doctor?"

"Tomorrow, I think, if her condition hasn't improved. I imagine a day or so of rest will put her to rights, though, sir."

Sophie stood suddenly, glancing at Carmilla, who was studying the chess board with interest. "I'll go see if Bettina needs anything," she said.

A few minutes later, the four of us – father, Adeline, Carmilla, and myself – had settled down for tea. Carmilla was eating with gusto. I watched her in awe, pleased to see her returning to the state she had been in when we met at Count Carlsfeld's fete.

Wanting desperately to engage her in conversation but unsure of how to begin, I held my teacup close to my lips and took frequent sips. Finally, I mustered up the courage to venture, "Miss Mueller, how have you occupied yourself since the Count's soiree?"

Her eyes held mine as she swallowed the last bite of her sandwich and took a sip of tea to wash it down. "Laura, please. I insist that you and your father call me Carmilla."

"Carmilla." I savored the taste of her name on my lips.

She smiled. "Well, unfortunately, my illness seized me very shortly after that pleasant occasion. My mother dragged me all around Austria, looking for a doctor who could help me. But the traveling only seemed to make things worse, so we returned to Styria. I believe she told you the rest. She wished to widen her search for a doctor, but she could neither take me with her nor leave me at home by myself. We thought it best to seek a gracious host, and as we remembered you both so fondly, we headed in this direction."

"Where *is* your home?" I asked.

"Not far from here." She helped herself to another sandwich.

"Yes, but where precisely?" my father asked.

"Well –" her tone suggested she was about to answer the question, but as she reached for the butter dish, she knocked over her cup and spilled tea across the table. She stood hastily, trying to stop the damage with her napkin. "Oh, dear!" she said.

"Don't you worry, miss," Adeline said, using her own napkin to help Carmilla. "I'll fetch Maria; she can bring a towel."

"I am *so* sorry!" Carmilla exclaimed. She sat back in her chair.

"It's quite alright," my father said. "We would be poor hosts indeed to be offended by an accident!"

"You're too kind, both of you," Carmilla said. Then she scowled. "I fear I am demanding too much of your generosity."

I covered her hand with my own. "Not at all. It is wonderful to have you here. We only wish we could do more to help your...condition."

An odd shadow passed over her expression. Then she smiled and stood up. "Laura, if you don't mind, I'd love it if you – and your father, of course – would show me around the house."

"If you're feeling up to it," I said.

"I am," she assured me. She took my hand, her fingers almost impossibly warm in mine, and I stood, ready to oblige her desire.

We wandered through the hallways, discussing the portraits and pointing out aspects of the architecture. Once we had exhausted these topics, she said, "You asked me at tea how I have occupied myself since the night we met. How about you? Have any notable events occurred in the Bancroft household?"

"Nothing noteworthy has happened *here*," my father said, "but did you hear about dear Emma? We told your mother about her, but you may not have heard, as you were quite insensible."

"Emma?" Carmilla asked. Her tone suggested she didn't recognize the name; it was like an arrow through my heart.

"Yes," my father said. "Miss Rheinfeldt, the General's ward. You must remember her; we were all sitting together at the Count's."

"Oh, yes, I remember her!" Carmilla exclaimed. Then she frowned. "What happened?"

My voice shook as I told her what we knew.

Carmilla brought her hand to her mouth in a perfect representation of shock. "How utterly *awful*. And you two seemed so close!"

I fought back tears. "We were. I don't think I've quite wrapped my head around her being gone."

"Nor should you." Carmilla reached out to touch my face in sympathy. She wiped a tear from my cheek with her forefinger and held it up, looking at it with interest. Then she swayed a bit on her feet, so that my father and I moved to support her. "I'm sorry," she said. "I fear I may have overestimated my recovery. I was just so excited to be up and about again."

I leaned down and let her put one arm around my shoulders while I wrapped an arm around her waist, my hand pressing into the solid ribs underneath her warm, soft flesh. The feel of her drove any thought of Emma from my mind.

"Thank you," Carmilla whispered. She kissed my cheek innocently, as though she were unaware that the brush of her lips on my skin set me aflame from my scalp to the soles of my feet.

On the Sunday morning ten days after her arrival, Carmilla arose earlier than usual. At breakfast, Adeline asked her if she'd like to visit the chapel with her and Martin. "No, thank you," Carmilla responded, a glint of amusement in her eyes. "I haven't been to church in a very long time, and I'm not about to start now." Adeline tsked, scandalized, but my father smiled as he sipped his coffee. Sophie, meanwhile, was staring at Carmilla coldly.

After Martin, Adeline, Maria, and Bettina headed to the chapel, my father retired to his office, and Sophie headed out for a walk, saying she needed to clear her head. Carmilla and I strolled around the garden, her hand clasping mine for support. Then we moved to the parlor to play card games.

The hours passed, and the other members of the household were still occupied elsewhere. Carmilla began to tire, and she asked me, after we had taken tea together, to accompany her to her room and read to her there. "It's deathly dull in the bedroom, you see," she explained, "and while I don't have the energy to read myself, my mind races such that I cannot sleep."

"What would you like me to read?" I asked. "My father has many things in his library."

"Oh, I don't know." She gave a carefree toss of her long-fingered hand. She was wearing a dress that, though made of linen and meant for daily wear, was impeccably fitted. Her breasts moved tantalizingly against the fabric as she gestured. "Whatever you like. Show me what *your* tastes are."

Having left to consult with Martin about an issue with the chicken coop, my father was no longer in his office. Carmilla and I perused the shelves. As I traced my finger along the spines of the books, she was beside me, so close her breath tickled my ear. I was finding it difficult to focus on the titles of the books, and I swallowed to regain my composure.

"Here," I said, affecting as much aplomb as I could muster and pulling a short, well-worn book from the shelf. "If you're looking to ease boredom, this will do the trick."

We went to her bedroom together. All the curtains were drawn, so that only the light from the fireplace lit the room, which was stuffy and hot. "Do you mind if I open the curtains?" I asked.

"I would rather you didn't. I know it makes it more difficult to read, but I'm beginning to tire, and the light hurts my eyes. But you may stoke the fire, if you wish."

I set the book on her bedside table and fed the fire with some of the wood pieces from the basket. Out of the corner of my eye I could see Carmilla stepping out of her shoes and slowly removing her dress, letting it pool around her feet before she picked it up and tossed it over a chair nearby. She was only in her shift now, and I marveled at the parts of her I hadn't seen before. White, shapely feet and ankles rising into rounded calves, arms that were long and surprisingly muscular, and the shadows of dark, hardened nipples through the thin fabric. My face burned both from my proximity to the fire and from the illicit thrill of seeing her body in this way. I tried not to leer too obviously, but she caught my gaze and smiled. Then she slipped beneath the covers of the bed and let her head relax against the pillow. She gestured to the armchair beside her, and I sat, arranging my skirts comfortably beneath me.

Before I could open the book and begin reading, there were several sudden, sharp raps on the door.

"Who is it?" Carmilla asked.

Sophie opened the door. "Excuse me, Miss Mueller, but have you seen—" When she saw me sitting beside the bed, her eyes widened with alarm. Then she straightened, her countenance stern. "Laura, my dear, you shouldn't disturb our guest. She looks tired."

"I'm just reading to her until she falls asleep," I protested. "It won't be long. I shall join you for dinner."

My governess paused, apparently reluctant to leave us alone. Finally, she nodded and closed the door. Carmilla's dark eyes were gleaming as she gazed at me, a small smile playing on her full, pink lips. I cleared my throat and asked, "Shall we begin?"

The book was a bawdy, rollicking adventure that centered around an unlikely romance between two hapless young nobles. It was one I had read many times before, and the characters were like old friends to me. Though my heart was pounding with nervousness at Carmilla's proximity, and though I felt my old shyness threatening to incapacitate me, I took a breath and began to read with gusto.

Carmilla was delighted. At times she threw her head back and laughed, her white teeth flashing in the firelight; at others she exclaimed with surprise at the unexpected developments in the overly-complex plot.

After an hour, however, my eyes and voice were exhausted from the effort, and I excused myself from reading further.

Carmilla sighed with pleasure. "That was divine. What a delight, to see you tell it so animatedly! I knew when I first saw you that your quiet demeanor was hiding a woman of passion and intelligence."

I blushed at the compliment. "There isn't much to do in this empty old house," I said. "I've read this story dramatically on numerous occasions, though this is the first time I've had an audience beyond my own mirror." She laughed again, and my stomach fluttered at the thrill of causing her pleasure.

She covered one of my hands with her own. Though she was warm, the touch sent a shiver through me. "I am tired, and I must ask you to take your leave. But will you read to me tomorrow? Please?"

She was indeed looking quite pale. Even her lips had lost some of their color, and there were dark shadows under her eyes. I wanted to make her laugh again. I straightened and feigned an air of importance. "Well, I'll have to check my schedule, but I believe I can accommodate your request." I was rewarded with a hearty peal of laughter before she bid me goodnight and turned away from me.

I left her room and hurried to my own, shaking with nervous excitement. After I had shut the door behind me, I leaned against it, trying to catch my breath, overcome by the intensity of it all – her shining eyes, her lithe body, her enthralling voice. I knew enough of the world to recognize what I was feeling, but I had never imagined that it would feel so utterly maddening. I had always assumed Cupid's age-old arrow was metaphorical, but here I was, struggling to draw breath like a deer wounded by a hunter. A very, very beautiful hunter. I shook my head as if to wake myself, but if it was a dream, it stayed firmly in place.

Even if it is a dream, I realized, *I don't want to wake from it.*

CHAPTER NINE
A DEPARTURE

A few mornings later, at breakfast, I picked at my food, trying in vain to focus on the conversation between my father, Adeline, and Martin, who were discussing what we would need to procure from Gratz and the Karnstein village to make it through the rest of the winter. Sophie was silent, watching me with a hawklike expression. I was getting ready to excuse myself from the table when something Martin was saying caught my ear.

"Excuse me, Martin, but I missed that last bit. What's happening in the village?" I asked.

"Oh," he said, surprised by my abrupt question. He shifted uncomfortably, then cleared his throat. "A strange sort of sickness. Just a few months ago, they lost two of their young people suddenly, in their sleep. And in the past couple of weeks several more of them have fallen ill. They're a superstitious lot, and they're beginning to mutter about the old Karnstein family curse."

"What was the curse?" I asked. "I remember Elias telling me something many years ago, but he didn't go into much detail."

"I wish I knew more myself, but even those who still live there don't seem to know much about it. All they know is that, more than a century ago, the village was bustling and prosperous, until some creature – or creatures – began to prey on the inhabitants one by one. The villagers believed that the Karnsteins were responsible for it somehow, even though one of the victims was the beloved young countess herself. The violence didn't stop until a man came from afar, killed one of the creatures, and destroyed the family's graves."

"Good God," my father said, crossing himself.

"It's a horrible story," Adeline said. She sent her husband a chiding look. "And one that certainly isn't suitable for the breakfast table."

"And they believe that the same thing is happening again?" Sophie asked.

"They are worried it might be, yes," Martin admitted. "Many of them speak of leaving, though they have nowhere else to go, and I fear that, soon, the little that remains of the village will be gone entirely."

"That is most troubling," my father said. "Do you think we should send for someone? A priest, or a doctor? Someone who can give them a rational explanation for these deaths?"

"I'm not sure it would do much good," Martin sighed. "As I said, they are a superstitious lot." Something in his voice suggested he didn't fault them for it.

"I see," my father said. "Do you give credence to their fears?"

Martin hesitated, and he and Adeline exchanged a worried glance. "I wish I could say no, sir," he admitted, "but I've lived too long in these woods to deny that there are things out there that can't be explained. Why, just last night I saw something that chilled me to the bone and sent me running for my torch and crucifix. I heard the animals in their pens, rustling about as if something had scared them. I went outside and saw a mist floating above the ground, a dark mist, like it was made from shadows rather than fog. When I approached, it moved quickly away from the pens and into the woods, and just before it flew out of sight entirely it seemed to form itself into the shape of a person, looking back at me with strange eyes."

Sophie and my father gasped. My spine tingled with icy terror, remembering my own frightful encounters.

"Why didn't you tell me immediately?" my father asked.

Martin shrugged. "When I woke up this morning, there wasn't anything amiss with the animals. It's not the first time I've seen something strange in these woods. I'm never sure if it's my own flights of fancy, a trick of the light, or something I'm not meant to see. And if it's the latter, what's there to do about it?"

That night, as I was preparing for bed in the firelight's glow, there was a knock on my door. I donned my dressing gown and called out, "Come in."

It was Sophie. The lines of her face were drawn tight with concern. "I apologize for calling on you so late."

"It's no matter," I said. "What is it?"

She looked behind her, making sure that the bedroom door was well and truly closed. "I'm not sure how you will take this. I've seen the way you look at her."

"Her?" I asked. There was only one *her* in my mind. "You mean Carmilla?"

She nodded somberly. My heart began to pound. Was she accusing me of something? Was she accusing *Carmilla* of something? "Go on," I urged.

"I..." her words faltered, and it was such a departure from her usual eloquence that I braced myself for what was coming. "I think you should stay away from her, Laura."

I was stunned. "Why?"

"There's something *wrong* about her. I don't know what it is, but..."

"She's ill, Sophie. I never knew you to be cruel."

"No, it's not that," she explained. "It's...the timing of her arrival and the things occurring in here and in the village. And her mother's strange behavior...I'm not sure what to make of it."

My eyes widened in shock. "You think she has something to do with the things happening in the *village*? A woman who can barely walk for more than a few minutes, who is shut in her bedroom all night and most of the day? I'm truly astonished to hear such things from you, Sophie."

"That's precisely it. I don't think she's sick. I think her illness is a pretext she's using to gain access to our house...and to *you*. Did you notice that Bettina became ill just when Carmilla's health improved?"

"You think she had something to do with *that*? Did you ask Bettina what happened?"

Sophie hesitated for a moment before answering. "I did. She doesn't remember anything strange happening."

I lifted my chin. "Sophie, I think you should leave my room and stop insulting our guest. Perhaps your head will be cooler and more rational tomorrow, once the chill of Martin's story has worn off."

"Laura, please," Sophie pleaded, stepping closer. "Did she ever tell you where she was from?"

I hesitated. We had been interrupted in the midst of her answer to that question, and it hadn't come up since then. Still, I didn't want to encourage Sophie's paranoia. "No," I said. "Do *you* know where she's from?"

"I don't. And I have never heard of her or her mother before, despite her mother's claim to be a Countess."

"Would it make you feel better if I asked her and found out once and for all?" I snapped.

She shook her head. "No, it would make me feel better if you stayed away from her."

I tried to swallow my rage. Stay away from her? When all I wanted to do was be near her? "Sophie, I demand that you leave my room this instant, unless you can come up with a *good* reason for your slander of Miss Mueller."

She sighed in resignation and turned to go. Before she opened the door, however, she sent one more remark over her shoulder. "She looks at you the way a cat looks at a mouse. Please be careful."

Now, my dear reader, you have no doubt already realized, because of the way I have framed my story, that Sophie was correct, and that Carmilla was indeed a pernicious and destructive evil. You may, in fact, be wondering why we ignored the signs that had been laid at our feet, signs that, *in hindsight*, would lead anyone directly to the conclusion that our guest was not what she seemed. But if my long years have taught me anything, it is this: when we hear of something terrible befalling other people, something that might have been foreseen if those people had paid attention to the evidence, we are wont to wonder, "Why didn't they notice?" or "Why didn't they do something sooner?" when the truth is that, *in the absence of hindsight*, the evidence was not at all clear. Why would I ever think that Carmilla and the deadly shadow creature (whose existence itself was so irrational as to defy belief!) were one and the same, when she seemed merely a sick, vulnerable, and beautiful woman? Indeed, as you will see, even when the evidence continued to mount against her, I was slow to accept the truth, up until the moment when I heard it from her own mouth. This was not just because I knew very little about vampires and would never have associated the object of my desire with such a creature, though that *was* part of it. No, I attribute it more to the mind's capacity for denial. By and large, if we wish *not* to believe a thing, we will shape reality to accommodate that wish, willfully misinterpreting everything that threatens to shatter our carefully constructed fortresses of delusion.

Especially when love is involved.

The next day, Carmilla was nowhere to be found. We were accustomed to her sleeping through the morning hours, but when she did not appear for tea, I made my way to her bedroom and knocked gently on the door. There was no response. I knocked again and called her name. Since she had been unwell when I'd taken my leave the night before, the continued silence filled me with dread. Deciding that ensuring her safety was more important than maintaining proper etiquette, I tried to open the door.

The knob didn't budge. The door was locked. I shook it a few times, feeling panic rise in my throat, and called her name again. She did not answer.

I ran to find my father, who was in his office. "Father, please come quickly!" I urged. "Miss Mueller's door is locked, and she's not answering. I fear the worst!" He removed the master key from his desk drawer and followed me back, pale with concern.

My heart was racing at the thought of finding her cold and motionless on the bed, but she wasn't in the room at all. The window was partially open, the curtains billowing slightly in the cold breeze.

"What in God's name?" my father asked. "She must be in here; she could only have locked the door from the inside."

But once we had exhausted every possible hiding place – and why would she have hidden? – and ruled out the idea that she had left through the second-story window, we called for Maria and Bettina to help us search the house. Sophie and Adeline joined us as well, the former scowling and the latter wide-eyed with panic. Our search led us out onto the grounds and even a fair distance into the snowy woods, but when the sky began to darken, we were forced to make our way back inside. Defeated and desperate, we were heading to our rooms to change out of our wet, muddied clothes when Carmilla swooped into the main hallway, dressed for dinner in a light blue gown.

"Oh!" she exclaimed. "Where were you all? I was so scared!"

My father frowned. "Well, Miss Mueller, we were out looking for *you*."

"What?" Her look of confusion echoed my father's. "I've been here the whole time, Mr. Bancroft." Her cheeks were flushed, and her eyes burned feverishly. There was a pinched air about her, as if she were in pain, and she seemed to limp somewhat as she approached us.

"The door to your room was locked," I said. I was so relieved to see her that the oddity of the circumstance was already fading. "We opened it and searched for you, but you weren't there."

"Oh, dear," she said. "Just a few hours ago, I was feeling exceedingly well, so I decided to dress up for tea and take a small tour around the schloss. I must confess, however, that I got a bit lost up in the attic. There are so many pictures up there in piles and in chests, you see, and I was utterly absorbed while perusing them."

"And you didn't hear us calling for you?" Sophie scowled. "We were loud enough to wake the dead."

"No, I'm sorry, I didn't hear anything."

"And the locked bedroom door?" Sophie demanded. "How do you explain that?"

Carmilla narrowed her eyes at her interrogator. Sophie returned the glare unflinchingly, and there was an uncomfortable period of silence. Then Carmilla shrugged and gave a girlish giggle. "Isn't that strange? I certainly didn't lock it; I don't have a key! Perhaps one of the servants saw that I had left and locked it to keep my belongings safe!" She placed her hand on my father's arm.

For a moment, his eyes seemed to lose focus. Then he nodded slowly and returned to himself. "It's no matter," he said. "We're all safe, and it's time for dinner."

Sophie was unappeased, a burgeoning protest pushing her lips into a tight circle, but my father raised his hand to stop her. "Come," he said. "Let's get ourselves changed and join Miss Mueller in the dining room."

Carmilla ate and drank with unusual gusto that night, engaging us all in conversation with an energy we hadn't seen in her before. Indeed, she seemed to have forgotten Sophie's uncordial interrogation entirely, for she drew my governess into conversation until even *she* appeared to have let go of the day's discomfort. The rapport between the two of them dissipated shortly after dessert, however, when Carmilla, swallowing the last of the ruby-red wine from her crystal goblet, said, "You know, Mr. Bancroft, the family you have gathered for yourself is most unusual. Most women of an age with Laura and me no longer have governesses at all, let alone the same ones they had when they were young."

Sophie's head snapped up, and she stared at Carmilla.

My father seemed not to notice the insulting implication. "Our household is unusual in many ways," he admitted. "Mademoiselle De Lafontaine is not simply Laura's governess. She is an important member of the family."

"Surely she must wish to make her own way in life," Carmilla suggested. "And Laura might benefit from other teachers. Perhaps more qualified ones?"

I felt a sharp pang of dismay at the unkindness of her words, and I thought suddenly of my governess's earlier warning to me. Sophie was shaking with the effort of keeping her voice level. "Don't you dare to presume what I do and do not wish for, Miss Mueller. I would be honored to stay here as long as Laura and Mr. Bancroft will have me."

"As you say," Carmilla said, shrugging off the knife's edge of Sophie's ire. My throat constricted with envy as she put her hand on my father's arm again. He continued eating, his face blank.

Sophie stood up and excused herself from the table. I considered following her, wishing to assure her of our affection, but as I put my silverware on my plate, Carmilla stopped me.

"Laura, my dear," she said. "Please stay with us."

I shook my head. "I feel I must comfort her. The words you spoke were unkind, Carmilla."

A flash of anger widened her eyes. Then she pouted. "Well, if my words are inspiring your departure, I regret them indeed. Stay, and I promise I will speak with Mademoiselle De Lafontaine myself once we have finished our dinner."

I hesitated and looked to my father for guidance. Still chewing his food, he gave me a bland smile. "Do stay, daughter," he said. "Sophie can wait."

Though I had lost my appetite entirely, I stayed.

Carmilla was true to her word. After dinner, I went to my father's library to select something for my bedtime reading. As I made my way up to my room, book in hand, I caught sight of Carmilla in the hallway outside Sophie's door, speaking to my governess in earnest whispers. Sophie was holding her door open, neither inviting Carmilla in nor coming out into the hallway herself. I hastened to hide myself in a shadowy corner. I couldn't hear what they were saying, but Sophie nodded in acknowledgement a few times and lowered her eyes with a soft smile. Carmilla extended a hand to her as if to ratify an agreement, and Sophie took it after a brief moment of hesitation. I leaned against the wall with relief and listened as Sophie's door closed and Carmilla's light footsteps padded toward her room.

Even once I had undressed, stoked the fire, and buried myself in my blankets, I found myself unable either to relax or to focus on the book. The tension between my governess and our guest chafed me, as it seemed to hint at a hitherto-unprecedented cruelty in each of them. And I couldn't stop thinking of the way Carmilla had touched my father's arm. I closed my eyes, imagining that touch on my own arm, the gentle pressure of her pale, slender fingers. I imagined her hands traveling over my body with soft insistence, her mouth warm against my ear as she whispered my name. I felt the same pressure and warmth between my thighs as I had experienced while watching Emma and Franz, so intense it was nearly unbearable. I writhed under my blanket as if in the grip of a fever.

My suffering was interrupted by a noise in the hallway.

I padded to my door and opened it just a crack, enough to see without being seen. Carmilla was standing in the dark hallway with my father and speaking to him with hushed urgency. Her back was to me, but in the meager illumination of the few lamps that had not yet been extinguished, I could just make out my father's expression. At first, he seemed not to believe what Carmilla was saying, but as she repeated herself, his face grew slack, and he nodded. She stopped talking and drew away from him. He stared straight ahead, his eyes blank, and intoned, "It will be done."

I closed the door before Carmilla could turn around and see me. My stomach knotted with anxiety. What were they conspiring about?

I slept fitfully and woke in the morning to the sound of aggrieved shouts. Rushing to my window and looking out upon the courtyard, I saw Sophie, who was trying to stop Bettina and Maria from dragging a large chest – her chest – to the waiting carriage.

"You can't be serious, Edward!" Sophie shouted.

I threw on my dressing gown and ran outside. "What's going on?" I asked, breathless in the chill air.

"Your father is throwing me out!" Sophie cried. Her eyes were wide and wounded as she pointed at him. He stood calmly beside the front door with Carmilla just behind him.

"Father?" I asked, unable to believe that such a thing could be true.

"She insulted and threatened Carmilla," he said evenly. "Such behavior toward a guest is unacceptable in this household."

"What are you talking about?" Sophie shrieked. "I did no such thing! I made peace with her, though it's clear now that shouldn't have!"

I glanced at Carmilla, whose lip was quivering with what seemed to be genuine fear and dismay. She clasped my father's arm and said nothing.

"Are you suggesting that our guest is lying?" My father's voice was emotionless. "I've seen the way you've looked at her since she arrived, like she's some criminal. I don't understand the reason for your hatred, but you cannot deny its existence."

Troubled as I was at the prospect of Sophie leaving, I had to admit that this, at least, was true. Hadn't I been angry with my governess for precisely the same reason?

"She's jealous of me," Carmilla ventured from behind my father's arm, her tear-streaked face indignant. "When I went to apologize to her last night, she called me a monster and threatened me."

The lie jolted me. That's not what I had seen. Sophie began cursing in French and trying to drag the chest away from Bettina and Maria.

"Mademoiselle De Lafontaine," my father intoned. "You will cease this undignified display and remove yourself from the premises immediately."

Though my heart ached to see Carmilla's fear and pain, my mind was spinning to reconcile what I had seen with what she claimed. In my periphery, I saw Martin and Adeline rushing out from the caretaker's cottage. "It's not true," I ventured, my voice barely audible in the commotion.

"What do you mean?" my father asked.

I gestured at Carmilla. "It's not true, what she said. I saw them last night. They came to an agreement. They shook hands and left each other in peace."

Sophie nodded vehemently. Carmilla tilted her head and narrowed her eyes at me, not unlike a bird of prey, before indignation returned to her lovely face. "My dear Laura, you saw our first meeting. But you must have been in your room for the second. She came to *my* room and told me what she thought of me. She even accused me of attacking Bettina and some villagers in some godforsaken town I've never heard of. She's out of her mind, and she's a danger to all of us!"

"That never happened!" Sophie protested.

I wanted to believe my governess. After all, while the second encounter could have occurred before Carmilla's conversation with my father (when she must have been telling him about Sophie's accusations), wouldn't I have heard it? On the other hand, Sophie had mentioned those same accusations in her private conversation with *me*. How would Carmilla know that unless she had been told the same by Sophie herself? My trust in my governess began to waver.

Sophie saw the doubt flickering over my features and shook her head wildly. "No," she said, quietly at first, then louder and louder. "No...no...no! So many years together, so much history, such a family we have created, and you believe *her* over me?!" My father stood immobile as a statue. She turned her pleading eyes toward me and took my hands. "Laura, *please*." She was weeping. So was I.

My eyes darted between her and Carmilla. Adeline began to hiccup with sobs. Carmilla's injured and tear-streaked face – and the memory of my own tense interaction with Sophie – finally swayed me, though my heart was breaking. "I'm sorry," I said to Sophie. "I love you, and I will always appreciate everything you have given me. But if my father says you must leave, I will not gainsay him."

She released my hands and stepped back, her face blank with shock. "Very well, then," she said grimly. Bettina and Maria were loading her chest onto the carriage.

"Martin," my father said. "If you don't mind, Mademoiselle De Lafontaine needs a ride to Gratz."

"Yes, sir," Martin said. He glanced hesitantly at his wife before moving with wary steps toward the horses. Sophie sent one last longing look at the schloss, glared at Carmilla (who returned her icy stare), and mounted the steps into the carriage, closing the door and the curtain behind her.

Within minutes, my governess, the woman who had been my companion and guide since I was six years old – and the one person who was trying to protect me from Carmilla – was gone.

CHAPTER TEN

THE ATTIC

With Sophie gone, only those who fell easily under Carmilla's sway remained. My father responded to everything she asked for with blank acceptance, as did Adeline and Martin. Indeed, all of them acquiesced to her suggestions that she and I be left alone. In hindsight, I should have realized that this was exceedingly strange behavior on their part.

I didn't realize it, though, because I was too preoccupied with wanting *her*.

Desire is a wonderful thing, but a terrible one, too. It drives us out of our wits, filling our senses with nothing but the object of our desire. And my senses were *full* of her. My vision tunneled, focused on her slender form, her dark, cascading hair, her obsidian eyes that sparkled with wit and laughter, her pale, graceful limbs. My ears rang with the throaty sound of her voice. Sometimes she would sit and play the piano for me, her voice soaring forth in a German or Italian aria while her fingers skillfully ran over the keys, the beauty of it bringing tears to my eyes. The sweet smell of her perfumed skin and coiffed hair lingered on me even as I slept, causing me to dream only of *her*. As for *touch*...when we went for walks around the property, she would trace her fingers lightly down my arm before clasping my hand in hers. When we picnicked in the garden, she would softly say "Come, Laura," and encourage me to place my head in her lap, where she braided my hair, the gentle tugging sending chills from my scalp down into my nether region. When we dressed for dinner, she would help me adorn myself with jewelry, her fingers lightly stroking my collarbone and neck, her breath stirring against my ears as she cooed about my beauty. My sense of taste alone remained free of her, though as I gazed entranced at her full lips and the tongue peeking wetly between them as she spoke, I wished desperately to remedy this.

She seemed to have recovered entirely from her illness, but at her insistence I continued to read to her before retiring to my bedroom for the night. Though I always turned away from her while she changed into her nightdress, I could not help but see her naked body in my periphery, a vision that, without fail, caused my heart to pound and my cheeks to redden with astonishing intensity. At first, I wondered why she always asked me to join her in her room *before* she changed, why she did not send me out into the hallway and recall me once she was ready, but the sly smile that played on her lips when she caught me glancing at her made me hope that she *wanted* me to see her.

Two months after her arrival, the dire cold of winter began to loosen its grip on the land. One night, when I had just finished reading a novel that ended, as many of them did, with the marriage of the protagonists, Carmilla asked, "And why aren't you married, dear Laura? I

would think there would be no shortage of suitors seeking your hand."
She was propped up prettily on her pillows, her eyes wide with earnest
curiosity.

I thought sadly of Elias, recalling his disappointment on that day
in the clearing. "I do not wish to be married," I answered simply.

Her gaze was steady upon me. "Why not?"

I hesitated for a moment, reluctant to spoil the pleasant atmosphere in the warm room. Then, haltingly, I told her about my mother's
death and my own experiences on that fateful day. When I was done,
she drew in a long, shuddering breath, her eyes welling with tears. "Oh,
my sweet friend," she said softly, "I am so sorry for what you went
through. Your father told me what happened to his late wife, but I
didn't know...how *awful*."

"At any rate," I continued, "even if I were not intent on avoiding
death in childbirth, the idea of joining my life to a man's has never
appealed to me. To be honest, I am quite stunned by how *insensible*
women seem to become when they're around their beaux. Not that I
would know for myself," I clarified, "but Emma used to relay all the
court gossip to me." The feeling of Emma's name on my lips sent a
pang through me.

"Oh, I agree with *that* sentiment!" Carmilla exclaimed.

"Is that why you are unmarried, as well?"

"Something like that." Her long, dark lashes swept the tops of her
cheeks before her gaze fixed again on mine. "Besides, my appetites have
always been...unusual."

I inhaled sharply, and the muscles of my inner thighs clenched.
Carmilla's dark eyes remained locked on mine for a moment before she

lowered them to my mouth. She moistened her lips with the tip of her tongue. Then she smiled. "Goodnight. I'll see you in the morning."

I was on fire. I couldn't sleep – my heart was pounding too hard! – so I paced my room, trying to calm myself but only managing to work myself into more of a frenzy. *Unusual appetites*, I thought. That was certainly how I would classify my soul-shaking desire for her.

Did she feel for me the way I felt for her? Many of her words and actions could be interpreted as flirtation, but I'd also seen her interact with *other* people with the same ribald candor and affection. She seemed to go out of her way to touch me, but I had seen her touch my father on several occasions, too. And an admission of her unusual appetites didn't necessarily mean she felt them for me. What if she was confessing such a thing to me merely as a friend, and I was reading too much into her sly smile? I remembered dancing with her at the Count's fete, and my pulse quickened. Would she have done that if she hadn't wanted to touch me the way I was aching to touch *her*? But Emma had danced with me, too... What if my own desire was causing me to misinterpret things she meant innocently?

There was another problem, too: giving in to our love, even if it was reciprocal, would be exceedingly dangerous. We could never be accepted in society, which considered such desires worthy of censure and punishment. If I confessed my feelings to Carmilla and she didn't reciprocate them, she would likely shun me. Yet hadn't Sophie introduced me to the works of Sappho, the brilliant poetess whose desire for other women had been celebrated by the ancients?

As sleep was out of the question, I decided to write, hoping it would calm my mind. I lit a candle and sat at my desk, pulling out sheaves of paper, my quill, and inkwell. But what was there to write about besides her? I tried to summon up some other story – a sequel to one of my previous supernatural endeavors, perhaps – but the only thing that came into my mind was Carmilla. Carmilla. Carmilla. The memory of her sly smile was pulsing through me with every beat of my heart.

I began to do something I had never done before. I wrote about desire.

The scene I wrote was taken from my recollection of Emma and Franz in the hallway at the Kepners' house, but instead of the two of them pressed against the doorway, satiating their need for each other with their hands, it was Carmilla and myself. As Franz had done, I leaned against the doorway with one hand, pleading with Carmilla as she smiled knowingly up at me. Her hand found its way underneath my skirts and her fingers moved eagerly against my sex. I kissed her hungrily, her mouth, her neck, her breasts, and I slid my own hand underneath *her* skirts...

I threw down my quill and tore the pages into pieces. This was *not* helping.

Outside my window, the moon provided enough light for me to make out the shapes in our garden and the forbidding edge of the forest. With a start, I realized that there was someone moving away from the house on the dirt path that led to the road. Though I could not make out the person's features, I recognized the white nightdress and dark hair as Carmilla's.

I stood in alarm, nearly knocking my chair over in the process. "Carmilla?" I asked in a loud whisper, placing my hand on the window.

She stopped walking and turned slowly, lifting her chin up toward my window. *Is it her?* I wondered. There was something different about her eyes. Or was the darkness simply playing tricks on me? A chill prickled through me, and I reached for my candle, but by the time I looked back at the pathway, she was gone. Only darkness upon darkness remained, the shadows of the trees barely distinguishable from the pathway itself.

Wondering if I had, in fact, nodded off at my writing desk, I slipped on my dressing gown, took up my candle, and hastened barefoot down the hallway to Carmilla's room. Overcome with worry as I was, I didn't even knock before opening the door. She was lying sound asleep in her bed, her slackened, peaceful face impossibly beautiful in the firelight.

Seeing her there ought to have calmed me, but it only filled me with greater dread as I walked back to my room. If Carmilla was safely in her bed, who had been on the pathway? And what sort of being could disappear so quickly? Or was it simply that my tired, lustful mind was so full of her that it was making me hallucinate her presence in places that she couldn't possibly be?

Neither option was desirable. When I finally slept, it was fitful.

The next day, I was exhausted. Noting my distinct lack of energy while we breakfasted alone in the dining room, my father asked me if I was quite well.

"I'm fine," I lied. "Just tired."

He tilted his head and appraised me. "Perhaps a bit bored, too? I know the winter weather has made it difficult to get out the past few months. And just when we thought we were in the clear..." He gestured with his hand at the heavy rain drenching the grounds outside.

"It's always tedious between Christmas and Easter," I said.

"At least Miss Mueller seems to have brought you some relief from the tedium," he noted.

Relief was not the word that I would have used for my feelings towards Carmilla, but the last thing I wanted was to confess such a thing to my father, so I nodded in agreement.

As if summoned by the sound of her name, the woman herself breezed into the dining room, looking even more beautiful than usual, her cheeks flushed pink and her skin glowing.

"Good morning to you both!" she said. She pulled back her own chair, sat, and began filling her plate as though she were ravenous.

"Good morning," my father replied before returning to his own plate of food.

"Good morning," I echoed weakly. Carmilla speared a piece of white asparagus on her fork, took part of it tenderly between her teeth, and then closed her lips around it as she broke off the bite. She hummed with delight and chewed it with her eyes closed, then opened her eyes and levelled her gaze directly at me.

My appetites have always been...unusual.

I cleared my throat. "Father, is there anything you'd like done around the house, since it's so dreary outside? Anything I can help you with?"

"Oh indeed, I'd love a project!" Carmilla added, cutting into a sausage.

My father smiled at Carmilla. "It's good to see you feeling so well. As a matter of fact, I was *just* speaking with Adeline about such a thing. Remember when we talked about changing the pictures last year, Laura? We never got around to it, despite our agreement that it ought to be done, and I think now is a perfect time. Adeline agreed to help me over the next few days, but we'd appreciate help from the both of you, too. The more numerous the hands, the more swiftly a task is completed."

"Changing the pictures?" Carmilla asked.

"When we moved in, the previous occupants had left all their paintings and portraits. Many of them are on the walls, but there are many more stored away in the attic."

"Oh yes!" Carmilla exclaimed. "I remember seeing them when I went up there!"

"At any rate, Laura and I have been looking at the same pictures since we moved in more than fifteen years ago, and it occurred to us that we might replace them with others from the attic. I'm sure it will make this place seem quite new."

"What a charming idea," Carmilla agreed. "I'd love to help! It'll be fun, won't it, Laura?"

I nodded, swallowing the last bite of my food with difficulty as I tried to stop looking at the spot where her slender neck sloped to meet her white shoulders.

Once we had set upon our task, the day flew by. My father and Adeline started in the attic, uncovering the pictures, dusting them, and sorting them by size. Carmilla and I were commissioned with making a list of the number and size of pictures that would be replaced throughout the rooms and hallways. With a quill and a piece of paper in hand, using an old book as a hard surface on which to write, I followed her as she glided through the house, admiring the current paintings as we gathered the information.

"This one's lovely," she said, gesturing at a pastoral landscape hanging in the parlor, a quaint, sunlit meadow with a small, round cottage, a pleasant dotting of sheep, and two brown figures with hats leaning on staffs. "It puts me in mind of *Daphnis and Chloe*. Have you read that in your studies?"

"I have heard of it," I said, avoiding mention of Sophie, "but I never had the chance to read it. That picture's always been one of my favorites. I've written a few stories set there."

"You know, Laura, I'd love to read some of your compositions, if you'd let me."

My stomach clenched at the thought of it. What if she didn't like them? What if I wasn't as talented as Sophie and Adeline had led me to believe, and Carmilla thought less of me once she had read them? I didn't respond, but she didn't seem to mind. She was walking along the perimeter of the room, tracing her finger lightly along the walls and bringing it to rest on each picture frame as she came to it.

"Who's this stern fellow?" she asked, laughing at a particularly large and detailed painting of an old man with pointed eyebrows and a white wig. His expression was one of disgust, as though he'd considered posing for the painter to be undignified.

I laughed, too. "I don't know! He must have been a patriarch of one of the families that used to live here."

She came to me, brushing my arm with her fingers as I wrote on the sheet of paper. "Did you write a story about him, too?"

I blushed. "No, but I used to imagine conversations between him and the others."

"The others?"

"The other portraits. They were always having very lively conversations in my head!"

She laughed at first, then her expression sobered. "It's been a lonely existence here for you, hasn't it?"

I swallowed. "It has."

She nodded. "I know something about that myself." The melancholic strain in her voice, so different from her general vivacity, startled me. I wanted very badly to ask her what she meant, but she had already moved to the next portrait in the room and asked, "Another of the former inhabitants, I suppose?"

I tried to swallow the hard lump that was suddenly lodged in my throat. The woman in the painting was beautiful, with dark hair and pale skin and features very much like mine. I put the paper and quill down on the piano. "Ah, no. I'm afraid that one will have to stay there. It's my mother, you see."

Carmilla gasped and looked more closely at the portrait. "I can't believe I didn't see it immediately. You are very like her, except for the color of your hair."

"So I've heard," I shrugged. I kept my gaze fixed on the oriental rug beneath our feet. I had spent many hours as a child looking at the portrait, basking in the beatific smile of my radiant mother. But over the years, her expression had seemed to take on a sardonic quality. Now her eyes seemed to me to glitter rather coldly, as though that smile masked a painful understanding of life's bitter ironies.

Carmilla drew near and placed her hands gently on my crossed arms. "I'm sorry. I didn't mean to cause you pain."

I shook my head and took her hands in my own. "You don't need to apologize. You didn't know."

She smiled ruefully and turned to look at the portrait again, her hands still in mine. "She was very beautiful," she said. "Almost as beautiful as you."

I felt like I was balanced on a precipice, my mouth suddenly dry. I pulled away from her, retrieving the paper and quill. "Thank you," I said. "Shall we continue?"

Once we had completed our inventory of the pictures throughout the house, we made our way up to the attic, where Adeline and my father had uncovered, dusted, and organized what must have been at least a hundred other pictures. I gasped at the sheer volume. "My goodness, why would anyone need so many paintings?"

Adeline scoffed. "When it comes to luxuries, my dear, *need* has nothing to do with it."

My father chuckled before turning to me and Carmilla. "The inventory, if you please." I handed it to him, and he perused it, his brow furrowed. "Now, if you ladies wouldn't mind going through these piles and selecting the ones that you particularly fancy, we can start figuring out what goes where. I'm going to go speak with Martin, to see what we can do to get the old ones taken down and stored."

He left me, Carmilla, and Adeline in the dusty room, our noses itching as we sat on the floor and thumbed through the piles of paintings. Carmilla kept glancing at me and Adeline as we chatted about the images, expressing our approval or disdain or, sometimes, when even a flatteringly-drawn portrait could not hide the unfortunate countenance of its subject, our amusement.

Carmilla broke into our idle chatter with a low but oddly powerful voice, like a deep bell whose ringing sets the body thrumming with its vibration. "Madame Perrodon, you should join Mr. Bancroft downstairs."

Adeline did not argue. She didn't even seem to register the words that Carmilla had spoken to her. She simply stood and hastened out of the attic, as if she had forgotten something.

I was shocked by her unblinking obedience to Carmilla's words, and under normal circumstances I might have questioned what had just occurred. But these were not normal circumstances, for Carmilla was suddenly crouched beside me on the floor, and she was taking my face gently between her hands.

"Laura," she breathed, her voice quavering, "my love. I cannot stand it anymore. I must kiss you or I feel I will die. Will you kiss me? Say you will. I dream of you day and night." The naked vulnerability of her confession and the loss of her customary poise was unsettling, and a thrill ran through me to know that I was not the only one who dreamed of our embrace. Her lips were mere inches from mine, her breath warm, and I wanted desperately for her to close the distance between us. Then I realized she was asking me to show her how *I* felt.

I closed the gap.

I had had no experience of kisses before this, and the intensity and passion of that kiss, the sheer pleasure of it...it went beyond anything I ever could have imagined. She kissed me softly at first, almost teasingly, her lips barely brushing against mine. Even this lightest of touches sent small jolts of sensation through me, but when she pulled me against her tightly and opened my mouth with hers, her tongue softly flicking the tip of my tongue, heat flared in my belly, and I groaned.

"Stand up," she said urgently. I obeyed, clasping her body to mine as she pressed me against the wall, our hands entwining in each other's hair, our kisses growing deeper and more passionate. It was as if we needed to swallow each other whole, as if nothing else would suffice. She broke from me, her breath ragged, and her lips teased the edges of my earlobes and the line of my neck, one hand sweeping from the back of my head to my nipple, which was erect beneath the cloth of my dress. I arched my back and gasped with pain and pleasure as she pinched it. She was beginning to loosen the laces at the front of my dress when we heard footsteps coming up the stairs.

I panicked and pushed her away, straightening my laces. She gave me a conspiratorial smile, then went back to her pile of paintings. By the time Adeline and my father appeared, we were both attending to our task dutifully. I was sure that they could read it on my face – my cheeks were *burning* – but they didn't seem to notice.

"Back so soon?" Carmilla asked casually.

"Martin asked me to check and see if there were any wires to hang the pictures up here," my father replied. "Oh!" he exclaimed suddenly, his attention fixed on a shadowed corner of the attic. "We seem to have missed one!" He crossed the room to retrieve a small portrait that had been half-hidden behind a chest.

Dismay clouded Carmilla's features.

"My word," Adeline said as he brought it over to her. "It's the spitting image of Miss Mueller!"

I would have expected Carmilla to be intrigued by this. Instead, she seemed to be trying to avoid the conversation entirely.

"Let me see," I said, standing up and brushing my dusty hands on my skirt. "Oh!"

It was her. It had to have been her, the likeness was so exact. She was sitting in an old-fashioned scarlet dress, her chin lifted as she smiled haughtily, her eyes penetrating the viewer. I turned the painting over and read the words from the label aloud: "Fraulein Karnstein, 1716." I turned toward Carmilla. "I could swear this was you!"

"It can't be, though, can it?" she said brusquely. She stood as if annoyed by the disruption and looked at the picture and its label. "Strange," she remarked. "It does look like me. You know, I heard a rumor once that someone who lived in this schloss was one of my great-great-great-grandmother's lovers. Her name was Mircalla Karnstein, and I have heard repeatedly that my looks favored hers. Her lover must have kept this as a memento."

"Your looks favor hers?" My father said in disbelief. "Why, you could be twins!"

Carmilla shrugged. "As I never met her, I can't comment on whether the painting renders her accurately."

"Wait a minute, did you say Karnstein?" Adeline ventured. "As in...*the* Karnsteins?"

Carmilla sighed. "Yes, Madame Perrodon, the very same. And before you ask, no, I don't know what happened in the village so many years ago. Only that it was something so terrible that the surviving members of the family scattered and changed their name to Mueller out of shame." She took the portrait from my father and placed it face down away from the other piles. "Now, shall we get back to work?"

CHAPTER ELEVEN

POSSESSION

Anyone who is familiar with my previous work might be surprised at the level of detail with which I have described the lustful encounters in my account thus far. But I must be truthful about all the ways in which Carmilla entranced me, for without understanding how deeply I was possessed by her, my reader will not be able to grasp the dire nature of the dilemma that I eventually faced.

That first kiss in the attic shook me to my core. After an awkward dinner, I shut myself in my room.

Is this really happening? I wondered, pacing. *If it is, should I allow it to continue?*

I was guilt-ridden at the thought of my father's disapproval. And yet there was no way I could *stop* loving Carmilla. The memory of the kiss came flooding back to me. It had felt so *right*, so unbelievably *right*. And I wanted more.

There was a soft knock on the bedroom door. I knew it was her; I could feel her presence like the heat from a fire. I hesitated for a moment, my heart pounding. Then I let her in.

She swept into the room and clasped me in a tight embrace that nearly unbalanced me. I shut the door behind her. "I'm so sorry, my dearest," she whispered in my ear. "Did I frighten you today?"

The sensation of her body against mine, her arms warm around my back, was driving all rational thought from my mind. "No." Then anxiety seized me again. "Well, maybe a little."

She pulled away. "Do you not want me, then?"

"That's not it," I said breathlessly, grasping her hands. "I want you desperately. It's just...is it not...unnatural?"

She stroked my cheek. "Does it feel so to you?"

I shook my head. "No, it feels *right*. It feels...inevitable. Like the pull of the earth on the leaves as they fall, like a bird's wings propelling it into the air."

"God, you're lovely," Carmilla sighed. Then she kissed me. Hungry, insistent.

My head spun. My legs trembled beneath me. I broke from her. "It's just...I've never...and I don't know how..." My heart was pounding so loudly that I was sure she could hear it.

She smiled. "I understand completely." She rubbed the tips of my fingers lightly with her thumbs, then caressed my arms as she moved her hands up into my hair, pulling my mouth close to hers again. "Just kiss me again. That's all I ask."

Nothing in the world could have persuaded me to deny her. I ached as she kissed me, her tongue teasing mine and her fingers caressing my jawline. I wrapped my arms around her back and pulled her so tightly against me that she gasped, the pressure of her hips sending heat blossoming through my nether regions. We kissed again and again, the sensation both increasingly thrilling and increasingly maddening. It wasn't enough. I wanted more. Yet I was terrified of what "more" meant.

I broke from her, breathing raggedly. "*Just* kiss you?" I asked.

She laughed. "You caught me, my love." We breathed together silently for a moment. "So...do you want me to stay with you tonight or not?" I hesitated, my stomach a knot of anticipation and anxiety. She sighed and stepped back. "I didn't think there was anything that could make me want you more than I have been wanting you these past months, but I was wrong. I will wait, my dearest, until you can give me a resounding 'yes.'"

She closed the distance between us again, took my earlobe between her teeth, and nipped it gently, her breath warm on the sensitive skin there. When I gasped, she chuckled and pulled away. "Goodnight," she said devilishly as she headed for the door.

I immediately regretted letting her go.

At breakfast the next day, she avoided my eyes as she engaged my father in small talk.

"What a beautiful morning!" she exclaimed.

My father glanced out the window. "Indeed it is. The sun always seems to shine more beautifully after the rain, doesn't it?"

"And it's so warm already," she said. "I'm of the mind to take advantage of such weather."

"How so?" my father asked.

"Well, I thought maybe we could pack a picnic and take the horses out. You've said there's a stream nearby; there ought to be a lovely place beside it somewhere, no?"

"The horses could do with some exercise," Adeline said, coming in with Bettina to clear the dishes. "Martin was just saying so yesterday during the storm."

Just then, I noticed that Bettina was avoiding Carmilla, skirting around her with a nervous countenance. *Now what could that be about*? I recalled what Sophie had accused Carmilla of. Had she said something to Bettina that had made her wary? But my attention was drawn back to the conversation about the picnic.

"But there are only two horses," my father said. "I'm afraid that we won't all three be able to ride."

"Oh, well then perhaps we can all walk instead!" Carmilla suggested.

"Nonsense. You and Laura can go without me! She knows these woods well; she and Elias used to go out constantly. Besides, I've some business to attend to." He was preparing for an upcoming trip to Gratz, both to meet with his accountant and to seek news of the General, from whom we had still heard nothing. My father had written to their acquaintances in every major city, to no avail.

"If you insist, I suppose," Carmilla said. Then her eyes met mine, and she raised an eyebrow. A thrill of anticipation ran through me.

Two hours later, we were on our way to the stable. I was carrying the picnic basket that Maria had packed for us while Carmilla chattered beside me, two riding crops in her hand. My father had always felt that the current riding etiquette for women was not only inconvenient but also dangerous, and so he encouraged me to wear breeches and ride astride. Carmilla, utterly charmed by this, asked to borrow some of my riding clothes. The loose riding shirt fluttered appealingly at her neck, while the breeches accentuated her small waist, curving hips, and the devastating cleft between her legs. Her dark hair spilled from her broad hat down her shoulders. I gulped nervously and looked away.

Martin had saddled the horses. As we approached, he raised a hand in greeting. "They're ready for you!"

We'd had both horses, a dapple grey named Stella and a dun named Holtz, for several years, and in all that time they had never displayed anything but a calm and easygoing temperament. As Carmilla drew near, however, they shied and tossed their heads up, stumbling backward and showing the whites of their eyes.

"What in God's name?" Martin asked, trying to calm them.

"Easy," Carmilla cooed. She placed the riding crops on the ground and reached out to both beasts with her outstretched hands. At first they whinnied with alarm. Then her hands touched their noses and they stilled, their nervousness replaced with an uncanny placidity.

"My word," Martin said. "I don't know what got into them. Just restless, I suppose."

Carmilla shrugged. "No matter, they're under control now." She retrieved the crops and handed one to me, then mounted Holtz with a fluid motion and took the reins from Martin confidently. "Shall we, Laura?"

It was an exceedingly pleasant ride. The horses were happy to be outside, their steps springy as they released the pent-up energy they had accumulated over the winter months. I myself had not ridden in ages, and at first I was disoriented by the height and power of the horse beneath me. Soon, however, I remembered how easy it was – and how wonderful – to move in concert with such a magnificent creature.

Carmilla rode like a dream. Holtz seemed to anticipate her desires and acquiesce to them immediately. They moved smoothly through the trees as though they were one beast rather than two. Carmilla and I chattered away about any topic that came to mind – books, birds, Austrian politics, our fears, our dreams – and our laughter echoed from the rocks and trees around us. Meanwhile, I was becoming increasingly aware of the growing ache between my legs, which was being fueled both by the sight of Carmilla's hips undulating as she moved with Holtz and by the rocking pressure of the saddle against my sex.

Finally, we came to a well-shaded grove beside the creek.

"Beautiful!" Carmilla exclaimed. "What do you think?"

"I think it's wonderful, though it may be a bit cold. Shall we find someplace sunnier?"

"Oh, no, I prefer not to be in the sun. My skin is quite sensitive to it."

"Very well, then." I swung my leg over Stella's back and tied her lead to a nearby branch. I pulled down the blanket and basket that had been tied to the saddle behind me and sought out a flat stretch of ground. Carmilla went down to the creek's edge and squatted, dangling her fingers in the water.

"It's so cold!" she said. "I had thought maybe we could dip our feet in, but that might need to wait for summer!"

I unrolled the blanket and spread it on the grass. "Do you think you will be here in the summer?" My heart leapt at the prospect.

She frowned, staring at the creek. There had been no word from her mother, and I suspected – though she had never said as much – that this was troubling her deeply. But now she turned to me and smiled. "A girl can hope."

She certainly can, I thought as I unpacked the picnic basket.

Half an hour later, we were reclining on our elbows on the blanket, our stomachs full of food and our heads fuzzy with wine. Carmilla took off her riding hat and shook out her long, dark hair. "Ah," she sighed as the breeze fluttered the wispy hair at her temples. The image of her just then, her slender body stretched out on the blanket in riding gear, her hair falling freely like a dark waterfall to the blanket, her eyes closed with the pleasure of our surroundings...she was so beautiful that it hurt. I inhaled sharply.

She opened her eyes and appraised me. "That hat is quite fetching on you. Actually, I have no complaints with this entire ensemble."

My cheeks grew hot, and I averted my gaze.

"Don't look away," she said, her voice low and urgent. She balanced herself on one elbow, turning my face to hers with her other hand. "Come here."

As I moved closer, she laid back on the blanket, and I arranged my body beside hers, my neck resting on her outstretched arm. She brought her face very close to mine and removed my hat, then traced my hairline with her fingers, as lightly as the breeze itself.

No more words were needed.

I kissed her slowly and deeply, opening my lips against hers and drinking in the marvelous warmth of her mouth and tongue. She returned my kiss with ardor, melting softly into me. I was shaking with desire. I wanted to plunge into her, to disappear. I encircled her with my arm and pulled her body against mine, our breasts pressing against each other. But she wasn't close enough. I lifted my leg over her hip, and she bent her knee between my legs, grasping my buttock to slide me closer. The pressure of her thigh on my pubis was exquisite, and my hips began to move of their own accord, seeking the sensation again and again.

I groaned and threw my head back, gasping for breath. Her hand traveled to the front of my shirt, unlacing it just enough to uncover one breast. The cool air hardened my already-erect nipple, and Carmilla sighed in appreciation, stroking me with her thumb. "So beautiful," she said, sliding down far enough that she could take my nipple in her mouth.

Her warm, wet, flicking tongue seemed to pull on an invisible string between my breast and my sex, sending shocks through my body that made me pant with need. She moved upward and found my mouth with hers again, drawing my breath into herself. Then she pushed me onto my back, straddled my hips with her legs, and pressed my hands into the blanket with hers. I could feel the heat of her as she moved her hips back and forth, tantalizingly skimming me with her pubis. When I groaned with frustration, she moved one of her legs between mine and pressed her sex against my thigh. She began to move her hips again, maddeningly slowly, and I whimpered as each forward thrust of her weight sent pleasure coursing upward from the nexus between my legs.

She had lifted herself up on one arm and was beginning to loosen the laces at the front of her shirt when I felt a stinging pain at my ankle.

"Ouch!" I cried out.

She froze, puzzled. "Did I hurt you?"

Another sting. "Ouch!" I shouted again, sitting up and pushing her away from me in panic. I scrambled to pull up the hem of my breeches and discovered to my horror that ants were crawling on the skin just above my boot. I shot to my feet. "Ants!"

A line of the insects had found its way across the picnic blanket and into the basket before making its way to us. I struck frantically at those that had crawled onto my ankle.

"Oh, of all the ridiculous..." Carmilla began. Then she threw her head back and laughed. I stood stunned, my heart sinking with disappointment at the interruption of our tryst. "We should go back," she said. Her nimble fingers tied the laces of my shirt, then she bent to pick up the picnic basket and shake out the blanket. "But I do hope we can continue this later."

She maintained chipper conversation all the way home, but I found it difficult to focus on anything but my pounding heart...and throbbing sex.

When we arrived, Martin asked me to help him put away the tack and brush the horses. Normally I would have jumped at the chance to help the caretaker, but today my thoughts were elsewhere. I watched glumly as Carmilla walked back to the house with the empty picnic basket, the riding breeches accentuating the curve of her buttocks.

Once I had finished taking care of the horses – Stella had a rock wedged near the frog of her hoof that took some digging to remove – I made my way inside, hoping to find Carmilla.

My father intercepted me in the front hallway. He held up a letter that must have arrived while Carmilla and I were out. "Laura, I've heard from Colonel Barragan, in Gratz. He knows no more about the circumstances of the General's current whereabouts than we do, but he *did* see him briefly a couple of months ago. He says the General was leaving in a hurry."

"Where was he going? And why?" I asked.

"I don't know. But the Colonel has suggested some contacts who might have more details about the General's departure. It is my intent to question them when I go to Gratz."

"I hope you find some answers."

I made as if to continue toward my room, but he raised his hand to stop me. "One more thing. The Colonel and his wife are throwing a fete next month in honor of their daughter's engagement to Leon Kepner."

Franz's older brother. Remembering Franz made me remember Emma. I swallowed down my sudden grief. "Oh?" I managed.

"He has invited us, as well as Carmilla (I told him that she was in our care when I reached out to him). I wondered if, since I am making the trip to Gratz anyway, you two might join me and accompany me to the fete." He looked out the window. The sky was bright blue and sunny now, but there were grey clouds looming in the distance. "I expect we'll have some weather over the next week; we'll have to wait for it to run its course before we depart. Perhaps two weeks hence?"

I swallowed again. I didn't know if I was ready to immerse myself in that world again, the world where Emma, sparkling so brightly, had been my guide and my anchor.

"Do you not wish to go?" he asked, his grey eyes full of genuine concern. "I thought it might be welcome to you. It's been so long, and we've been so cooped up here. We can use the General's flat there; he long since offered me use of it whenever I wished. I even have a key." He held up his key ring as if to prove it to me.

"I...we'll have to ask Carmilla," I replied. The memory of the night I had met her at the Count's fete came to me unbidden. How she had danced! How she had laughed! How ravishing she had looked in that garnet dress! The thought of attending a fete with her again, this time as companion rather than stranger, thrilled me. "I'm sure she would love the diversion, but I hesitate to speak for her."

"Are you talking about me?" Carmilla asked, emerging from the study with a book in her hand. She had changed into a simple linen dress and arranged her hair in a bun, though a few dark wisps had escaped and were framing her face charmingly.

"Ah, Miss Mueller," my father said, "we are indeed. We've been invited to a fete in Gratz next month. As I am heading there anyway in a fortnight, I wondered if you and Laura would like to join me."

I had expected her to respond to the invitation eagerly, but she paled.

"Do you not wish to go?" I tried to hide the disappointment in my voice. "We can stay here, if you prefer."

"Of course I want to go! It's only..." she trailed off as though at a loss for words.

"Are you worried about your health?" my father asked. "There are fine doctors in Gratz, should you need them."

She shook her head. "No." She seemed to be searching for the right words. "I just...Well, how long will we be there? I worry that my mother will return here in my absence and panic when she can't find me."

"That depends on how long my business takes. Ten days, at least, for the fete. But surely Adeline and Martin can inform your mother of our whereabouts, should she arrive here while we are gone."

"I suppose you're right," Carmilla admitted. Worry still lingered in her eyes.

I desperately wanted to ask what was troubling her, but I didn't want to embarrass her in front of my father. "Carmilla," I ventured, "would you like to join me in my room? If we're going to a fete, I need to inspect my wardrobe and see if I can find something satisfactory."

"Forgive me," she said, rubbing her forehead with her fingertips. "Our ride, though lovely" – she smiled wanly at me – "seems to have exhausted me. I think I'll retire to my room."

Without waiting for our response, she left.

My stomach was in knots at the thought that I had done something to distress her. By dinnertime, however, she had regained her customary aplomb. She conversed freely as she consumed every morsel of food that Maria brought out to us. She and I sat across from each other, as we often did, and beneath the table she moved her foot against mine, reminding me of the feeling of our bodies pressed together. My cheeks flushed, and I fixed my gaze on my plate. My father, blissfully unaware of the situation, commented on the deliciousness of our meal and began to list the things we would need to bring with us when we journeyed to Gratz.

The time before we could retire to our bedrooms seemed interminable. Father invited us to the parlor after dinner and challenged me to a game of chess while Carmilla played the piano, then he read aloud to us from a book of poetry he had acquired recently. Carmilla sat beside me on the chaise, surreptitiously stroking my fingertips with her own when my father was engrossed in the lines he was reciting.

Finally, he stood and announced that it was time for him to retire, and we assured him of our plans to do the same. As we left the parlor and went our separate ways, Carmilla drew me close, her breath warm against my ear as she whispered, "I will come to you."

Though I had already bathed after changing out of my riding clothes, I used the wash basin again before slipping into my nightdress. I paced my bedroom for a while, then tried – and failed – to distract myself with a book. I alternately stoked and damped down the fire, anxious about whether the temperature of the room was right. My blood was thundering in my ears.

Finally, there was a soft knock on the door.

She flew into my arms and instantly ignited me with fierce, deep kisses. As she pressed me backward toward the bed, she opened her mouth and tasted my tongue, wrapping one hand in my hair.

When the back of my legs struck the bed, our faces collided uncomfortably, and I winced and pulled away.

She stepped away and looked at me in concern. "I'm sorry." Her breath, too, was coming in ragged gasps. "I cannot help myself. I never want to stop kissing you."

I licked my lips, tasting a drop of coppery blood. Her eyes widened, and she exhaled a soft "oh." Then she stepped forward and took my blood onto her tongue.

"I'll ask you again, Laura." Her voice was tight with anticipation. "Do you want me to stay with you tonight?"

My whole body was trembling with longing. "Yes," I said. "*Please.* Yes."

"Good." She brushed her lips against mine, her warm whisper tickling my skin. "Because I don't want to spend one more moment of my life not knowing the way you taste."

I've been writing for a long time, and I am reasonably sure of my descriptive abilities. Yet now, as I attempt to describe what it felt like to make love to Carmilla, I realize that there is no way to do it justice. How does one capture in words something that was at once heartbreakingly tender and frighteningly powerful? At once miraculously new and as comforting as coming home after a long absence? My mind cannot comprehend it, let alone find words to explain it. Yet I remember that night so vividly that I can still feel her, still taste her with a potency that brings tears to my eyes.

I remember the unselfconscious way she removed her nightgown and helped me out of mine. The curve of her breasts and the dark areolas against her pale skin. Her sigh of appreciation before she cupped my breasts in her hands and then bent her head to take one nipple in her mouth, then the other. The warmth from the fire on our naked bodies as we spread out on the pillows, kissing hungrily. The softness of her skin as I explored her breasts, her hips, her thighs with my fingers. The warm, wet circles that lingered on my torso as she kissed my neck, my collarbone, my belly, my pubis. Her dark hair spilling over my thighs. The shock of pleasure that ripped through me when she parted my nether lips with her tongue. The shuddering climax that seized me mere moments after she had begun her skillful lavishments. Her hands clasped around my thighs, holding me firmly in place though my body tried to writhe away from the unbearable intensity of it. The moans and whimpers that escaped me as she kept pleasuring me until I was nearly insensible. The musky taste of my sex on her tongue when she moved up and kissed me again, straddling my thigh so I could feel her wetness. The thin sheen of sweat on our bodies as I pressed her back against the bed and slid my body down hers. The smoky taste of *her* when I found her slick, warm center with my tongue. Her murmurs of encouragement as I sought to please her the way she had pleased me, though the newness of it made me worry that I was going about it clumsily. Her throaty groan when I drove her to the brink of ecstasy and, finally, over the edge. Her thighs quivering around my face while the waves crashed within her.

Afterward we lay facing each other, kissing softly, our bodies slackened with pleasure and glistening with perspiration. She smiled.

"I've been wanting to do that since the night we met at Count Carls-feld's fete. But it was even better than I imagined."

"So have I," I agreed. "Though I didn't know what to imagine."

She chuckled. "You've never made love before?"

Heat flooded my face. "No. And what I thought I knew about lovemaking didn't involve tongues being used like *that*."

She stroked my flushed cheeks. "You don't need to be embar-rassed. It just surprised me. You're remarkably good at it."

"I merely followed your lead."

"Clever girl." She rolled onto her back and stretched. This afford-ed me a generous view of her pert breasts and the dark triangle of hair between her legs, and I felt desire stirring within me again. But the question she had asked me – and the way she had asked it – was troubling me.

"I take it *you* have had other lovers?" I ventured. Despite my efforts to the contrary, the words sounded querulous rather than casual.

She heard the edge in my voice and hesitated before answering. Finally, she rolled to face me again, her nose inches from mine. "Yes," she admitted. Then she enfolded my hand in hers and raised it to her lips, kissing my palm tenderly. "But I promise you, it's never been like *this*." Her eyes were shining with tears, and even now, I still believe that she was telling the truth.

Then she released my hand and reached between my legs to tease the still-tender flesh there. I gasped, and she smiled against my mouth. "Now, do you want me to show you what we can do with our hands?"

The two weeks before our departure passed in a haze. We were possessed, we were consumed, we were blissfully happy. We ought to have been exhausted, since our nights were filled with more sex than sleep, but we were fueled by the giddy intoxication of being together. Even during the day, we found ways to embrace, to kiss, to touch whenever we were alone, parting from each other hurriedly and smoothing down our dresses when we heard footsteps approaching.

The most devastating part of it all, though, is that our infatuation wasn't just about physical pleasure. It is one thing to feel overwhelming desire for someone, and certainly desire alone has ruined better people than I. But it is another thing entirely to give yourself to someone whose presence soothes your spirit, whose devotion makes your heart feel like a cup that has been filled beyond the brim.

Just being in the same room with her was a source of contentment, but we also comforted each other in times of need. One morning I found her in her room, tears of distress marring her cheeks. "What's wrong, my love?" I asked.

"My mother," she said. "I miss her. And I worry about her."

I took her in my arms, embracing her in silence, letting her vent her worry. Warm tears fell on my shoulder.

"What would I do without you?" she sniffled. "My dearest love."

A few days later, I was suffering gravely from the pains that always attended my monthly bleeding. Carmilla tucked me into my bed and fetched a hot water bag to put on my abdomen, then rubbed my feet solicitously.

"Thank you," I sighed. Her ministrations were surprisingly effective.

"You're welcome," she said. "You know, I've never done this for anyone else. It would never even have crossed my mind."

"Oh? Why not?"

"I don't know. I am quite unpracticed in kindness, you know. But I'm inspired by the certainty that *you* would do it for me. If circumstances allowed, anyway."

I realized that there had never been any signs that *she* was menstruating, though she had been with us for months now. "Your illness?" I asked.

She nodded. "I have not bled since it first took hold of me."

I raised an eyebrow. "So it's not all bad?"

She laughed. "Indeed." She released my foot and moved up the bed. She kissed me, her lips soft, tentative, but I began to flush with desire nonetheless. "Whenever you're up for it," she said, "there's something else I'd like to do to make you feel better." My eyes widened in surprise, and she smiled and kissed me again. "My love, did you think a little blood would deter me?"

That's what it was like between us. As tender as it was consuming, as warm as it was unbearably ardent. Whether we were reading or walking or picnicking, our conversations, our laughter, and the fit of her hand in mine made my heart soar. I cherished each second with her. Nor could I pinpoint exactly what it was about her that made our souls fit together so happily. She was beautiful and charming, yes, but there are many beautiful and charming people in this world, and I have yet to find another whose eyes, whose voice, whose body could enflame me in this way. Nor do I understand what she saw in *me*. Next to her, I felt like a candle beside a roaring fireplace, neither as beautiful nor as worldly nor as clever. Yet she, too, seemed to cherish every second we had together.

You could read every book that has ever been written, and you would never find a satisfactory explanation for how love can wound so quickly and so penetratingly, nor why it chooses the victims that it does. Indeed, sometimes the arrow pierces *so* deeply that almost nothing can shake it from the heart, not even the shocking discovery that one's beloved is a monster.

CHAPTER TWELVE

GRATZ

In the driver's seat, Martin clicked his tongue, encouraging Holtz and Stella with his customary gentleness. Inside the carriage, Carmilla and I sat on one bench, our thighs pressed tightly (and rubbing together with a maddening friction as the carriage bounced over the rough roads). Across from us sat my father, who, though clearly anxious about the object of the visit, was nonetheless willing to contribute to our conversations. A few times, I caught him smiling as he watched Carmilla and me bantering playfully. When we stopped to stretch our legs and relieve ourselves, my father beckoned to me.

"It's good seeing you so happy," he said. "I'm pleased you've found such a close friend in Miss Mueller."

I fought back the urge to giggle at the word *friend*. Was he so blind to what was happening?

We were drawing nearer to the city now; the road was smoother here, and the rough bouncing became gentle swaying. My father's eyelids drooped, then his head, and soon he began to snore. Carmilla leaned over and kissed my neck, then my earlobe. She caressed my cheek with one hand, turned my face towards hers, and tasted deeply of my mouth. Ignoring the flood of desire that was causing my fingernails to dig into the bench cushions, I broke away from her. "He'll see," I protested.

She continued kissing my neck. "Watch him. If he starts to wake, I'll stop. In the meantime..." She deftly reached beneath my skirts and moved her hand up my leg, finding that most sensitive spot and massaging it in wide circles with a pressure that was nearly – but not quite – too intense. I whimpered, covering my mouth with a hand to muffle the sound and struggling to keep watch on my sleeping father when all I wanted to do was throw my head back and give in to the sensation.

He didn't wake until we arrived at the General's flat in Gratz in late afternoon. As he helped me out of the carriage, I was certain that he would notice my legs shaking underneath me or the conspiratorial smiles that Carmilla was sending my way.

He did not notice.

Martin helped Carmilla down and began unloading the luggage with my father. Since we could walk nearly everywhere in Gratz, and other forms of transportation were readily available should we desire them, Martin was planning to return home with our carriage and come back to fetch us three weeks hence. Once the luggage was unloaded, he tipped his hat and bid us farewell. "I'm off. I'll spend the night at Elias' flat, then head back home in the morning."

Elias. As always, the name brought with it a twinge of loss. How was it that someone who had once been my dearest friend could now be a stranger to me? Suddenly, I wished very much to see him.

"Elias!" my father exclaimed. "Oh, how I miss that boy!"

"No boy now," Martin chuckled. "He's taller than any of us!"

"True!" my father laughed. "At any rate, please give him our best, and urge him to come visit us next holiday."

"Please do," I echoed. "The schloss is not the same without him."

Carmilla looked at me quizzically. I hastily turned my attention back to Martin, who assured us that he would convey our sentiments to his son.

We carried our luggage to the second floor of the building. My father had written ahead to the housekeeper, so the dust covers had already been removed from the furniture, the linens on the beds re-placed, and all surfaces cleaned to a high shine.

"How quaint!" Carmilla exclaimed. She turned around in the small space and admired the simple decorations, then moved to the windows and opened the curtains that faced the street. Bright light streamed in, and she cringed and shut the curtains again. "It's a bit too bright today. But how fascinating to be right on the street like this! I feel I could spend days just sitting and watching people as they pass by."

"Yes, it's quite different from our home, isn't it?" my father said. "It usually takes me a couple of days before I can sleep through the clatter and hum."

The housekeeper, hovering at the door between the kitchen and the living room, cleared her throat to get our attention. "Good afternoon, Mr. Bancroft. I'm Mrs. Bohm, and I'll be attending to you while you're here."

"It's a pleasure to meet you, Mrs. Bohm," my father replied. "This is my daughter, Miss Bancroft, and our guest, Miss Mueller."

Her gaze lingered overlong on Carmilla. "Yes, sir," she said finally. "Shall I bring some tea?"

"That would be lovely," my father replied. "Girls, while we wait, let's make ourselves comfortable in our rooms."

There were three rooms in the flat. In previous years, I had shared a room with Emma, while Josef and my father – or Josef and Sophie, depending on who our chaperone was – occupied the other two. Father took the smallest room at the end of the hall, while I chose the room that Emma and I had always shared, which was furnished with a large bed and a small window. My father showed Carmilla to Josef's room, the most spacious of the three, which boasted a huge window and a balcony above the street. But Carmilla, finding that the curtains did very little to block the light, clicked her tongue and shook her head. "It's far too bright in here, Mr. Bancroft. Even at night, the streetlamps and moonlight will stream in. How will I sleep?"

"Oh," he said. "Well, I would be happy to change rooms with you, if you prefer."

She rested a hand on his arm. "There's no need to undergo the hassle of moving your things; I'm sure Laura wouldn't mind sharing a bed with me, the way she and Emma used to do."

She said it like it was the most natural solution to the problem. My father nodded blankly and moved her chest into my room. Carmilla smiled at me, her eyes dancing with anticipation.

With more than a week until the Barragans' fete, we had plenty of time to explore the city. While my father was called away by business and his search for news about Josef, Carmilla and I strolled through the streets, parasols shielding us from the sun, visiting restaurants and shops before returning to the flat in time for tea. As pleasant as it was to be in the city, my experience was darkened somewhat by a startling discovery (the first of many that would soon unfold): my beloved Carmilla had a mean streak.

One day, while we were waiting to be seated at a café, a young gentleman entered, heading toward a table where his friend was waiting. As he passed us, he jostled Carmilla. It was unintentional, and he apologized profusely, so I expected her to brush it off. But she glowered at him throughout our meal. When he and his friend got up and headed for the door, Carmilla stuck her foot out as he passed and tripped him. He fell heavily, crashing into one of the wooden tables – which was thankfully unoccupied – and sending the table settings flying. There was a collective gasp, and several patrons moved to help him. He picked himself up and shakily assured everyone that he was all right, though he was gingerly holding one elbow, where blood was beginning to seep through his shirt.

Carmilla smirked. I was stunned.

"Why did you do that?" I asked, once everyone had settled back down to eat and the usual ambient noise had returned.

She speared some salad on her fork. "What do you mean?"

I pitched my voice low. "You know what I mean. You tripped that man."

Carmilla put her utensils down and leaned back in her chair, looking at me coldly. "Why on earth would I do such a thing? The oaf must have stumbled over his own feet. He should be more careful."

I saw you, I thought, and my heart twisted in my chest at how casually she had lied. But I knew that I would accomplish nothing by pressing the matter further.

Yet another example of her cruelty manifested itself a few days later. We were visiting the grave of my mother and brother, as we always did whenever we happened to be in Gratz. The cemetery was quiet, and my father and I gazed solemnly at my mother's marble headstone – *Emilia Bancroft, 1794-1820, beloved wife and mother. Sit tibi terra levis* – our hearts heavy with the renewed sense of loss. Carmilla stood beside me, one arm hooked through my elbow, the other holding her parasol, and her warm presence was like a balm to my suffering.

Before long, we began to hear the sounds of wailing and lamentation, distant at first, but growing steadily louder. A funeral procession was approaching. The keening cries of the attendees pierced the air around us, and when I saw how small the coffin was, I understood the wild, helpless quality of the mourning. It was one thing to escort an adult to their resting place, quite another to do so for a child. Tears stung my eyes, and I saw my father wiping his cheek with his hand. But Carmilla scoffed with disgust.

"Such a fuss," she complained. "I'd like to leave now; this hurts my head."

I was astonished at her indifference. "It's a *child*, Carmilla."

"Children die every day," she shrugged. "I'm not sure what made *this* one so special."

Some of the women in the procession were muttering to each other as they passed, and an icy chill went through me when I heard their words. The child had died in her sleep, apparently drained of all her blood.

From the nearby church, bells began to ring in honor of the deceased. "Ugh!" Carmilla exclaimed, covering her ears with her hands. "*Must* they?"

I was disappointed by this behavior, but I told myself that it was not a true reflection of my beloved's character. This lie was made easier by circumstance, for Carmilla fell ill again shortly after we arrived in the city. Her face took on a grayish cast, and the languor that had plagued her when she had first come to our schloss began to weigh down her limbs. Her mind was as eager and restless as ever, and she urged my father and me to keep accompanying her on outings. But the strength of her body was quickly depleted, and when we returned to the flat for tea she would retire to the bedchamber, complaining of a headache and sleeping until dinnertime.

One afternoon, after a long morning of shopping had sapped Carmilla's strength, we came back to the flat, where my father was writing some letters. With one glance at Carmilla's strained expression and paler-than-usual face, he stood up, concerned.

"Is anything wrong, Miss Mueller?"

She gave an unconvincing smile and headed straight for our room. "I'm afraid I'm just suffering from another headache." Then she closed the door behind her.

"Shall we fetch a doctor for her?" my father asked anxiously.

"I know she would say that there's no use, but perhaps we should. At least here it's an easier task to find one."

He finished folding his last letter. "I'm heading out to post these anyway; I'll ask around for a doctor while I'm at it."

After he had gone, the flat was entirely silent but for the bustle of the street outside. Mrs. Bohm, I assumed, was likely at the market procuring items for dinner. I knocked tentatively on the door to the bedchamber and heard Carmilla's weak "Come in."

She really did look terrible. There were deep shadows under her eyes, and her chest rose and fell shallowly as she breathed in soft gasps. I sat beside her on the bed, taking one clammy hand and enfolding it between both of mine. She smiled wanly.

"I remember when my father suggested coming here, you didn't seem too thrilled," I said. "Is this what you were afraid of?"

She sighed. "Yes. I...How can I explain it? This happens sometimes, whenever I travel away from...whatever place I currently consider home."

I lifted her hand to my lips and kissed her knuckles. "I suppose I should be charmed that you think of our home as your own, but I'm too busy being worried about you. You're not yourself. My father is going for a doctor."

"As you wish. He'll not find anything to help me, I can assure you. But if it will help you and dear Mr. Bancroft feel more at ease, then..."

"It will. If we should fail to do everything in our power to help you, we would never forgive ourselves."

This time her smile was broad and genuine, and she squeezed my hand. "You've always been so kind to me, Laura. Even when I'm being terribly ill-natured." Was she ashamed of her recent behavior?

"I love you," I said simply. "Why wouldn't I be kind?" I stretched out beside her on the bed. "Now, is there anything I can do to make you feel better?" I kissed her, tenderly at first, then, when she seemed receptive to my advances, deeply enough to elicit a groan. "There's no one else in the flat, you know..."

Unfortunately, I was mistaken. When I emerged from the bedroom half an hour later, Carmilla's loud moans of pleasure echoing in my mind, I came face to face with Mrs. Bohm, who had been standing outside the door listening. Her jaw was hanging open in shock.

A hoarse "No!" escaped from my lips. She started to turn away, and I reached out to stop her. "Mrs. Bohm, please." She resisted my grasp, her arms stiff. "It's not what it sounded like."

"It's exactly what it sounded like," Carmilla's calm voice came from beside me. She stood tall, chin raised. I could feel the tension in her, like a cat preparing to pounce. "It doesn't matter, though, Laura, because she's not going to tell anyone." She stepped forward and placed her hand on Mrs. Bohm's arm. For a moment, the housekeeper trembled, agitated. Then she became utterly still, just as the horses had done a few weeks prior. I had often wondered at the way creatures and people reacted in Carmilla's presence, how she seemed to get what she wanted so easily with just a touch of the hand and a calm voice. But it had never bothered me before. This time, the hair on the back of my neck stood up. The housekeeper's eyes were locked on Carmilla's, and they grew wide and wild with fear, as though she had seen something horrifying in my beloved's face. "You're not going to tell anyone, are you?" Carmilla asked, tilting her head.

"Tell them what?" Mrs. Bohm replied hollowly.

Carmilla smiled and released her arm. "You see, my love," she said to me, "there's no need to worry. Mrs. Bohm is simply going about her business as usual."

But I was very worried. My skin prickled as I watched Mrs. Bohm walk stiffly into the kitchen.

None of this, however, could hold a candle to the act of sheer cruelty that Carmilla perpetrated the next day.

The doctor had come and gone, admitting reluctantly that he could neither diagnose nor treat her. Afterward, Carmilla claimed to be overtired and asked us to forgive her if she chose to sleep the day away. My father went to Colonel Barragan's house, both to help his friend with the final preparations for the fete, which would take place the next day, and to get more information about the people who claimed to know something about General Spielsdorf's departure.

I read in the living room all morning, checking on Carmilla every half-hour, but she continued to sleep peacefully. When Mrs. Bohm peeked out from the kitchen and asked if she might make me lunch (nothing in her manner suggesting that the events of the previous day had transpired), I decided that I'd prefer to go out, though I promised to be back by tea time.

I walked down the street to the nearest café, where I purchased a torte that I wrapped in a napkin and carried to the banks of the river. I found a pretty bench at the river's edge where I could enjoy my simple repast and the warmth of the sun. I watched people passing by: young couples dressed in finery, old merchants, women whose clothes and bold manner suggested that they were prostitutes, boatmen transporting their wares. Children played loudly and happily in the street, some well-dressed, others dirty and destitute. The smell of urine and unwashed bodies wafted potently around me every time the breeze blew, but so did the smell of baking bread and tree blossoms. A young man whistled at me, then laughed when I blushed and waved him and his friends away. Finally the sun's heat radiating through my hat became uncomfortable, so I brushed the crumbs from my clothes and made my way back toward the shops, determined to find something pretty to bring Carmilla.

When I returned to the flat, Carmilla was standing in front of the window in the living room, having donned a silvery gown and blood-red earrings. Her cheeks were pink and her eyes bright, and she rushed across the room to take my hands as I entered.

"You look quite recovered!" I exclaimed.

"I *feel* quite recovered, my dear! And I'm dreadfully bored. I have such a lovely idea for how we might spend the evening. Will you come with me?"

"Of course," I replied. "Shall I have Mrs. Bohm get us some tea?"

"Oh, I'm afraid the poor woman has taken ill. She could barely stay on her feet, so I sent her home. Not to worry, though. My plan involves finding something to drink. Do you want to get changed? I'm going to go see if the doorman can hire us a carriage. Or shall we walk?"

"How far is it?"

"I have no idea!" she laughed.

Her plan, as it turned out, involved patronizing The Gilded Mare, the most notorious tavern in Gratz, whose existence had apparently been revealed to her by Mrs. Bohm just before her sudden illness. Knowing that I would refuse to go if she told me what type of establishment it was, she kept it secret until we had hired a carriage and paid our way to the other side of the city.

"No," I said, looking dubiously at the sign hanging above the tavern's entrance and frowning at the startling amount of noise that was spilling out into the street.

"Come on," Carmilla pleaded. She was pulling me toward the door. "It'll be fun! When will we get another chance like this?"

"My father would be mortified if he knew we were here."

"Your father would be mortified if he knew other things, too, but that doesn't stop you from doing them," she said with a wicked smile. "Please, Laura. For me? We won't stay long, I promise. I just want to try it!"

A few moments later, I was surrounded by drunk strangers, overwhelmed by the loud music from the band of musicians in the corner and the even louder laughter of the patrons, choking on the smell of cigar smoke and beer...and face to face with Elias.

He was standing at the bar, stein in hand. I recognized his sandy hair and firm jawline, but he had grown broader and more muscular than the last time I had seen him. As he turned to find his table, he caught sight of me and froze in place, aghast.

"Laura?"

My initial shock transformed into a flood of joy. "Elias!" I released Carmilla's hand and flung myself into Elias' arms, causing his beer to slosh onto the back of my dress. He stood stiffly at first, then put his stein on the bar and tenderly enfolded me in his arms.

"What on earth are you doing here?" he asked. He stepped back and glanced around the room as if to catalogue all the ways in which our current location was unsuitable.

"Oh," I said, turning to Carmilla and gesturing for her to come forward. "This is my friend, Miss Mueller." At his look of surprise, I shrugged. "This was her idea."

"To judge from the squeal I just heard," she said coolly, her low voice somehow cutting through the noise of our surroundings, "you must be the famous Elias Fischer."

Elias' eyes widened. He gingerly took Carmilla's extended hand and lowered his head in a bow. "Miss Mueller, my father told me of your beauty. I'm afraid his description fell quite short of reality."

"Doesn't it always?" she said. She dodged a drunk patron who stumbled in her direction. "Are you a regular here?"

"Well, not *very* regular," he answered, "but I do come here occasionally. I'm currently with some friends." He gestured toward a table of craftsmen who had a rugged look about them.

"We won't bother you if you'd like to stay with them," Carmilla said, "but do you know if there's a corner somewhere that's a little more...private?"

Elias chuckled. "Only a fool would choose the likes of *them* over the two most beautiful women in Gratz. And yes, I do know where we can go. Shall I buy you both a drink first?"

A few minutes later, beers in hand, we headed to a table in the back corner of the tavern. The sound was dampened there, and at first I was surprised that no one else had chosen it, as it offered a pleasant reprieve from the raucous noise. But the view of the musicians was obstructed, and these musicians in particular seemed to be attracting a great deal of interest.

"He's wonderful," Carmilla said, gesturing at the young violinist who had taken center stage to play a rousing Viennese Waltz. We could not see his face from where we were seated, but his whole body moved with the music as he played.

"He is," Elias agreed. He slurred the words somewhat, and I realized that he was already well on his way to being drunk. "They say he has a bright future." He gulped his beer greedily.

Carmilla smiled at him and sipped her own beer more methodically.

Hours passed. We talked and laughed and drank. Elias told us of his life in Gratz and peppered us with questions about the schloss and his parents. Carmilla asked him what I had been like as a child, and we were sent into fits of laughter as he recounted our adventures. After a while, my head was swimming, and it was difficult to focus on what my companions were saying. My attention strayed again and again to the young violinist, who was now – as the lateness of the hour urged many of the patrons to leave – playing a melancholy tune, an unaccompanied lamentation whose simplicity stirred my soul.

Carmilla and Elias noted my distraction and stopped talking, enraptured by the skilled performance. When the song was over and the musician bowed to scattered applause, Carmilla took my hand and brought it to her lips, kissing my fingertips. "Are you enjoying this, my love?"

Elias was quite drunk by now. His head swayed upon his neck and his eyes stayed closed overlong when he blinked. But I saw him sit bolt upright at this, the realization plain on his face. His eyes sought mine, and the plaintive expression in them asked, as clearly as if he had spoken the words aloud, *Is it true*?

I didn't look away. After a moment, he did.

Carmilla smiled wickedly. "Elias, would you like another drink?"

He nodded silently.

"I don't think he should have another drink," I said. "I think we should leave."

"Nonsense." Carmilla motioned the waitress over to refill Elias' stein. "We're only young once, after all."

The waitress left. Carmilla stroked my face teasingly, then pulled me in for a kiss. I broke away, glancing around to see if anyone was watching us, but the tavern had emptied out considerably – I wondered what time it was – and the patrons who were still there were too drunk to notice two women kissing in a dark corner. Carmilla kissed me again, and despite the pained look on Elias' face, I found that, as always, I couldn't resist her.

Elias downed his beer, then gestured for another. Carmilla gripped my thigh beneath the table, a smug smile playing on her lips.

"Carmilla, I think we should go." My voice shook with anxiety and shame.

She ignored me and leaned toward Elias. "Elias, do you still love Laura?"

He closed his eyes as if the words had pained him. Then he swallowed, opened his eyes, and looked at her as levelly as his intoxication allowed. "I do."

"Even though she rejected you? How romantic."

How did she know about that? I wondered. I had never mentioned Elias' proposal. My head was spinning. "Carmilla, stop," I pleaded.

"I do," he repeated drunkenly. "And I always will."

A sob caught in my throat and nausea roiled in my belly at the pain in Elias' eyes.

Carmilla rose from her seat and stood behind Elias, placing her hands on his shoulders. "You poor man. I, of all people, understand your infatuation." She bent and brushed his ear with her lips. "Did you know that she's never been with a man?" I stifled a gasp. He squirmed beneath her hands. "It's a shame, isn't it?" Carmilla continued. "A woman as beautiful as she is? You know what? You should ask her."

"What?" Elias slurred miserably.

"Ask her to fuck you."

Tears stung my eyes, and I dashed them away, shaking my head in disbelief. "Why are you doing this?"

I might as well have said nothing at all. Carmilla whispered in Elias' ear again, "Ask her."

His head shook as the words came out, as though they were being ripped from him against his will. "Laura," he begged, his voice choked. "Will you...?" He stopped, lowering his head in disappointment.

"No," I whispered, my eyes fixed on the sticky wooden table before me.

Carmilla threw back her head and laughed, then slipped back into her seat beside me. "Now," she smirked, "watch this." He watched helplessly as she cupped my face in her hands and kissed me deeply. Shame and desire flooded me simultaneously.

She pulled away, her breath hot against my lips as she spoke. "You see, Elias? She won't fuck you, but she'll fuck *me*."

His face crumpled in agony. I shot out of my chair, running heedlessly out of the tavern and down the street. The night air was cold, but I didn't care. I was sobbing, my breath coming in ragged gasps.

Suddenly, Carmilla was standing in front of me, impossibly still, as if she had been waiting for me, though she must have run to catch me there. She grabbed my arms. "Laura," she said calmly as I struggled against her. "My love, come here."

"Let go of me!" I screamed, ignoring the curious looks of the few passersby who were still on the streets at this hour.

"Please," she pleaded. Her eyes, so smug in the tavern, were now full of fear.

I pushed her away. "Leave me alone!" I spat. "Why? Why did you do that?"

She was silent. I lowered my face into my hands and wept. When I looked up again, she was gone.

I had determined to walk back to the flat, but I began to regret this decision half an hour later when I realized how late it was and how much farther I had to go. As if summoned by my thoughts, the carriage that we had hired to take us to The Gilded Mare pulled up beside me. "Miss Bancroft," the driver said, "Miss Mueller sent me to bring you home, if you so desire."

I glanced warily at the carriage window. "Is she with you?"

"No, miss. She hired a different carriage for herself."

I climbed into the carriage. By the time we had reached the flat, most of my drunkenness had worn off. My father was pacing nervously in the living room when I entered.

He cried out with alarm and relief. "Laura! What were you doing out so late? And without a chaperone?"

"Carmilla convinced me it was a good idea," I sighed. "I'm so sorry. I didn't mean to worry you."

He enfolded me in his arms. "I'm just glad you're unharmed."

I'm not sure "unharmed" is quite the right word for it, I thought bitterly. I returned his embrace, thankful for his quiet strength.

He pulled away to look at my face. "Did you and Carmilla have a row? She arrived a few minutes ago looking quite distressed. She assured me that you were ok and that you would arrive soon, but she wouldn't say why you were traveling separately."

"We did. I'd rather not get into the details of it. Suffice it to say that I will need to find Elias tomorrow and apologize to him."

"Elias?"

"Yes. He was at The Gilded Mare. Carmilla was...she was very unkind to him, Father. Do you know where he lives?"

"I do, and I'll help you get there tomorrow morning. We just need to make sure you're back before the fete."

"I expect I will be." A wave of exhaustion crashed over me, and I turned to go to the unused bedroom, wishing to avoid Carmilla. But then I remembered why my father had left us alone in the first place. "Oh!" I exclaimed. "Did you find any useful information about Josef?"

My father shook his head sadly. "I'm afraid not. I'm wondering if this was a fool's errand, after all."

I nodded, sharing his disappointment, then excused myself and went into the empty bedroom. Realizing with a sigh of exasperation that all my clothes were in the bedroom currently occupied by Carmilla, I took off my dress and laid down in my shift, which was grimy and still smelled like the tavern. I tried in vain to quiet my mind and relax into sleep, but Carmilla's cruelty and Elias' agony kept replaying in my mind, like some sort of perverse theatrical performance that I couldn't turn away from.

There was a hesitant knock on the door. My heart flooded with anger at the thought of seeing her. "I'm not ready to talk to you yet," I said bitterly.

She didn't respond. I could feel her presence on the other side of the wood, waiting anxiously. Two breaths, three breaths, four. Then her footsteps retreated down the hall.

Finally, I slept.

CHAPTER THIRTEEN

FRANZ

I awoke the next morning with a pounding headache, my stomach roiling with nausea. I moaned and turned away from the sunlight that was streaming through the small window. My luggage had been brought into the room, and a few dresses had been hung over the chair. A wash basin, a pitcher of fresh water, and a hairbrush had been set on the dresser.

Having availed myself of these amenities, I made my way shakily out into the common area, where my father was sitting with a newspaper. When he caught sight of me, he arched an eyebrow. "How are you feeling this morning?"

"Awful," I admitted. "Is there food? I need something to settle my stomach."

He gestured to a tray of pastries and sausage, and I put a few things on a plate and ate them tentatively, swallowing down the nausea.

"I take it Mrs. Bohm is feeling better?" I asked. "It was kind of her to bring my things into my room."

My father shook his head. "She's still ill, I'm afraid. She's here, but she looks frightfully pale. Her niece came with her to help make breakfast. And," he continued, his eyes sliding to the door of Carmilla's room, "I don't believe Mrs. Bohm was the one to bring your things to the other room."

I swallowed. I appreciated the unseen act of kindness, but I still wasn't ready to forgive her. At least she seemed to be showing some remorse. "Is she awake?" I asked.

"No. She was up for a little while earlier, but she went back to bed. She's not feeling well either, and I don't think it's just the hangover." I winced at the mention of it, my own head still pounding, though my stomach had settled a bit. My father continued, "Hopefully she'll feel well enough for the fete this evening."

"Indeed," I said, though I was anxious at the thought of attending the event with her.

"Are you ready to go find Elias?" my father asked. "I've hired a carriage."

Though my father often seemed cold and distant (especially in our first years in Styria), and he didn't always have the presence of mind to understand the things going on around him – as the affair with Carmilla suggests – he was also remarkably compassionate. This became particularly clear to me during that carriage ride. He never pressed me to divulge what had happened, nor did he try to distract me with inane chatter. He simply sat in silence and gazed out at the city, occasionally sending a reassuring glance in my direction as my fingers twisted the seat cushions. When we arrived at the dismal apartment building where Elias lived, he asked if I wanted him to accompany me.

"No, I think it's better if I speak to him privately." I squeezed his hand as I stepped out of the carriage. "But I do appreciate the offer. Now which one is his?"

He chuckled. "You know, if it were anyone but Elias, I would have qualms about sending you into a man's apartment alone. It's number five."

I stood frozen in front of Elias' door. What could I even say? Was there anything that would make what had happened last night any better? Would I only make things worse by reminding him of what had transpired without being able to explain Carmilla's cruelty?

Finally, steadying myself with several deep breaths, I knocked.

He looked awful. His sandy hair stood up in all directions, his clothes – the same ones he had been wearing the night before – were disheveled, and his eyes were bleary. He was leaning heavily against the doorframe. When he saw that it was me, he cringed. Then he steeled himself. "Good morning, Laura." His breath was rancid, and I tried not to wince.

"Good morning. May I come in?"

He didn't move at first. Then he pushed himself away from the door frame and stepped backward with a perfunctory welcome gesture.

His flat was small and untidy. I wrinkled my nose at the stale smell.

"Would you like some water?" he asked. He poured some into a glass for himself and gulped it down greedily.

"I'm fine," I said. "I won't be here long."

He waited, pouring himself another glass of water while I tried to figure out where to begin. My headache was suddenly much, much worse, and I brought my fingers to my forehead as if pressure would ameliorate it.

"Before you begin," Elias ventured, "I want to say that I don't remember much of what happened last night. I remember feeling sad and...embarrassed. And I remember you crying out and leaving the table. But I can't remember the details of our conversation." Relief washed over me. Then he continued, "Did I...did I say something to hurt you?"

Tears stung my eyes. How could he think that *he* had done something wrong? I drew closer to him, raising a hand to the side of his face comfortingly. "It wasn't you. I don't think it could *ever* be you. You are too kind."

"Carmilla, then?" His jaw clenched.

"It's probably best if we don't go into details about the conversation last night. I wish it had never happened in the first place. But I want to apologize to you for putting you in such an awkward situation."

He nodded and took another large gulp of water, then drummed his fingers nervously against his glass. "I do remember enough to know that she is your lover. You both made that abundantly clear."

I winced. "Yes." It was strange to admit it openly.

Elias sighed and sat on his rumpled bed. "I suppose I should be thankful. It sheds some light on your refusal of me."

I nodded. "It was never about *you*, Elias. I love you dearly. Just...not as a wife should love her husband."

He took my hand. "That will be a tragedy to me until the day I die. But I'm sorry for the way I behaved after I proposed. It was petty. I miss your friendship."

"And I yours." I meant it.

His eyes darkened again. "Does she make you happy, at least? I worry for you. Last night she was looking at you the way a hawk looks at a hare."

I thought of Sophie's warning, and goosebumps prickled my skin. "She's not normally like that," I said. "I don't know what got into her last night. She has been ill lately. But...yes, she makes me happy. Deliriously so."

He winced, then gave a rueful smile. "In that case, I'd be a piss-poor friend if I faulted you, wouldn't I?"

I swallowed the lump in my throat, dazed by the unexpected gift. Then the reality of the situation doused my joy like cold water. "I'm relieved to hear you say that, Elias. But many others *would* fault us, you know? You must speak of this to no one."

He nodded soberly. "I understand. You can trust me, Laura."

The conversation with Elias had softened me toward Carmilla, and by the time we returned to the flat, I was ready to speak with her. But my equanimity was dashed to pieces as soon as we crossed the threshold, for we were greeted by the acrid smell of panic and a distraught Carmilla.

"Thank God!" she exclaimed. "Mrs. Bohm just collapsed! Please, you must take her to a hospital quickly!" She pointed to the kitchen door; someone was sobbing behind it. My father hurtled in that direction, and I followed. On the other side of the door, Mrs. Bohm was lying motionless on the floor, as white as a sheet. Her niece was cradling her head in her lap and crying.

"Is she breathing?" my father asked, kneeling.

"Yes," the niece said, "but barely. Please help!"

Without delay, my father rushed downstairs for the doorman's assistance, and within a few minutes they had bundled Mrs. Bohm and her niece into a carriage. I watched from the window as the carriage thundered away. My heart was pounding.

"What happened?" I asked, turning toward Carmilla, who was sitting on a chaise behind me. She was already dressed for the fete. Indeed, she was wearing the same garnet gown that she had worn on the night I met her, and her dark hair was elaborately coiffed. She looked stronger and healthier than she had in several days. Her cheeks were rosy and her dark eyes sparkled, though her brows were knitted in concern.

"I don't know," she said. "I was getting ready when I heard Mrs. Bohm's niece screaming, and I rushed in and found her there, motionless."

I turned to look out the window again. "I hope she'll be alright." There was no sign of the carriage now.

An uncomfortable silence stretched between us for a moment. Then I heard the rustling of Carmilla's dress as she stood from the chaise and approached me. Her tentative footsteps and the halting way she brought her hands up to touch my arms conveyed her contrition before she gave voice to it. "Laura," she whispered, her voice trembling, "I'm *so* sorry."

Angry tears blurred my vision. "Why did you do it?"

Her voice was strained, thick with despair. "I don't know! I don't know what came over me, why I felt the need to hurt your friend so cruelly. I have no excuse, not one that will ever suffice. But the way I feel for you dashes all rationality from my soul. I was overcome with jealousy thinking about how long he has been your friend, about how he wanted you to be his wife, about how he was confident enough to ask you."

"He shouldn't have been. And you should have talked to me about all of this before making assumptions."

"I realize that now." She paused, weighing her words. "Laura, before I met you, all I knew of love was that it was a cruel power. Before I met you, I thought that desire and pain had to go hand in hand, that being in love meant one had to wound and be wounded. Perhaps you don't believe me. I will explain it all soon, maybe when we're back at the schloss." She clasped my hands in hers urgently. "But you have shown me a different way. You have shown me that love can be kindness, that it can be a bright, warm light unsullied by shadows. And I *so* deeply regret that pain I have caused you. You are the last person in the world who deserves it, and I swear to you on my very *soul* that I will never intentionally hurt you – or anyone you care for – again. Just please"—her voice cracked as tears streamed down her cheeks—"*please* forgive me."

The wall of anger within me collapsed under the weight of her sincerity, the earnestness of her tears. I hated seeing her in despair. I pulled her into an embrace, my own sobs welling up in response to hers. "I forgive you, Carmilla," I said softly into her dark hair, feeling her tears fall hot upon my shoulder. "And I love you. Desperately and deeply."

She sighed with relief and pulled me closer. "Oh God, I thought I had lost you. I never would have forgiven myself."

"I am yours," I said. I kissed her, the salt of our tears lingering on our lips.

We held each other close for several breaths before she broke from me, wiping her tears away with the heel of her hand. "We must get you ready for the fete."

"But my father..." I protested.

"He may very well be back before it begins. If he isn't, don't you think we should still go without him?"

I nodded. "I suppose it would be rude if *none* of us showed, and at the very least we can explain his absence to the Barragans."

"My clever girl," Carmilla smiled. "By the way, do you recognize the dress I'm wearing?"

I chuckled. "Do you think I could forget the dress you wore on the first night you set me aflame?"

Her eyes shone with the compliment. "I was thinking you could wear the same dress that you wore that night, the emerald-green one. It set off your golden curls so beautifully."

"It's a lovely idea, but I didn't think to bring it with me."

She smiled slyly. "*I* did."

She had packed the green dress with her own belongings and folded it over the chair in her room to remove its wrinkles. She led me by the hand to the bed and urged me to sit down. She began to undress me, slipping off my casual shoes and my thick stockings, kissing my bare feet and legs with her warm lips as she uncovered them. Her fingers deftly unlaced my simple linen dress, and as she pushed it off my shoulders, the palms of her hands brushed along my clavicle, down my arms. She leaned forward to kiss the tops of my breasts, then traveled up my neck to my mouth, tasting of me deeply with her tongue. I hummed in anticipation and reached for the front of her dress, but she laughed and pulled away. "No time for that now. We must get ready."

"You started it," I murmured. She slipped on my silk stockings, slowly running her hands up my thighs along with the garments. I ached for her hands to touch my cleft, but she turned and reached for my underclothes instead, swiftly maneuvering the various layers onto my body. Then the dress itself, with its layers of green silk. I raised my hands so she could drape it over me. It was like diving into cool water, and she kissed me as my head broke the surface. Then she pulled away again and fastened me where I needed to be fastened. The light caress of her fingertips against my spine made me shiver. Then she fetched the jewelry and hair pins with which to adorn me.

She stepped back after she had clasped an emerald necklace around my neck. "You are so breathtakingly lovely. Look." She drew a hand mirror from the dresser and held it facing me. Seeing myself in a mirror held by her hand, my green dress contrasting vibrantly with her red one, my blonde hair shining beside her black tresses, I felt a shock of overwhelming joy. The last time we had been dressed in this way, I had been intoxicated by her, but I had been forced to keep myself at a distance, aching, because she had been a stranger to me. To see her in the dress again and realize that now she was *mine*...it was thrilling.

As if she had read my mind, she put the mirror down behind her and said, "Seeing you like this again, it's..." She came into my arms, kissing me frantically and pushing me back against the bed, reaching under my skirts and pushing them up over my thighs.

"Carmilla," I gasped. "You just dressed me. And, as you said, we'll be late."

"I don't care. I need you *now*." She was wetly kissing my inner thigh, making her way higher...

We heard the front door of the flat open. "Carmilla?" my father called. "Laura?"

We stood hastily and smoothed down my dress. "Yes, Father?" I answered. "We're in here!"

He opened the bedroom door. "Ah, good," he said, looking rather harried. "You're both ready. I'll just be a minute or two, then we must go to the Barragans'. I've got a carriage waiting for us outside."

"Is Mrs. Bohm well?" I asked.

"She's fine. Or, at least, she will be, according to the doctors. She just needs some rest and nourishment."

Carmilla and I cooed with relief and urged him to get ready. We applied powder and lipstick to our faces and gathered our necessities into small handbags that hung from our wrists. I was dizzy with the frustration of our interrupted passion.

We were somewhat late to the party, but there were still a few other guests trickling in, and dinner had not yet been served. My father introduced Carmilla and me to the towering Colonel and his petite, plump wife, both of whom welcomed us with enthusiastic kindness. Then we met their daughter, Hannah, and her fiancé, Leon Kepner, who looked very much like Franz except that his hair and mustache were darker than his brother's. I glanced around the room to see if I could find Franz, but I was forced to return my attention to Hannah when she started asking Carmilla and me about our dresses.

The Barragans' mansion was stunningly immense and well-appointed, decorated according to modern tastes. They had hired a tenor and his accompanist – both apparently well known, to judge by the excited whispers of the other young women – to provide the entertainment before dinner, and a full ensemble for the dancing afterward. The food and the wine were excellent. After we had finished the elaborate feast at our table, small trays with champagne and dessert cakes were circulated around the dancing hall. The toasts given in honor of the soon-to-be-wedded couple were heartfelt and eloquent, and there was very little ill-mannered chatter and gossip (as often occurs at such events); everyone seemed genuinely happy to see a couple so well-matched and so clearly in love.

I couldn't tear my eyes away from Carmilla. It was a marvel to me how easily she engaged in conversation with everyone, how charmingly she managed to fend off the suitors who swarmed her, how gracefully she danced. I tried to channel some of her confidence, and found to my surprise that I, too, was beset with admirers, and that I could banter with them as wittily as she did. Whenever a new young man asked us to dance, we aligned ourselves close to each other so that we could brush our gloved fingertips together as we promenaded around our partners. Finally, we begged their forgiveness and found ourselves a corner and some flutes of champagne to consume, breathless and giggling and bright with the joy of being young and wanted.

Suddenly, I caught sight of a familiar sandy head. "Franz!" I exclaimed, nearly dropping my goblet. I hadn't seen him at dinner. He looked like he didn't want to be there. Dark circles shadowed his eyes, and he gave only terse smiles to the friends and family members who were trying to engage him in conversation as he passed.

I was tempted to approach him, but Carmilla put a hand on my arm. "Laura, look! Your father!"

My father, who had been conversing with Colonel Barragan on the edge of the room, was being tapped on the shoulder by one of the Barragans' servants. The servant spoke to him urgently, and my father leaned toward the Colonel to excuse himself before rushing off in the direction of the front door.

"Come on," I said. I took Carmilla's hand and led her in the same direction.

When we reached the foyer, we were shocked to see Martin standing there. Breathing hard with exertion, he handed a letter to my father, who ripped open the seal without delay, glancing in our direction only long enough to say, "It's from the General." He read it silently at first, then handed it to me.

My dearest friend,

I tracked the monster to London, but have since lost her scent. I have enlisted the help of a Baron Johann Vordenburg, who is knowledgeable in such matters. However, he is as much at a loss as I. I hesitate to ask this, for I know how dearly you will miss your daughter if you leave her for an extended period of time, but I am in dire need of your help. You know London better than I, and you proved your strength and intellectual acumen on more than one occasion when we served together. Please, help me bring my Emma's killer to justice. Come as quickly as possible. I have lodged at the Baron's house; you can ask for me there. I fear that time is running out, that any delay may lead the monster to strike again.

Josef

I covered my mouth with my hand, stunned by both the dilemma and the request. I read it again, trying to make sense of the shocking and inexplicable words he had used. Monster. Emma's killer. *Her*.

Carmilla, who was reading over my shoulder, gripped my arms tightly with her hands.

"The letter arrived at the schloss yesterday," Martin said, still trying to recover his breath. "I left this morning and came here without stopping."

"I have to leave *now*," my father said urgently.

My mind ran over the words again. Why hadn't Josef explained what he meant? Why had he written as though my father already knew what he was talking about? "Father, what does he mean?"

"I don't know." His voice quavered with desperation. "I don't *know*."

"What's going on?" Colonel Barragan said, coming into the foyer.

My father showed him the letter, and the Colonel's eyes widened. "You must leave as soon as possible," he said.

"But the girls," my father protested.

"They can stay here with us tonight," the Colonel assured him, "and then we will personally ensure that they return to your schloss in the coming days."

My father nodded. "Martin, can you take me as far as Calais? I can book passage from there. I know it will take you away from your duties at home, but...dammit, this is more urgent!"

"Of course, sir," Martin said. "Adeline can take care of things while I'm gone. That woman has more sense than I do."

My father turned to me and grasped my shoulders. "Laura, is it alright with you if I leave? I don't know how long I'll be gone."

"Father, I want nothing more than to see Emma's killer brought to justice." *Emma's killer. Her.* Whoever *she* was. I was still reeling from it. Seeing the concern on his face, I added, "And I won't be lonely, not with Carmilla around."

"That settles it, then. I apologize for my early departure, Colonel."

"No apologies necessary, Edward," the Colonel said. "Please let me know if we can assist you in any way. And Godspeed."

In mere minutes, my father was gone. I knew he was doing the right thing, but I couldn't escape the anxious pit that had lodged itself in my stomach. After all, if things didn't go well – if his ship was caught in a storm or he was besieged by bandits or the murderer they were chasing proved too powerful for them – I might never see him again.

For the second time in two days, I got *very* drunk. The champagne was flowing freely, and soon my anxiety on my father's behalf was replaced by an all-consuming desire for Carmilla, who looked so ravishing in that blood-red dress that it was everything I could do to keep from touching her. The glances she kept throwing my way and her constant small touches – a hand on my waist when she came to bring me more champagne, a caress on my cheek under the pretext of wiping away a stray eyelash, a surreptitious caress of my buttocks as she passed me on her way to the dance floor – enflamed me even more. As the night wore on, the crowd grew thinner. The tenor had retired for the evening, and the musicians were playing more softly now. The remaining guests were scattered in small groups at tables, playing cards or drinking and smoking cigars. I was seated with Hannah and Leon, who were giggling drunkenly and trying (unsuccessfully, due to their inebriation and my own) to teach me how to play Karnöffel. Carmilla breezed up to our table and took my hand. "Miss Barragan, Mr. Kepner, please excuse me, but I need Miss Bancroft for something."

"Hopefully it's not too urgent," Leon slurred. "Is there anything I can help you with?"

Carmilla flashed him a bright smile. "Oh, no, it's very kind of you to ask. It's...well, it's women's business," she said with mock seriousness.

Leon held up a hand. "Say no more. I don't know much about women's business, I confess, but I know enough not to defile the sacred mysteries!"

Hannah blushed and giggled beside him. Carmilla tugged my hand insistently, and I followed her, stumbling a bit in my efforts to keep up.

She brought me to a darkened corner of an empty hallway, pushed me hard against the wall, and kissed me deeply. I was startled at the violence of it, and I turned my face away, struggling to catch my breath. She grasped my jaw with a hand and forced my mouth to hers, her tongue tasting mine again and again. My body responded of its own accord, my hips driving forward against hers.

"Someone will see," I panted, finally managing to break free from her hungry embrace.

"I don't care," she whispered. Her kisses scorched a line down my neck and breasts.

"I do," I said weakly.

"Enough to stop?" As she waited for me to answer, she bent down and slipped one hand beneath the hem of my dress and traced a line from my ankle to my thigh. She stopped just before she had reached my sex. The warmth of her hand being so close – and yet not touching me where I was desperate to be touched – made me throb with desire. She brought her mouth to mine again. My need for her gnawed at me like an insatiable, ruinous hunger.

I glanced around the hallway. No one was here. We seemed to be near some sort of storage room, the kind of place unlikely to see any traffic at this hour. And perhaps it was the champagne, but the laughter from the party sounded unfocused and far away.

"No," I said finally. I kissed her ardently, drinking her smile as if it could quench the ache deep inside me. "Keep going."

Her hand found its target between my legs. "You're so wet," she groaned. Trying to suppress the sounds of pleasure that were being ripped from my throat as she worked her fingers skillfully, I broke our contact just long enough to tease up the hem of her dress and find *her* cleft – warm and wet with anticipation – with my own hand.

When we finally re-entered the grand room, we did so cautiously, trying not to draw too much attention to ourselves. As it turned out, this effort was unnecessary. Things were winding down in earnest now, and the remaining guests were in no condition to notice that our cheeks were flushed and our lips redder than usual.

Colonel Barragan, slouched in a chair by the fireplace, was the first to catch sight of us. He sat up straighter, raising his hand to get our attention. "Miss Bancroft! Miss Mueller! I just realized that I never showed you to your room! We've put some spare nightdresses in there for you, too. Hopefully it will be enough for you until we can escort you back to your flat in the morning. Martha!" He looked around anxiously for his wife. "Martha! Damn, she must have gone to bed already. Come, I'll show you myself."

We went up the sweeping staircase to the second floor, where several bedrooms were arrayed along one hallway. The Colonel gestured to the last door. "You're here, next to Leon's brother Franz."

"Franz?!" I exclaimed.

"Indeed, though I believe he's gone to bed already. Poor chap. Did you hear what happened to his fiancée? Oh!" he exclaimed in horror, looking very much like he wished he could retract his words. "I forgot she was your friend. I'm *so* sorry, Miss Bancroft."

"Please don't trouble yourself," I said. "It was devastating, to be sure, but your words do not make it more so." *Or less,* I thought bitterly.

"We appreciate your hospitality," Carmilla cut in, "but we should turn in now. Right, Laura?"

I nodded, and the Colonel bowed and left us alone. In the bedroom, we undressed and slipped on the borrowed nightgowns (too big by far, but suitable enough for one night). We lay in the bed, our arms around each other and our legs entwined, our noses nearly touching as we breathed together, cherishing the silence.

"Is something wrong?" Carmilla asked quietly.

"No, why?"

"You just seem...troubled." She kissed the tip of my nose. "Is it because the Colonel brought up Emma?"

"Yes," I admitted. "I was hoping I could talk to Franz. He might know something about what led up to Emma's death. She wrote to him every day. I don't want to wake the poor man, though. And who knows if he'll be up and about by the time we leave in the morning."

"Could you write him a letter? Once we're back at the schloss?'

"I suppose so." My eyelids felt impossibly heavy.

She traced my eyebrows with her fingertips, sending me deeper into relaxation, and kissed my nose again. "Goodnight, my love."

It had been a long time since I'd been troubled by a nightmare, and it was so pleasant at first that I didn't initially recognize it as one. Carmilla and I were walking from our schloss out into the vegetable garden, wide sun hats on our heads and baskets slung over our arms. We chatted and smiled at each other with frank, open devotion, and my father and Adeline and Martin, who had been waiting for us, didn't bat an eye when Carmilla leaned over to kiss me. The freedom of it thrilled me. We bent to our task, picking vegetables from vines and lattices and furrows. The vegetables were overripe, huge and soft and discolored, but I continued picking them until my basket was nearly full. When I looked up at the others, however, their baskets were still empty. I stopped to watch as Carmilla pulled a potato from the earth, leered at it, and dropped it back on the ground. Then she stepped on it with her boot until there was a wet *pop*, and blood gushed around her foot and soaked into the dirt. The entire garden was stained dark red, and I suddenly realized that she and the others must have been doing this with everything they picked.

"What are you doing?" I asked, my voice as weak as an echo.

Carmilla smiled crookedly. She picked a tomato, held it up high in the air, and squashed it in her fingers, the bright red juice becoming dark blood as it streamed in rivulets down her arm and onto her white bodice.

"Oh no," she said calmly, "I seem to have ruined my dress." She untied the laces, shrugged it from her shoulders, and began peeling it stickily from her chest.

My father, Adeline, and Martin were unbothered. They continued to pick the vegetables and explode them into bloody puddles on the ground. The ground shook, trembling with delight at each new offering.

Carmilla was now uncovering the skin beneath her pale bosom, and I froze in horror. Her white, smooth belly had been replaced by a gaping hole stuffed with worms, centipedes, and beetles, hissing and writhing as they crawled over each other to burrow deep in her guts. A few of them fell to the earth with soft *plops*, and I reeled backward and fell on my elbows, nausea roiling in my stomach.

Carmilla walked slowly toward me, her smile stretched wide beneath cold eyes, handfuls of the squirming creatures dropping upon the blood-slick ground with every step. "What's the matter, Laura?" she hissed, the inside of her mouth dark with the shiny, wriggling backs of insects. When she spoke again, her voice was no longer hers, but a deep, thunderous growl, with a rattle like the beating of small, hard wings. "Don't you want to taste me?"

I awoke shaking and nauseated, vomit rising in my throat. In a panic, I scanned the bedroom for a solution. I made out a large porcelain bowl that had been placed on the dresser for use as a wash basin. I scrambled and grabbed hold of it just as my stomach heaved and emptied itself. Again and again I retched, shocked by the sheer volume that my body was expelling.

That was a lot of champagne, I thought. I wiped my mouth with the back of my hand and turned to make sure I hadn't disturbed Carmilla's slumber.

She wasn't there. The bed was empty, sheets rumpled and pillows displaced. I looked frantically around the room. "Carmilla?" I called out.

I needed to take the bowl downstairs and outside to empty it. The smell was too putrid to keep in the room, and I didn't want any of the Colonel's servants to have to deal with it in the morning. I put my hands around its sides and lifted it up, willing the contents not to slosh as I made my way out of the bedroom, down the hallway, down the stairs, and out into the cool air. Having completed my task, I scanned the courtyard – in vain - for any sign of Carmilla. The dim light of pre-dawn and the utter silence of this in-between time – after the party, before the day – might have been charming if I hadn't been distraught by her disappearance. I turned and headed inside, my bare feet silent on the stairs as I made my way back to our room.

I heard the soft click of a doorknob at the end of the hallway and froze, straining my eyes to try to make out shapes in the darkness.

It was Carmilla, and she was leaving Franz's room.

My face went numb and my arms shook around the bowl as I watched her slip back into our bedroom like a shadow. My gorge rose again, and I ran back outside and vomited into the bushes. When the sickness had passed, I sat in the grass next to the bowl, shaking weakly.

"Laura!" I heard her exclaim behind me. She crouched beside me. "What's wrong? Are you ill?"

"Yes," I said numbly. "It must have been all the champagne."

"I was so worried! I came back to the room and you were gone!"

I lifted my face. "And where were *you*?"

"What?"

"You said you came back to the room. Where were you?"

"Oh," she said casually, "I couldn't sleep, and I was hungry, so I went to the kitchen to find something to eat."

She lied so easily.

I wasn't planning to let it go, but I also didn't want to cause a scene at such an early hour and at someone else's house. "Let's go back to bed," I said stiffly. "It's too early, and we have the journey home ahead of us."

CHAPTER FOURTEEN

DISCOVERY

A couple of hours later, the Barragans' household began to stir. Carmilla, who had slept peacefully once we returned to our bed, was eager to avail herself of breakfast when the smell of sausages wafted into the room, and she quickly changed out of her nightgown and back into her evening dress. As I had been too tortured by resentment to find sleep again, I had neither the energy nor the appetite to join her. "Are you sure?" she asked, brow furrowed in concern.

"I'm sure. Go without me. Would you mind asking Colonel Barragan about our conveyance to the flat? I'd like to return home as soon as possible."

"I will. Get some rest, my love."

I lay in bed for an hour, wishing that I could snuff out the sunlight like a candle. A servant knocked politely on the door and offered me some cool water, then asked if there was anything else I needed. When I assured her that there wasn't, she added, "Miss Mueller asked me to relay that the Colonel will have your carriage ready within a quarter of an hour."

I thanked her, and she excused herself. No doubt she had many other things to attend to in the aftermath of the festivities. I stripped off the borrowed nightdress and slipped on the emerald-green gown, still a bit sweat-damp and wrinkled from the previous night. My feet felt too swollen and sore to put back in my dress shoes, but I had no other footwear, so I forced them in and hobbled my way out of the bedroom. I paused outside Franz's door. As angry as I was about whatever had happened between him and Carmilla, my questions about Emma still burned in my mind.

I knocked. There was no response. I knocked again, clearing my throat and calling hoarsely, "Franz?" Still no response. Either he was no longer in his room – which I doubted, as I had been awake for hours and had not heard him leave – or he was sleeping drunkenly. If the latter, he would not thank me for disturbing him, and it would be better if he were in an amenable state before I peppered him with questions about his dead almost-fiancée. I sighed and made my way downstairs.

Twenty minutes later, Carmilla and I were in one of the Barragans' carriages. Our driver was a young man named Johannes, who had a shock of hair so blonde it was nearly white. Once we had returned to the flat to retrieve our things (which Johannes, smiling shyly at Carmilla, insisted on carrying down to the carriage for us), we set out for the schloss. The Barragans' cook had been kind enough to pack us a basket of sandwiches. Shortly after we had left the flat, Carmilla delved into the provisions with her customary enthusiasm.

"Are you sure you don't want any?" she asked me for the third time.

I shook my head.

"What's wrong?" she asked, wrapping her sandwich in a napkin and placing it back in the basket beside her. "You've been so cold and quiet this morning! Are you worried about your father?"

Gratz was slowly fading into the distance behind us. The empty road stretched before us. Johannes was singing to the horses in a high, sweet voice. Now was as good a time as any to broach the topic. I steeled myself. "Yes. But I'm more worried about the fact that you were in Franz's room last night."

She grew very still, her eyes fixed on the floor. Then she laughed, a touch too brightly. "Oh, that?! Nothing happened, my dear." She leaned forward and clasped my hand in hers. "I promise."

I scoffed. "Nothing happened? So what exactly were you doing in there?"

She released my hand and leaned back on the bench. "I...Well, if you must know - "

"I must." My voice was low, but as sharp as a knife. It surprised even me with its vehemence. Carmilla hesitated, as if realizing the precariousness of the moment.

"As I mentioned before, I was hungry," she began, "so I went down to the kitchen. But I wasn't the only one awake at that time. On my way back up the stairs, I ran into Franz, who was heading outside with his pipe. We passed each other without saying anything at first, but I kept thinking about what you had said, about how you wanted to ask him about Emma's correspondence. And eventually I worked myself up into thinking it was a good idea to ask him myself, since you were asleep."

Anger swelled like nausea in my stomach. "You took it upon yourself to do this without asking *me* first?"

She bit her lip and lowered her eyes, then continued her explanation. "I waited for him in the hallway, and when he came back inside, I asked him if we could talk in private."

"And he refused, I'm sure!" I scoffed.

"He did, at first," she replied, ignoring my sarcasm. "But I assured him that my intentions were not inappropriate, that I merely wanted to ask him something on your behalf."

I pressed my eyelids with the heels of my hands. It sounded too convenient to be true. But I loved her so much that I wanted to believe her. And I was burning to know the outcome of the conversation. "And?" I urged.

She covered my hand with hers again. "I'm sorry, Laura. He said that Emma stopped writing him letters more than a month before she died. He has no idea what happened to her."

Tears stung my eyes, and a small, wounded cry escaped from my throat. Carmilla leaned forward and embraced me, holding me while I shook with sobs, and she didn't let go until long after they had passed.

I wiped my eyes. "I'm sorry. It's just...I was hoping there would be something to help make sense of it."

She stroked my cheek. "I know. I understand. And *I'm* the one who should be sorry. Sorry he couldn't shed any light on your darkness, and sorry I did it without consulting you first."

"And that you lied to me?"

She stiffened. "What?"

"When you found me outside last night, and I asked you where you had been, you said you went to the kitchen for some food. You didn't mention Franz."

"I..." she stopped, sitting back and looking fixedly in her lap.

"Carmilla?" Her eyes, filled with regret, met mine. I grabbed her hands. "If you love me, you *have* to be honest with me. I don't want to be with someone who doesn't respect me enough to tell me the truth. Do you understand? I *love* you. There's nothing you could tell me that would break my heart more than a lie."

How naïve I was! I could not have imagined then how deeply horrifying the truth would turn out to be.

Carmilla nodded and brought my fingers to her lips. "I won't lie to you again, I promise. I don't want to lose you. I couldn't bear it."

And then we lost ourselves in each other as the carriage rocked and Johannes' blithe voice danced around us.

Adeline ran out to meet us when we arrived, her eyes wide as she took in the unfamiliar carriage and driver. "Girls!" she exclaimed, reaching out her hands to help us out of the carriage as Johannes attended to the horses and luggage. "It's so good to see you. But...Mr. Bancroft? Martin? What did the letter say?"

Of course she wouldn't know, I realized. They wouldn't have opened the General's letter without my father's consent.

"The General begged my father to come to London to help him track Emma's murderer. Martin took him straightaway. I imagine he'll come back once he's seen father off safely."

Adeline crossed herself. "Lord preserve and keep them. This business is so ugly, isn't it?"

Bettina and Maria were coming out of the house now, too. When Bettina saw Carmilla, she hastily lowered her eyes. This was the second time I had seen her react to Carmilla with what seemed to be fear or embarrassment, and I resolved to ask Carmilla about it later. Meanwhile, Adeline was pulling me into a soft embrace. I was taller than she was – I had been for nearly a decade – but she had an uncanny ability to make me feel like a small child in a safe, warm place.

"I missed you, my dear. The house is not the same without you."

"I missed you too." I hugged her tightly. "I saw Elias," I added.

She pulled away from me. "Oh? How is he?"

Obviously, I couldn't tell her the truth. "He's well enough. Though I think it would do him good to come back here more often."

"Can't say I disagree with that!" she laughed. "Come on, let's get you girls settled back into your rooms."

Carmilla, who was cringing in the late-afternoon sunlight, voiced her approval of this proposition.

"Bettina!" Adeline added, as she and Maria took hold of the luggage. "Show the driver – what's your name, young sir?"

"Johannes," he piped.

"Show Johannes the stable and the guest room in the cottage."

"Yes, ma'am," Bettina said. She was still studiously avoiding eye contact with Carmilla and me.

As we walked back to the house, trailing behind Adeline and Maria, Carmilla surreptitiously took my hand and squeezed it, smiling. I could tell she was thinking the same thing I was. *It's good to be home.*

In the bustle of reinstating ourselves into the household, I forgot my resolution to ask Carmilla about Bettina. After we had helped each other unpack our clothing in our respective rooms and carried down the dirty laundry, Carmilla groaned, holding her head. "I'm so sorry, my dear, but I think I need a nap before dinner. My head is *aching*!"

I chuckled sympathetically. "I would do the same, except I worry that I would sleep right through to morning!" There was no one else in the hallway, and she kissed me softly before retreating into her bedroom.

Struggling to fend off my own exhaustion, I tried to make myself useful. As our return home had been unexpected, Maria was struggling to put together a proper dinner. I offered to help her – as I had many times as a child – and she accepted. It felt good to work with my hands, cutting potatoes for the Gulasch and running to fetch whatever Maria needed. She laughed good-naturedly at my imprecise cuts.

Once dinner had been prepared, we all ate at the table together, even Johannes. Adeline asked us dozens of questions about the Barragans' fete and the rest of our time in Gratz. Carmilla answered most of them, her eyes sparkling, her wit and laughter drawing smiles from her rapt audience. Even Bettina gave a reluctant smile on occasion, though for the most part she kept her eyes fixed sullenly on her plate, and when she had finished eating, she excused herself.

The dishes were cleared, and everyone went their separate ways: Adeline, Maria, and Johannes to finish the last of their daily tasks,

Carmilla and I to our bedrooms. I was truly exhausted, my limbs heavy with fatigue and food. When Carmilla kissed me outside my bedroom door, her tongue sliding languorously against mine, I sighed and reluctantly pushed her away.

"I'm so sorry, my love, but I really must sleep tonight."

For a moment, her eyes darkened. Then her frown disappeared, replaced by a compassionate smile. "It's been an overwhelming few days and nights."

I raised her hand to my lips and kissed her fingers. "Tomorrow?"

"I'll be dreaming of you until then."

I was asleep moments after my head hit the pillow. Unfortunately, the blissful oblivion didn't last long; I was awakened near midnight by the desire throbbing between my legs. I moaned and shifted in the bed, hoping to ignore it and find a way back into slumber, but to no avail. Every time I closed my eyes, I thought of her breasts...her wet mouth...her deft fingers...her legs wrapped around mine...her throaty groans urging me on as I pleasured her with my hands or my mouth... It was no use. I wouldn't be able to sleep until my need for her had been satisfied.

I rose from the bed, donned my dressing gown and slippers, and padded down the hallway to her room. I knocked softly, but there was no response. Fearing that a louder knock might wake Maria or Bettina and knowing that Carmilla wouldn't mind the intrusion, I turned the knob and carefully opened the door.

She wasn't there.

The hair on the back of my neck prickled, and I was suddenly struck by the number of times she had disappeared in this way. "Carmilla?" I called, feeling a sense of déjà vu from the previous night. There was no response.

I searched the house for her. I even ventured into the attic, remembering what she had claimed the first time she disappeared. But there was no trace of her. As I passed through the dining room for the second time, a movement outside – far off, near the stable – caught my eye. I ran to the window and peered in that direction, my face so close to the glass that it fogged with my breath. I could see nothing out of the ordinary. I decided to investigate further.

The night air was cool. I drew my dressing gown more tightly around myself as I headed toward the stable. My slippers were getting hopelessly dirty, and I would no doubt get a scolding from Adeline, but donning my boots would have been a waste of time. When I got to the small, low structure, I saw that the two horses who had drawn our hired carriage were strangely restless, the whites of their eyes showing as they stomped and whinnied nervously in their stalls.

"What's the matter, dear hearts?" I asked. My eyes scanned the dark corners in vain.

Then I heard a cry from the woods behind the stable. It sounded like someone in pain. I hesitated. It was not the sort of sound one ought to go *toward* in the middle of the night, but I had to find out what was going on.

I made my way around the building and into the shadowy realm of trees, cursing every stick that cracked beneath my feet. As I recall it now, I shudder at the horror of what I was about to encounter, and I wish I could reverse my younger self's steps, make her return to the house, make her stay blissfully unaware, if only for a short while longer.

Johannes was standing pressed against a tree, his face contorted in pain beneath his shock of blonde hair. In front of him, I recognized Carmilla's white nightdress and the long waves of dark hair that spilled down her back. But there the familiarity stopped: her graceful hands had become gnarled claws, digging into Johannes' shoulders. I gasped, and she turned to face me, tearing herself away from her prey. A gaping wound in his neck spurted blood, black in the dim light. Her face was stretched to skeletal thinness, her mouth and chin dripping obscenely with Johannes' blood, her eyes – I recognized those eyes! – shiny and hard, like a beetle's carapace. The eyes widened when she caught sight of me. Then she parted her blackened lips in a grotesque grimace, revealing unnaturally long, sharp teeth that extended beyond her lower lip. Drops of blood hung from them like venom before falling and staining the white dress at her bosom. Still grimacing, she began gliding toward me, the tips of her clawed toenails floating just above the ground.

Released from her clutches, Johannes slumped to the earth. I screamed and scrambled backward. My limbs were heavy and numb with terror, and I felt myself fall, my head striking a rock with a resounding *thunk*. Black dots swam before my vision and pulled me backward through a narrow tunnel. Fighting to stay conscious, I shook my head vigorously, and pain shot down the back of my neck. Carmilla – the creature that had once been Carmilla – was kneeling before me now, wiping the blood from her face with her forearm. She craned her neck upward and closed her eyes, groaning with effort as she fought to return to herself. Her hands and fingernails unclawed, the terrible, skeletal rictus became a woman's face again, her teeth slowly retracted back into her gums. Her eyes blinked quickly as they morphed from opaque, impossibly-stretched black ovals to the beautiful dark eyes rimmed with full lashes that I knew – or thought I had known – so well.

"Well," she said sadly, "you *did* say you wanted to know the truth." Black unconsciousness pressed upon me again, and this time it consumed me.

CHAPTER FIFTEEN
THE BEGINNING OF THE TRUTH

I woke up in my bedroom. Sunlight streamed through the windows. It was cool and quiet, and I could hear the faint sounds of activity outside: Adeline talking to someone, a horse whickering. For a moment, I wondered if it had all been just another bad dream. Then I turned over in my bed and saw Carmilla slumped in the chair by the fireplace.

"Good morning," she said grimly.

The tone of her voice confirmed it. "It wasn't a dream, then."

She shook her head slowly. "No, it wasn't a dream."

Fear coursed through me like lightning. I shot from the bed and ran to the window on trembling legs. I hit the glass repeatedly and screamed, "Help! Help me, please!"

Adeline and Bettina were in the courtyard, shaking out linens in the sunshine. They didn't seem to hear my shrieks. Carmilla rose from the chair and walked toward me. I cried out as she drew near. The window vibrated with my panicked poundings.

One of her hands enveloped my wrist, and suddenly I could no longer move my arm, no matter how vigorously I thrashed. I brought my other fist forward to strike her, but she locked that one, too, in her strong grip. It was like being held in a stockade. Her face remained unmoved as I struggled against her, though her eyes were dark with despair. "Let go of me, you monster!" I shouted. "Adeline! Adeline! Help me!"

"They won't hear you." Carmilla slid her eyes toward the unperturbed figures of the women outside as if to prove her point.

"Why not?!" I shrieked, still pulling violently – and in vain – against her. Despite how steadfastly she was holding me in place, her grip around my wrists was soft.

"Because I don't want them to."

My knees buckled, and I hung suspended for a moment before she lowered her arms, guided me to the floor, and released my wrists. I retched and sobbed, terror coursing through my veins, my heart pounding in a panicked rhythm. "No," I whispered. "No, no, no." My protestations grew louder and louder, and, as if my own words were giving me strength, I found my feet beneath me, stood up again, and fumbled at the window latch.

I froze.

Johannes was in the courtyard, bringing the horses from the stable and hitching them to the carriage. He looked as strong as ever, if a bit pale, and he smiled shyly at Bettina as she came to help him. There was no trace of the bloody gash at his throat.

My jaw dropped in disbelief.

Carmilla stood beside me and looked out the window, a grim smile on her face. "He won't remember what happened last night. He'll recall that he and I had a...pleasant rendezvous, but nothing else." My mind was still reeling, but the sadness in her eyes rooted me to the spot. "Laura, if you want to flee from me, or if you want me to go away, I understand. You're right to be afraid; I *am* a monster. But if there is anything left of the love you once felt, I beg you to at least believe *this*: I don't want to hurt you, nor anyone else in this schloss, for that matter." I flinched as she reached for me. She winced and stepped back, her eyes welling with tears. "Please. Please believe me."

I swallowed. The memory of her – her blood-stained mouth, her distorted features, her clawed feet floating above the ground – flooded my mind unbidden. It wasn't just fear coursing through me now; anger and betrayal were there, too. "Why should I believe you?" I hissed.

Her expression hardened, and she lifted her chin. "Because if I *had* wanted to hurt you, you wouldn't be standing here right now."

My mind wavered between stupefaction and the primal urge to flee, between fear and curiosity. And my heart...the Carmilla standing before me now was the woman I loved, not the creature in the woods from the night before. She turned away from me, resting her head on the windowpane and closing her eyes in pain.

There was truth to her words, wasn't there? I had seen what she was capable of last night, had felt the strength in her body just now when she held me immobile, like an owl flying soundlessly through the air with a mouse struggling in its grasp. And clearly her powers went beyond the physical, if Adeline and Bettina could be made to ignore the sights and sounds around them and Johannes could be made to forget such a grave wound. I cringed, wondering if she'd ever influenced *me* to ignore or forget anything. At any rate, it was true: if she had wanted us dead, we would be dead already.

I put a hand to the back of my head, remembering my precipitous tumble to the ground. How had I gotten back to my room? And why was there no bruise or lump?

I had so many questions.

"I don't want you to leave," I said finally, and Carmilla took a shaky, relieved breath. "At least, not yet." In truth, I was helpless in the face of her monstrosity, and it was foolish of me even to pretend I had any control, but her evident distress gave me hope that she wouldn't harm me. "But you need to tell me everything," I continued. "Who you are, *what* you are, and why exactly you're here, to start."

She nodded. "I promise I will tell you everything you want to know."

Adeline was calling us down for breakfast. I frowned. We needed to talk in private, and I didn't want to interact with anyone else while I was in my current state of shock.

"If you want," Carmilla ventured, "I can make it so that no one hears or disturbs us."

"No! Don't...don't *manipulate* them like that."

"We must find somewhere else to talk, then. Get dressed, and let's take a walk in the woods." She moved from the bedroom so swiftly that the air in her wake pulled at me where I stood. I took several shaky breaths, trying in vain to collect myself. Following a monster into the woods was a stupid idea, and if logic were the only thing driving me,

I would have refused. But though some part of me – the animal part – was still quaking with fear, in my heart, I believed that she wouldn't hurt me.

I dressed myself, let Adeline know that we were heading out for a walk, and met Carmilla in the front hall. We set off in a northerly direction, strolling in the shade of the trees. We didn't speak for a long time, not until the schloss was no longer visible behind us. Then she began.

"You asked me who I am, what I am, and what I'm doing here. To answer the first question, my real name is not Carmilla Mueller. It's Mircalla Karnstein."

I gasped. "The portrait!"

"Yes, I am the subject of that portrait."

"But it was dated to 1716!"

She nodded. "I was born in 1682."

I stumbled over a rock, and she was beside me in an instant, her arm underneath my elbow, keeping me upright. "How...how is that possible?"

"That brings me to your second question. You saw me feeding from Johannes last night, so you must have some idea of what I am."

I swallowed. I knew of many supernatural creatures who fed on human blood, but none that walked in the sunlight in perfect mimicry of a normal human being. I shook my head.

Carmilla sighed. "We have been called many things throughout the ages, but the word you might be familiar with is *vampire*."

A shudder passed through me. "Vampire," I whispered, the word heavy and strange on my lips.

"It means that I must drink blood to survive," Carmilla said, her voice tinged with sorrow. "And it means many other things, as well, the most important of which is that I am immortal."

This stopped me in my tracks. "Immortal? Are you saying you *cannot* die?"

"I *can* die, but not of old age or sickness. And I heal very quickly, so even wounds are no threat to me, except those which are impossible to heal from."

"Such as?"

Carmilla raised an eyebrow. "Surely you can't expect me to answer *that*, can you? At least, not before I'm sure you don't want to kill me?"

We stood still for a moment, studying each other. Her confident façade was belied by a worried shadow in her eyes, and I realized with shock that she was just as nervous as I was. *I don't want to lose you*, she had said to me in the carriage. My heart ached to see her so vulnerable. Heaven help me, I loved her.

"I don't want to kill you," I said quietly.

She dashed a tear from her eyes, then made a motion with her hand that suggested we should keep walking. I willed my feet to continue their forward movement. "Burning," she said finally, once we had walked in silence for several moments. "And beheading. And a weapon through the heart, though it must remain there to prevent the heart from healing itself."

I looked up at the patches of blue sky peeking through the leaves, marveling at how well the dense foliage blocked the light of day. "But not sunlight? I thought that vampires were vulnerable to sunlight."

"Not in the same way the stories would lead you to believe. We do, however, have exceedingly keen eyesight, along with our other senses, and bright sunlight can be painful, even disorienting."

"Crosses? Holy water? Sophie told me such things are effective against...supernatural beings."

She chuckled. "The priests would like to think they're effective, I'm sure. I would be a weak creature indeed, if sunlight and water could harm me."

She certainly wasn't weak. "Did you carry me from the woods last night?"

Was there a glint of pride in her eye? "You *and* Johannes. I am preternaturally strong. It is one of my gifts, besides immortality."

"And the others?"

"I can move very quickly, almost faster than a human eye can follow. I can float above the ground, as you saw last night, or even fly if I have fed recently. I can also shapeshift into shadowy forms. But I suppose you could have guessed that one."

"The servants at Count Carlsfeld's house," I realized numbly. "You killed them."

"Yes," she admitted sorrowfully. "I was...it's difficult to explain, but...I had been asleep for over a decade, and I was still in the process of awakening, which means that I was unusually weak. It took all my powers to attend that fete, and I overestimated what I was capable of. I didn't mean to kill them, but I couldn't control myself." She lowered her eyes, her voice nearly a whisper now. "I don't like to kill, not if I can help it. But sometimes I *can't* help it. It is the greatest cruelty of my...condition."

Condition. The image of her distorted features as she fed on Johannes flashed before my eyes. It was hard to imagine that he could have forgotten that. How much had she made *me* forget?

"Have you ever...have you ever fed from me?"

She paused for a moment before answering. "Only once. And not recently."

The memory came flooding back to me. My head swam, and I staggered backward against a tree, the bark rough and cold against my back. "It was you!" I gasped. "When I was a *child*...it was *you.*"

She lowered her eyes in shame. "It was."

Anger roiled in my belly. The rough bark of the tree dug into my palms as I willed myself not to scream.

"I'm so sorry," she said, her voice so weak it was nearly imperceptible. "I know it must feel like a betrayal."

It is *a betrayal*, I thought bitterly.

She drew close and took my hands, though I struggled against her. "But my love, you must listen to me. I don't regret it, because without it, I would never have come to love you."

"What do you mean? I was eight years old!" It was sickening enough that she had preyed on me; even more sickening was the idea that her predation had gone beyond the simple – if horrifying – thirst for my blood.

"Please calm down," she begged. "Let me explain."

My breath was burning in my chest, but I stilled myself and nodded.

"As you already know from this morning, my abilities go beyond the physical. I can read people's thoughts, change their perceptions, influence them to think what *I* want them to think, even change their memories. When you and your father moved here, I was nearby, and I heard the activity going on at the house. I could hear your father's thoughts, and Martin's and Adeline's and Elias' and Maria's. And I knew you were there, because I heard them thinking and talking about you. But I couldn't hear *you*. I was intrigued. So I came to your bedroom one night. I saw you sleeping, so peacefully, like a little angel. Then my terrible thirst urged me to drink from you, and when I did, I felt your soul touch mine. You were young, yes, but there was something in you that called to me, a darkness...and a sweetness. I couldn't explain it then, no more than I can explain the way I feel for you now. But it's why I stopped, why I withdrew, and why I stayed away from you for over a decade, waiting until you were old enough to reciprocate my love sincerely. And that's the answer to your third question, Laura. That's why I'm here. You see, it's not just that your soul calls to mine; it's that I cannot hear or influence your thoughts. Whatever you feel for me, it comes from *you*. Do you understand? I have no power over you, and so we can truly be equals in love. I never thought that would be possible for me. I haven't believed in God for a long time, but the fact that you are *you*, and you are *here*, and you feel the way you feel about me...it's the nearest thing to a miracle I can imagine."

No power over me? If only she knew. My defenses were beginning to crumble. As awful as it was to think of what she had done to me as a child, she had *stopped*. She had loved me enough to stop. She had *waited*. For years, she had waited.

"Why didn't you tell me sooner?" I whispered.

"The same reason I don't tell *anyone*. Self-preservation. Would you have accepted the fact that I am a monster, if you had discovered it before you came to love me as a woman?"

Of course I wouldn't have, I thought grimly. She couldn't have done anything differently, not without losing me. I cleared my throat. "What is it you want from me?"

"Just to be with you," she pleaded. "Just that, and nothing more. For as long as you want me and as long as you live, whether that be a short time or..." She stopped, and, though she didn't say the words aloud, they hung in the air above us.

I was still stunned. Could anything she was saying even be real? I was caught between wariness at her dangerous nature and a desperate affection for the young, beautiful woman standing before me, baring her heart and trembling with the fear that I might break it. Part of her was a monster, it was true. I shuddered, remembering the carapace eyes, the jagged mouth dripping with dark blood. Would I ever be able to erase that image from my mind altogether? But it was also true that she loved me, and that she didn't want to hurt me. I could see it in her, could feel it as her dark, tear-filled eyes shifted nervously between my face and the ground. And Johannes was perfectly fine, wasn't he? Didn't that show that she was able to exist in her...state...without harming anyone irreparably?

I wasn't sure what to do yet, not in the long term. But right now, as she stood before me, I was overwhelmed by a desire to comfort her. I stepped forward, pushing aside the image of her distorted, bloody face, and kissed her tenderly. Her mouth was salty with tears, and she shook with relief as I embraced her. Her breath caught in her throat when we finally broke apart, and she rested her forehead against mine.

"This is a lot to wrap my mind around," I said. "It might take me some time to understand it, and I'm not sure if I'll be able to accept it. But I do love you, Carmilla. Even if I am frightened."

She stifled a sob. "This is what I saw in you," she whispered, "even all those years ago. I knew you could see...that you could see *beyond,* that you could see who I *really* am, through this...this *curse* that has been forced upon me." She cupped my face and pulled me in for another kiss, opening her mouth as if to drink me in. My body flushed with desire, and all rationality, all sense, all understanding of the danger I was in were driven from my mind like darkness fleeing the dawn.

There was a rustling in the underbrush nearby, and we broke apart and whirled toward it in alarm. To our relief, it was only a rabbit, who ran back into its burrow as soon as it saw us, its potential predators. *The rabbit has more sense than I do,* I thought.

"Must you drink human blood?" I wondered aloud. "Can you not survive on animals?"

She sighed. "I can *survive,* but just barely. It does not give me strength or vitality, it merely keeps me from shriveling away into a state of torpor. I would that were not the case. It would be so much easier to live off animals; it would make me not so very different from the rest of you."

I realized that turning my head sharply had not caused me any pain, and I raised my fingers to the back of my head. "Why don't I have a lump on my head, or a bruise? I remember falling on a rock last night."

"My ability to heal myself is something I can share with others, so long as the wound is minor. A few drops of my blood on Johannes' neck – and your head – and it was as if nothing had happened at all."

The image of the gaping, spurting gash on Johannes' throat came unbidden into my mind. *I wouldn't consider that a minor wound*, I thought.

"What you said about not being able to...hear or influence my mind? Is that...I mean, has that ever happened with someone else before?"

"Yes. In fact, I've met several others, though I tend to avoid them when I can. One of them was the man who tried to kill me more than a century ago, and it was the reason he almost succeeded. Another was Sophie."

"Sophie?" I exclaimed.

She grimaced. "Yes. That's why I had to find a way to get her out of the house. I couldn't control her, and I could tell she was deeply suspicious of me. I was worried she would turn you against me."

"She tried," I admitted. "But I'm not pleased at how you handled it. She's my friend, and I miss her."

Her eyes flashed. "I could have killed her instead, you know."

I shivered. Did being in love with her mean that I had to be grateful when she refrained from killing the people I loved?

"Do you want to ask me anything else?" Her voice was soft, apologetic.

So many things. My mind reeled. "You said you were near the schloss when my father and I arrived. Why? Shouldn't you be thriving in Paris or Munich, making use of your charms and your abilities to live your immortal life to its fullest?"

She responded bitterly. "Because I am bound to this place, Laura, and leaving for any significant period of time makes me weak."

"Gratz," I gasped. "That's why you were so ill there?"

She nodded.

A terrible thought came to me, and I flinched. "Mrs. Bohm?" I asked. "And..." I stepped back, my hand covering my mouth as I remembered that awful funerary procession, the parents and other family members grieving for the young girl whose death had come far too soon. "The funeral in Gratz? Was that...was it because of you?"

Carmilla sighed. "My clever girl. I regret those things terribly. It is so difficult for me to control myself when I'm weak..."

I was aghast. What could I say? What could *she* say? "Why were you so ill when you came to *us*, then?"

"My mother had briefly brought me with her to Vienna to seek someone, anyone, who might know a cure for my...confinement. And I had been in hiding for months before that, a circumstance which always weakens me. In truth, though," she admitted, lowering her eyes contritely, "I was not quite as ill as I put on. I wanted you and your father to feel pity for me. I'm sorry for that deception."

I recalled how Sophie had accused Carmilla of pretending to be sick to gain access to me. *How right she was,* I thought. Then another realization struck me. "Your mother!" I gasped. "Is she a vampire too?"

"Yes, though she does not suffer from the same limitation I do. Come, keep walking with me," she urged. "I want to take you to what was once my village. And I will tell you along the way how I came to be what I am, and why I am cursed not to be able to enjoy it."

CHAPTER SIXTEEN

CARMILLA'S STORY, PART I

I was born to Count and Countess Karnstein in 1682. The village was very different then. Lively, thriving. My father and mother were so respected by the villagers that, though I was a girl, my arrival was heralded with a great deal of celebration. I was cherished and coddled by everyone around me. They knew my name, brought me gifts as I toddled through the marketplace or to church services. They cheered when I made appearances – dressed in the finest silks, my hair coiffed and tied with elaborate bows – at the lavish celebrations hosted at our house.

Then my father died. His death caught us by surprise, for he was young and strong, and when the influenza had swept through our village, it had seemed, at first, to claim only the lives of those who were naturally weak. We lost many children in those months. I myself was gravely ill. I remember the doctor and the priest coming to my bedside, my mother and father weeping. I pulled through, though my lungs never fully recovered, and I remained prone to coughs and fevers throughout my life (at least, my mortal life). But my father succumbed to it quickly and irreversibly. We were all devastated. I can still see his body stretched out in his coffin, my mother weeping hopelessly.

So I grew up without a father. But we were lucky to have a warm and compassionate community around us. After that first deep cut of grief, my life was marked by the love and attention of the villagers. Distant relatives came to visit frequently, filling our house with laughter and warmth. I became a silly girl, obsessed with parties and pretty silks, more interested in playing the piano charmingly than in learning anything of substance.

Her expression darkened.

As the years passed, my burgeoning womanhood began to bring me the less desirable sort of attention. I didn't know how to handle the leering smiles and snide comments, and instead of placing the blame where it belonged, I felt deeply ashamed of myself. My mother was a devout Catholic, and we spent many hours a week at church. I sought the guidance of our priest, Father Wagner, begging him for help. He was a balding man in his fifties, with fat fingers and pale, watery eyes. He had always been so kind to me and my mother, so good to the community. But when I told him about my predicament, he didn't comfort me. He told me I was right to feel ashamed, that my body had clearly been built as a vessel for temptation, a means for Satan to test the men of the village. He told me I needed to pray to God, to cleanse myself of the lust with which I was infecting those around me. And he told me that I must let him touch me, as only his hands – sanctified as they were by God – would be able to draw the demon out of me.

She stopped speaking for a moment, tears welling in her eyes. Then she took a shaky breath. "I was fourteen." I seized one of her hands and pressed her knuckles to my lips. She continued, her gaze steely.

It started with his hands. I would go to him for "confession," and he would touch me. At first, it was just my breasts. He would grope and pinch them, ignoring my whimpers of discomfort, his breath ragged as he pressed his erection against my leg through his robes. After a few minutes, he would moan and shudder before pushing himself away from me and scolding me for tempting him again. "The devil is strong within you, Mircalla," he would say. "You must continue to pray to God." Eventually, merely touching my breasts was not enough to satisfy him, and he began to touch me between my legs – clumsily and painfully – or instruct me to touch his pudgy, straining cock. When his seed spilled in my hand, I cried, and he chastised me for crying at receiving God's blessing.

I know now that I should have told my mother. But he made me so sure that it was all my fault. And he was so well-loved and well-trusted. I thought if I accused him, all he would have to do to discredit me was to claim that the devil was working through me, and everyone would believe him. I kept trying to avoid our private meetings, but he threatened to condemn me publicly as a witch unless I obeyed him. The saddest part is how unfairly I underestimated my mother. I know now – because we have talked about it since then – that she not only would have believed me immediately but would have punished Father Wagner as he deserved to be punished. As it turns out, I took care of that myself. But we will get there in due time.

The abuse continued for years, and it became more and more severe. By the time I was sixteen, Father Wagner would make me kneel as if I were going to give confession, then stand before me and force his cock into my mouth. I still remember the pungent smell of him, the acrid taste as he spilled his seed in my throat. By the time I was seventeen, he was sodomizing me, seemingly spurred on by my cries of pain. He started fucking me shortly after that, always being careful not to spill his seed inside me.

Still, in every other regard my life was enviable. I enjoyed my lessons with my governess. I had friends in the village. My mother threw fetes frequently, some of them quite large, with people coming from Gratz and Vienna or even farther away. My mother was the epitome of grace, a wonderful hostess who could dance and tell jokes and play cards, and I learned from her how to shine brightly in a room full of people, how to impress with my accomplishments and seduce with my charms. People came from miles around to hear me play the piano and sing, and I had a bevy of suitors whom I delighted in teasing and driving to the brink of madness.

On my eighteenth birthday, my mother had a lavish fete planned, to celebrate not only my adulthood but also the arrival of the new century. I was recovering from a nasty cough (a condition that often plagued me after my bout with influenza) and was unusually exhausted. I nearly begged my mother to call the whole thing off. But as we sat eating breakfast, there was a knock on the door.

He was dark-haired, dark-eyed, and exceedingly handsome. Though he was not particularly tall (indeed, he and I were of a similar height) his presence made him seem imposing. When my mother saw him standing outside, she gasped in surprise, her eyes gleaming with delight. He smiled, took her hand, and brushed his generous lips against her knuckles. "Hello, Anna, my dear," he said, smiling. "It's been far too long." I could hear some of the servants whispering excitedly behind me. Who was this strange man that they all seemed to know?

"Indeed it has, Alexander," my mother replied breathlessly. "I didn't expect to see you. You've been away for so many years."

I was surprised by this, as he didn't appear to be much older than I was. He smiled. "I hope you don't mind."

"Not at all," my mother reassured him. "You're welcome to one of our guest rooms. Do you have your carriage with you?" She peered over his shoulder into the courtyard, where there was indeed a vehicle waiting, drawn by four black horses. It was long enough to be a funeral carriage. "We'll have some of the servants bring your things inside. You're just in time, you know. Today we are celebrating my darling Mircalla's eighteenth birthday." She gestured toward me, and he took my hand and kissed it, his dark eyes dancing. He moved like a cat, so graceful it was nearly predatory. "Mircalla," my mother said, "this is Alexander Karnstein, a distant relative of your father's."

"It's a pleasure to meet you, little cousin." His voice was like velvet. "I'm not surprised that you're as beautiful as you are, given who your mother is, but surely it is not fair to the rest of the world for two such gems to be hidden in the same house!"

"You shouldn't say such things," my mother purred. "Come, I will show you to your room."

Puzzled by Alexander's sudden and mysterious appearance, I stayed in the foyer, listening to the excited whispering of the servants and watching in disbelief as a coffin was carried from the driverless carriage up to the guest rooms.

That day, I discovered the truth about my family. Alexander, our "distant relative," was more than two hundred years old, and he was a vampire.

My mother explained it all to me in the hours before the party. Over two centuries ago, he had been born and raised in our very house, and he had eventually found great success as a lawyer in Munich. At the age of twenty-six, however, he had been attacked by a vampire and had become one himself. Ever since then, it had been our family's mission to provide him with shelter whenever he returned to the village and to help him keep up his lifestyle discreetly. The last time she had seen him was over twenty years prior, just after she had married my father and moved into this house. She, too, had been surprised to learn of the Karnstein family secret at first. "It didn't take long for him to win me over, though," she admitted, blushing. "You'll see for yourself, I'm sure."

I certainly did. Alexander's presence at my party was dizzying. He danced like a dream, sweeping across the floor with me in his arms as if I were lighter than paper. He poured drinks and told stories of his travels, soon accumulating a crowd of admirers, both male and female. The night wore on and intoxication hung heavy in the air. Many of the guests had already gone home, but a handful remained, including a few of my suitors. We sat in a tight circle around Alexander, my mother on one side of him, me on the other. He smiled at me beguilingly as he talked politics with my suitors. His hand brushed my thigh or breast as he gesticulated along with his arguments. Somehow, even though the topics being debated were controversial, all participants laughed and spoke good-naturedly. I wondered if Alexander's enthralling presence was the cause. Just as my eyes were beginning to droop, he stood up. "I'm going to bed," he said. Then he raised an eyebrow. "Would anyone like to join me?"

My jaw dropped as two of the women and one of the men sitting in the circle stood up and followed him to his bedroom. My mother and the other guests seemed unbothered; they all either settled down on the couches to sleep or headed for the front door. After sitting in shock for a few minutes, my curiosity got the best of me, and I made my way to Alexander's room. Standing outside the door, my ear pressed against the wood, I heard the undeniable sounds of pleasure. My heart pounded with shock and – I will not deny it – excitement, and I tore myself away reluctantly.

The next morning, I heard hushed voices in the hallway. I dressed quickly and rushed from my room, overwhelmed with curiosity about what had happened to Alexander's bedfellows. I found them in the foyer, bidding my mother and Alexander goodbye, their faces as placid as if nothing had happened to them the night before but a pleasant night of sleep. Once they had gone, Alexander turned to me and, with a wry smile, said, "Good morning, Mircalla. Did you enjoy your birthday party?" And he swept me into his arms and kissed me like I had never been kissed before, as if we were the only people in the house, as if we were the only people in the world.

I am not ashamed to say that I fell in love with him, Laura. It was hard not to. And my mother was quite pleased with the situation, though sometimes she seemed a bit envious, too. No doubt if she had been twenty years younger, she would have been the object of his affections (indeed, I later discovered that this had been the case in the years before I was born). Seeing our infatuation must have been painful for her, if only because it was a reminder of her own age and mortality.

But it was nothing like what I feel for you, my dearest. It was not real love; I know that now. He was handsome and charming and powerful, but his soul did not speak to mine the way yours does. And he could be cruel, too. He delighted sometimes in showing me how naïve and unworldly I was, laughing condescendingly when my wit was not sharp enough to keep up with his. Sometimes he would use his abilities to make me do things against my will. He especially loved to make me watch him with his victims, who were often friends or suitors of mine. He would hold me frozen, powerless to look away, while he seduced and drank from them. When he fed, his face would contort into a skeletal rictus, his teeth and fingernails extending to sharp claws, and it terrified me, but he would not let me even close my eyes. At other times, he would make his voice sound loudly in my mind, driving me to distraction whenever I was trying to talk to a friend or practice my music. When I expressed my displeasure and frustration at the way he disregarded my volition, he always apologized profusely and promised never to do such a thing again. Alas, those promises were frequently broken. I was too young and inexperienced to understand that the way he was treating me was not love by any definition of the word. His manipulation seemed unimportant to me then, for I was so enthralled with him that I considered myself lucky just to be his chosen one. And he taught me about many things. About the world, about what his life was like as a vampire and, most importantly, about pleasure. My only previous experience with sex had been with Father Wagner, and obviously that had soured my opinion of the act. But Alexander...Alexander showed me what a gift it can be. We made love day and night. I thought of nothing else; I was addicted to it. Indeed, it became difficult for me to bear it when he used sex as a means of gaining access to his victims, as was his wont.

He occasionally drank from me, too, though never enough to weaken me. Eventually, he allowed me to drink from him, not enough to change me, but enough to feel the intoxicating effects. One day, I asked him to make me a vampire. His eyes darkened. "No. I would not wish this on anyone."

"Why not?" I pouted.

He embraced me. "You have seen only the pleasures of it. But I can never stay in one place for very long, can never form attachments – other than the ones I have here – and must always be on guard against those who fancy themselves vampire hunters. It was one such man, in fact, who drove me to return to this house, and I am ever wakeful, ever watchful, in case he follows me here. And sometimes"— he shuddered — "the thirst drives me to do terrible things. No, Mircalla, I would not wish to burden you with such an existence."

The man who was pursuing him, a Moravian who had killed Alexander's sire several years before, tracked Alexander to the village less than a month later. Alexander fled, his driverless carriage conveying him and his coffin away from our house in the dead of night. The Moravian appeared on our doorstep the next day, a tall, stooped man who introduced himself as Antonin Bruzek. He peppered us with questions about Alexander, though both my mother and I feigned ignorance. The villagers were of little help, too; although many of them had found themselves in Alexander's clutches, none of them could recall anything unusual.

Still, Bruzek's questions caused the townspeople to whisper among themselves. They began to cast suspicious looks in our direction. Perhaps in an attempt to restore our reputation as good citizens, my mother decided that she and I ought to begin attending church again, a practice we had stopped when Alexander was with us.

Father Wagner had been disturbed by our lack of attendance; he had even come knocking at our door more than once, only to be turned away by our servants. But I found that, suddenly, I didn't care. After years of pain at the hands of a so-called godly man, and weeks of joy and pleasure in the arms of a so-called demon, I was beginning to understand that Father Wagner's threats against me – and his assertions of his own sanctity – were nothing but the nonsensical ramblings of a bloated pederast. He called me to his office to chastise me and force me to "repent." I followed him into the room, hoping to tell him what I thought of him once and for all. I stared at him in defiance and let him see the disgust in my eyes. I suppose it was foolish of me to think that I could do so with impunity.

He attacked me. As loathsome and cowardly as he was, he was still bigger and stronger than I. He overpowered me easily, knocking me to the floor and covering my mouth with one hand as the other fumbled beneath my skirts. And then he raped me, as he had done many times before, only this time with a violence that made it feel as though he were ripping me apart. He left me bleeding and trembling on the floor, and, even worse, sticky and dripping with his seed.

I didn't tell my mother what had happened – I had been silent for so many years; how could I begin to speak now? – but I refused to attend church again. A few weeks later, when I missed my monthly cycle, I realized (having heard enough gossip from the servants to know how such things worked) that I was with child. I didn't cry, or scream, or faint at the realization. Instead, my heart turned to iron, and I resolved to rid myself of the thing. I had heard rumors of a woman who lived on the outskirts of town – they called her a witch, though in truth she was merely an herbalist – and I set out to find her the very next day. Wrapped in a shawl to protect against the bitingly cold winter wind, I passed through our bustling marketplace, responding cheerily to the villagers who greeted me and wished me well. The Moravian and his small band of men were there, too. They had stayed in town under the pretext of waiting for better traveling weather, but my mother and I knew that he was waiting for Alexander to return. I was alarmed at how easily he seemed to have integrated himself into the life of the village. As he walked through the marketplace parallel to me, he, too, received many friendly greetings. He kept glancing at me, and under my breath I cursed his watchful eye for robbing me of my Alexander. Apparently, he wasn't suspicious enough to follow me all the way to the herbalist's house, for he turned to join his men in the market once I had made it to the far side of the town square.

The herbalist was surprised to see me. "Mistress!" she exclaimed, taking a step back from her door. She was younger and more beautiful than I had expected (the word "witch" does tend to evoke a certain image in one's mind). When I told her of my dilemma, she embraced me, cooing sympathetically. Then she pulled away and warned me, with shadowed eyes, "I can help you rid yourself of the baby, but it comes at significant danger to yourself. It is not unlikely that you will die in the process. Think, Mistress. You are wealthy, and you have a loving mother who would do anything for you. Can you not hide your pregnancy, then give the child away in secret, as is often done? There are women in the village who cannot conceive, and they would be pleased to foster a child as beautiful as yours will be."

I shook my head. "I will spare you the details regarding the circumstances of this conception, but they are such that I cannot bear the pregnancy."

"I understand." She looked me up and down. "Well, at least it is very early on. That makes things less precarious, as the fetus should come loose more easily." She turned matter-of-factly to her herb jars and began to put together a sachet for me.

"I suppose it goes without saying that you must speak of this to no one."

"I wouldn't be in business long if I were the type of person to divulge other people's secrets," she said, handing me the small packet. "There'll not be a word from my lips."

After I had paid her, she instructed me to drink the herbs after steeping them in hot water. She warned that I would be very sick, possibly for days, and that I must be prepared to be in a great deal of pain. I nodded curtly and thanked her. As I turned to leave, I heard her mutter a prayer for my safekeeping.

Apparently, God did not see fit to answer her prayer. A few minutes after drinking the concoction, I was racked with an unspeakable pain.

I doubled over on the floor as I vomited again and again. My mother cried out and ran to my side. And then I lost consciousness.

I don't remember much of the next three days, the final days of my mortal life. I was violently ill, with a high fever that made me delirious. Blood seeped from between my legs – at least the herbs had been successful in attaining their object, I thought – and continued to do so even when it seemed impossible for there to be any blood left to lose. I could neither eat nor drink, and I repeatedly vomited bloody bile onto my bedsheets, too exhausted even to raise my head and aim for a bowl instead. My distraught mother summoned a doctor, who asked me urgently if I had eaten or drunk anything unusual. When I didn't answer him, he pronounced solemnly that there was nothing he could do to help me.

I was dying.

I heard my mother keening beside me, felt her cool hands on my skin, heard her calling my name and begging me to come back to her, but I couldn't swim my way up to consciousness. And part of me didn't want to. I was hovering on the edge of a precipice. Before me lay peace and quiet, behind me pain and anger. I was beginning to feel disconnected from the physical torments of the past few days, and it was such a relief. I wanted to sink into it, into that weightlessness.

Suddenly I heard Alexander's voice in my mind, clear and strong. Mircalla, I am here. *I found the strength to open my eyes and saw him there, clutching my hand, his eyes wide with worry. My mother was beside him, looking back and forth between him and me. He bent low over me and drew in a deep breath, nostrils flaring.*

"This is no illness," he said to my mother. "It's poison. I can smell it in her blood."

My mother gasped, covering her mouth with her hand. "Poison? But who?"

I did not want to answer that question. Alexander could easily read my thoughts, but, mercifully, he stayed quiet. I swallowed and tried to speak, but my voice was too weak. I addressed him in my mind. What are you doing here?

"I heard your distress, and your mother's. I had to come."

You cannot be here. Bruzek has been waiting for you.

"You think I would just leave you like this?" He smiled sadly and kissed my hand. Then he turned and looked at my mother, as if asking her permission for something. She nodded her head slowly. "Mircalla," he said quietly, "do you want me to stop you from dying?"

A moment before his arrival, I had been considering letting myself slip away. Now, seeing him and my mother, feeling their distress, I remembered what I had to lose. I nodded.

Alexander sat up and began to unfasten his shirt sleeves. "What happens now?" my mother asked.

"She must drink from me. She must drink as much as she can, and if there is enough of my blood in her when she dies, she will be resurrected as a creature like me. It will weaken me, so we must be vigilant about Bruzek. If I have to leave suddenly and she does not die of the poison naturally, you must kill her yourself. I know it will be difficult, Anna, but you must."

He drew a long fingernail across the opposite wrist, then pressed his forearm against my lips. The blood was warm and salty, and I choked on it at first. But I finally managed to swallow, fighting down the nausea that threatened to send it back up. He grunted as I grabbed his arm with my hands, latching greedily and gulping again and again. I pulled away, falling back against the pillow and trying to catch my breath, and he pressed his wrist to my mouth again. "More," he urged, though I could hear in his voice that it was beginning to weaken him. "You must drink more. Otherwise this will all be for naught." I was just starting to pull from his vein again when there was a loud shout in the hallway.

Alexander and my mother jumped to their feet. "Bruzek!" my mother exclaimed. "Alexander, you must go!"

The Moravian came barreling into the bedroom with his men, each of them holding a crossbow. They let the arrows fly at Alexander, and he cried out in pain as one of them pierced his chest, just shy of his heart. His body whirled and changed, becoming a dark mass of shadows, but in his wounded state he had difficulty maintaining the illusion, and his body became solid again. Then he crashed through the window and was gone.

I heard Bruzek and his men shouting as they ran to the window, my mother's cries of distress. I felt myself falling away, and I heard...and saw...and felt...no more.

I awoke in a darkness so complete that it was as though I hadn't opened my eyes at all, a darkness like a thick, velvety blindfold pressed around my head. I was so disoriented that, if it hadn't been for the harsh press of wood at my back, I might as well have been hanging in midair, and I reached out with my hands, feeling for something – anything – that might indicate my location. My hands had barely moved from my sides when they encountered a wooden barrier that prevented them from progressing farther. I squirmed, trying to maneuver myself into a different position, but I was confined on all sides, and when I tried to sit up, my nose and forehead immediately struck something cold and hard.

I screamed.

The force of my voice shook the coffin (for I now realized that was what it was), and I struggled to quell the panic in my breast. I could hear the wriggling of small creatures in the dirt surrounding me. I knew I was several feet deep in the earth, but I could feel raindrops striking the ground above me and the pressure of footsteps. I could smell coppery blood running through veins. A terrible thirst overwhelmed me, and I raged, thrashing in my prison as my face and teeth distended painfully, my fingernails becoming as long and hooked as talons. I dug my nails into the wood with a newfound, frenzied strength, and it splintered around my fingertips. I thrilled at the power I could feel coursing through me, a power driven by that awful thirst. I heaved against the lid of the coffin, pushing it upward. With each inch of space, I could leverage my arms better, could press it even higher. Wet mud came pouring in, and I panicked as some of it filled my mouth, but I spat it out, shook my head, and kept pushing until there was a wide enough gap that I could climb up through the mud. I struggled through that cold, smothering blackness, the inability to breathe sending frenzied shocks of desperation through my limbs.

I broke the surface, gasping as I pulled myself from my own grave. For a moment, I lay motionless on the ground and reveled in the feeling of the rain on my face and the cool, fresh air that was flooding into my lungs. Then I opened my eyes and saw two stunned faces looking down at me. Two of our servants. But their familiarity meant nothing in the face of my monstrous appetite. Before they could even scream, I was upon them. I tore the throat from one while I held the other immobile in my impossibly-strong grip. Wet, hot blood gushed into my mouth, and I pulled it vigorously from the vein, glorying in the taste of it and the indescribable pleasure it sent pulsing through my body. The other servant screamed ineffectually against my hand as I let the dried husk of her friend fall to the ground. Then I was tearing at her throat, too. My thirst seemed unquenchable. I drank and drank, swelling with strength like a bloated tick. When I was done, I discarded her effortlessly. She fell to the earth with a wet thud, her limbs tangled beneath her torso, her neck bent at an unnatural angle.

The thirst began to subside, and in its wake, the horrible realization of what I had done – what I had become – crept in. The rain was coming down hard, plastering my hair against my skin and washing the blood from my chin and neck down into my dress. The stain spread over the fine fabric like watercolor over a blank page. I realized that I was at the family burial plot, just over a small hill from the house. I wondered briefly what the servants had been doing at my grave; I looked around and saw two baskets filled with flowers nearby. My head was spinning from the blood I had consumed. I could hear and see and smell and feel everything, my awareness stretching around me for what seemed like miles. The thoughts of hundreds of people clamored in my mind, an overwhelming cacophony that I tried unsuccessfully to shut out. Remorse for the violent murder of my own servants was welling up inside me, choking me with sorrow. I held my head in my hands and moaned.

What have I done?

My feet seemed to move of their own accord, taking me toward the house. It was dark and quiet, and I did not encounter anyone as I made my way to my mother's room. My wet feet and dripping hair left muddy, pink-tinged puddles where I stepped. I knocked on her door and stood shivering as I waited for her to answer. I could hear her thoughts loud and clear. She was annoyed, assuming that a servant had come to ask her about some menial thing. She opened the door, her tear-blotched face dark with anger.

When she saw me, soaked with mud and rain and blood, she stumbled backward. "Mircalla!" she cried. And then she was clasping me in her arms, sobbing. "I thought it didn't work! We waited for three days, but nothing happened! Oh, my daughter!" Her voice trembled with a mixture of relief and sorrow, as if she didn't know whether to be happy or sad that I had returned. This was, it just so happened, a sentiment I shared.

CHAPTER SEVENTEEN
CARMILLA'S STORY, PART II

Carmilla and I had reached the village now. We stood at the top of a crest, looking down at the blackened church and the empty Karnstein schloss. I remembered when Elias had brought me here. Briefly, I wondered if his friend Matthias, the woodcutter's son, still lived nearby. Carmilla's harrowing story made me look at her former house more attentively. Tattered curtains billowed from broken windows, giving the impression of movement. I tried to imagine what it had been like during Carmilla's childhood, full of life and music and people, warm light spilling from the windows in the evenings. Behind it, I could see the clearing where her grave must have been – a few worn gravestones were still barely visible. I shuddered at the thought of her gruesome awakening.

I looked at the blackened husk across from the Karnstein house. "What happened to the church?"

Her lips parted in a devilish grin. "Me."

We sat down on a fallen log under the dense, shady foliage of a beech tree, and she continued her story.

I was a vampire, but there were two major problems that confronted me. First, I didn't really know how to be a vampire, and Alexander wasn't there to guide me. This meant that I had no way of solving the second problem, which was the fact that everyone in the village thought I had died. They had been to my funeral, had mourned me. I couldn't pick up my life where I had left it, at least not without the ability to influence people's memories, especially since Bruzek was so watchful of the village. He himself had disappeared when Alexander fled, but he had left a few of his men behind. While it was likely that I could overwhelm them with my newfound strength, I had no idea what tricks they might have hidden up their sleeves, what vulnerabilities of mine they might exploit. For these reasons, I had to remain hidden in the house. Taking their cue from Alexander's practices, my mother and the governess – the only other person whom we trusted – brought my coffin to my room and filled it with dirt from my grave. They buried the two dead servants under my headstone. They brought me animals to feed on, which did little to slake my thirst. I grew ever more frustrated and lonely. I screamed at my mother, who promised that she would find a way to get us out of our predicament.

"Let me make arrangements," she said, "and we will go somewhere else. To Paris, maybe, where no one knows you. And then we can start anew. But it will take some time. You must be patient." Traveling with me, especially with the need to transport my coffin at the same time, was no easy task.

I reached out with my mind to try to find Alexander, sending my frenzied thoughts wildly into the ether, screaming soundlessly and hoping he would hear me. One evening, I felt him, though only faintly.

Mircalla. *A flood of relief.* It worked.

It worked. But I need help.

I will come as soon as I can. It's not safe now.

I didn't know where he was, but he was clearly far away. Maintaining a conversation over such a distance was difficult, and I broke the connection. I grabbed the edge of my dresser and sent it crashing loudly to the floor. I felt the surprise in the minds of the servants on the floor below me, heard my mother making an excuse to them ("I left the window open in Mircalla's room; how thoughtless of me! I will go close it myself"). I recalled what Alexander had said, about how he wouldn't wish his existence on anyone. How right he had been. I was desperate for human contact and angry at the iniquity of my fate, so angry that my whole body was vibrating with it.

And I was ever so thirsty.

There had to be something I could do about that, *at any rate. Alexander had turned himself into a weightless shadow, hadn't he? I closed my eyes and willed my body to dissipate. Nothing happened at first, and I wondered if maybe I was not strong enough. But I tried again. I took deep breaths and imagined my body dissolving into the air, imagined weightlessness and darkness spreading through me like warmth from a fire.*

It worked. My body began to fall away. The floor disappeared beneath my feet, and gravity released its hold. I stretched my hands out before my eyes to see if they were still there. Shadowy tendrils had taken their place. A thrill of amusement ran through me. I knew exactly where I wanted to go.

I waited until past midnight, when the village was enveloped in silence and I could blend into the utter, moonless darkness. I slipped under doorways and made my way to the church, gliding soundlessly over the ground like a rolling fog. I poured myself through the keyhole in the big wooden doors at the entrance, then reconstituted myself on the other side, my bare feet cold against the stone floor. A few candles were glowing at the altar, illuminating the figure of Jesus on his crucifix. The pews stretched silently on either side of me as I made my way forward. How many times had I listened to Father Wagner preach about godliness from the pulpit, as though he hadn't spent years molesting me? I stretched my mind toward his now. He was sleeping in the bedroom beside the sacristy, and – fittingly – he was dreaming of me. I laughed, the sound of it echoing through the empty sanctuary.

I was really going to enjoy this.

But I was feeling weak now; the animal blood I had been subsisting on was not enough to maintain my strength for long. I reached out with my mind to the nearest house, where four people were sleeping soundly. The Brunners. I knew them from church, and I recalled that the youngest child, Lucy, was frequently ill. If she was a bit weak and pale the next morning, no one would give it a second thought. I took on my shadow form, slipped out of the church and into the Brunners' modest home, and made my way to Lucy's bedside. The thirst was rising in me now, and I fought against the monster within me as I brought my lips to her neck, trying to refrain from ripping her throat open. She stirred with discomfort when my teeth pierced her skin, then relaxed as I sent a pleasant dream into her mind. Her blood was potent, and I nearly lost control of myself – and of her – as it filled me with dizzying strength. The beat of her pulse rang in my ears and through my veins. Soon it began to weaken, and, though it took every ounce of willpower in me, I pulled away. I didn't want to kill her; I just needed to replenish my strength.

Back in the church, I hid myself in a dark enclave and called to Father Wagner with my mind. I felt him awaken, heard his footsteps hurrying toward the sanctuary, and watched him enter. His face loomed in the darkness, lit by the candle he held before him.

"Hello?" he ventured.

I was silent. He looked around with trepidation, his gaze pausing on the altar, where the flickering candlelight was making shadows dance upon the nearby surfaces. Then he shook his head and began heading back toward his bedroom. In my shadow form, I slipped toward the altar and knocked over a candelabrum, sending it clattering to the ground. He shouted with surprise and whirled toward the noise. The candle shook violently in his hand.

"Who's there?" he asked. My laughter echoed through the vaulted room. He whirled, unable to pinpoint where the sound was coming from. "Show yourself!" he commanded.

I floated up and coalesced on the altar. His jaw dropped, panic and confusion clamoring loudly in his mind. Then I seeped down off the edge and began skimming along the floor toward him. He stumbled backward, tripped on his robes, and crashed to the ground. His candle skittered away from him. He cried out and raised his hands to shield himself as I drew nearer. But I wasn't quite ready to end his misery. I sent myself in all directions, my shadows extending outwards and up the walls. I reveled in the look of abject terror on his face as I disappeared into the vast, empty space above the rafters. He couldn't see me now, couldn't discern between the natural and unnatural sources of darkness. His heart was pounding, his mind paralyzed with fear. It was delicious. *I reconstituted myself into human form, crouched on one of the crossbeams just above the crucifix, and leaned down far enough for the candlelight to reach my face.*

"Hello, Father," I said.

He scrambled to his feet, his eyes wide. "No. It's not possible. I saw you laid to rest." I could feel his urge to flee. His heart thrashed like an animal throwing itself against the bars of a cage. But I willed him to be immobile, rooting his feet to the floor.

"Not possible, you say?" I leered at him, then poured myself down-ward, grasped the crucifix below me, and climbed headfirst down to the floor. I stood and brushed off my dress as if I had dirtied it on Jesus' wooden likeness. Then I walked toward him. "Perhaps you don't know as much about the world as you claim. I mean, even I know that God is against raping children, but that was a concept that your *mind was too feeble to grasp."*

His heart beat even faster now, and my thirst swelled at the sound of blood rushing in his veins. As I drew closer, my face and teeth and fingers began to distend. He screamed, and the sharp odor of urine filled the air. I shook my head and clicked my tongue in disgust. Then I was upon him, my hand around his throat. He tried to scream again, but I was crushing his windpipe. He cast his eyes up at the ceiling, and in my mind I could hear his desperate prayers for God to help him. I brought my lips to his ear and hissed, "I don't think He's listening to you."

I dragged him to the dais and propped him against the crucifix, then tore the cloth from the altar and tied one end of it around his ankles, looping the other end over the top of the cross and using it to hoist him in the air. He dangled in the air face-down, a perfect inversion of his savior. He moaned in pain and begged me to let him go.

I said nothing. I tied off the end of the cloth and grabbed one of the candles from the altar. I tore the nightshirt from his body, placed it underneath the back row of pews, and set it alight. The flames from the cloth flicked upwards and caught the wooden benches. While they crackled, I made my way swiftly around the room and touched the candle to everything else that could burn – curtains, tapestries, cushions. Soon fire was raging all around us. He sobbed as he watched his church burn, and I stood before him, grinning as his pain washed over me.

Finally, I'd had enough. I slit his throat with one of my talons, and blood spurted violently outward, showering my clothes. "You always did like seeing me on my knees," I grinned. Then I knelt and opened my mouth to catch as much of the spray as I could. He wriggled like a fish on a hook for nearly a minute, his body spasming as it fought against the inevitable. Then his body stilled, and his mind went dark, like a candle being snuffed out. The absence of him filled me with indescribable joy.

The fire was beginning to come closer, its heat nearly unbearable now. I swirled into my shadow form and flew upwards, reconstituting myself just long enough to crash through one of the stained-glass windows and into the night. The fire roared up behind me.

Shortly thereafter, it began to rain. The deluge was heavy enough to extinguish the blaze before it spread beyond a few of the nearest houses. They found Father Wagner's body the next morning, a charred lump beside the ruined crucifix. Since the flames had consumed the cloth with which I had bound him, everyone thought he had died trying to rescue the cross from the fire. No one ever suspected that he had been murdered.

Carmilla paused, losing herself in the memory, her face smug as she gazed at the blackened church.

I was aghast. I did not begrudge her the revenge against Father Wagner, but there was a cruelty in the way she had gone about it that troubled me. "Carmilla," I asked tentatively, "why did you feed on Lucy Brunner first? Why not just drain and kill Father Wagner without hurting anyone innocent in the process?" I couldn't help but think of her attack on *me* when I was a child, how deeply it had terrified me and the rest of my household.

She scoffed. "I didn't really hurt her. She made a full recovery, as far as I know."

"And the church? You didn't know it was going to rain; you're lucky the whole village didn't burn to the ground."

She shrugged. "I suppose so."

Her flippancy troubled me. I lowered my eyes, trying to conceal my disappointment. "Don't you think...?" I stopped, cleared my throat, and started again. "Don't you think it was a little unnecessary, killing him like that?"

She levelled her gaze at me. "Laura, what I said to you before was true: I no longer enjoy killing, and I don't wish to harm you or anyone else now. But I also do not feel the need to apologize for the things I have done in the past. My entire existence is predicated on the need to prey on people. Before I met you, any restraint I showed was purely a matter of self-preservation. I was not squeamish about causing pain, especially to those who deserved it. Indeed, once my thirst had returned, about a week after Father Wagner's death, I considered dispatching the herbalist, too."

I gasped. "But she hadn't done anything to harm you!"

"Hadn't she?"

"You sought her out! She told you it was dangerous!"

"She must have given me too much. It was careless of her. At any rate," she said, dismissing the topic with a wave of her hand, "she was saved by Alexander's return to the house."

Bruzek had tracked Alexander all the way to Munich. Though Alexander had managed to kill several of the Moravian's company, Bruzek himself escaped by covering Alexander with lamp oil and setting him ablaze. Alexander had found a rain-filled ditch in which to extinguish himself and had hidden there until he was strong enough to make his way back to the village. Bruzek disappeared, possibly to find reinforcements, though Alexander didn't know for sure, as the man's thoughts were unreadable.

"That happens sometimes," Alexander explained to me upon his return, "often with people who have an unusually strong connection to the spirit world. I have met several others in my life, though never one who was trying to kill me."

He explained other things to me, too. He taught me to shut out the cacophony of thoughts around me, to pick and choose the ones I wanted to hear. He taught me that, because I had been buried before my resurrection, I would always be bound to my coffin and the dirt in which I was buried. "Not that you can't be away from them," he said. "You will just be weaker when you are not in their vicinity. Thankfully, it's easy enough to transport grave dirt and even" – he gestured toward his carriage outside the window – "a coffin, especially when you can influence people not to notice it." He taught me the trick of this, too. Planting suggestions into people's heads or making them perceive things a certain way was surprisingly simple. Memories, on the other hand, were much harder to alter, especially on a large scale. Though we often left our victims with memories of pleasure rather than pain, trying to get a whole village to forget that I had died was much more challenging. We influenced their perceptions instead: when they saw me, they did not realize that I was identical to the girl they had once known. I took the name Carmilla, and we told them that I, like Alexander, was a distant cousin of Countess Karnstein. This was remarkably effective, even among the household servants.

My life as a vampire began in earnest, and I no longer dreaded the fate to which I had consigned myself. Alexander and I traveled throughout the continent and across the channel. I was dazzled by the splendor of the cities we stopped in, charmed by the lovers – both men and women – we took for ourselves, and enthralled by the music and food we consumed. We were able to feed without killing, to live without fear. We had to avoid those individuals who could resist our influence, of course, but that was easily done. We even met other vampires along the way, who enthralled us with tales of their long and adventure-filled lives. After fifteen years, however, a letter from my mother cut our adventures short.

She was ill. Dying, the doctors said. Alexander and I raced back to the village, neither of us questioning what needed to be done.

I was the one who turned her. She drank my blood until I was nearly too weak to stand, then I smothered her with a pillow to complete the process. I sat beside her dead body for a whole day, waiting for her to awaken as a vampire, leaving her unburied in the cold bedroom so that she wouldn't have the same limitations Alexander and I did. Since no one else knew she had died, we were able to convince the servants and doctors that she had recovered miraculously. We decided to stay in the village for a while to let her adjust to her new existence.

That's when I met Max.

He and his family had moved into what is now your schloss a few months prior, and he came with some frequency to the marketplace in our village. He was very young (still a teenager) and very sweet, and he fell head-over-heels in love with me. I humored him, for Alexander was, of late, occupied with instructing my mother about the intricacies of vampiric life. I began to visit him and his family regularly. They encouraged our connection, hoping that I might someday deign to marry the boy. I fed from them all. Never enough to hurt them (I did care for them; it was not entirely an act), but it was a welcome change not to prey on my own villagers for once. And Max...he loved me in that infatuated way youngsters do, stumbling over himself and writing me torrid love poems. He commissioned that portrait of me, the one that is still in the attic. He nearly cried the first time we made love!

At any rate, my acquaintance with Max proved to be useful when the Moravian returned to the village. We had found that drinking from people while they slept in their own beds was the best practice, as it ensured there would be less suspicion cast at our home. One night, as we were venturing out to sate our thirst, the Moravian caught us by surprise.

Hiding just outside the front door, he swung an axe at Alexander as we stepped across our threshold. I remember Alexander's head bouncing as it rolled away from us, the body twitching and spasming while it fell. I shrieked and flew at Bruzek, but he pulled a stake from his belt and drove it into my chest, narrowly missing my heart. My mother grabbed me, knocked the stake from my chest, and swept me away from there.

She flew with me in her arms to Max's schloss and hid us behind the stable so I could heal. We wept for Alexander, keening into the darkness even though we knew it might give away our location. His absence, his loss, was a graver wound than the one the stake had inflicted, and in my distress I was having trouble healing myself. I summoned Max and he came to us. His eyes widened under his tousled hair when he saw the gaping hole in my breast.

"We need a place to hide, Max," I gasped. I was too weak to try to manipulate his mind, and my mother was less practiced in the art. So I told him everything, trusting the strength of his feelings for me. And God bless him, Laura, he didn't falter. The villagers were well aware of my attachment to Max's family, so we could not hide in his house. But he had another place for us, a place Bruzek would never find, halfway between the village and his schloss. He took us there and let me feed from him, giving me the strength I needed to continue the healing process.

My mother, meanwhile, slipped away to see what was happening in our village. When she came back, she was trembling. "Bruzek told the villagers what was going on. They burned Alexander to ashes and destroyed his coffin. He is gone, daughter." We wept together in the cold, black womb of our hiding place. Then my mother continued, "That's not all." She took a deep breath to steady herself. "They found the coffin in your bedroom and burned it. Then they dug up your grave (and the bodies of the servants we put there), took handfuls and shovelfuls of the dirt, and scattered it all into the wind. I'm not sure what that means."

We found out soon enough. It means that I am bound to this place, or at least to its near vicinity. My grave dirt and coffin are still here, though they are not in a form that allows me to transport them. Thus, I will always be weak if I go more than a few miles away. My mother and I tested this many times, but even Gratz was too far, and I could only tolerate staying there if I drank a great deal of blood. Even then, I was still plagued by headaches and lethargy.

My mother has spent over a hundred years trying to find a cure for me. She has contacted many of the vampires Alexander and I met during our travels, has consulted every witch doctor. All of it has been to no avail. Yet she never gives up. I, meanwhile, could not fathom continuing to feed on the village and Max's family so extensively; it seemed unfeasible at best, cruel at worst. Once I had healed, I influenced Max to leave us alone.

And then I spent most of the past century sleeping. We vampires can sleep for decades, if we want to. It lets us conserve our strength without needing to feed more than once every few years. While I slept, Max's family died, or perhaps they simply left. Another family moved into the schloss, then another. My mother would occasionally wake me and force me to feed, lest I shrivel to such weakness that I could not move of my own accord, an awful fate Alexander had once warned us about. It was on one of these occasions that I fed from you, Laura. And after I had seen your soul, I knew that I wanted to wake for good when you came of age. I came out to catch glimpses of you from time to time, to make sure you were well.

But I didn't try to return to full strength until Count Carlsfeld's fete. My weakness drove me to feed on the servants there, and when I killed them unintentionally, I was ashamed. My mother and I knew we had to try one more time to find a cure for my limitations. We headed for Vienna first, having heard of a powerful witch there who might be able to help. But I became sick again almost immediately. That was when we made the decision to bring me back here, so she could go without me.

Her story was over. She stood apprehensively, awaiting my response. I was stunned by all of it – her suffering, her joy, her ferocity, her overwhelming loneliness. *Over a century of loneliness.* It was impossible to fathom. I was terrified of her monstrosity, of her cruelty and flippancy toward human life. But despite the terror of the things she had done, the terror of her very existence, she stood before me now as a woman, a beautiful, charming, flesh-and-blood woman who was capable of tenderness and passion. I didn't know how to handle the incredible burden of the truth, let alone how to respond to it, so I latched onto something smaller.

"What do you mean, you came out to catch glimpses of me?"

She smiled. "Sometimes when you came out of your house at night to walk, I would walk beside you, half-hidden in the woods, wishing desperately I could hear your thoughts, though it did not take a mind-reader to see that you were troubled. Sometimes I heard you and Elias playing during the day. I even heard you speaking Latin once. Vergil, I believe? There was one night, too, when Adeline's thoughts were so strange that I felt compelled to come to the schloss, and I saw you and Adeline and Sophie in your bedroom, performing a séance. You caught sight of me and ran toward the window, and I fled."

A small sob caught in my throat.

"What is it, my love?" She peered into my downcast face solicitously.

"I thought...I thought you were my mother."

She gasped. "Oh, I'm sorry! I shouldn't have said anything."

I shook my head and squeezed the tears from my eyes. "No, it's better to know." *Is it?* "When I thought she was there, always just out of sight, I wondered why she wouldn't talk to me, why she ran away. It's a comfort, really."

Even I was not convinced by this.

The sun was low in the sky. We would have to head home soon. I could see a few villagers milling around below. This reminded me of what Martin had told us before Sophie's departure.

"Carmilla, I know that you were exaggerating your illness, but you *did* say you were somewhat weak when you first came to us."

"Yes," she confirmed.

"How exactly did you become strong again? From whom did you feed?"

She hesitated. Then, reluctantly: "Bettina was the first. Then I realized that preying on the few people who lived in the house was a terrible idea, so I began to come here and feed on the villagers instead."

"No wonder Bettina was so skittish around you. Did she remember it, then?"

"No, I influenced her to believe we had made love."

This bothered me. Carmilla had stopped preying on the members of my household, to be sure, but for practical – not moral – purposes. And she seemed entirely too willing to manipulate the minds of my loved ones. I swallowed my objections for the moment, however, because another question had come to me.

"Are you still feeding on the villagers?"

"Every so often. Once I returned to my full strength, I was able to feed less frequently. Just in time, too, for the villagers were beginning to make it very difficult for me."

"Oh?"

"Do you remember the day I disappeared from the house, and I told you I had been exploring the attic?"

"Yes! We were so worried!"

"I had gone out the previous night to the village, but after several successive nights of my predations, they were wary. They were waiting for me, ready to fight. I was overconfident, which made me careless, or else I would have read their minds and anticipated their plans. I got away, but they managed to wound my leg quite seriously. I had to stop to let myself heal, and that's why I wasn't back in my bedroom at my usual time."

"I remember you were limping."

She nodded. We were silent, watching the shadows of the trees lengthen as the sun continued to sink.

"We should go back," I said finally. "It's getting late; Adeline will worry."

"She doesn't have to," Carmilla suggested.

I sighed. "Carmilla, I really wish you wouldn't manipulate the people in my household. They deserve to be in control of their own thoughts."

She threw her head back and laughed bitterly. "Oh, my dear girl, do you really think there's any way you and I can be together unless I change their perception of what's going on? Would your father leave us alone or let us sleep in the same bed together, if he knew how passionately we desire each other?"

My heart sank. She was right. Our situation was not the same as hers and Max's had been; *that* union had been deemed acceptable.

"Let's go home," I said grimly. The journey back was utterly silent.

CHAPTER EIGHTEEN

EUPHORIA...AND ITS RUIN

Once we were home, I asked Carmilla to give me some time to think. I couldn't rush back into the intoxicating euphoria of our passion until I had grappled with my fear of her, my revulsion at the things she had revealed to me.

Could I ever inure myself to it? *Should I?* Could I know what she was, know what she had done, and still accept her presence in my life as though she were a mere woman? On the one hand, she was unrepentant about the things she had done in the distant past. On the other hand, she seemed genuinely contrite about what she had done to me and my household. And when she said she didn't want to harm us, there was nothing in her words or demeanor to suggest she wasn't telling the truth. And if she had lied to me in the past, wasn't it because she'd had no other option? There was a monster inside of her, a monster that impelled her to drink blood from living humans and to manipulate them in various ways. But there was a woman, too, a woman who was vulnerable and affectionate, bound unfairly by the limitations of her *condition* and so, so scared that she could never truly be herself without alienating the one she loved. Me.

I loved her. Every second that I wasn't with her, my flesh and my heart cried out to be reunited with her. But I feared her, too. She claimed that she didn't want to hurt me or my family. But was that a promise she could make? She had killed Count Carlsfeld's servants in a moment of weakness. Could she promise not to do something that was out of her control? I worried, too – I couldn't deny it – about what would happen if I said I never wanted to see her again, given what she was capable of when she was angry. Wasn't it better to accept her for who – and what – she was, if rejecting her would undoubtedly endanger me *more*?

I thought of Bettina. While it galled me that Carmilla had manipulated her mind and fed from her, in the end, no lasting damage had been done. Bettina was as hale as ever, and she had only been left with a false (and undoubtedly pleasant) memory. Did such a situation warrant discarding the ardent, blissful, all-consuming love I felt for Carmilla?

For days I wrestled with it. Carmilla mainly stayed in her room, though sometimes she wandered the halls, silent and sulking, her eyes watching me warily as I passed. Finally, I made up my mind: I couldn't deny my love for her, even in the face of her monstrosity. As terrifying as her story had been, as frightening as it was that she could kill with such apparent ease, I truly believed that she did not wish to harm me or my family, and I could forgive even her manipulations of the people in my household – and the lies she had told for the sake of self-preservation - if it meant we could be together.

I found her in the parlor, dangling a book carelessly from one hand as she looked out the window. She turned as I crossed the room, her eyes wide with anxiety. I stopped before her, not knowing what to say, and she groaned with frustration. "How I wish I could read your mind, Laura!"

"You must promise me," I implored, "that you will try not to hurt *anyone*, not just the people here in the schloss."

Hope flared in her eyes, and her words came out in a rush. "I promise. Oh, I promise! You didn't even need to ask. I don't *want* to hurt anyone. I just want to be with you. Do you understand? I don't want to be a monster anymore. I want to be *yours*."

I took her hand tentatively. She was trembling. "And you must never lie to me again."

"I won't!" she vowed. Her other hand found my cheek as she moved closer.

"I know I cannot ask you to refrain from influencing minds. You're right; it's not feasible. But maybe...maybe you can do it as little as possible? Just as much as we need to...to stay safe?"

"Whatever you want, my love."

No other words were necessary. I took her in my arms and marveled at the softness and warmth of her body, the *rightness* of our embrace. I kissed her tenderly, lips brushing hers. Then I opened her mouth with mine and tasted her tongue. She whimpered, clutching me to herself.

I broke the kiss. "Here?"

"No one will bother us," she assured me. She went to the windows and drew the curtains halfway closed, dimming the room but leaving enough light for us to see each other.

We helped each other undress, our fingers trembling with urgency. The swell of her breasts beneath her shift tormented me, and I tore at the cloth that covered them. Her shift fell to her feet and she stepped out of it, her naked body a wonder. I finished removing my own shift, then took her face with one hand and pulled her to me, hungrily kissing her mouth, her earlobe, her neck...I bit her neck playfully, and she gasped.

"You *tease*."

Then she moaned as I took one nipple in my mouth and sucked greedily. We moved to the chaise and I laid her back upon the cushions. I explored every inch of her – down to her very toes - with my hands and mouth until she was begging for release. When I parted her nether lips with my tongue and tasted her, she arched her back in ecstasy. I moved upward along her body, kissing and teasing until my mouth found her breast again. I slipped two fingers inside her slick, warm sex and pressed my thumb against her swollen pearl. As I flicked her erect nipple with my tongue, she rocked her hips against my hand, gasping each time my fingers drove into her and my stroking thumb found purchase.

When she climaxed, she let out a loud cry and convulsed beneath me, the walls of her sex tightening in a steady rhythm. I withdrew from her and gazed down at her naked body. Her chest was heaving as she tried to catch her breath, her eyes closed in ecstasy.

After a moment, she opened her eyes and gave me a wicked smile. "Come here." Then she reached forward, lifted me – as though I were as light as a feather! – and positioned me so that I was straddling her face. I held on to the back of the chaise as she pleasured me with her tongue. Her arms were wrapped around my thighs, supporting me when my quivering legs threatened to give out from the intensity of the sensations that were tearing through me. When I felt myself precipitously at the edge of climax, I lifted myself away from her mouth.

She groaned. "Why are you stopping?"

"I want you to drink from me," I said.

She grew very still. Her eyes went from shock to disbelief. "Are you sure?"

"I trust you."

She shut her eyes tightly, as though I had pained her. Then she opened them and smiled with a tenderness that shook me. "God, I love you." She guided me down over her mouth again, then turned her face slightly to the side, kissing my inner thigh. "Are you ready?"

I was trembling with anticipation and (I will not deny it) with fear. I nodded.

"Look away," she said. She didn't want me to see her in her inhuman form. I looked up at the ceiling, but I still felt her face shifting and changing against my skin.

There was a hot sting of pain as her teeth pierced the flesh of my inner thigh, but the discomfort was fleeting, and then...suddenly our minds were connected, and all the pleasure that she felt as my blood spread through her was something that I could feel, too. Our hearts pounded together, our minds hummed with reciprocal joy. She opened my nether lips with her thumb and stroked me as she drank, the physical pleasure magnified by spiritual euphoria as she pulled the blood from my vein. My climax, when it came, was so deep, so intense, that I wept, shaking uncontrollably while the waves crashed over me again and again.

I was beginning to feel lightheaded. Carmilla sensed it and pulled herself away. As she breathed hard against my leg, I felt her face shifting, transforming back to its human appearance, and I looked down. Blood was streaming down my inner thigh still. Carmilla bit her finger, drawing a dark drop of her own blood from its tip and applying it to the wounds. They immediately began to close. She ran her tongue along my skin to consume the last traces, and I shivered at the tickling sensation. Then she chuckled and plunged her tongue between my slick, sensitive folds. My sex was so tender that I jumped away, and she laughed even harder.

I grinned, stretched my body alongside hers, and kissed her again. Her mouth tasted of my blood and musk together, like copper and smoke. Languid, we lay in each other's embrace, gently tracing patterns on each other's skin with our fingertips.

"Was it hard for you to stop?" I asked.

"A little," she admitted, "though not as hard as I thought it would be. My desire not to harm you, it turns out, easily overrides my desire to consume every drop of you."

To consume every drop of you. Why did those words thrill me?

A sense of awe hung between us. She had laid herself bare when she told me about herself, and I had reciprocated by giving myself to her, by trusting her not to hurt me, and by sharing my mind with her through our blood connection. We were different now, opened to each other in a way we hadn't been before.

The time that followed was the happiest of my life. We enjoyed the house and its grounds as though we were the only people in the world, basking in the truth of each other, surrendering ourselves to it entirely.

"You could make a living as a writer!" she exclaimed one day after she had read one of my stories. We were on the chaise in the parlor, my head in her lap, the dip between her legs tantalizingly warm against my ear. "Can you imagine? We could live here together, and you could write and provide for us! We wouldn't need anyone else, we could just be *us*."

The thought charmed me, but I was in an impertinent mood. "Indeed. And what would *you* provide?"

"I'll show you." She drew me upward and kissed me deeply.

She drank from me with some frequency, always allowing time for me to heal in between. The ecstasy of it – both hers and mine – was addictive. I sometimes dreamed that she was, in fact, consuming every drop of me, and I would wake from these dreams confused by the mixture of terror and arousal they engendered in me.

The day after my birthday (which Carmilla arranged to celebrate with a small cake and a day of playing games with Adeline, Maria, and Bettina), three weeks after we had left Gratz, Martin returned. After

Adeline had embraced him warmly, he assured us that he had seen my father safely off from the harbor at Calais, though there was no plan yet for his return. His arrival without my father reminded me of Josef's dire situation, and anxiety kept my stomach in knots for much of that day and the next. Sensing this, Carmilla suggested we go for a stroll together. We made our way into the woods, and she tried to keep me distracted with small talk. When my feet grew tired, we found a tree to sit against, resting our heads together. She reached up and playfully tugged on my curls.

"Laura?"

"Yes?"

She hesitated.

"What is it, my love?" I asked. "Don't be shy."

"I was just wondering...would you like to drink from *me*?"

I was astonished. "What...what would that do?"

"It wouldn't make you a vampire, if that's what you're wondering. I was thinking you could have just a little bit. It's...well, it's quite pleasurable. You would get to feel what I feel, if only for a few minutes."

I couldn't deny that it was an intriguing idea. "I...yes. Yes, I think I would like to try that."

She used a fingernail to open a thin line on her wrist. When the blood began to seep out, she guided my mouth to it. I balked at the salty heat of it, its unpleasant thickness, but it was a temporary discomfort, for she pulled away after I had taken only a few drops.

When it hit me, I reeled back against the tree trunk. The sky spun and yawned above me, and I felt my awareness stretch wide in all directions. The ground beneath me was shaking with the movement of small creatures. My nose prickled, overwhelmed by the scent of leaf and animal. The sound of the wind blowing through the trees was unbearably loud, and I covered my ears with my hands, but there were sounds in my head, too: Carmilla's thoughts – she was worried about me – and the thoughts of everyone in the schloss, swirling together like the buzzing of bees.

"Shhh." Carmilla pulled me away from the tree and laid my head in her lap. "The worst of it will pass; you will adjust."

I took deep, ragged breaths, trying to slow my heart, which I could feel pounding in my fingers and toes. Then a calm came over me, the frenzied discordance of the world around me receded, and *then...*

The world was dancing with energy, a life force that lit everything from within. I could see a line of ants on a tree trunk fifty meters away, could hear the sap moving in the trees. I could hear Carmilla's heart pulsing in her veins, could smell her blood and her sex underneath the layers of clothes. The wind whistled in my ears, and I found I could cast my awareness along its path, tracing its route back to the tops of mountain peaks, where birds circled and cartwheeled in the air.

It was like nothing I had ever felt. It was the heady, weightless rush of whirling on the dance floor after too much wine, except that the whole world was open to me, and I was aware of everything that moved and breathed. I could feel Carmilla's love for me radiating through her pores, and I wanted to weep with the intensity of what I felt for her in return.

"*This* is what it's like?" I said breathlessly.

"Yes. Although one becomes somewhat desensitized to it after a while."

It was hard to imagine such a thing. I laid back and tried to take in the enormity and eternity of the world around me. Tears streamed from my eyes.

"My dearest love," Carmilla whispered after a few minutes, "do you want to become a vampire?"

It was unfair of her to ask me when I was in the euphoric grip of intoxication. Nevertheless, I managed to keep enough of my wits about me to consider her question rationally. I was, of course, terrified of dying. This was even more the case now that I knew my mother's spirit had not appeared to me after all. Had she been consigned to oblivion or, worse, eternal punishment? It was a pretty thought to imagine her in heaven, but the utter uncertainty of it all tormented me. Spending eternity with Carmilla instead, ageless and giddy with all the pleasures a life with her would entail, was a tempting proposition indeed.

Yet I couldn't accept the idea that I would need to harm others to satisfy my own thirst, nor did I wish to *become* capable of accepting it (as would inevitably happen if I chose monstrosity over humanity). And what of my father? Would I have to spend the remainder of *his* life manipulating his mind? Would I watch him, and everyone else I knew, grow old and wither away before my eyes, while I remained unchanged?

"How would that work?" I asked. "With my father, I mean. And how would we stay...I mean...where would we..." I gulped. It was an awful thought. "How would we find enough blood?"

"We would need very little, if we were here. A visit to the village now and again, and no need to kill anyone. As for your father, it would be easy enough to shield him and the others from the truth. There are so few of them. Though he loves you enough that I wonder if we could tell him. After a while, anyway."

I was tempted. I am not ashamed to admit it now. An immortal life...and with *her*? But then the image of my own face distorted into that monstrous rictus flashed in my mind. I shuddered and shook my head. "I'm not ready. At least, not yet."

Our idyllic life together continued until a fortnight after Martin's return. After dinner, Carmilla and I sat together in the parlor. She played a lovely invention by Bach, and I listened, enraptured, smiling at her in frank adoration. Her eyes caught mine occasionally, and a small smile played on her lips as her fingers caressed the keys. Suddenly, she cried out and doubled over in pain.

I ran and knelt before her. "What's wrong?"

She stayed hunched over for a minute, silent, then the pain seemed to pass and she straightened up, her eyes wide with worry. "My mother," she whispered.

"What?"

"Something has happened to my mother." She stood up from the piano bench and rushed to the window, as though she might be able to see what was happening.

"Where is she? Can you hear her thoughts?"

"No, she's in London. Too far away. For me to feel anything at all from her, it must have been...it must have been bad."

London. It struck me suddenly that my father had gone to London to help Josef search for Emma's murderer, and that Josef had referred to this murderer as a "monster" and as "her." Seeing Carmilla's distress, however, I pushed down the suspicion.

"What if...can I help somehow? If you feed from me, can you reach out to her?"

"We can try it." Her bosom rose and fell with panicked breathing.

I offered her my wrist and turned away as she changed. Her teeth pierced my skin, and I grimaced while she pulled greedily from the vein. Once she had taken several deep gulps, she let me go. After a few moments she touched my shoulder, indicating that she had changed back into her human form. I watched as she stood at the window, her hands on each side of the frame, her eyes shut in deep concentration. She was silent for a minute...two minutes...

Finally she stepped back, shaking her head. "I can't find her. And I don't know if it's because she's too far away or because she's...gone." She dashed worried tears from her eyes. "God, it's maddening being stuck here!" She struck the wall with her fists. Small cracks spidered away from the impact.

I pushed away my fear of her torrid strength and pulled her into an embrace. "I'm sorry, my love. I'm sure she is fine. Perhaps it is only the distance."

"Perhaps," she responded, but her voice was cold. When she stepped away, her eyes were still wild with concern.

Two more weeks passed, and her anxiety about her mother never left her. She made love to me with an ardor that grew ever fiercer, ever more desperate, as though she feared that our days together were numbered. I didn't understand the reason for this at the time, but I realize now that, when she suspected that her mother had died, she also suspected – rightly, it turned out – that my father and the General would soon be arriving at the schloss, bringing the whole truth (and thus the end of our love) with them.

Troubled by the change in her, I finally got up the courage to ask her the question that had occurred to me that night in the parlor. After exchanging blood and making love, we were sprawled on the bed in our usual stupor when I ventured, "Carmilla, did your mother kill Emma?"

I wasn't sure how to interpret the coldness in her eyes. Was she disappointed that I could suspect such a thing? Angry that I had discovered the truth? "No," she said curtly. I felt the truth in her words. I embraced her, trying to bring warmth back to her expression. We made love again, fiercely, our anxieties somehow sharpening our desire.

The next morning, it all came crashing down. If she hadn't been distracted, she would have heard them coming a long way off. Their thoughts would have given them away, and she would have left long before the carriage thundered up the path. But, as it happened, her attention was entirely on me. We were in bed together, naked. As the first grey tendrils of the early morning sun began to illuminate the small gap between my curtains, she stirred behind me. She drew herself close to me, the warmth of her body pressed to mine, her nipples hard against my back. Then she lifted the hair from the back of my neck so she could kiss me there. I hummed with pleasure, and she moved her lips slowly downward, tenderly planting warm, wet kisses down the length of my spine. Having finished her netherward journey, she moved up again and whispered in my ear, "You are mine, you shall be mine, you and I are one forever." She pulled my hips back until my buttocks were pressed into the tops of her thighs, her hand tracing my hip and the lower curve of my belly before finding its way urgently between my thighs. I moaned and arched with pleasure.

Then we heard the pounding of hooves drawing nearer to the house. We scrambled from the bed, pulled our nightdresses on frantically, and threw on our coats and boots before hastening out to the courtyard to meet the unexpected arrival.

The carriage was large, drawn by six massive horses who were wet with perspiration. They panted the rest of the way to the house until the driver brought them to a halt and jumped down from his box. Martin was already running to help with the horses. He grasped one set of reins and shouted something at the driver. Beside me, Carmilla's face blanched. Then she ran inside.

The door to the carriage box swung open, and my father jumped down. My heart soared at first, until I saw the worried look on his face, which was drawn and darkly-shadowed with exhaustion. He hurtled toward me and took me in his arms.

"You're alive!" he gasped. "Thank God you're alive!"

"Why wouldn't I be?" I asked, stunned. Over his shoulder, I watched as Josef came out of the carriage, followed by two men I didn't recognize: a tall, lanky man with a hawklike nose and eyes, and a shorter man with kind eyes wearing a priest's tunic. I *did* recognize him; it was Father Schmidt, our former priest.

"The creature!" Josef bellowed. "Where is she?"

"Father, what's going on?" I asked, though my heart was sinking with suspicion.

Josef, Father Schmidt, and the tall man were heading for the front door. I pushed my father aside and hurtled after them, foolishly imagining that I could head them off before they found her.

But they didn't need to hunt for her. She was standing in the foyer, waiting for them, her demeanor so calm that she might have been welcoming guests at a fete. Josef cried out and lunged in her direction, but she raised her hand, bringing everyone except me and the stranger to a standstill. She frowned when she realized that her powers had been ineffective against the tall man; the others writhed in her invisible grip and shouted in frustration as their feet refused to move. The tall man hesitated, appraising the condition of the others, and in this moment, I managed to put myself between him and Carmilla. He scowled, pulled a sword from inside his coat, and advanced upon us.

"What's going on?" I asked again, louder.

"She's a monster!" The tall man shouted as he drew near. He stopped and lowered his sword, clearly unwilling to endanger me. "She must be destroyed!"

"I know what she is" – I cringed at the look of betrayal on my father's face – "but she won't hurt us. Right, Carmilla?" I glanced over my shoulder; fury was distorting her features. Bettina and Maria emerged from the kitchen, cried out in shock at the scene before them, and flattened themselves against the kitchen door as if they could disappear. I heard Maria's voice muttering urgent prayers.

"No, Laura, you don't understand!" Josef spat, still struggling against his immobility. *"She's the monster who killed Emma."*

Something broke inside me.

A ringing began in my ears, nearly imperceptible at first, then louder and louder until it was unbearable. Adeline screamed, frozen in the front doorway.

"It's not true," I whispered.

Carmilla, did your mother kill Emma?

No.

"It is true," my father said with a pleading expression. "She has fooled us all."

I turned slowly to look at her. Tears were welling up in her eyes, and she lowered her gaze, unwilling to answer the wordless entreaty in my face. "It's not true," I said. "It can't be true."

She said nothing. My heart wrenched in my chest, and I groaned and stepped away from her as if she were a foul thing. She winced and inhaled sharply, then let her hand drop. Released from her invisible clutches, Josef and my father launched themselves in our direction, pulling large wooden stakes from their belts just as the tall man was raising his sword again and shouldering past me. But the vampire swirled into her shadow form – in the orange light of the morning, it was like smoke rising from a fire – and slipped upwards. She glided high above our heads and through the front doorway before dissipating into the open air.

My knees shook below me, as numb and disembodied as though I had been standing too long in icy water. My fingernails dug into my palms. A roar of anger and grief rumbled through me before ripping forth from my throat.

"Look to Miss Bancroft!" Bettina's voice, hoarse with shock. She and Maria were running toward me, their hands outstretched as if to catch me. But I wasn't falling, was I? Then the floor was rushing up to meet me, and I knew no more.

CHAPTER NINETEEN

THE REST OF THE TRUTH

I was alone for several hours while my father, Josef, Father Schmidt, and the tall man brought their things out of the carriage and into the house. The truth had sunk deeply into my breast, souring and dashing to pieces all the joy that had been mine over the past few months. It hurt too much. When Adeline came into my room to bring me some tea, I threw myself into her arms and sobbed uncontrollably. She held me and stroked my hair, cooing with sympathy.

"Oh, my dear child. You've had quite a blow, haven't you? Nobody will blame you for weeping, least of all me."

"I was a fool," I said bitterly.

"For what?"

"For trusting her."

"Why *wouldn't* you trust her? I know you cared for her, and she seemed to care for you, too. Don't blame yourself. She had *all* of us fooled."

"But I knew…I knew what she was." I pulled away and pressed the heels of my hands against my eyes as if I could stop the tears.

For a moment, Adeline considered my words silently. Then she reached out for me again and pulled me back into her embrace. "So your emotions got in the way of your reason. You aren't the first, and you won't be the last. There is anger to be felt, certainly, but it oughtn't be directed at yourself."

A flurry of movement outside caught my attention. I walked to the window and peered down into the courtyard. Martin, my father, and the General had unloaded huge bags full of white powder from the carriage. Under the direction of the tall stranger, they were taking bucketfuls of the substance and pouring it onto the ground in a continuous line that ran parallel with the front of the house.

"What are they doing?" I asked.

"Salt," Adeline replied. "Baron Vordenburg – that's him there – says an unbroken circle of salt will keep the creature out."

We watched them silently for several minutes.

Adeline cleared her throat. "When you're ready, Father Schmidt would like to take a look at you, to ensure you're in good health. And the Baron would like to speak with you, too."

I sighed. I didn't really want to see *anyone*. My heart clenched at the memory of my father's expression when I had revealed that I already knew what Carmilla was. I wasn't looking forward to explaining myself further, either to him or to the stranger he had brought. But I *did* want to hear from Josef about what had happened to Emma, and I was curious about what they were planning to do about Carmilla.

"I'm as ready as I'll ever be, I suppose," I said. Adeline nodded and left the room.

A few minutes later there was a knock on the door, and Father Schmidt entered. His face had aged since I had seen him last, but he had the same calming presence and kind expression, with deeply-furrowed smile lines beside his mouth and eyes.

He took my hand and bowed slightly. ""Miss Bancroft, I don't know if you remember me, but my name is Father Schmidt."

"I remember you. You cared for me when I was just a little girl and I had been attacked by the vampire."

"I'm surprised you remember that so clearly."

"She herself reminded me of it."

"I wondered if it was the same creature," he said. I feared he would ask me why I had been so ready to defend her, then, but he only smiled kindly and asked, "May I take a look at you? Make sure you are physically well? I can ask Madame Perrodon to attend us, if it makes you more comfortable."

I nodded. He opened the bedroom door and summoned Adeline, who had been waiting in the hallway. She sat beside me on the bed and held my hand while the priest inspected my arms and neck and legs.

"No bite marks," he said finally, "and you seem to be in good physical condition. Did she feed from you?"

"Yes," I admitted. "With some frequency. But never enough to hurt me," I added, hearing Adeline's sharp intake of breath.

"And yet you have no marks?"

"She used her own blood to heal them." I was surprised at how calm and collected my voice sounded.

Father Schmidt lowered his head, grasped the crucifix at his neck, and uttered a prayer under his breath. "I am very sorry, Miss Bancroft, that the creature compelled you to suffer such indignities, though I thank God in heaven that you are alive and healthy despite them."

I could have let him and the others continue to believe that Carmilla had compelled me. It would have been easier, certainly, and far less shameful. But something in me balked at the lie. And there is something healing in the act of confession, isn't there? I steeled myself, then confessed: "She did not compel me."

"Pardon?"

"She did not compel me. I offered myself to her."

Adeline's grip tightened on my hand, and Father Schmidt's eyes widened. Adeline's voice was breathless with disbelief. "You...why would you do such a thing?"

Tears pricked the back of my eyes, and I swallowed the lump in my throat. "Because I love...I loved her. I wanted to please her."

Father Schmidt's eyes flickered nervously toward Adeline before he asked the next question. "Miss Bancroft...Laura...was your relationship with Carmilla carnal in nature?"

There was no going back now. "Yes." I kept my eyes firmly fixed on my lap, trying not to meet his gaze.

"And you're sure she didn't compel you in this?"

"I'm sure. She told me she could not. And I have no reason to think she was lying. If she could have compelled me, she would never have mentioned it at all, I think. No, Father Schmidt"—I finally raised my eyes to his—"I truly loved her. It's possible I still do, as angry as I am. And I believe that it was not one-sided."

He nodded slowly, digesting everything I had told him. I could see the disappointment in his eyes, and in Adeline's, too. *Of course* they disapproved of the fact that I had willingly given myself to a vampire. But I suspected that her *gender* was nearly as troubling to them. "Well, my child," Father Schmidt said finally. "God will forgive you, as He forgives anyone who comes to Him with a repentant heart."

Adeline crossed herself and looked pleadingly up at the heavens.

Do I have a repentant heart? I wondered to myself. I thought it wise not to voice the question out loud.

"If you don't mind," he continued, "I will summon the Baron Vordenburg. He is anxious to meet you."

I stood. "I'd rather meet him in the parlor, if he doesn't mind. Would you ask Josef to join him?" Having people come to my bedroom like this made me feel like I was ill, and I wanted to feel strong.

"As you wish." He inclined his head humbly as he left.

I turned to Adeline, who was still sitting on the bed and carefully avoiding my gaze. "Well," she said, standing briskly. "I ought to go see if there's anything I can help Maria with. She'll have to prepare a much larger dinner than usual."

Her voice was as chipper as ever, but there was something in her manner – her nervously-shifting eyes, her forced smile – that suggested that she didn't want to be alone with me. *Well, so be it*, I thought bitterly, *I am not the woman she thought I was. I have made my bed; now I must lie in it*. Still, it hurt when she walked out of the bedroom and left me alone.

All four men were in the parlor by the time I had finally composed myself enough to meet them there. Father Schmidt was conveying the things he had learned in our conversation to the other three. My father was holding the mantel with one hand and looking into the flickering fireplace with an anguished expression.

I cleared my throat. They turned to face me silently.

The tall man approached me, hand outstretched. His fingers were ice-cold when I shook them. His voice was stern. "Miss Bancroft, I am Baron Johann Vordenburg. I have been commissioned by General Spielsdorf to hunt down this creature, whom you know as Carmilla. Indeed," he said, his eyes flashing, "it seems you know her *quite* well. If what Father Schmidt has told us is true, you have experienced some of her more, shall we say, *abominable* tendencies yourself."

I withdrew my hand from his, flushing and feeling myself prickle. Did he really intend to begin by embarrassing me? To my dismay, neither my father nor Josef seemed to find his approach troubling.

"And what is it that makes *you* an authority on the subject?" I asked coldly.

"I come from a long line of vampire hunters on my mother's side," he said. "In fact, one of my ancestors killed Carmilla's sire, Alexander Karnstein."

The Moravian, I realized. "Antonin Bruzek?" I ventured. The Baron was taken aback. I raised an eyebrow and explained, "As you said, I know Carmilla quite well."

He glowered. "With that being the case, we would very much appreciate any information you have about the creature. We have already dispatched her mother – another menace who has devastated the world for over a century – but it is our intention to destroy Carmilla, too."

Her mother. I felt an unexpected swell of sympathy for Carmilla. I tried to swallow it down, reminding myself that she had killed Emma, as if feeling the impact of *that* blow again could help drive out my love for her.

"Baron Vordenburg, is it true that the circle of salt will keep Carmilla out?"

"Yes. So long as the circle remains unbroken, it will protect the enclosed area both from the creature herself and from her powers. I myself have witnessed its efficacy on several occasions."

"If that is the case, then before we speak any further about how to deal with her, I should very much like to hear from General Spielsdorf regarding what happened to his ward."

He scoffed. Clearly, he saw such a delay as unnecessary. But after he looked at me, really *looked* at me, narrowing his eyes in appraisal, he understood that I wasn't going to budge.

He threw up a hand dismissively. "Very well. I have plenty of things I can prepare in the meantime. Father Schmidt, please join me."

Father Schmidt assented, and they headed for the door.

"I'll join you, too," my father said. "I already know this story." His voice was cold, and he was looking at me with what I can only describe as wariness. My heart sank.

And then Josef and I were alone in the study. He sat in the chair opposite mine, his gaze cast down, deep lines of grief etched in his face. I was stunned by the change in him; he had always been so full of life, his rotund body dancing with a boisterous energy that spilled out into his genial smile and booming voice. But now he sat hunched, his skin far paler and his hair far greyer than I remembered.

He sighed. "Laura, my Emma loved you so deeply, and I know you returned her affection. It pains me to have to speak of this to you, although I realize that, had I only written to you before I left, we would not be in our current predicament. I fear it will take me a long time to forgive myself for such an oversight."

I placed my hand comfortingly over his. He returned the gesture, then continued.

"A fortnight after the fete in honor of Grand Duke Charles, Anna and Carmilla Mueller appeared at our estate. They had been traveling around the area, they claimed, and hoped we might accommodate them for the night. We were happy to acquiesce, having enjoyed their company immensely at the Carlsfelds'. I am ashamed to say, too, that I was quite taken with Madame Mueller, and that my intentions toward her were not entirely gentlemanly.

"They ended up staying with us for several weeks. I realize now, from what the Baron has told me, that they must have enchanted us, for we never questioned the longevity of their stay or the strange things that happened while they were there. Many of our servants became ill. Countess Mueller and her daughter kept us so entertained, however, that even if we hadn't been victims of their hypnotic powers, I doubt we would have suspected anything was amiss. Carmilla and Emma became inseparable, talking and laughing and playing music together all day.

"One day, however, Emma awoke very ill indeed. We summoned a doctor, who could not tell us the reason for her illness, but who warned that she was very much in danger of dying. Carmilla"—a sob caught in his throat—"Carmilla played the role of concerned friend very well, weeping in distress and throwing herself upon Emma's bed, promising to sit beside her and pray on her behalf. Looking back on it now, I think that is the most horrifying part of it. If she was thirsty for my Emma's blood, if she wanted her dead, why didn't she just come in the night and kill her without any of us realizing she was there? Why put on the façade of kindness? Why draw it out so long? It's as if...it's as if she *enjoyed* it. And I never suspected a thing. I even encouraged Carmilla to stay beside Emma's bed throughout the night, not realizing that in doing so I was condemning my dear ward to death."

He paused for a moment and wiped a tear from his eye.

"Emma's illness worsened each day. When she was still strong enough to speak, she told us of the harrowing nightmares that tormented her when she slept, dreams where death lurked around every corner, waiting to seize her and enfold her in its shadowy embrace."

A shiver ran through me. Hadn't Carmilla told me that she could send pleasant dreams to those she fed on? Why, then, had she plagued Emma with nightmares? It couldn't have been purposeful, could it?

"The morning she died," Josef continued, "I woke up early, before the sun. The Countess, who had been in my bed – God forgive me! – was gone, and I had an odd feeling that something was wrong. I made my way to Emma's room to check on her, and when I opened the door, there was Carmilla, feeding on my Emma, her face distorted, her eyes...I can't begin to describe those eyes. She looked up from Emma's neck, her mouth dripping with blood, and she *laughed*. Then she changed into a mist of shadow, like she did earlier today, and escaped through the window. I was torn between running to help Emma and chasing the creature. But I could see that Emma was dead. Her eyes were like glass, fixed on the ceiling in a lifeless stare. Her skin and lips were as white as paper, her mouth contorted in an unmoving grimace of pain. The puncture wounds on her neck were seeping blood slowly; her heart was no longer beating."

His voice broke, and he stopped, shaking with tears. I, too, was beginning to weep as I imagined what Emma had suffered. We mourned together for several minutes, our heads and bodies bowed under the weight of our anguish. Finally, Josef continued, though his voice still shook. "I ran frantically after the creature, but by the time I got to the courtyard she and her mother were already in their carriage, the horses galloping away. Her mother must have been waiting; I suspect they planned it all ahead of time.

"You can see, perhaps, the reason for my haste, and why I didn't pause to inform you and your father of what was going on. I didn't want them to get away from me. I lost their trail in Vienna. I stayed there a few days, asking around and looking for any clues about their whereabouts. It was there that I wrote my first letter to you and your father, explaining everything that had happened."

"We never got a letter," I said.

"I know. I imagine they had something to do with its disappearance, for I realize now, after speaking with your father, that at that time they had come *here* to leave Carmilla with you. From there, Anna came back to Vienna alone and drew me back into the chase, bringing me farther away from you. She always left enough clues in each new city to keep me searching, although she remained ever out of my reach. Not that I ever could have caught her by myself, and, if I had, I certainly couldn't have hurt her. At the time, however, I didn't know the extent of what they were. I didn't realize they could easily control my mind, could easily rip me to pieces if they wanted to. Indeed, looking back on it now, I wonder why Anna didn't just kill me. It would have been easier than allowing me to continue the chase. And you and your father would never have found out the truth about Emma and Carmilla." He stopped, lost in thought. This perplexed me, too. Why had they risked things turning out the way they did, when removing the problem entirely would have been so simple?

Josef continued: "Whatever the reason for its continuation – perhaps she was enjoying the game of cat and mouse – my pursuit seemed to stretch on interminably. From Prague to Berlin, from Brussels to Paris, then north to London, where I lost all trace of her entirely. In the meantime, I had heard about the Baron, a renowned vampire hunter from the Order of Perseus, and I went to him for help. As soon as I had told him my story, he knew what – and whom – we were dealing with: Anna and Carmilla Karnstein, who had once escaped the clutches of his vampire-hunting ancestor. He told me what he knew of them, what they were capable of, and asked me if there was anyone I could trust who might help us in our endeavor to hunt them down. I sent for your father, and for Father Schmidt, with whom I've long been acquainted.

"After your father arrived in London and told us that Carmilla was here with you, we panicked. Indeed, we wanted to return here as quickly as possible to ensure your safety. But the Baron convinced us that we should dispatch the mother first, to keep her from returning to Styria and joining forces with her daughter, since it would be exponentially more difficult to handle the two of them together. Your father wanted to write you a letter warning you of the danger, but we worried that, if it were to fall into Carmilla's hands, she would lash out against you pre-emptively. We decided that the best approach was to deal with the mother quickly and then return home posthaste. In the meantime, Father Schmidt had received some information from a fellow priest that there had been some unusual activity in one of the catacombs, and we had good reason to think it was the Countess, as there had also been reports of wounded vagrants nearby.

"We waited until morning, when she most likely would be resting, and made our way down into the catacombs. It didn't take long for us to find the coffin she was using as a resting place. It had been freed of dust and cobwebs, and its former inhabitant – now a desiccated mass of bones – had been deposited on the floor beside it. This seemed strange to me. As far as I know, she never rested in a coffin when she stayed with me, though I suppose she could have manipulated my memory somehow."

I confirmed his suspicions. "She didn't need a coffin."

He sighed. "Well, I suppose she was less likely to be seen and recognized in a catacomb than in a hotel. At any rate, we knew she could change herself into a mass of insubstantial shadows, and that she could escape quickly in such a form. But the Baron had assured us that surprising her would give us an advantage. She might be able to escape in her shadow form, but she could not feed on or harm us when she was incorporeal. If we took her by surprise and angered her, she would want to fight. And in order to fight, she would have to stay corporeal.

"The plan worked. We pushed open the coffin's lid, and she awoke immediately, screaming in fear and anger. Though she used her ability to morph and fly to her advantage, whenever she attacked one of us (and was thus in her corporeal form), the others were able to strike. Eventually, the four of us together were able to overwhelm her. Once she had been weakened enough that she could no longer transform herself, your father wrapped a wire around her neck, choking her, and the Baron and Father Schmidt forced her to the ground and held her still. I myself struck the killing blow, severing her head from her neck. We burned her body, and then, tired though we were, immediately hastened to Dover, trying to get back here as quickly as we could. We stopped in Gratz only to gather supplies, like the salt. While we were there, we were told that Franz Kepner had been found dead at the Barragans' house the morning after his brother's engagement party. The rumor was that he had committed suicide in his distress over Emma's untimely demise. But your father reminded us that *she* was in the house with him that night..." He trailed off.

My blood felt like ice water in my veins. "She said she went into his room to talk to him," I whispered. "And I...I can't believe I was such a fool as to believe her." My heart sank with shame at my own naivete and anger at yet another of Carmilla's betrayals.

Josef continued. "Your father was so worried that we would be too late...I've never seen him so upset. When we got here and saw that you were still alive..." He stopped, choking on a sob. "I can't imagine what my life will be like without my Emma. If we had lost you, too..."

Tears were streaming down my face. To see my father's closest friend in so much pain, knowing that, henceforth, he would ever be burdened with grief and guilt...I felt a pang, too, at the thought of my father's distress, especially since it seemed to have transformed into disappointment when he learned the truth about me and Carmilla.

"Laura," Josef said kindly, as though he had read my thoughts, "I know well how charming Carmilla can be, even without the added power of her supernatural abilities. Father Schmidt told us about your feelings for her, and I wouldn't dare blame you for them, nor for your willingness to accept the lies she undoubtedly told you about her past." He patted my hand. "Your father will come around. He was surprised, that's all. And I think he considers himself responsible for the whole situation, no matter how unfairly; I know *I* would. Talk to him."

I nodded.

His expression became grave. "No matter what your feelings have been for her, though, we need your help." He leaned forward in his chair and clasped my hands. "My dear, will you help us? Will you tell the Baron everything you know?"

I thought of what Emma had suffered, of how unnecessarily cruel Carmilla had been to her. I wondered how many times Carmilla had lied about other cruelties. She had said she didn't like to kill, that she only did it when she had to, but Emma's murder told a different story. Was what she and I had shared – as wondrous as it was – worth risking the lives of those I loved for the clearly naive notion that she could change? *My God,* I thought, *how did it come to this?*

"I don't know how much help I will be," I responded, "but I will do what I can."

We ate our dinner mostly in silence, weariness and worry taking their toll on our spirits. After the plates had been cleared, however, the Baron sat forward in his chair and pulled a small notebook from his pocket. "Miss Bancroft," he said, "tell me everything you know about Carmilla."

It was late, and I was tired, but I knew that sleep was out of the question. I related the story Carmilla had told me from start to finish, in more detail than I needed to (Father Schmidt looked particularly troubled by the account of Father Wagner). Then, reluctantly, I explained how my relationship with Carmilla had developed.

"You drank from her?" My father said in alarm when I had finished. "Does that mean...Baron, does that mean Laura will become a vampire?"

"She said it wasn't enough," I said. "But I don't know if she was telling the truth."

The Baron nodded. "It is true. The change only occurs after a large amount of blood, and death must follow shortly thereafter, within a few days at the most."

My father sat back in his chair, relief flooding his face.

"You said that you and Mademoiselle De LaFontaine are immune to her mind powers?" the Baron asked me.

"Yes."

The Baron looked over his notes. "Most interesting. And yet she ensnared you anyway. Well, you are young after all, and a woman."

I bristled. "And I suppose no man has ever fallen in love with someone he shouldn't?"

Josef's mouth twisted upward in a wry smile, and Father Schmidt's eyes crinkled with amusement.

The Baron cleared his throat. "Never mind. Now this is really important, Miss Bancroft." He leaned forward in his chair, his sharp eyes fixed on mine. "Do you know where her hiding place is?"

I shook my head. "No, I don't. I wouldn't think it would be difficult to find, though. There isn't so much space between this schloss and the Karnstein village."

The Baron ran his fingers through his jet-black hair. "And yet my ancestor Bruzek looked for it for *years* and never found it. I have his notes, you see."

Everyone was silent for some time, absorbed in thought.

"What's the plan, then?" I finally ventured.

"Well, until we know where she is, there's not much we can do," the Baron said. "So we'll have to wait for some indication of her location, or for her to show up here."

"But the salt?" I asked.

"The salt will keep her out for as long as we want it to. In fact, we may need to break the circle in order to face her."

"How can salt work against her, if crosses don't?" I queried.

The Baron chuckled. "The protective power of salt is primordial, Miss Bancroft; it has been a defense against unclean entities since long before the Christ appeared."

"Why not put the salt circle *inside* the house, where it will not be destroyed by the elements?"

"An apt question," he noted, somewhat begrudgingly. "Beyond the difficulty of dealing with all the doors opening and closing inside, the perimeter we have chosen gives us some room to maneuver. We can get in and out of the carriage, which we've placed just outside the door, without endangering ourselves. Only the person tasked with getting the horses will be in peril, if we need to make a quick escape."

Poor Martin, I thought.

"In addition," he continued, "we will be able to empty the chamber pots and gather vegetables from the nearest garden plot without worrying about being snatched by the creature, which your servants will be glad for. And it will be easier to keep watch for her out in the open."

I nodded. "I see. But when we do face her, what if she keeps taking on her shadow form and eluding us? We don't have her trapped in a catacomb, nor do we have the element of surprise, the way you did when you dispatched her mother."

"Regretfully, that is something I have yet to figure out. The key is to wound her; it makes it much more difficult for her to use her powers. But we must get close enough to do so. Do you have any thoughts on the matter?"

I considered for a moment, then shook my head. "Not yet." I noticed that the others around the table were nodding off. "Perhaps we should continue this discussion tomorrow."

The Baron looked around the table disdainfully and grunted in agreement. "Indeed, we should." He stood from his chair abruptly, the noise of it startling the others awake. "Who will keep an eye on our barrier?" he asked.

"I'll do it," I volunteered. "I can't imagine I'll be able to sleep anyway."

My father looked like he was about to protest at first. Then he sighed, giving in. "If you start to get tired, you can wake us."

"She'll do no such thing," Adeline said. She had been listening in the doorway. "You need rest, Mr. Bancroft. I'll watch with the girl."

The girl. As if I wasn't a woman grown who had just been thrust into an unimaginable situation.

"That's settled then," the Baron said curtly. He stalked up the stairs and headed for the room to which he had been appointed. My father and Josef followed, walking side by side in silent companionship.

Father Schmidt groaned and stood from his chair slowly. "A night of rest will do us all some good. My bones are too old for riding in a carriage all day long, let alone for many days."

Adeline said she would be in the kitchen if I needed anything. When everyone had gone, I sat by myself in the dining room, listening to the minutes ticking by on the grandfather clock. My mind raced, struggling to grasp the various shocks it had received over the course of the day.

I was angry at Carmilla, so angry that I could feel the rage sticking in my throat like honey. But I was angry at the others, too. The way Father Schmidt had said I could repent, the way the Baron had suggested that my relationship with Carmilla was one of the facets of her abomination...these reactions had not surprised me, but the more I thought about them, the more they troubled me, like a sore in my mouth that grew worse every time I passed my tongue over it. Carmilla was a monster, I couldn't deny that. But she was a monster because she was a *murderer,* not because she was my lover. If her carnal love for me had been a symptom of her monstrosity, as the Baron had suggested, then wouldn't that make me a monster too, since I had reciprocated that love? Perhaps I was simply unwilling to admit my own faults, but I couldn't accept that. My love for her – and her love for me (it was real, I *knew* it was) – had been a source of joy, a slice of heaven in the lonely existence my father and I had built for ourselves here. Who had been hurt by our love for each other? How could our smiles, our kisses, our moans of pleasure...how could they have been evil?

And yet, I could never forgive her for what she had done.

I went outside.

The air was misty, and a thin, white fog clung to and shifted over the ground. I found the line of salt and walked along it, looking out into the darkness beyond and hoping that the Baron's assurances of the salt's efficacy weren't misguided. Soon, though, the steady rhythm of my shoes on the damp earth worked its magic: my mind began to still, shedding its anxieties into the air and the moonlight and the rustling of the trees.

"Laura."

She was there, less than a meter away from me on the other side of the salt line. Her white nightdress seemed to fade into the mist, but her dark hair and eyes loomed out of the whiteness, framing a face twisted in anguish. My heart jumped in my breast, but I quelled my panic and turned to face her calmly, bringing my toes to the very edge of the line, so close that I could feel her breath on my face as her shoulders rose and fell.

"I need to talk to you," she said. Her voice was thin and quavering. A young woman's voice.

I felt strangely disconnected, as if I were standing outside of myself and watching the scene unfold from a distance. I glanced over my shoulder at the darkened windows of the house. "Not here," I said. "If they see you, they will try to kill you."

"Where then?"

I couldn't break the barrier of salt and allow her in. I doubted she would have any qualms about killing anyone inside the house. But I knew she wouldn't kill *me*. I could see it in her eyes, could hear it in her trembling voice. Our little chapel – so infrequently used by me and my father – was just beyond the circle of protection. I gestured toward it with my chin. "In there."

Her eyes widened. Was she surprised that I was willing to endanger myself? Then she nodded, and we walked in silence into the chapel. It was even smaller than I remembered it, though that may have been because I had grown significantly since the last time I'd been there. There was a simple podium with a plain wooden cross behind it, and six short rows of pews. The ceiling sloped upward in mimicry of a larger church, but the windows were small and unadorned. No stained glass or elaborate architraves here. There was enough moonlight spilling in for me to make out Carmilla's form, but her expression was deeply shadowed and, thus, inscrutable. I wondered if my face was as unreadable to her. Or did her keen, predatory eyesight eliminate the disadvantage of darkness?

There was no longer a line of salt between us, but that didn't mean that every barrier had been removed. We stood untouching, the distance between us as icy and insurmountable as a yawning chasm.

"My mother?" she asked.

"She is dead," I confirmed.

She hunched forward with a high, keening cry. Again I felt a surge of sympathy for her. I had only known my mother for five years; she had known – and loved – hers for a century and a half. That sympathy was erased, however, at the next words she uttered: "I *told* her we should kill him. I *told* her he would continue to be a danger to us if she let him live. But she *cared* for him too much. And she thought if she could only find the cure before he found her, we could escape his clutches together. And now she is dead, doomed by her own sentimentality!" She was raving, tearing at her hair, her voice shaking the air in the small space. "Tell me how they did it, Laura. Please, you must tell me!"

I shook my head slowly. "I have a better question for you, Carmilla." She became utterly still, her breath held as she waited for my words. I whispered, "*Why?*"

She winced and fixed her gaze on the ground, fully aware that I wasn't talking about her mother anymore. When her voice came, it was nearly inaudible. "Laura, *please.*"

I wasn't going to be dissuaded. "Why did you kill my friend?"

She drew a shaky breath before answering. "Because I saw the way you two looked at each other at Count Carlsfeld's fete. I saw that you loved each other, even if it was only the love of friendship, and I...I wanted you for myself. I thought she would stand in our way."

I stepped away, bitter rage rising in me like bile.

"I'm sorry," she pleaded. She reached out for me, then cried out and flinched away when she saw my face.

"You really are a monster," I breathed.

"No, Laura," she begged. "I've changed. You've changed me!"

"Have I? What about the way you treated Elias? And the girl you killed in Gratz? And...oh God, what about *Franz*?"

"He would have told you," her voice shook childishly. "He would have told you what Emma had written to him...about *me*. Not the whole truth, but that I was there with her."

"You always have some excuse, don't you? You may think you've changed, but I don't think you have. I don't think you *can*." The sharp edge of my anger had worn off, replaced by a hopeless sense of desolation, the realization that there was no way to salvage this.

"Laura, I —"

"When you showed me your cruelty in Gratz, when you told me of it in your confession, I ignored it. Because I wanted to, and because I could. It wasn't directed at me or my family, so I turned a blind eye to it. But I was a fool. You told me that you were a monster, and I didn't listen. And do you know what the worst part of it is? If you had just left Emma alone, everything would have been alright. Your mother would still be alive, and there wouldn't be an angry mob hunting you, and I..." I trailed off. How could I express how utterly she had lost me? "You weren't just cruel, Carmilla. You were so blinded by your cruelty that you ruined *everything*."

"Come with me," she begged, her voice shrill with panic. "We can be together, just the two of us, and I promise I will never hurt you – or anyone – again. I'm sorry, my love. I'm sorry! I'm *sorry*!" She repeated the words over and over again, pacing wildly through the chapel like a caged beast before falling to her knees in front of one of the pews, as if in prayer.

My chest ached so intensely I thought it might burst and spill forth the black bile of my anger. My voice, however, was steely. "How many times did you think you could hurt me with impunity? How many times did you think I would forgive you? Listen to me closely now, and know that, unlike you, *I* mean what I say: no matter how much I love you, I would rather die than be with you."

She stopped crying and stood up. I couldn't see the expression on her face, but her voice cut through the darkness like a knife. "If that's the case, then there's nothing to stop me from killing everyone in this schloss."

A shock of fear sent blood roaring through my veins, and she tilted her head to the side, listening to it. If there had been any doubt that she was irredeemable, her icy voice and predatory gesture erased it. And suddenly I was very scared of the dangerous predicament in which we had all placed ourselves. My mind raced. Was there anything I could do to stop what was coming? "So be it," I said, as bravely as I could muster. "But do not think they will go easily. In fact, you are very much in danger, Carmilla. Listen to me: I will never forgive you for what you did to Emma, but I don't wish to see you – or anyone else – dead. Can't you influence them to make them forget that they want to kill you? My father and I will leave this place, and you never have to see any of us again."

She shook her head. "It would be too difficult to erase their memories in a way that would keep them from resurfacing. Memories are a tricky thing. Besides, the tall man..."

"Baron Vordenburg."

"Like you, he is immune to my powers. He will not forget me."

I thought of what had happened in the foyer earlier today – today? It felt like weeks ago! – when the Baron had resisted the immobility that Carmilla was inflicting on the others. "Then just keep hiding," I said. "They don't know where you are. You don't have to hurt anyone."

My skin prickled at the rage I could feel emanating from her, like heat from a blazing fire. If I could see her eyes, I wondered, would they look like embers? "I'm tired of hiding," she growled. "Besides, they killed my mother. What kind of daughter would I be if I let them live?"

Her body melted into shadows, spreading through the air like ink through milk, and then she was gone.

CHAPTER TWENTY

FIRST BLOOD

"I don't think we have to worry about her running away," I said the next morning as I walked into the front hall, where the Baron and the others were laying out and taking inventory of the weapons at our disposal. Two large axes; several swords and daggers, glinting coldly in the light from the windows; four crossbows and an enormous pile of arrows; sharpened stakes, both wooden and iron; even a few guns (my father's hunting shotguns, and Josef's trusty pistol, which he insisted on carrying himself). There were also several large bags of salt still, as well as barrels of oil. *No wonder they brought such a large carriage*, I thought. I shuddered at the warlike atmosphere that had suffused our home.

The Baron turned to face me. "What do you mean?"

"She wants to fight," I explained. "She's angry about her mother's death."

He narrowed his eyes. "And how, precisely, do you know this?" The others – my father, Josef, Father Schmidt, even Martin and Adeline – stopped what they were doing and listened.

I told them about my conversation with Carmilla the night before. Adeline gasped when I described how she had first appeared to me, and my father's eyes were wide with worry. When I got to the part where she threatened to kill everyone, Adeline, Martin, and Father Schmidt crossed themselves. By the end of it, the Baron was inexplicably angry.

"You foolish girl!" he spat. "Why didn't you summon us? We had a chance to wound the creature, and you let it pass!"

"How did you want me to summon you? With a shout? By running back to the house to get you? Do you suppose she would have stayed there and waited for you to throw on your dressing gowns and run outside with your weapons?"

The Baron scoffed. "At the very least you could have summoned me immediately upon your return. We could have followed the creature's trail."

I shook my head. "There was no trail. And did you really intend to chase the shadow creature *at night*, and in your state of exhaustion?"

He didn't admit that I was right, but he refrained from further complaint. "Nevermind. Let's focus on the most salient thing. Did she really say she would kill everyone?"

I nodded.

"Now I want you to consider this carefully, Miss Bancroft," he said, "because it's important: do you think that she meant she would kill *you* too?"

I closed my eyes, trying to ignore the urgent expressions on the faces around me as I remembered and weighed Carmilla's words and expressions. "No," I said finally. "I don't think she will."

There was something in his eyes that I hadn't seen before. Was it admiration? "I think you're right," he said. "And we must use this to our advantage. If she can't read your mind, and she won't kill you, we have a distinct advantage if you are with us when we hunt her."

"No! I won't put her in danger!" My father objected. "Not again." His words knocked the wind out of me. Had Josef been right? Was my father avoiding me because he was disappointed in *himself* rather than *me?*

The Baron rounded on him, his eyes flashing. "She will be less endangered than the rest of us, Edward. And her presence will cause the beast to hesitate, giving us a better chance of overcoming her. Don't you see?" He looked at me again. "Miss Bancroft, what do *you* think?"

I hesitated. It was one thing to give them the information they needed to hunt her. It was another to confront her myself and to witness – or even commit – the violence that would undoubtedly unfold. But the Baron was correct about my usefulness, and the conversation with Carmilla had made one thing very clear: if I wanted my family to survive, Carmilla would have to die. "I'll do whatever I can," I said finally.

There it was again, in the brief smile that played on his lips. Admiration. My father, meanwhile, was looking fixedly away from us, struggling not to let his terror show.

"We have reason to believe she might be in the Karnstein village," Josef said as he wiped down one of the guns with a rag. "What do you think of this hypothesis, Laura?"

"It makes sense. She'll need a place where she can feed, and she won't want to go far."

"Our thoughts precisely," the Baron agreed. "Dangerous though it may be, one of us must go and investigate; if it turns out she's there, we'll go after her together."

"I'll go," Martin said.

"Absolutely not," my father protested. "This is not your fight, Martin. You have served this household tirelessly and selflessly for many years, and I will not permit you to put yourself in danger on our behalf."

"It's just as much my fight as it is yours," Martin said calmly. "This is my home, and the creature is a threat to my family, as well. Besides, I know these woods like the back of my hand, and I know the people in the village. I can make quick work of it."

My father sighed and shook his head. "I don't like it, but you're right."

"Good," the Baron said. "That's settled. Go now, Martin, while it is still morning, as the creature is more likely to be in a state of rest."

"Why can't you all go?" Adeline asked.

The Baron frowned. "It will take quite a bit of effort to get all of us there with our arsenal. If she's not there, that effort will be wasted, and that is something we cannot afford."

"I don't like this," Adeline said anxiously. She embraced Martin. He kissed her forehead and spoke reassuring words under his breath, and she nodded, tears streaming down her cheeks. Then he parted from her, slung a crossbow and a quiver of arrows over his shoulders, and headed briskly through the front door, over the salt line, and into the woods.

Once he had disappeared from view, the Baron turned to me, gestured toward the arsenal of weapons, and asked, "Miss Bancroft, do you know how to use any of these weapons?"

I shook my head.

"Well," he said, "now may be the only time we can remedy that. General Spielsdorf, bring that shotgun here."

Martin surprised us all when he returned in an hour and a half, gasping for air as though he had run the whole way. Adeline threw her arms around him in relief when he made it over the salt line and into the courtyard, where we were practicing shooting crossbows.

"She's there," he panted, putting his hands on his knees. "I didn't even have to go all the way into the village. I came across a woodcutter's family on the outskirts of the village, fleeing in this direction. I told them, sir, that they could come here, and that they would be given shelter. I hope you don't mind."

"Of course not," my father assured him.

Martin gratefully took several deep gulps from a cup of water Adeline had offered him. "The eldest son, Matthias, told us that the creature returned last night and settled herself in the old Karnstein schloss. First she woke nearly everyone in the village with her inhuman shrieking. Then she held everyone in the village in an invisible grip. Their feet were frozen to the ground, though they screamed and fought with all their might to escape. Then she called one of the men to her, forcing his legs to bring him into her house. He did not come out again. Then she called a woman...then another woman...then a child...Her thirst must have let up finally, because near dawn the callings stopped, and an hour later the villagers found themselves released from her grip. They gathered as many of their things as they could and fled in different directions. Well, most of them. Matthias said that the family members of those who were summoned have remained, clinging to the hope that the creature's victims might still be alive."

"She must have fallen asleep," the Baron said. "We have no time to waste. Quickly, everyone, gather your weapons. Father Schmidt, bring a lantern and some vessels of oil, so that we may burn the creature when the time comes."

Martin, still out of breath, immediately began scanning the arsenal of weapons we had brought outside. Adeline and my father exchanged a glance.

"You must stay here," Adeline urged her husband. "You are tired already; what good will you do?"

Martin opened his mouth to argue, but my father interrupted. "Yes, Martin. You are needed here at the house. Otherwise, who will receive and protect the villagers who make their way here?"

Martin bowed his head, his expression a mixture of disappointment and relief. "Yes, sir." Adeline inclined her head appreciatively at my father and led Martin into the house.

The rest of us gathered our weapons and set forth, crossing the barrier of salt and heading in haste toward danger and – for one of us – death.

The village was eerily still, its silence unnatural in the bright daylight. As we drew closer, however, this silence became less absolute, peppered with the helpless sobs of the villagers who had imprisoned themselves in their houses at the outskirts of town (as if a locked door would keep them safe). A few of them watched from windows or doorways as we walked by. They shouted at us with relief and alarm.

"Please, save my Lena, if you can," one woman begged. Her tears had left white streaks down her dirt-smeared face.

"We will try our best," Father Schmidt replied. "You must turn your thoughts to the Lord and pray for us."

The Baron hissed, "We must be quiet. Remember the plan."

We had argued the plan on the way to the village, with the Baron suggesting that I go into the house alone to find Carmilla. If I could not lure her outside, I could at least inform the others of her location. But my father and Josef had flatly refused to send me into the house by myself.

"If the creature plans to attack the girl," the Baron had protested, "she is not less likely to do so if the rest of us are nearby. Meanwhile, if we all go in without knowing her location, and she finds *us* before we find *her*, it will be that much easier for her to slaughter us."

"I don't care!" my father had shouted, and the determined set of Josef's face beside him suggested that the General was entirely in agreement. "I will not send my daughter in alone!"

"She will hear us all as soon as we enter!" the Baron had complained.

"She will hear you all anyway," I had noted. "She can hear your thoughts from miles away when she is at full strength. And if it's true that she has fed on those villagers she abducted, I have no doubt that she *is* at full strength."

The Baron had pondered this for a moment, and the sound of the twigs crunching beneath our feet had suddenly seemed very loud indeed.

"Mightn't that be to our advantage, Baron?" Father Schmidt had ventured. The incongruity of a priest walking with a gun slung over his shoulders, holding a lantern with which he hoped to set someone aflame, struck me again, as it had done several times since we left the schloss. I felt the incongruity no less sharply as I looked down at the unfamiliar crossbow in my hands. I had chosen it for its relative lightness (it was the smallest one the men had brought), and because I hadn't managed to acquire the skill of reloading a gun in the brief minutes I had been given to practice doing so. The bag over my shoulder was heavy with bandages, rope, and a sharp dagger. Its weight was too real for this to be a dream.

"It might," the Baron had responded. "It's possible that in her rage she has fed to excess. I have no experience with the feeling myself, but I have heard that the act of blood-drinking renders a vampire intoxicated." He had looked at me for confirmation, but I had avoided his gaze. "At any rate," he had continued, "it may be that, after glutting herself, she is suffering from the effects of over-intoxication."

"Well then," my father had said, "we must pray that this is the case."

"Once we wound her, even if it is only a minor wound, her abilities will begin to falter," the Baron had continued. "If we are persistent in our attack, if we can overwhelm her with several small injuries, eventually we can disarm her powers of compulsion and limit her to her human form. And then we will have the opportunity to destroy her."

We had planned, then, to enter the Karnstein house as quietly as we could manage. If she was asleep, we reasoned, she would not necessarily be alarmed by our thoughts, but physical noise would be likely to rouse her. Then we would spread out in search of her, shouting out to the others if we found her. This was all assuming, of course, that we were right about her potential intoxication, and that she wasn't already lying in wait for us, in which case she'd be able to silence any of us well before we could alert the others. My skin crawled at the thought, and my stomach fluttered with the animal instinct to flee.

Now, the house loomed silently as we approached, and it seemed entirely possible that Carmilla was indeed asleep or otherwise incapacitated. There was no sound coming from within its walls, no movement but the occasional fluttering of tattered curtains in the windows that had long since been broken. Terrified of what was to come, I found myself hoping that we would enter the house and search in vain, discovering that she was no longer there.

The front door was hanging open slightly. Why shouldn't it, when the only danger was *inside?* The Baron put his ear to the opening for several seconds, then shook his head to indicate that he didn't hear anything. Pushing the door open the rest of the way, we moved cautiously into the house. We fanned out in different directions and crept through the hallways, holding our weapons before us. My father stayed close behind me. Each door we opened let out the cold, musty breath of long abandonment. Father Schmidt opened the door to the kitchen, and the squeaking of what sounded like hundreds of rats pierced the air. The Baron and Josef disappeared down the hallway in the other direction. My father and I made our way up the stairs. One of the steps creaked beneath my foot, and we froze, holding our breaths and straining our ears for the inevitable sound of Carmilla swooping down upon us. When it did not come, we pressed on.

I found her in the second room on the left. The door swung open to reveal a jumbled mass of limbs on the bed, arms and legs tangled, feet and hands sticking out at odd angles. Atop the mass was a white-clad form, face-down, dark hair spilling down the grotesque pile.

I shouted for the others, turning to allow my father access to the room. But he was frozen in the act of peering into the bedroom, his eyes unseeing, his ears unhearing.

The white-clad form began to move, slowly raising itself atop the pile. The black hair swept up along the bloodless face of one of the corpses, a young girl's face, unmoving as the hair passed through her gaping mouth and over her glassy eyes. Carmilla rose up on her hands and knees, then sat back on her heels. She tottered slightly as if balancing on the pile was difficult. Then she sighed, smiled serenely to herself, and looked at me. When she spoke, her words were slow and syrupy. "Oh, my love, I knew you would come."

There was something coiled in her, like a serpent preparing to strike. I grasped at my father behind me, desperately trying to shake him to consciousness. I shouted in alarm again, but there was no reply. She must have immobilized the others, too. Icy fear ran up my spine. Where was the Baron?

She laughed then, a girlish giggle that was belied by the gleaming, utterly black voids of her eyes. Her long, sharp teeth were stained with blood, and she licked them with her tongue, moaning with pleasure. "Did you think you could *surprise* me, Laura?" She flopped back on top of the bodies, stretching languidly over them as though they were pillows.

"Why didn't you stop us, then?" I asked, my heart racing. "Why not kill us long before we reached this house?"

"Because I'm ever so tired," she whined. "It's hard work, you know, slaughtering innocents." She laughed again, and I realized that the Baron's supposition had been correct. She was deeply intoxicated. But how could I use it to my advantage?

"Carmilla, you know we came here to kill you?"

"Yes." She rolled off the pile and abruptly pushed it over, spilling the corpses off the bed as easily as if she had been shaking out a sheet. The thud of limbs and skulls upon the floor sickened me, and I averted my gaze from their sprawled forms. "And you must know that you all will end up like *them*," she said calmly. She bent her head back and stared up at the ceiling, her eyes nearly rolling back in her head, and then she moaned. Her feet lifted from the ground and she hovered, suspended several inches in the air. "It's so *much*," she whispered to herself as the glut of blood overwhelmed her.

I fought to push down the terror that was threatening to immobilize me. Someone had to do this. Someone had to deal with her. "Do you really mean to kill *all* of us? Even me?" I asked. "You promised you would never hurt me."

Her feet touched the floor again, and she stared at me in consternation, saying nothing. The thin patches of daylight streaming through the threadbare curtains darkened as a cloud passed over the sun. She smiled and raised an eyebrow just as the Baron barreled into the room, raising his crossbow. Her body shifted, swirling into her shadow form, and she slipped through the shattered window. The Baron's arrow lodged itself in the wall on the far side of the room.

Behind me, my father jerked and gasped, released from Carmilla's compulsion. I grabbed his hand and pulled him in the direction of the stairs "She's outside! She's outside!" I shouted through the echoing halls.

The Baron hurtled down the stairs beside us. "What took you so long?" my father asked him.

"She compelled Josef to grab me!" he exclaimed.

Josef and Father Schmidt met us at the bottom and raced with us through the front door and into the street.

"What happened?" Josef asked.

But there was no time to tell him, because now Carmilla's laughter was coming from behind us. We clutched our weapons and whirled in panic. She was perched on the roof, sneering down at us.

"Now!" The Baron called. The men raised their weapons and sent a volley of arrows and bullets at Carmilla.

She dodged everything with ease and shrieked with glee as they all bent to reload. "I don't know if I'm more impressed by your courage or astounded by your foolhardiness, thinking you could come here – to *my* village – and overtake me. I thought for sure I would have to come to *you*; I was waiting for the rain to wash away that charming little barrier of yours. Although"—she looked up at the dark clouds that were gathering in the sky—"it looks like that may be happening sooner rather than later."

Fear shot through my chest like an arrow. If it did rain, if the salt were washed away, she could get back to the schloss much more quickly than we could, and everyone there, including the villagers seeking refuge, would be in danger.

The Baron sent another arrow at her chest, but she swatted it away like a fly. "Baron Vordenburg," she said appreciatively. She crouched on all fours as if to get a better view of him, sniffed deeply, and gasped. "Oh! You are descended from Bruzek! How marvelous. I never got to kill that son-of-a-bitch, but it seems he did not escape my grasp entirely after all!"

"We have to get her down from there," the Baron muttered. "We can't make headway against her like this."

"But how?" my father demanded. "She's toying with us, and she has no reason to come closer. If she waits us out, we'll tire long before she does."

"It's quite a predicament you're in!" Carmilla sent down smugly.

"I think I know how," Josef scowled, stepping forward. Then he called out to the creature on the roof, "Miss Mueller! Do you remember me?"

She rose from her crouched position. "It's Karnstein. And how could I forget you, General Spielsdorf? I remember your little ward, too. Such *sweet* blood she had."

My heart twisted in my chest. Josef's stern face wavered for a moment, but he pressed on. "Did you know that we found your mother in London? It took us a while – she was cleverer than you, I think – but we finally found her." Carmilla's gleeful smirk twisted into anger; she had already read Josef's thoughts and knew what he was going to say. Nevertheless, he continued. "And it was *I* who severed her head from her body and sent her to hell where she belongs."

She threw her head back and screamed, an inhuman howl that shook the ground beneath us. Pain pierced my eardrums, and I dropped my crossbow and tried (unsuccessfully) to shield my ears with my palms. The others cried out in pain but managed to keep hold of their weapons. Now Carmilla was hurtling at Josef, shadows swirling behind her like huge black wings, her clawed fingers outstretched as she plummeted down. He began to raise his pistol, but he was not fast enough; I realized with horror that she was going to take him down before he could pull the trigger. Another gun roared, and Carmilla was knocked sideways and to the ground just before she had Josef in her clutches. Small red scratches blossomed on his face from where her claws had brushed his skin. The pellets did little harm beyond the initial impact, and she stood up and rounded on Father Schmidt, from whose shotgun wisps of smoke were curling.

"A priest?" she said in mock disbelief. Then she grinned again. "My favorite meal."

A volley of missiles from the others wiped the grin from her face. She howled in pain, staggering backwards with each impact. When they stopped to reload, she turned and ran toward the outskirts of town, impossibly fast. She seemed to be trying unsuccessfully to take on her shadow form, crying out in frustration as darkness sparked from her in a jerky rhythm.

"You were right," I said to the Baron, reaching down to pick up my crossbow. "She is weakened."

She headed toward one of the houses that still had villagers hiding in it. "Not for long," the Baron said grimly. "Come on."

We ran as fast as our burning legs and lungs would allow, but long before we had reached the house, the anguished, terrified screams of her victims spilled out into the road. "No!" I cried out, but my protest was in vain. She was already pulling out one of the house's inhabitants, still alive. We could see the crumpled, drained bodies of two others inside. Her face was that distorted, horrible mask, the bone structure distended upward, the carapace eyes hard and unfeeling, the sharp teeth stretched past her lower lip. We raised our weapons and took aim, but she held the screaming woman (Lena's mother, I realized) in front of her, preventing us from shooting. Draining the two people who now lay dead inside had restored some of her strength, though she had several wounds that were still dripping blood. She flew over the road, dragging the woman's heels in the dirt all the way to the church. The blackened front door swung open as she approached, and she and the struggling villager disappeared inside.

We ran again. By the time we reached the church, Carmilla had deposited the woman's body – now drained, the glassy eyes wide with terror – just inside the door. We gingerly stepped over the corpse to enter the chapel. We held our weapons in front of us and scanned the charred nave. Much of the church's structure was still standing, but the pews and the altar had been irreparably damaged. The ceiling of the church soared upward into shadow, a few wooden rafters still crossing the empty space between the two side walls. What must have once been magnificent stained-glass windows now gaped open, and small pieces of colored glass littered the floor, like gems. I wondered if the fire had not been hot enough to melt them, or if they had been saved by the rain. There was no sign of Carmilla, and I sent a questioning look toward my father, who was, as ever, beside me. He shook his head, just as perplexed as I.

Our group crept cautiously forward, breath held in fear and anticipation, charred bits of wood and glass crunching beneath our shoes. Suddenly a chorus of high-pitched screeches came from above us. We froze, our panicked eyes locked on the dark recesses above the rafters, and an amorphous cloud of small, shrieking, fluttering creatures swooped down from the shadows upon us. *Bats.* We waved our hands in panic to ward them off. They swirled around us before skittering upward and pouring through the open windows.

Carmilla's laughter echoed above us, emanating from that dark region whence the bats had come. We aimed our weapons in the direction of the sound, and she stopped abruptly. Silence. One breath...two breaths....three.

The mass of shadows plummeted down at the Baron, coalescing into solid form and stretching forth its harpy-like talons as it obliterated the distance between them. Her claws plunged into his shoulder and neck before a bolt from my father's crossbow struck her between the shoulder blades. She flew upward again, tearing away chunks of the Baron's skin from his flesh as she went. The Baron stumbled back and landed hard on the ground. He clutched at his neck as blood poured between his fingers.

"Don't let her out of your sight!" My father shouted to Josef. The two of them trained their weapons on the space above the rafters, while Father Schmidt and I ran to the wounded man and rummaged through our packs for some clean cloths.

"I've got it," the Baron said. The white cloth he was holding against his own neck was becoming saturated with blood alarmingly quickly. "You two must fight."

I turned to join the others and cried out in surprise to see that Carmilla was fully visible now, sitting casually on a rafter with her white legs dangling. But my father and Josef weren't shooting at her, and Father Schmidt, though he had raised his gun, couldn't pull the trigger. Sweat beaded their brows as they fought against her compulsion, unable to master themselves. Behind me, the Baron gasped with fear.

I stared at the arrow whose tip I could see peeking through the skin at the bottom of her neck. It had gone in too high to pierce the heart. "How?" I cried. "You're supposed to be weakened!"

Carmilla looked down at the arrow. "Oh, this?" She grasped the tip and pulled it forward through her body with a sickening squelch.

She tossed it down, then followed it herself, floating down from the rafter to the ground. She walked calmly past my father and Josef as they grunted in frustration. "I *am* weakened. But I'm still stronger than you ever could have imagined. You see, I've just consumed quite a lot of blood in a short period of time." She drew closer to Father Schmidt, her eyes dancing in anticipation. "And I'm about to consume even more." I raised my crossbow and let the bolt fly, but she swatted it away with ease. "Really, Laura, it's like you're not even trying."

She knocked the gun from Father Schmidt's hands and took him into her deadly embrace, clutching him as she flew back up into the rafters. Our shouts of despair echoed ineffectually through the chapel. My father and Josef cursed their inability to move, the Baron, immobilized still by his wound, hurled vehement insults at Carmilla. Father Schmidt screamed in agony once. Then we heard the creature gulping and moaning with gluttonous pleasure.

Then silence.

A sob caught in my throat.

Father Schmidt's lifeless body crashed down into the blackened pews. His limbs, as limp as a scarecrow's, splintered the wood with the force of the impact. I screamed. Carmilla jumped down after him, stood on his chest, and straightened, her black eyes fixed on Josef. "Now," she growled, "for the man who killed my mother."

I hurled myself at Josef and knocked him over with my momentum. He grunted in pain, and my elbow hit the ground with a crunch, but I ignored the agony shooting through my arm and whirled to face Carmilla, shielding Josef's body with my own. "No!" I screamed.

Her face danced with amusement, her clawed hands stretched out at her sides. "You think you can stop me?"

I reached into the bag hanging at my hip, frantically seeking the knife I had hidden there. The edge of the knife sliced my fingertip when I clumsily grabbed at the handle, and I cried out in pain, but she was closing the gap between us impossibly fast. I grasped the knife, held it before me with both hands, and pressed the tip into Carmilla's chest as she leaned over me.

She looked down at it and raised her eyebrows. "You wouldn't."

"Wouldn't I?" My arms were trembling uncontrollably. She leaned forward, daring me to hurt her. Blood welled around the knife tip. Mustering every ounce of strength within me, I thrust it forward, feeling it sink wetly into her flesh.

It didn't kill her; I hadn't thrust deep enough. But it hurt, and, more importantly, it surprised her. Her eyes widened with shock, and she yelped, jumped away, and lost her hypnotic control of the others. My father let fly an arrow from his crossbow. It pierced through her neck, the arrowhead bursting from the other side with a spray of blood. Josef rolled me from his chest, sat up, and aimed his pistol at her face. The shot exploded next to my ear, knocking me sideways. The bullet tore half of Carmilla's face away. One eye was gone, replaced by a pulpy mess of pink flesh and white bone, and her nasal cavity and jaw gaped through ragged red holes. She fumbled in vain at the arrow in her neck, and the scream of panic that ripped forth from her bloody maw shook the very rafters above our heads. Her body was flickering between shadow and substance; she was trying to take on her incorporeal form, but her injuries were sapping her strength. The

Baron shouted to my father and Josef to shoot her again, and they bent forward and hastened to reload.

Carmilla dashed away from us, hissing, and quicker than lightning she was gone. The door of the church swung wildly in her wake.

We sat in silence, trembling. The Baron rested his head on the floor and closed his eyes. He was horrifyingly pale. The cloth at his neck was completely saturated, and dark blood dripped onto the floor. My father and Josef panted, trying to catch their breath. I lowered my head into my hands, feeling sorrow and desperation well up inside me. Even without looking at him, I couldn't shake the image of Father Schmidt's bloodless, broken body from my mind. We had failed. I wanted to scream.

"We'll have to try again, and soon," the Baron wheezed. "She is wounded badly enough that we might have a chance."

Josef scoffed.

My father gestured at Father Schmidt's body. "If she's going to go through us like *this,* we're going to need more help."

CHAPTER TWENTY-ONE
REINFORCEMENTS

"Sophie," I said. I rubbed my temples and stared through the parlor window at the line of salt outside. It was, thankfully, still intact, though the rumbling clouds underscored the precarious nature of our safety. Our return from the village, hindered by Father Schmidt's corpse and the Baron's weakness, had been much slower than our initial departure, and now night was drawing itself across the sky. "We need Sophie. Then at least there will be another of us who can resist Carmilla's compulsions."

Baron Vordenburg, who was reclining in the chaise as Adeline changed the bandage at his neck again, grunted in assent. For the first time in twenty-five years, my father had needed to recall his skills as an army medic to give the Baron a rudimentary set of stitches. The bleeding had stopped, though he was so weak and pale that we were gravely concerned about his recovery.

"Do we have time?" My father asked.

"We might," the Baron whispered weakly. "I imagine it will take Carmilla some time to heal. And the sky appears to be holding...for now."

"I suppose it depends on where Sophie is," I said. "Does anyone know?"

My father shook his head. "No, and I'm afraid she won't be willing to help us anyway, given the circumstances of her departure."

We heard the shuffle of feet outside the parlor door, and then Maria's voice, speaking to one of the villagers who had arrived seeking refuge. In our absence, our servants had made haste to prepare the unused guest rooms for the new arrivals, but the additions to the household only added to our anxieties. The situation felt worrisome at best and unsustainable at worst.

Adeline cleared her throat. "I know where she is. At least, I know where she might be." My father's eyebrows lifted in surprise. Adeline continued. "We've been exchanging letters since she left. She's in Gratz. Or, at least, she was quite recently. She was planning to depart for Munich, last I heard, but I don't know if she's managed to make all the arrangements."

Gratz! It was so close. My spirit soared with hope.

"And will she help us, do you think?" my father asked.

Adeline shrugged. "She may indeed, sir. Regardless of her feelings toward *you*, I'm sure she would appreciate the opportunity to get her hands on the creature." She shook her head. "I'm such a fool. She wrote so vehemently about Carmilla, and I always shrugged it off as no more than a personal grudge."

"I'm sure we all have reasons to regret our past ignorance," Josef said grimly from the chair by the fire. "There's naught to do about it now but to make sure the things we suffered have not been in vain."

"Indeed," my father said. He pressed his lips together in determination. "I have an idea. Adeline, do you think Martin would accompany me to Gratz?"

"I'm sure he would, sir."

"Good. It would be safest if we leave immediately, while the creature is still healing from her wounds. We'll take the large carriage together with the small one, so we can transport the villagers to the city. We don't need to endanger them, too."

"Leave now?" Adeline protested. "It's already night."

"We have no time to waste."

"I'll fetch Martin and tell our guests to ready themselves for departure," Adeline said. "Shall I ask Bettina and Maria if they'd like to leave, as well?"

"An excellent thought, Adeline. What about you?"

She smiled. "I could not leave my husband, sir, and I know he will not leave *you*."

I worried that I wouldn't be able to sleep, given my father's absence and the dire nature of the situation, but I was exhausted, body and soul. Bettina, to my surprise, had chosen to stay with us, though Maria had made the more prudent decision to leave. Bettina had explained that the outside world held no refuge for her, despite our urgent entreaties that she ought not to endanger herself. I was thankful for her presence now, for she had set a cloth and a fresh basin of water on my dresser. After washing myself, I lay on my bed and wept with deep, aching grief. I mourned for Carmilla's victims, nausea rising in my throat as I thought of the pain and fear they must have felt as their lives slipped away in the creature's clutches. But I mourned for myself and for Carmilla too, for the loss of what I had thought she was, the loss of our joy together. Soon, I felt myself slipping into unconsciousness.

I awoke the next morning surprisingly refreshed, though I was anxious about what had transpired during my slumber. I glanced outside and noted with relief that the clouds, though still ominous, had not yet broken. The salt line was still there.

The halls of the house were empty, the faint clanking of cooking utensils in the kitchen the only thing that suggested anyone was still with me. It reminded me of the lonely mornings from my childhood, and I felt the loss of Carmilla's company – Carmilla the woman, not Carmilla the monster – even more sharply.

I found Josef and the Baron still in the parlor. Josef was sitting at the window, his eyes deeply shadowed with exhaustion. He must have kept watch all night. The Baron was snoring lightly, still propped up in the chaise.

Josef smiled wanly as I entered. "I can keep watch now," I said gently. "You need to get some rest."

He shook his head. "I don't think I could sleep if I tried. Besides, Father Schmidt needs to be buried."

I wavered on my feet. "I will help you."

Josef gave me a skeptical look, knowing full well that I hadn't dug much of anything before, much less a grave. "You don't need to, Laura. I can do it myself."

"I know you can. But I *want* to. I want to help lay him to rest."

We forced down some breakfast, shouldered two shovels from the arsenal in the front hall, and headed outside. Unfortunately, the limited diameter of the salt circle made it impossible to bury him in the small cemetery that was just beyond the chapel, but we found a quiet spot on the side of the house, within the protective barrier, that would suffice for now.

Once Josef had shown me how to use the shovel most effectively and had marked out the plot, we applied ourselves to the mournful task. My elbow still ached from my crushing fall the day before, and I was unaccustomed to such physical labor; it wasn't long before my arms began to tremble and blisters began to swell on my hands from the wooden weight of the shovel. *My hands never held a weapon before yesterday, either,* I thought. Still, my lot was preferable to Father Schmidt's, and it would dishonor him to complain about the effort it took to ensure he was buried properly. I pushed down the physical pain and drove the shovel into the earth with even more effort, grunting as I lifted each pile of dirt from the ever-expanding grave. Josef's wide face, so tight with determination that it was nearly a scowl, dripped with sweat. He, too, worked in silence. After an hour or so, Adeline brought us some water, which we drank gratefully before returning to our task. She watched us work for several minutes, went into the house, and came back with her own shovel to help us.

We finished near noon. Josef carried Father Schmidt's slight, canvas-wrapped body to the grave himself, though there was no graceful way to lower him in. The irony of burying the one person who could perform funeral rites properly was not lost on any of us. Nevertheless, Adeline and Josef tried their best, and I did not think that Father Schmidt would fault their efforts. Then came the awful task of covering the body with the mounds of dirt we had excavated. The finality of it – the way the earth seemed to swallow him, erasing any trace of his existence – shook me, and I gazed regretfully at the grave for a long time, resting my hands atop the shovel handle.

"There's one thing I don't understand," Josef said quietly, after Adeline had gone back inside. Then, with an ironic chuckle, "Well, I guess there are many things I don't understand. But one thing that maybe *you* can help explain."

I turned to face him.

"My servants didn't remember anything about Carmilla or Anna. The whole time they were at my house is like...like a blank spot in their memories. Did they...did they change their memories somehow?"

Carmilla's words from two nights before rang in my mind. *Memories are a tricky thing.* I remembered, too, her account of her rebirth as a vampire, how she and Alexander had had to influence the villagers to perceive her as someone new rather than try to change their recollection of her death and funeral.

"They might have. But Carmilla told me it can be difficult to erase memories – especially the memories of many people at once – in a way that keeps them from resurfacing. It's more likely they did something to change your servants' *perceptions*, making it so that the memories could never form in the first place."

"I see. Well, I guess my question is: why didn't they do the same to me? It seems like a lot of...*this*"— he gestured vaguely —"could have been avoided."

"Carmilla made a lot of choices I don't understand," I remarked bitterly. Then I sighed. "I suspect it had something to do with Anna's feelings for you."

"What do you mean?"

"Carmilla told me that *she* wanted to kill you, but her mother wouldn't allow it because she loved you. If that's the case, then Anna probably chose not to influence you, either. She would have wanted to know your feelings for her were real. It was one of the things Carmilla said she loved about *me,* the fact that I couldn't be influenced, the fact that I desired her of my own accord."

"Much good it did either of us," he noted darkly.

We went back into the house. I washed myself in my bedroom, grimacing at the pain of scrubbing the dirt from the blisters on my hands. After donning fresh clothes, I joined Adeline and Josef and the Baron in the parlor, where Bettina brought us some simple sandwiches for lunch. The Baron's state had improved, and he spoke occasionally to us as we ate, though he himself was limited to the consumption of broth. Eventually, Josef nodded off in the chair beside the window, and Adeline put a finger to her lips to silence the Baron so that Josef could rest.

An hour later, we heard the clatter of hooves approaching. Roused by the noise, Josef stood hastily, muttering that he needed to close the circle after the carriage wheels broke it. Adeline and I ran outside – I whimpered at the stiffness of my aching muscles – and met the small carriage as it came to a halt in the courtyard. Martin was in the driver's seat, looking very much like he hadn't slept at all since last I saw him (nor would he have, I realized, if he had driven the whole way). Adeline took the reins and whip from him as he climbed down, then enfolded him in a relieved embrace. My father opened the carriage door and hopped out, then immediately turned to offer his hand to someone who was inside. A slender, long-fingered brown hand clasped his, and Sophie stepped down from the carriage.

Relief surged through me, and I ran forward to embrace her. She had never been effusive with her affections, even in the best of circumstances, and she held herself somewhat stiffly in my arms now. "I'm so sorry," I whispered.

She patted my back. "Nevermind that now."

I stepped back so I could see her face again. "I was worried you wouldn't come."

"When I discovered the truth, how could I not? I cannot fault you or your father for decisions you made under her influence. And," she continued, the slightest hint of a smile reaching her eyes, "I will not deny that it is good to see you again, my dear girl, though I wish it were under better circumstances."

My attention was pulled away from Sophie when I realized that someone else was coming out of the carriage, too, someone sandy-haired and burly. *Elias.*

I flew at him, nearly knocking him off his feet. He stood immobile for a moment. Then he chuckled and enfolded me in his strong arms.

My ear was pressed against his chest, and I could hear the steady thumping of his heart. Hot tears stung my eyes.

I stepped back and looked up into his face. "Why did you come? You didn't need to endanger yourself for my sake, not after...everything."

"Who says I'm doing it for you?" he teased. "You know my parents live here, right?"

I lowered my eyes, chagrined. He pulled me into another hug, resting his cheek on the top of my head. "Ah, I shouldn't tease you so. You know me better than that, don't you? Even if my parents weren't here, I would have come. I'm not one to sit idly by when...when someone I love is in danger."

Gratitude and relief flooded through me. The fact that *either* of them had come was astonishing, and the unexpected gift of it made me wonder if we actually had a fighting chance against Carmilla.

Everyone who had arrived in the carriage retired to their bedrooms, having had little sleep since the previous day. Josef offered to keep watch again at the parlor window, but his head fell onto his chest shortly after he sat down. The Baron and I kept watch in his stead. I knew that it pained the Baron to speak, so I refrained from conversation. But when he broke the silence to marvel at the fact that the weather was still holding despite the menacing clouds in the sky, my curiosity got the better of me. I asked him about the Order of Perseus. He explained that it was an organization dedicated to ridding the world of evil supernatural entities. Every male member of his family from Bruzek onward had been blessed with the ability to resist psychic compulsion, making them extraordinarily valuable to the Order, and he had been raised from infancy with the expectation that he would devote himself to their mission, too.

"And was this what you *wanted* to do with your life?" I asked.

"I never knew any different. And I can't imagine something more worthy. Who knows the number of human lives that have been saved by the actions of the Order?"

"Where is this Order? In London, where the General found you?"

"Not solely. There are outposts in every major city in Europe. Our numbers have been dwindling, however. As our efforts have found success around the world, the demand for our knowledge and skills has lessened. I am one of the few members of the Order who remain in London, and the only one who was able to answer the General's call for help so quickly. Still, I can't wait to inform the others of the death of the Karnstein beasts."

I swallowed, even now discomfited by how nonchalantly he spoke of their demise.

He cleared his throat. Then, tentatively: "You know, you're not what I expected. The way you protected Josef in the church...He told me you were a shy thing."

I raised an eyebrow. "Well, perhaps in the future you will know not to confuse introversion with weakness."

"Indeed," he said with a snort. Then he winced with pain, and, with a gesture toward his throat, indicated that he wished to speak no more.

There were nine of us now, so putting together a dinner was no small feat, especially when there was little time to plan, dwindling supplies, and no Maria to contribute her expertise. Nevertheless, Bettina and Adeline accomplished it neatly, and a fragrant meal had been set in the dining room by the time the clock struck eight. We conversed with remarkable cheer as we consumed the food, the imminent danger urging us to take pleasure while we could. For my part, burying Father Schmidt had caused my lifelong anxiety – the understanding that death was an indifferent entity that could strike suddenly and without compunction – to rear its ugly head. As if to defy this anxiety, I gazed gratefully at the faces of those around the table and drank in their words. Sitting beside me, Elias squeezed my hand warmly.

Finally, Sophie brought us back to the task at hand. She leaned back in her chair, placed her napkin on her plate, and asked, "So, how do we proceed?" My father had used the time in the carriage to inform her and Elias of what had transpired thus far, but none of us had yet voiced any suggestion of what might happen next.

Everyone looked at the Baron expectantly. "We will wait for her here," his voice rasped. "She will undoubtedly come. She wants Josef's blood...and mine. If we're lucky, we'll have more time before the rain destroys the circle. If we're luckier, we'll have even more time while she heals herself. We must use this time to rest and prepare ourselves as best we can. But eventually she will come. There are a few things we learned in our previous confrontation with her that are important for us to know: first, she is powerful enough to control *all* of us with her mind at once, except for me and Miss Bancroft and – if the creature's own words are to be trusted – you, Mademoiselle De LaFontaine. Because I am wounded, it will be up to you both to find a way to wound her. It's a pity that we don't have someone with greater physical strength than the two of you to rely on for this."

"The strongest man in the world would be nothing compared to Carmilla," I reminded him.

"I suppose you're right, Miss Bancroft. Laura." His wound still made speaking at length difficult; he cleared his throat and took a drink of water before continuing. "But if you two can find a way to weaken her, it will loosen her control on the others."

Sophie drew in a shaky breath and looked at me nervously. "Well then, I suppose that's what we'll have to do."

"Do you have any experience with weapons, Mademoiselle?" The Baron continued.

"No."

The Baron tsked. "Well, let's hope the rain holds off long enough for us to give you at least a rudimentary acquaintance with them."

"General Spielsdorf and I will see to that," my father volunteered, and Sophie bowed her head in appreciation.

"Is there anything else?" Elias asked.

The Baron shook his head.

"I believe there is," I ventured. Eight faces swiveled toward me in surprise. "When we were in the church, Carmilla could easily have pushed me aside to get to Josef. But she didn't. I have an idea for how we might use this to our advantage."

"Tell us."

I shook my head. "If I tell everyone, she will be able to read it in their minds. I will tell you and Sophie in private, and when the time comes, the others must simply do as we ask."

We stayed up past midnight so that my father and Josef could instruct Sophie in the use of some of our weapons. Being painfully aware of my own deficiencies in matters of violence, I joined them, as did Adeline and Bettina. The Baron, exhausted after the dinner conversation, stayed inside; the rest of us practiced in the cool night air of the courtyard, creating an arena of sorts by arranging lanterns in an ellipse around us. Elias had brought his smith's hammer, and I was astounded at his strength as I watched him swing it.

"That could do some damage," I marveled.

"Only if I get close enough," he said. "From what I understand, that's the difficult part. I wish I had more skill with the longer-range weapons, but I never really used a gun or a bow, even when we were hunting. It's too bad we can't make use of my snares."

"She is much larger than a rabbit, unfortunately," I noted.

He placed his hammer on the ground and crossed his arms. The two of us were standing at one end of the makeshift arena. At the other end, Adeline aimed a crossbow, fired at a target, and shouted excitedly when she hit the mark. "I don't know what's stranger," Elias said, "the existence of the vampire or the fact that my mother is shooting a crossbow."

"You're in remarkably good spirits."

He shrugged. "It's strange to say, but it's good to be home."

"It's good to have you here. It reminds me of simpler times."

His eyes danced mischievously. "You certainly know how to complicate things."

I chuckled. "You see? That's what I mean. It feels good to laugh."

He smiled, though there was a tinge of sadness in his eyes. "Surely you must have laughed with *her* sometimes."

Grief seeped coldly into my limbs. "I did. But it feels so long ago, or like it was never real in the first place."

He clasped my hand, and we continued watching the others practice.

He cleared his throat. "I meant to tell you. I have...there's a...there's a woman I'm courting. In Gratz."

"Oh?" I was surprised to feel tears stinging my eyes.

"Her family owns a bakery. Her name's Sara. I think you and your father would really like her."

"Well then, I hope we get the chance to meet her someday."

There was something in his expression I couldn't read in the obscure light from the flickering lanterns. Regret, perhaps?

"That's a good place to stop for the night," my father said from the other side of the arena. "If our luck holds, we can resume tomorrow. For now, we ought to get as much rest as we can."

"Let's set up a watch in shifts," Josef suggested. "If it starts raining or anything else changes, we'll need to know it."

"An excellent idea," my father said. "Laura, will you take first watch with me?"

"Yes, Father," I said with surprise. As he assigned the other shifts, my mind raced, wondering what on earth we could say to each other now.

The Baron was sleeping in the parlor, the fireplace blazing beside him. We did not wish to disturb him, and the light from the fire made it difficult to see the dark realm beyond the windowpane, so we decided to keep watch outside the front door instead. It was as dark as pitch, for the clouds were blocking both moon and stars, but it was not particularly cold. We sat on a pile of blankets and donned light jackets to keep us warm. Eventually, our eyes adjusted to the darkness, and we found that the dim light spilling from the windows of the house was enough to discern a good stretch of the area before us.

We were silent for a long while. Finally, my father spoke. "How are you, my dear?"

The warmth in his voice surprised me. "As well as can be expected, I suppose," I replied.

He didn't speak again for several breaths. Then he cleared his throat and continued. "I've been wanting to speak with you. I should have done so long since, but the situation has been so...so hectic." He paused, as if summoning strength. "At any rate, it seems imprudent to wait much longer. After all, we don't know what tomorrow will bring."

I felt a pang. Would he survive the next encounter? Would I?

He sighed and shifted on the blankets. "It seems I've been a fool, as Adeline and Josef informed me before dinner today. I didn't realize that my manner toward you had given you the impression that I was disappointed in you."

"Is that…is that not the case then?" The tightness that was binding my chest like a corset loosened ever so slightly.

He shook his head. "Truthfully, I *was* a little disappointed at first. When you said you already knew what Carmilla was, when you told us of your love affair and that you had let her drink from you…It surprised me, I suppose, because I didn't understand it. And I blamed myself, too, for putting you in this situation in the first place and for not recognizing the monster for what she was."

"And now?"

Even in the dark, I could see his cheeks move upward. "I still don't understand it, but neither did I understand my feelings for your mother, nor her feelings for me. And you are a sensible girl. If you say that your feelings were true, I trust that they were."

I inhaled shakily, stunned by his acceptance.

"I have *also* realized," he continued, "that if I had been in a similar situation – if I had found out your mother was a vampire when we were first falling in love – I wouldn't have pushed her away. To be honest, I would probably have begged her to make me a vampire, too, so we could be together forever." He sighed. "There is no limit, no moderation when it comes to love. No reason, either. How could I blame you for behaving the same way *anyone* would have?"

A sob caught in my throat, and I moved closer to him, resting my head on his shoulder. "I'm sorry. Even if what you say is true, even if I am not *to blame*, everything that has happened is still *because of* me."

"No." He lifted my chin with his hand so that I could see the earnestness in his face. "It's because of *her*. And you? The way you are standing up to her now...it's a sight to behold, Laura. I don't know how you have found that kind of strength. I know I never would have."

"I don't *feel* strong," I sighed. "Just scared. And sad." I laid my head on his shoulder again and looked out into the courtyard.

Something moved at the tree line. I stiffened, straining to see in the darkness.

"What is it?" My father asked.

"I saw something."

We held our breaths, watching and waiting in silence. A slender, white-clad form slipped from between the trees and began walking toward us with slow, sure steps. My father tightened his grip around his shotgun, even though Carmilla couldn't cross the salt barrier. I could still see the marks from where she had been wounded, but she must have completed most of the healing process, for she had two eyes again. She paced along the perimeter of the circle like a restless, caged animal, leering at us, and then at the sky. Her message, though unspoken, was clear: *This won't hold me forever.*

"Well," my father said grimly, "at least we know that, once it rains, we won't have to wait for long."

Somehow, this observation failed to bring either of us comfort.

CHAPTER TWENTY-TWO

CRISIS

The next morning was, by some miracle, still dry. On the one hand, the postponement of our fight against Carmilla left us anxious and restless; we were eager to achieve *some* sort of resolution. On the other hand, the delay gave the Baron the opportunity to recover more fully, as well as allowing us additional time to practice with our weapons. After breakfast, the Baron stayed inside, resting, while Bettina cleaned up the kitchen and began preparing our next meal. The rest of us practiced outside for hours, looking anxiously at the edge of the woods, though Carmilla had vanished with the dawn. Still sore from the labors of the last few days, I stopped after a mere half hour of target practice and sat in the same place where my father and I had kept watch the night before. I laid my head on the cool stones behind me, listening to the pleasant – if somewhat nervous – chatter between Elias and his parents, between Josef and my father and Sophie. A twinge of worry took my breath away. How many of us wouldn't live to see the light of another day? Should I have taken Carmilla's offer to stay with her, thereby ensuring their safety? I shuddered; I could never consign myself to existence with her, knowing her lies, her disregard for the sanctity of life. There was no guarantee that she would refrain from seeking vengeance on her mother's killers anyway. And I knew that every single person here would prefer to die than to see me become a monster, too.

A low growl of thunder rolled in like the distant rumble of galloping horses before it boomed over us, shook the ground beneath our feet, and echoed away across the tops of trees. We fell silent, our pulses quickening with the understanding of what was about to occur.

A drop of rain hit my arm, then another. Water splattered on the foliage around us, first at intervals, then in a crowded cacophony as the clouds opened and poured forth the long-awaited deluge. We scrambled to gather the weapons and strained our voices to communicate over the howl of the storm. We watched in horror as the line of salt melted away.

Once in the foyer, we armed ourselves and spread out along the windows at the front of the house, straining our eyes for any sign of Carmilla. The Baron hobbled in from where he had been resting in the parlor. Water dripped from our hair and clothes as we waited, and our panicked breaths fogged up the glass.

"I don't see her," Adeline said.

"We need to station someone at the back of the house," the Baron said. "She may try to enter that way."

"I'll go," Sophie said. "And Laura should stay here at the front. That way one of us can sound the alarm before she puts the others under compulsion."

"Don't forget the plan," I urged. "As soon as we see her coming our way, we need to get into our places."

Sophie nodded, then headed for the back of the house. Adeline, Martin, and Elias volunteered to go with her, leaving me with Josef, the Baron, my father, and Bettina, who was trembling violently as she and I went together to the dining room.

"Are you sure you want to do this?" I asked. "It's not too late for you to hide somewhere, stay out of sight."

"I'm sure." Her voice quavered. "From what you've told me, that wouldn't do much to keep me safe anyway."

I desperately wished there was something more I could do to keep her out of danger. Still, I appreciated her steadfast attention while we watched through the window for any movement.

We waited for half an hour, but there was no sign of Carmilla. From her behavior the night before, I had expected to see her marching – or flying – across the grass as soon as the protective circle dissolved. Indeed, that was what we were all prepared for. But this? This was much worse. It made me wonder if she was planning something that we hadn't anticipated. Not being able to see or predict the movements of one's enemy was a terrifying disadvantage. My stomach knotted with anxiety.

"Stay here," I said to Bettina. I ran to the front hall where the Baron and my father were stationed and asked, "What's happening?"

"Maybe she's asleep?" My father ventured.

"It's possible," the Baron said. "It's more likely she's toying with us, though. As soon as we look away, as soon as we relax in our vigilance, she will strike unseen. We mustn't let that happen. We must keep watch, must force her to give up her location."

"I'll tell the others," I said.

I made my way around the house, conveying the Baron's words to Josef – who was stationed in the parlor – and to Adeline, Martin, Elias, and Sophie, who had spread themselves between the kitchen, the rear entrance, and my father's office. Then I joined Bettina at the window in the dining room again. She nodded, wide-eyed, when I relayed the Baron's words to her. She tried to smile bravely. "Luckily, Miss Bancroft, I am very good at waiting."

So we waited. And waited. There was no movement outside but the splashing of rain and the swaying of branches in the wind. Occasionally, lightning flashed and the rumbling of thunder followed. When our legs started to ache, we pulled up chairs so that we could rest while we watched.

The horses in the stable whinnied, a high-pitched scream that cut through the sounds of the storm.

"Does that mean something, do you think, Miss Bancroft?" Bettina asked.

"It could. They could also just be nervous from the thunder."

The horses' agitation continued, and the repeated, distressed whinnies – so very akin to screams – only heightened our own anxiety. Beside me, Bettina sat back in her chair and closed her eyes.

"Perhaps I should go outside," I said. "To try to lure her in? I'm not sure how."

"Perhaps you should," Bettina responded. Her voice was lower than usual, from weariness, I thought. She stood and moved to the table, collapsing in one of the chairs there and resting her head on her folded arms, her knife clutched in one hand.

The skin on the back of my neck prickled. "Are you alright, Bettina?"

"I'm just so tired of all this," she said. "Aren't you tired of it, Laura? Don't you ever wonder...what's the point of fighting?"

A bolt of fear pierced my chest. Bettina had never called me Laura before. And her voice was lower, stronger. I raised my crossbow and aimed it at her. She lifted her head and grinned at me, and I shuddered to see Bettina's features twisted into an expression that was undeniably Carmilla's.

She stood up and walked toward me, dragging the point of her knife along the table. "When I thought you wouldn't wound me in the church, you proved me wrong. But I know...I *know*...that you will not harm *this* body. Thankfully, *I* feel no such compunction." She brought the edge of the knife to her opposite arm, punctured the tender flesh of the wrist, and sliced downwards. Blood pooled around the tip of the knife and spilled in ragged streaks along her white skin, dropping in a rain-like patter upon the floor.

I screamed for help. There was an immediate response, shouts of panic followed by hurried footsteps. I wondered why she hadn't made the others immobile. Had she reached the limit of her powers by occupying Bettina's body in this way?

"I do hope General Spielsdorf makes an appearance," she smiled. She raised her knife and turned to face the footsteps that were pounding in our direction. "I'd like to get a shot at him before *this* one bleeds out."

"Josef, no!" I screamed. But my warning came too late. The door flew open. My father was the first to fly into the room, with Josef following closely behind. The knife hissed through the air and lodged itself firmly in Josef's shoulder. He fell backwards, clutching the wound, and collided with Sophie, who was streaming in with the others. I pointed at Bettina. "Grab her!" My father and Martin took hold of her and forced her to her knees while Elias attempted to bind her hands behind her with rope.

"There's so much blood," Elias gasped. He kept trying to pull the knots tight, but his fingers were slipping in the dark blood pouring from Bettina's wrist.

Sophie was sitting on the floor just outside the doorway, supporting Josef, who winced as Adeline knelt to check his wound.

Bettina – Carmilla – was laughing.

The Baron stepped over Josef's legs as he entered the room, his expression fierce. "What happened?" he asked.

"She's *in* her somehow," I cried. "Controlling her like some kind of puppet."

The astonishment on the Baron's face made it clear that he hadn't been prepared for such a possibility. Terror seized me again. We were not ready for this. How could we ever be? "You said she fed from her once," he said. "That must have created some sort of bond between them."

"What do we do?" my father asked. Bettina's body struggled against the restraints.

"Nothing," the Baron said. "The way she's bleeding, she will die soon, and Carmilla will have to find someone else to possess."

Bettina's face was rapidly growing paler. The puddle of blood expanded inexorably beneath her. "On the other hand," Carmilla said through Bettina's mouth, "a human body *does* have its limitations." As if to make her point, she bucked against the ropes. Finding that she still could not budge them, she grunted in frustration. She went rigid, her neck straining impossibly upwards. Then Carmilla's expression vanished from Bettina's features, leaving behind something entirely human and very much in pain, and Bettina collapsed onto the ground.

My feet slipped in the dark pool as I knelt to comfort her. "Cut her loose!" I urged.

"No! It could be a trick," the Baron said. "She could be waiting to possess her again."

Bettina was losing consciousness. My father fell to his knees beside me and began slapping her cheeks to try to keep her awake. "If she does, we will bind her again!" I screamed. "But we can't just let her die!" Elias pulled his knife and sawed at the knots until they burst open, sending droplets of blood everywhere.

My father inspected Bettina's wrist and shook his head. "I can't sew it up. Not quickly enough, at any rate. The wound is too long, too deep."

"Is there anything we *can* do?" My voice was nearly a whisper.

"I'll try bandaging it, but it may not help. She's lost so much blood already." He removed a roll of linen from the pack that was slung across his body and set to work, wrapping her wrist tightly. Each layer of white cloth was already soaked with dark blood by the time the next layer was applied. "Go check on Josef," he said grimly.

My legs shook beneath me, but I stood.

"Mr. Fischer," the Baron said to Martin, "you and your son must keep watch. While we are tending to our wounded, the vampire may find another way to attack."

Martin hastened to the window; Elias headed into the hallway to keep watch from another viewpoint. Adeline was getting ready to pull the knife from Josef's shoulder as I approached. I was relieved to see that he was alert and that the knife had inflicted only minor – if painful – damage. He was even giving Adeline suggestions for how to do it most effectively. Sophie was still sitting behind him, supporting him.

"What can I do?" I asked.

Sophie handed me the wad of clean linen she was holding. "Here. You're at a better angle."

With a grunt and a curse from Josef, Adeline pulled the knife out. Once she was clear of the wound, I applied the cloth. Adeline discarded the knife, unrolled some lengths of bandaging, and looped it around Josef's shoulder and arm until it was secure.

"Can you stand?" Sophie asked.

He sat forward and took my and Adeline's hands, and we heaved against him to help him up. Sophie stood up behind him, brushing down her skirts. "It looks like she didn't get me this time," Josef said with a relieved smile. The rest of us felt a rush of relief, too, until we glanced in my father's direction.

Bettina was dead.

Before we could register our grief, Martin shouted in alarm. A thin, sinuous tendril of shadow was seeping through the bottom corner of the windowpane. Martin lashed out at it with his hand, and, for a moment, it swirled away like smoke in the wind. Seconds later, however, it had reconstituted itself, continuing its menacing crawl in our direction. He ran across the room to join us and put a hand out to shield Adeline.

Then Elias gave a shout of alarm from the other side of the house.

"Everyone, go!" the Baron commanded.

We began to run toward my father's office, but what we saw in the front hall brought us to a halt. There were tendrils of shadow stretching through every keyhole, every window of the house. My stomach lurched. We were a ship being enveloped by some ghastly creature from the deep. "The plan!" I screamed. I grabbed Josef's arm as Sophie ran up beside me. "Josef, you're coming with us. The rest of you, don't engage Carmilla. Hide yourselves...and be ready to come to us when we call."

The shadowy tentacles were seeping together and coalescing into a low, creeping black fog that skimmed along the ground toward us. Sophie, Josef, and I ran upstairs and shut ourselves in my bedroom, panting with exertion.

"I suppose you still can't tell me what the plan is?" Josef ventured. I shook my head. "Very well," he sighed. "I am in your hands, ladies."

Sophie clasped her long knife with one hand and concealed herself behind the curtains. I urged Josef to sit in the chair by the fireplace. I paced across the floor, waiting.

We didn't have to wait long. As softly and silently as if she were coming to me for an amorous tryst, Carmilla slipped into the bedroom. She saw Josef in the chair and grinned. "Did you think you could hide him from me, Laura? After all this? Or perhaps you thought to lure me in here, then shout to the others for reinforcement?" She waved a hand dismissively, not waiting for me to answer. "Well, they won't be coming. I am holding them all immobilized. Him too." She nodded toward Josef, who was wide-eyed with panic, frozen in the chair. "You know, it's a bit upsetting that you didn't think this through."

She went at him. I flung myself upon her, trying to wrench her away. She could have batted me away like a fly, but she didn't. Apparently, my instincts had been correct: she didn't want to hurt me. As she had done on that day after I saw her with Johannes, she held me in her grip, keeping me from wounding *her* but refusing to fight me, letting me struggle, perhaps hoping I would eventually wear myself out.

Distracted by my violent struggling – as I had hoped she would be – she didn't see or hear Sophie emerging from behind the curtain. When Sophie plunged her knife between Carmilla's shoulder blades, the vampire gasped and dropped my wrists. Her face contorted in shock and agony, her eyes darkened, becoming hard and inhuman, and her face and teeth distended. She twisted around, frantically trying to remove the blade that was lodged in her back. Josef stood up from his chair and raised his own knife. Carmilla's spell had been broken.

I called out for the others and immediately heard footsteps pounding up the stairs. Josef lunged and stabbed Carmilla in the neck. An unearthly screech tore from her mouth as he pulled the knife out and stabbed her again and again, his blade making dull *thwacking* noises as it pierced her blood-slick flesh. She pushed him away, sending him reeling backwards, and managed to twist her arms far enough behind her to dislodge Sophie's blade.

She whirled on Sophie. "*You*," she hissed, blood spraying from her mouth. Then she threw herself at Sophie with outstretched claws.

The door flew open, and my father and the Baron barreled in, crossbows at the ready. The Baron loosed his arrow with a *twang*; it pierced through the back of Carmilla's neck, propelled her forward, and pinned her to the wall just beside the window. Face crushed against the hard surface, her breath gurgling, she moved her arms and legs frantically, trying to free herself, but the arrow was stuck fast. Sophie, who had jumped out of the way just in time, stared slack-jawed.

The Baron pulled a knife from his belt and ran toward Carmilla. "Don't just stand there! She is not defeated yet!"

I could hear the others' footsteps coming up the stairs. Sophie scrambled to pick up her bloody knife from the floor. My father, the Baron, and Josef rushed at Carmilla, but before they could reach her, she put both hands flat on the wall and pushed, and the shaft of the arrow disappeared into her neck as she tore herself away. She whirled and knocked the knives from their hands, and they stepped back, realizing their sudden vulnerability.

Elias, Martin, and Adeline were coming through the door now, their weapons at the ready, and the Baron turned to say something to them. Striking like a snake, Carmilla wrapped her arms around the Baron and propelled him backwards with her through the window, which shattered outward into the storm. Shards of glass rained down as Carmilla and the Baron thudded upon the wet earth. We raced to the open window. The gale drenched our hair and faces as we watched Carmilla drag her prey's limp body across the courtyard. He was shouting with pain and fear, but seemed unable to move his limbs, perhaps paralyzed by the fall. Once she was out of range of our weapons, she dropped him disdainfully like a cat leaving a dead mouse on the doorstep. His cries for help echoed through the night air. Then she crouched down and drained him until he cried out no more.

"Oh, God," Adeline breathed. Martin enveloped her in his arms. Sophie groaned and brought her hand to her mouth. My father and Josef were cursing under their breaths. My heart was already pounding from the panicked rush of our confrontation, and now the shock of losing Bettina and the Baron was filling my body with numb horror and an overwhelming sense of helplessness. Elias put his hand on my back as if to comfort me, but I could feel his own distress in the trembling of his muscles.

Carmilla stood and wiped her mouth, leering at us. Then she disappeared into the woods.

"What are we going to do now?" I whispered. "That was our best chance."

"I don't know," my father said. "But we'd better think of something fast."

We sat in the front hall, exhausted and despondent. We had brought some chairs into the large space, and while most of us were sitting near the stairs, far from the front entrance, Elias stood beside the front door and kept watch through one of the windows. Like the rest of us, he had realized by now that the things we had hoped would keep us safe were completely ineffective in the face of Carmilla's strength. "Yet," he told me, "I cannot bring myself simply to give up."

The loss of Bettina and the Baron still weighed heavily on us, but our feelings of panic and helplessness had been eased somewhat by the fact that there had been no sign of her for hours. The storm had let up, so the pounding of rain and the rumbling of thunder no longer pressed upon our senses. My father and Josef were discussing potential next steps. Adeline was making sure everyone was supplied with wine and bread and fresh water. Despite the anxious nature of the situation, I found the low hum of voices to be calming. My father and Josef were leaning toward each other, their heads nearly touching. They were reminiscing about the last time they had been in a situation like this, during the war. I began to doze in my chair, occasionally opening my eyes to catch a glimpse of my father as he spoke to Josef, or of Elias' watchful profile as he looked out the window.

Suddenly, a ripple of unease woke me. *Something is wrong.* I opened my eyes and glanced around the room. Elias was still standing at the window, but his expression had changed. His eyes were wide, his face slackened in terror.

Goosebumps prickled my skin. *Something is wrong.*

I leaned forward in my chair. "Elias? What do you see?"

He said nothing, but his whole body was shaking now. He reached down, took the knife from his belt, and began – slowly – to raise it.

Cold horror propelled me to my feet and launched me in his direction. "Elias!" The others heard the panic in my voice and snapped to attention.

The hand holding the knife rose higher and higher, moving toward Elias' throat. He was struggling against it, grunting and sweating with the effort. Adeline and Martin cried out, rose from their chairs, and hurtled in our direction.

"It's her!" I yelled. I grabbed his arm and tried to pull it down, but it continued to move upward, my weight seemingly having no effect at all. *Damn his strength!* I thought, my mind reeling with panic.

The whites of his eyes flashed in the dimly-lit hall. "No!" he gasped. "Don't do this!" His voice was thick with anguished tears, shrill with panic. "Please don't do this!"

Just as Adeline and Martin reached us, Elias slit his own throat.

It was a deep wound, and ragged. Blood sprayed outward and splashed my face; more of it – an impossible deluge - gushed down over his collarbone, soaking his shirt. Adeline screamed and grabbed at him as he fell forward, his weight knocking me to the floor. Martin pulled him over onto his back and tried to stanch the bleeding with his hands. Adeline threw herself against the wound. Their hands slipped ineffectually in the overwhelming spray of blood. Elias was trying to breathe, but the air kept catching in his throat with a sickening, wet gurgle. His throat moved as he tried to swallow the blood away.

I saw him realize he was going to die. His eyes widened in helpless terror. Tears of anguish spilled forth unbidden, cutting white tracks over his blood-spattered cheeks. Then he grimaced and squeezed his eyes shut as his body spasmed from lack of oxygen.

Adeline and Martin were weeping, still trying to stop the flow of blood, though it was seeping out more slowly now. Someone was screaming. I reeled backward, putting my hands to my ears to try to shut out the awful noise, until I realized it was coming from me. My father put his arms around me and tried to pull me away, but I shrugged him off and threw myself forward, clasping Elias' hand in my own.

"Elias!" I screamed. I felt like the whole world was collapsing around me.

There was no response. His hand was limp in mine. He was gone. For a moment, stunned silence gripped us all. Then Adeline emitted a low, keening moan, the cry of a heart shattering irrevocably into a thousand pieces. She rocked back and forth on her knees, holding Elias' other hand to her cheek and sobbing. Beside her, Martin sat frozen. Tears streamed down his face, anguish distorting his features beyond recognition. Sophie turned her face into my father's chest and shook silently. Josef's face was a mask of rage.

Carmilla's deep, taunting laughter came to us from outside.

Josef strode to the pile of weapons and selected an axe. "It's me the creature wants," he spat, "and it's me she'll get, although she might find that I'm more than she can handle."

"Josef, don't!" my father protested. When Josef didn't stop, my father grabbed a shotgun and followed him outside, calling to Sophie, "Bring a lantern! Perhaps we can destroy the creature with fire."

I took the knife from where it had landed beside Elias. It was still warm and slick with his blood. Then I shakily made my way to my feet.

It was cold and dark outside. The clouds had opened like a curtain upon the night sky. The crescent moon shone in a black tapestry bejeweled by stars. We couldn't see Carmilla.

We clutched our weapons and scanned the grounds anxiously for any trace of her. *What do we do now?* I wondered. Searching for her in the woods would be both dangerous and futile.

"Carmilla!" Josef shouted, his voice booming in the still night air. "You coward! You'll fight us through trick and shadow, but not face to face? You must resort to turning our own minds against us? Are you afraid of us, you bitch?"

Her laughter rang out above us. As we looked up, she hurtled down from the roof like a falcon barreling down upon its prey. She landed in a crouch on Josef's shoulders. As he stood immobilized, his eyes rolling wildly with panic, she clasped her hands underneath his chin. Before we could react – and what could we have done, exactly, without putting him at risk, too? – she strained upward, screaming, until, with a loud crack, she tore his head away from his neck. Josef's body collapsed upon the ground. The headless stump, ragged with sinew, landed at my father's feet. Carmilla flew over us with a shrill, inhuman shriek. The head clutched in her hands splattered us with a rain of blood.

My heart plummeted. *Another one*, I thought miserably. I was dizzy with disbelief and misery, and my knees were shaking beneath me, but I refused to fall down this time. My father cried out, the sound of his grief reverberating through the air before transforming into a roar of utter, terrifying rage. He pried the axe from Josef's limp hand and hurled it at Carmilla, who was flying toward the woods, still holding the head by its hair. The axe sank into her side with a *thunk*, and she dropped to the ground. She landed hard on the blade in a way that pushed it farther into her body. She cried out in pain, and Josef's head rolled from her grasp.

"Sophie! The lantern!" My father shouted. The two of them ran at Carmilla and reached her just as she was pulling the axe from her side. Sophie swung the lantern and brought it crashing down on her as she struggled to stand. The oil sprayed over her body and the flames blazed forth. Carmilla screamed and staggered around wildly, hurling herself on the ground to try to put out the flames. My father aimed the shotgun at her and pulled the trigger, and she bounced with the impact of the pellets, still screaming in agony from the flames. She rolled again and finally managed to quench the flames in the wet grass. Then she was on her feet, running haltingly into the woods. Even badly wounded, with charred skin and an axe wound pouring blood, she was still faster than any of us. We had to let her go.

"At least we'll have some time," Sophie said somberly. "I imagine it will take her a while to heal."

"Time for what?" I groaned. "We still don't know how to defeat her, and our numbers are dwindling." Bitter grief pierced me again as I glanced, nauseated, at the General's headless trunk.

My father's resolve crumbled, and he collapsed to his knees beside his friend's body. He sobbed "I'm sorry, Josef, I'm so sorry" in an endless litany. There was anguished weeping coming from inside the house, too. *Elias.*

The agony of our losses filled me, choked me, threatened to swallow me whole. How was it, I wondered, that being the one who was still alive could feel so much like dying?

CHAPTER TWENTY-THREE

THE VAMPIRE'S END

We spent the next two days preparing the bodies for burial and digging the graves. Since we no longer cared about establishing a protective circle for ourselves (whether because we trusted Carmilla would not attack again until she had healed or because our losses had driven us to apathy), we put them in our small burial plot near the chapel.

My father leaned on his shovel after we had finished the last grave. "Once this is over, I...or someone else, if I don't make it...will have to write to their families, and"— he nodded in the direction of Father Schmidt's grave beside the main house —"to the diocese. They may wish to give them their final resting places elsewhere." His voice was steady, but I could see the deep sorrow in his eyes, especially when we lowered the bodies into the ground in their canvas wrappings.

Adeline and Martin stood at the edge of the small clearing, weeping in silence. The frantic edge of their grief had subsided, and all that was left was a deep, throbbing pain that seemed to have turned them to stone. My heart, already broken, ached even more profoundly when I thought of the agony they would carry with them for the rest of their lives.

In truth, it was too much to bear, and I found myself alternating between feeling it intensely and going so numb that even my senses were dulled. When my father and Sophie spoke over the bodies – my father reading from the Bible, Sophie reciting some beautiful Latin poetry about grief and love – their voices came to me as if through layers of cloth, as if I, too, had been wrapped and laid in the earth. I helped to cover the bodies with dirt. I hammered the wooden crosses into the earth above their heads. I clutched Adeline's elbow to support her as we walked back to the house. I went to my room. I bathed and changed my clothes.

I looked in the mirror as I smoothed my hair back into a loose bun. Even freshly bathed and wearing clean garments, my reflection disturbed me. My face was pale and thin, darkly-shadowed with exhaustion and sorrow. It was like looking at a ghost in the mirror. With a start I remembered that séance nearly a decade ago and the young man who had appeared to me in the mirror, urging me to leave the house because I was in danger. He must have lived here once, I realized, and from the way he was dressed and the kind innocence in his face, I wondered now if it was Max, Carmilla's former lover. Carmilla had claimed to be ignorant of his fate, but his bleeding throat suggested he had died in a vampire attack.

Well, that wasn't the only *lie she told me.*

I looked down at the dress hanging loosely on my body. If I died here today, I wondered, would this be what I wore as I wandered the halls for eternity? Would I see Elias here, and Josef, and the others who had been laid to rest in our plot? I put my face in my hands, as if I could expel the morbid thoughts from my mind with the pressure of my fingers. I couldn't. With a grim irony, I imagined some future inhabitant of the house doing a séance and summoning *me*, imagined myself standing over her shoulder and warning her that she was in danger, Carmilla peeking through the window as the Latin words swirled through the darkness...

The breath was snatched from my lungs. What was it Carmilla had said? *I even heard you speaking Latin once. Vergil, I believe.* I suddenly recalled that day, years ago, when Elias and I had talked about death, when I had recited those lines from Aeneas' journey. I couldn't remember the lines exactly now, but I remembered where Elias and I had been standing. And hadn't Carmilla called her hiding place a "cold, black womb"?

I know where she is.

I ran to the dining room, where my father and Sophie were eating cheese and stale bread for lunch. They looked up in surprise as I stumbled in.

"I know where she is," I panted. "At least, I think I do. There's a cave in the craggy mountain just to the north of us. Its entrance is hidden; you must walk around the mountain's base toward the cliff on the other side in order to see it. I don't know why I didn't think of it before."

"And why do you think Carmilla's there?" Sophie asked.

I told them what had led me to draw this conclusion.

"It seems likely enough," my father noted. "Did you ever go inside?"

"Elias and I tried once," I said. "It's very deep and dark, so we didn't make it far."

"Do we go to her, then?" my father asked, his lips in a tight line. "And kill her before she has a chance to come back and kill us?"

"How?" Sophie asked. "There are so few of us now. How can we possibly hope to overtake her?"

I had been considering this very thing while we dug the graves, while we covered the corpses with dirt, while we walked back to the house, while I sloughed the dirt from my skin at the wash basin. "I know how to weaken her," I said grimly. "You won't like it, because it's something I have to do alone, but it's the only thing that might give us a chance."

"What is it?" he asked.

I shook my head. "I need you and Sophie there, waiting outside the cave. And since she'll be able to read your mind, Father, it's better if you don't know what I'm planning."

His eyes darkened, and he shook his head. "At least tell Sophie, then. I can't fathom sending you in there without *someone* knowing what's about to happen."

I nodded. "I'll need a lantern and a knife. You two should bring every weapon you can carry, but especially an axe. I can tell you this much: if all goes according to plan, it is likely that I will drive her from the cave. You must be ready to cut her head off."

They sat in silence, absorbing this terrifying thought.

Finally, Sophie sighed and stood up from her chair. "Well, what are we waiting for?"

We made our way to the cave, my father trailing behind so that I could tell Sophie the plan without him hearing.

She glanced back nervously at my father. "That seems awfully risky, Laura. What if she doesn't believe you and decides to rampage our way anyway? Or what if she *does* believe you, and she ends up taking things too far?"

"I'm worried about those things, too. But I can't see what other options we have. She will certainly overpower us unless we take advantage of her one weakness."

"Her one weakness being *you*."

"It seems so."

We walked in pensive silence. Finally, we reached the clearing and saw Wolf's Tooth jutting sharply into the sky. I showed them the entrance of the cave, so cleverly shielded by the natural topography of the place.

"I'll be damned," my father said. "No wonder Bruzek and his men never found it."

We stood in its empty maw, straining our ears for any sign of her. We were met only with silence and the cold breath of the gaping, invisible space beyond. If she *was* there – and for a moment I wondered if I had been mistaken – she was either deep within the mountain or she was choosing not to respond to our approach.

My father had brought the biggest lantern he could find, and he lit it and handed it to me, keeping a smaller one for himself in case they needed to enter the cave, too. I had a small bag with a knife in it slung across my torso. My father saw my reluctance as I turned to face the darkness and asked, "Are you sure about this? It's not too late to regroup at the schloss and come up with another plan. Maybe she won't even come after us; she has already killed those whom she blamed most for her mother's death."

My stomach roiled with nausea at the thought of traversing the void alone. It was impossible to tell how deep and complex the system of caverns might be, and I knew it would be easy to lose my sense of direction once inside. But *if* she was there, *if* I didn't lose my way, I was confident that my plan would at least give us a chance. I remembered Elias' words to me so long ago: *It doesn't matter how scared you are. You have to do it anyway.* Of course, he hadn't been talking about putting oneself directly in the path of a monster. Still... "She's a murderer," I said. "Nobody is safe. Bettina and Elias proved that once and for all. Besides, I can do this. Please, just wait for me here. Give me until sundown, and if I'm not back by then, you can come in after me." I took a deep breath, lifted the lantern higher, and pressed forward into the shadows. The path sloped downward and away from the cliff, burrowing into the earth.

It is difficult to describe the horror of making my way through that dark, soulless place. I saw my progress in ten-foot intervals, never able to glimpse what was beyond the reach of the lantern's light, never able to plan what my next move would be until the tunnel twisted suddenly. The stones pressed close around me, so dark I often couldn't tell the difference between what was void and what was solid. At times, the passage became so narrow that I had to hold my breath to squeeze through, and panic clawed at my throat at the thought that it might become even narrower, blocking my progress either forward or backward and crushing the life from my body. At other times, a small passage would empty into a yawning cavern whose bounds the lantern light could not reach, whose expanse was only suggested to me by the sudden coldness of the air and the echoes of my footsteps crunching the rubble below. Eventually, I reached a fork in the passage, my current path branching into two tunnels whose openings were nearly identical to each other in every way. I chose one and ducked into it, following it for several minutes until it began to close ever more tightly around me and ended finally in a solid wall of stone. The lantern was slipping in my sweaty grip by now, and my arm trembled with the effort of holding it aloft. In the close space I could hear my panicked breathing, could feel its hot moisture bouncing back from the stone. I headed back the way I had come, but when I reached the fork again, a wave of dizziness overwhelmed me. Had I chosen the left path or the right one? If I turned left now, would it take me to the other hallway, or send me back to the entrance? My pulse quickened and I fought down the terror that was rising in my throat.

"Breathe, Laura," I said to the blackness around me. "Get ahold of yourself and *think*."

I shut my eyes – not that I could see anything anyway – and tried to remember what I had done. Steeling myself, I made my choice and headed down what I thought was the *other* passage. It quickly became apparent that I had chosen correctly, for I began to hear the soft, echoing sounds of a woman's voice, growing louder as I pressed ever forward. I could tell that it was *her*, but I couldn't discern whether she was speaking or...singing?

As I turned a corner, a huge cavern opened around me, amplifying the sound, and I realized what I was hearing.

Carmilla was weeping.

There was light in this cavern. It filtered through a face-sized opening high up in the side, near the domed ceiling. The opening must be visible from the outside, I realized, as a hole in the ground or in some rocky outcropping, though I had not explored the area thoroughly enough to recognize it. The small source of light was enough to provide a dim view of the cavern, especially now that my eyes had adjusted to the darkness. I lowered the lantern. At the far end of the space was a wide, flat ledge free of rock formations. A straw mattress had been placed there, surrounded by piles of books. Some dresses were slung over a small stool. They were all things that she or her mother or Max would have had to transport through the narrow passageways of the cavern, though she herself (and her mother) would also have been able to use the small aperture above in their shadow forms. Max had been the one to tell Carmilla about this place, I remembered, which meant that *he* must have discovered it after exploring the cave system on his own. And Carmilla had spent more than a hundred years here, largely alone. I shuddered at the weight of it, the enormity of a century spent in cold and silence and shadow.

When I entered, Carmilla was lying on the bed, facing away from me as she sobbed. She was still wearing that white nightdress, though it had been drenched in blood and blackened in places by the flames, and her white skin peeked through the various holes made by bullets and blades. Seeing the light from my lantern on the wall and hearing the sound of my footsteps, she turned. Her face – the woman's face, not the creature's – was streaked with tears and puffy from prolonged crying. She looked so vulnerable, so very *young*. I suddenly remembered that she had been only eighteen years old when she became a vampire.

I can't do this, I thought. *I can't do this.*

Then I thought of the ease with which she lied, the malice with which she took lives. So many lives.

I have to do this.

She gave a brief, strained smile and said, in a voice that shook with a century of weariness, "You found me. My clever girl."

I approached her slowly, the heavy lantern at my side.

"I suppose you're here to kill me," she said. "I can feel your father outside. He seems to think you're going to lure me outside somehow so he can chop my head off with an axe." I didn't respond, continuing my steady approach in her direction. She rolled onto her back and sighed, her tears beginning anew. "It's for the best, anyway. What do I have to live for now? You were right, Laura. I've ruined everything." She covered her eyes with her hands and gave in to deep, hopeless sobs.

I froze. Would this be easier than I had expected? Could it really be that she wished to die? *No, it can't be that simple. She may wish to die, but the monster inside her certainly will not.* "What do you mean?" I asked.

"My mother's gone. And I've lost *you*. And I have nowhere to go, not without condemning myself to a life of pain and weakness."

I placed the lantern and my bag on the ground and sat beside her on the bed. "You haven't lost me," I said softly.

She removed her hands from her eyes and stared at me in alarm. "*How*? After all the things I've done, after Emma and..." she swallowed nervously "...and Elias? And the others?"

I suppressed the rage and grief rising in my gullet like bile at the mention of their names, focusing on the pity I had felt mere moments ago and summoning all the care I had once felt for her. "I will never forgive you for Emma," I said. That part was true; what followed was a lie. "But the others? Their deaths devastated me, but I also understand that you were defending yourself. You wouldn't have killed any of them if we hadn't sought you out. Truthfully, I hold *myself* largely culpable for their deaths." Her eyes were wide with disbelief. I took one of her hands in mine. "And when you refused to hurt me, even when I was attacking you with all my might...Carmilla, you proved that you were telling the truth about loving me."

She sat up in the bed and dropped my hand. Her eyes narrowed. "I don't believe this. It's some trick, isn't it? You said you'd rather die than be with me."

Careful, I thought. "I did say that. But I was angry. I was wrong. I love you, Carmilla. When I first found out what you did to Emma, the pain of that betrayal made me forget it. But over the past few days I have not been able to shake it from myself entirely. It has taken root in my heart too deeply. And as horrifying as it was watching you kill so savagely, I also regret that I put you in the position to do so in the first place."

She hadn't just killed savagely; she had killed *gleefully*, causing as much pain as she could in the process. And it was *that* which had closed my heart to her. But I found it surprisingly easy to say the words, as though they were professing feelings not so very far from my own. I could see from the earnest look in her eyes that she was nearly convinced. Perhaps her emotional distress was making it difficult for her to think clearly, to read the deception.

"Oh, Laura," she whimpered, "I can be good. I promise."

No you can't. "I know you can," I said. "Especially if we are together. I'll help you."

I leaned forward and kissed her. She hadn't expected it, and her lips and body were rigid at first. Then she softened into me, pulling me into her arms and holding me with aching tenderness, her lips moving against mine in a way that – I will not deny it – sent sparks of desire through my body. I broke from her, breathing raggedly. "I love you, and I'm sorry I hurt you." I placed my hand on the bare skin at her chest, where my knife had pierced through her clothing. She placed her hand over mine. "And," I continued, "I can think of no better life than one spent with you. I want you to change me."

She stiffened. "What about your father? The others?"

"We can compel them, can't we? Or simply send them away? We can live at the schloss together, just you and me."

"What about Sophie?"

I shrugged. "I will not be terribly distraught if she must die. She and I were never really that close, you know."

I realized immediately that this was a misstep. Carmilla couldn't read my mind, but she still *knew* me. She eyed me with skepticism.

"That wasn't true," I admitted hastily. "I would be very sad if Sophie died, but it's a sacrifice I'm willing to make. To be with you and...to be immortal. I've seen too many people die, and it terrifies me. I want to live forever, even if it means being a monster." I almost believed that part myself. "Change me," I begged. Tears filled my eyes. I couldn't believe it had come to this, couldn't fathom what I was about to do.

Her eyes searched mine for a long time. She shouldn't have believed me. But we are all more willing to accept the unbelievable when it matches our own desires. The silence of the cavern stretched around us, and my heartbeat pounded in my ears, impossibly loud. Finally, she spoke. "Now?"

"Now."

"You must drink from me, as much as you can, and then I must kill you."

"I remember."

"It might take some time for you to change," she warned. "I worry that your father will try to come find you."

"Sophie is with him. They wouldn't let me come alone, but I didn't tell them what was truly in my heart. While I'm undergoing the change, you can slip out of that opening" – I nodded at the aperture above us – "and deal with them. Spare my father, please; it's the only thing I ask."

She looked up skeptically. "I may not be strong enough to take on my shadow form once you have drunk from me."

Panic shot through me. This was, in fact, exactly what I was hoping, and everything would come crashing down if she realized I was trying to weaken her. "What if you drink from me first? Would that give you enough strength to bolster you through my transformation?"

"It's possible." She leveled her gaze at me. "Are you sure about this?"

In reply, I pulled my collar away from my neck, baring the skin there. She bent her head solemnly and put her lips to my throat. I felt her face change against my skin, then the sharp sting of her teeth. She moaned with pleasure, drawing deeply from me. As always, our minds touched as my blood flowed into her, and for a moment I worried that she might be able to see what I was hiding. But I had nothing to fear: her frantic need was blinding her to everything but the satiation of her undying thirst.

She pulled away, panting with the effort of it, her grotesque mouth dripping with blood as her eyes rolled back in her head. I didn't look away from her this time; I needed her to think that I could accept this fate for myself. But the carapace eyes, the skeletal face, the distended teeth...I struggled not to shrink from her as fear and disgust rippled through me. She proffered a pale, slender arm, enclosing the clawed fingernails loosely in her fist to hide them. With her other hand, she drew a nail along the vein of her wrist. Dark blood poured from the wound. "Drink," she urged.

My previous experiences with tasting her blood had involved very small quantities. Though the warm saltiness did not appeal to me, it had been, in those insignificant amounts, something I could stomach. This was another thing entirely. I pulled fiercely at the vein and choked down gulp after gulp of her blood, fighting against the nausea as my stomach rebelled. My senses expanded around me in a dizzying rush –

who knew there could be so many sounds in an empty cave? The scent of Carmilla's skin, the pounding pulse of her heart, the warmth radiating from her body...they intoxicated me. I felt her thoughts collide with my own, and my head spun with the poignant mixture of desire, joy, and fear that I was pulling into myself along with her blood. *The blood.* I tried to think of nothing else, tried to focus on the sensation of it sliding down my throat and sending strength through my limbs. Otherwise, she would surely hear my thoughts, and that would be a death sentence if it happened too soon.

I *was* growing stronger. I could feel it with each swallow, even as I gagged against the unceasing flood. She wavered beside me and tried to pull her arm away. "That's enough." But I clung to her with both hands, digging in with my teeth. I could feel her strength beginning to ebb, a heaviness creeping into the edges of her consciousness. I pulled harder at the vein, even though I couldn't stomach any more. I gagged and let the blood pour from my mouth. I spit each mouthful onto the ground before returning for the next one.

"That's *enough*!" she cried. Her voice was edged with alarm now, and she struggled with all her might against my grip, but she was growing weaker by the second.

My heart twisted in my chest. I was killing the monster. I was killing the woman I loved. *I have to do this.*

As her power ebbed from her, I was becoming suffused with it, and the bones of her wrist snapped in my unshakable grip. Her mind touched mine again, and she *knew*. A wave of crushing betrayal and desperation – *her* betrayal and desperation – coursed through me. With a roar that shook the walls of the cavern around us, she lashed out frantically, panic lending her enough strength to pull away from me. The force of it sent her tumbling off the mattress and onto the hard stone below. She stayed there for several seconds, so weak that she couldn't even lift her head. Then she pushed herself up on her hands and knees, trying in vain to stand.

I was still reeling from the blood, dizzied and weightless and painfully aware of every minute aspect of our surroundings. I could feel her panic, could hear her anguished thoughts, and my own mind, my own strength, seemed to have been swallowed by the cacophony of her distress. But I knew that this was my chance. Remembering my purpose, I dragged myself away from the brink of chaos, picked up the lantern beside the bed, and swung it overhead, bringing it crashing down onto her back. The oil splashed over her, and the fire leapt upon her skin as if eager to devour her.

I reached for the knife in my bag, ready to take advantage of her incapacitation, but pain sent her rocketing to her feet. An unearthly, awful scream ripped from her as she clawed at herself, trying to put the fire out with her hands. I screamed, too, for I could feel her pain as if it were my own. I collapsed onto the floor and tried desperately – in vain – to shut off my mind, to break the link between us. She ran from the cavern, shrieking, hurling herself through the passageways toward the entrance, trying to make it to the creek outside before she was consumed entirely. In my mind's eye I saw her scramble frantically through the twisting darkness. Her burning body illuminated the stone walls as she hurtled clumsily against them, and she kept roaring – again and again, endlessly – as the awful, blinding heat spread over and into her limbs.

The cave's entrance was ahead of her now, a bright oval in the distance. She could feel that she was dying, could feel her limbs growing heavy, the pain from the blazing heat growing duller, her nerves burning away. But she kept going, hoping that she was wrong, hoping that there was still some time for her to stop this. To *live*.

As she emerged into the afternoon sunlight, an arrow hit her chest and knocked her backward. She saw Mademoiselle De LaFontaine's face, grinning at her victoriously over a crossbow. The impact of her back upon the earth did nothing to quench the flames, which had crept down her arms and up past her ears. The odor of burnt hair filled her nostrils. Mr. Bancroft was approaching her now, swinging an axe over his head. With a surge of helpless despair, she realized that she was going to die.

The axe arced through the air and hissed downwards.

Then Carmilla was gone. The part of my mind where I had been sharing her consciousness was nothing but void, as dark and empty and cold as the cave around me. Trembling on my hands and knees, I vomited blood over the unfeeling stone. I felt myself slipping, swaying...I scrambled to my feet and stumbled through the cave, my heightened senses allowing me to see in the dark, like a bat. My feet churned forward, propelling me toward the entrance, until finally I was approaching the bright oval of light. I heard Sophie and my father calling out in alarm when they saw me emerging from the darkness, soaked in blood. I hurtled into my father's arms and my legs gave way. The sky spun above me. He clung to me as I screamed and screamed, my preternaturally powerful voice shaking the trees around us and echoing in the canyon below.

CHAPTER TWENTY-FOUR

THE AFTERMATH

We burned Carmilla to ashes right there before the cave. We scattered her over the cliff's edge. Then we trudged back to the schloss under darkening skies.

The vampire had met her end. But none of us felt like celebrating. Indeed, Adeline and Martin, when we told them what had transpired, only wept harder. It was hard to feel relief when the enormity of the loss was unchanged.

Exhaustion from the days of dire conflict and nausea from the massive amount of blood I had consumed kept me bedridden for days. I convinced my father and Sophie that I wished to be left alone, and, once they were sure I would recover, they departed for Gratz in our carriage, to send word of the Baron's demise to his companions in London and, along the way, to relate the heartbreaking news of Josef's fate to his household. My father helped Sophie into the carriage before climbing into the driver's box, and I noted with surprise that they held on to each other's hands longer than they needed to, a meaningful glance passing between them.

Understandably, Martin and Adeline were in no mood to converse. I was left alone in my bedroom, occasionally nibbling on the bread and water Adeline left outside my door, with no appetite for anything else. I wept and cursed and slept fitfully. I kept feeling the searing pain that I had shared with Carmilla as her flesh burned, kept hearing her panicked, pleading voice, kept seeing her face, twisted with the agony of betrayal and blackening as it was consumed by flames. The night after my father and Sophie left, I woke to find that my legs had brought me into the woods, to the very edge of the cliff where we had discarded the last trace of her. The wind whispered menacingly in my ear and pulled at my dress, beckoning me into oblivion. Goosebumps prickled my skin.

Is it so easy, then? I asked silently. I had said those same words so many years before, with Elias. I laughed bitterly into the frigid air. My senses were still heightened, my body thrumming as it drank in the cold, dark sky and its glittering stars. Carmilla's blood was still coursing through my veins. All I had to do was step off the edge into the darkness and put an end to this mortal body, and I would be resurrected as an immortal.

Immortal. I shivered with the enormity of it.

Could I do it? Could I live a life that required me to hurt others for my own benefit? Would it change me the way it had changed Carmilla? Her life had been long, yes, but it had been lonely. I swayed with the weight of my grief. I didn't regret killing her. I regretted the loss of what we could have been, if only she had been human. Would I lose myself, too, if I gave in to the dazzling promise of a life without death? Could I watch those around me grow old and die without the bitterness of mortality warping me into something inhuman? And what about my father? What would I tell him?

I can't, I thought finally. I stepped back from the cliff's edge, went back to the house, and wrapped myself in my blankets, trying in vain to shut out the desperate howling in my mind.

That moment on the cliff, that choice, brought me back to myself. The next day, I ate a simple but hearty breakfast and went out to the mounds of fresh dirt with wooden crosses at their heads. I knelt beside Elias'.

"I'm sorry," I said. "You didn't deserve this." *If only you hadn't come. If only you had stayed in Gratz with your...with Sara.* "If only you had left us all behind entirely."

I heard a soft sigh beside me, and I turned to see Adeline standing there, a rueful smile on her tear-streaked face. "Now, child, there's no sense in 'if only.' You know he couldn't have done anything but what he did. It wasn't in his nature."

I embraced her, leaning down to bury my face in her neck. "I know. But I wish it weren't so. Now we've lost him forever."

"Not forever, child. We will see him again. I have faith that it is so."

Her voice broke, though she was trying to smile. I clung to her and hoped her words were true.

Eventually the grief and pain lessened, not completely, but enough to allow us to return to some semblance of normalcy. My father and Sophie married, and for a year we stayed at the schloss, trying to make a happy life for ourselves there. But it was too haunted, too lonely. Thinking a change of scenery might do the trick, we traveled to Italy and explored its wonders for several months. The warmth of the Mediterranean air was a balm to my spirits, and I found that the crowds no longer frightened me. I suppose it's not surprising; I had been through the most terrifying thing imaginable, and I had come to know my own strength. I began to conceive of a different life for myself, one full of food and music and the company of other people.

We made our way to London then, to connect with the remnants of my father's family. Shortly after we arrived, we were contacted by the Baron's colleagues in the Order of Perseus, who were eager to learn more about our encounters with the last of the Karnstein vampires. I went to meet them alone. There were only three of them now (I will keep their identities private, in case the Order is, somehow, still operating), and they were aging and weak. They listened raptly to my account and took detailed notes for their records. After congratulating me on my accomplishment, they asked if I would be willing to join the Order. I would be an asset, they reasoned, with my ability to resist psychic compulsion and the knowledge I had gained from battling the vampire. I laughed at the irony of it, remembering how dismissive the Baron had been of my contributions at first. Then I refused their offer. "I'm terribly sorry, Gentlemen," I said. "But if I never see another vampire, it will be too soon."

We returned to the schloss briefly, but our travels had shown us a bright world far removed from the pain and isolation of the past. Soon, my father and Sophie announced their intention to move to Germany, where Sophie's family was, and they urged me and Adeline and Martin to come with them. But I wanted to make a name for myself, to shed the past like a skin and find myself anew. So I moved to Florence and began to write under the pseudonym Johnathan Karnstein. Adeline and Martin never left the schloss, saying that they wished to stay near Elias' grave. They must have died long since; I hope they found him in those empty halls.

Strangely enough, people relished the morbid stories that stemmed from my worst nightmares, and my success was instantaneous. My audience found a sort of escape in my writing, I suppose, blissfully unaware that the violence and gore in the "fiction" I published was inspired by the reality that I – and many others – had experienced (and will continue to experience, so long as there are such creatures on this earth).

My father and Sophie occasionally came to visit me in Florence, until they moved to America in 1845, after which we communicated only through letters. My father died in 1860, and Sophie and I corresponded rarely after that. She must have passed away by now.

The village Karnstein, at least, has recovered in the years following Carmilla's death. I have heard that it is a bustling center of trade again, a haven for woodcutters and their customers. The Karnstein house is occupied by a wealthy merchant and his family, and the church has been rebuilt. It reminds me of an occasion many years ago, when I walked through a swath of forest that had been destroyed by wildfire. The soil and trees were blackened and desolate, and yet small green shoots and bright purple flowers were beginning to climb through the ashes towards heaven, proof that joy and beauty can find their way even through the bleakest ruin.

We never sold our schloss. As far as I know, it sits there still, a silent ruin whose empty halls hold the ghosts of our sorrow in their dark recesses. Perhaps moss is creeping up its walls and creatures have taken up residence there, building their nests or burrowing into our old mattresses. I've never gone back. I don't need to. I still see *her* in my dreams every night, still catch glimpses of her in the shadows at my periphery as I write. Sometimes, too, I see Elias or Emma in my dreams. If I am very lucky, they are smiling.

You have the truth now, reader, all of it. You may judge me as you will, disbelieve me if you choose. I have been writing for a long time now, and I have amassed quite a fortune in my success. I have had many lovers over the years (I will not name them, for the world still does not accept such relationships), and I have experienced a great deal of pleasure, though nothing has come close to the all-consuming passion with which Carmilla and I burned. That suits me just fine. But with no one to leave my fortune to and no real ties keeping me here in Florence, I have decided it is time for me to see more of the world. And so, dear reader, this, my most important work, will also be my last. Through these words, the undying echoes of my pleasure and pain, maybe I will gain immortality after all.

EPILOGUE

May 28th, 1889

Dear William,

I must relate to you, brother, the very strange reception I received when I went to Florence to fulfill your request. I arrived at the address you had given me, a charming flat overlooking the Arno. I knocked on the door, expecting Laura Bancroft herself to answer, but instead it was a finely-dressed young woman, astonishingly beautiful, with blonde curls and dark, wise eyes.

"May I help you?" she asked.

"Good afternoon, miss," I said. "I'm looking for Miss Laura Bancroft."

"Who, may I ask, is calling?"

"My name is Daniel Woodson. I was sent by my brother, her publisher, to bring her the latest royalty check from her most recent book."

She frowned. "Oh. Normally it is forwarded here through her solicitor."

"Yes, miss, and I apologize for the unexpected nature of my call. It's just that...well, you must know that her book has done very well. My brother wished to send someone to give her the check in person with hearty congratulations."

"That's very thoughtful," the woman said, "but I'm afraid she's not accepting visitors at the moment."

"I'm sorry to hear it. Who are you exactly?"

"I'm Emilia, her caretaker." She smiled charmingly and shook my hand.

"I see. Is...is Miss Bancroft unwell?"

"I'm afraid so. She's been very explicit that she does not wish to see anyone."

"Would you mind asking her for me? I hate to trouble you, but I've come all the way from Cambridge to give this to her, and I'd hate to have wasted the trip."

"I'll...I'll ask her," she agreed hesitantly. "Give me just a minute." She closed the door, leaving me outside.

A few minutes later she returned, shaking her head apologetically. "I'm sorry, sir. She really doesn't wish to see anyone. In fact, she was quite chagrined to hear that William sent you, as it is outside the bounds of their agreement. She did, however, give me this." She handed me a page on which the following had been written:

I apologize for my reluctance to meet you in my current state, Mr. Woodson. Please do give the check to Emilia, as she represents me in all things, and send my regards to William.

Laura Bancroft

The signature was similar enough to those I have seen in her recent correspondence that I trust it was, in fact, her own. I hope I did not commit an error here, but after considering the situation for a few moments, I handed the check directly to Emilia. She stared at it in astonishment. "My word! Miss Bancroft will undoubtedly be surprised and pleased." Then she looked at me. "Mr. Woodson, are you busy this afternoon and evening?"

"No, miss. This was my only errand for the day."

"Well, would you like to go to the taverna next door with me? It's my afternoon off, and I can't think of a better way to spend it than making a new acquaintance."

I hope you do not think that my acceptance of this proposal was an impropriety, William. I certainly do not regret it, as my evening with her was delightful indeed. After she had briefly withdrawn into the flat to give Miss Bancroft the check and to retrieve her own coat, we walked to the taverna, which was rather more expensive than I am accustomed to, but well worth it for the charming company. We drank and ate and talked about many things. She had accompanied Miss Bancroft on her recent travels to India and Greece, and she described in detail her favorite encounters on those sojourns.

"May I ask you a question?" I asked, as the night wore on. We were both a little drunk at that point, I'm afraid, and it made me unwontedly bold.

She leaned back in her chair with a warm, expectant smile. "Of course."

"Do you think everything Miss Bancroft wrote about in the book is true?"

She chuckled. "It's hard to believe, isn't it? It *would* be a brilliant authorial conceit. Writing a horror story as if it were a memoir?"

"We have considered that very thing at the publishing house. Not that we mind. It's made us *loads* of money."

She laughed again, throwing her head back, an act which emphasized her marvelously elegant neck. Then she pressed her lips together and appraised me, as if deciding how she wanted to answer my question. "I've known Miss Bancroft for quite some time now, Mr. Woodson, and I am confident in asserting that the events that she wrote about are true. At least, mostly," she added with a mischievous smile.

The rest of the night passed in a blur. I awoke this morning feeling strangely weak, with a pounding headache and no recollection of how I got back to my hotel, although I can say at least that I do remember escorting Emilia to her flat. I am writing to you now so that you may know what transpired regarding Miss Bancroft's check, but I think I will stay a few more days to explore this lovely city. I must admit that I am also hoping to cross paths again with Emilia, who is a clever and enchanting young woman indeed. Please forgive my absence at the publishing house, brother. I promise I will work as diligently as ever upon my return.

Sincerely,
Daniel

AUTHOR'S NOTE

When I first read J. Sheridan Le Fanu's 1872 vampire novella *Carmilla*, I absolutely adored it. The Gothic atmosphere, the (surprisingly explicit, for its time) sapphic undertones, the genuinely sexy and genuinely scary monster. It's a unique specimen of early vampire literature that has managed to be both highly influential and criminally under-appreciated.

My desire to write my own version of this story, then, does not arise from any dissatisfaction with the original. For its own time, it's perfect.

But as a modern reader and writer, I immediately imagined a version of the story that gave its reader *more*. More of Carmilla. More of Laura. More of the love, more of the torment. More of the violence.

And I wanted to write that version.

Now, I am by no means the first person to undertake a "modern" adaptation of *Carmilla*. There are *many*. Nor will I be the last. But there were certain things I wanted my version to accomplish. First, I wanted it to retain the original setting in 19th century Austria. Second,

I wanted it to end as the original does (and as most vampire stories *should*), with the death of the vampire. Third, I wanted the love story to be *real*.

Though many people refer to *Carmilla* as the original "lesbian vampire" story and idolize the sapphic tension between the narrator and the vampire, Le Fanu certainly did not intend for this aspect of Carmilla's character to be idolized. Carmilla's lesbianism, in Le Fanu's original, is part of her monstrosity (a view echoed by Baron Vordenburg in my version). The author was, after all, a product of his time. Le Fanu's Carmilla brings Laura under compulsion immediately and begins to feed on her from the start. Thus Laura is Carmilla's victim, not her beloved.

In my version, I wanted Carmilla and Laura's love story to be genuine. This meant I had to take a page from *Twilight* and make Laura immune to Carmilla's compulsion. I also wanted to make it clear (unlike *Twilight*) that this love affair – however sexy – is a *bad idea*, because the vampire *is* a monster. Not for her lesbianism, but for all the, you know, *murder*. Violence, not love, is the problem.

The two guiding principles, then, are:

1)   Laura and Carmilla's love is real, and Carmilla is NOT a villain for desiring Laura

2)   Carmilla IS a villain

Making these dual ideas work together meant – fittingly – embracing and emphasizing a duality in Carmilla's nature.

As Laura puts it in Chapter Eighteen, "There was a monster inside of her, a monster that impelled her to drink blood from living humans and to manipulate them in various ways. But there was a woman, too, a woman who was vulnerable and affectionate, bound unfairly by the limitations of her *condition* and so, so scared that she could never truly be herself without alienating the one she loved."

This makes the outcome (I hope) both satisfying and tragic. What do we do when we love someone who is really, truly toxic? The answer is clear, but it sucks.

It was also important to me to make Laura's story more rewarding by modern standards. In the original, despite her narrative importance, she has no hand in the vampire's demise (she merely hears about it from others), and she never fully recovers from her encounter with the vampire. I wanted to give her an arc that took her from fear to strength, from desolation to longevity and success.

I do not know if I accomplished these aims successfully. I hope I have. I know some readers – understandably – have strong feelings about writers and filmmakers adapting classics. But the story took root in me and drove me to near-obsession until I had finished it, and so it is a relief and a pleasure simply to see it on these pages.

My sincerest thanks to my family and my friends for their undying support (see what I did there?). To my husband Kris, in particular, thank you for believing in me and urging me to write even though it means I'm too busy all the time. Thanks to Jacqueline Fellows, whose success in writing and self-publishing encouraged me to do it, too. Finally, thanks to my writing group: Andrew, Garrett, Julie, and Shelly, your support, feedback, and encouragement have been absolutely invaluable; this book wouldn't be here without you.

About the Author

Born to a family of dancers in Southern California, Reina was bitten by the creativity bug at an early age, whether she was writing fanfiction about her Barbies, composing music on the family piano, or choreographing dances to New Kids on the Block. Thanks to her bibliophile grandmother, she soon developed an enthusiasm for classical languages and literature, which brought her first to the Classics Department at UCSD and then– after a stint as an English teacher at a small private school – to the graduate program in Classics at CU Boulder. There, Reina fell in love with the mountains, and she refused to leave even after she had finished her Ph.D. She still teaches for the Classics Department in Boulder, while also devoting time to writing, exploring, and spending time with her family.

If you're interested in reading Reina's blog or discovering her other books, head to https://reinacallier.com.